I0739238

THE TALE OF TWO BARONS

LINDA RAE SANDE

Twisted Teacup
PUBLISHING

This is a work of fiction. The events and characters described herein are imaginary and are not intended to refer to specific places or living persons. The opinions expressed in this manuscript are solely the opinions of the author and do not represent the opinions or thoughts of the publisher. The author has represented and warranted full ownership and/or legal right to publish all the materials in this book.

The Tale of Two Barons

Copyright © 2018 by Linda Rae Sande

V1.1

ISBN: 978-1-946271-16-7

All rights reserved.

Cover photograph © Romance Novel Covers.com

Cover art by KGee Designs

All rights reserved - used with permission.

Edited by Marsha Zinberg

This book may not be reproduced, transmitted, or stored in whole or in part by any means, including graphic, electronic, or mechanical without the express written consent of the publisher except in the case of brief quotations embodied in critical articles and reviews.

https://www.lindaraesande.com

To Rachel Falk for being the best boss a writer could have.

ALSO BY LINDA RAE SANDE

The Promise of a Gentleman

The Pride of a Gentleman

The Holidays of the Aristocracy

The Christmas of a Countess

The Knot of a Knight

The Heirs of the Aristocracy

The Angel of an Astronomer

The Puzzle of a Bastard

The Choice of a Cavalier

The Bargain of a Baroness

The Jewel of an Earl's Heir

The Vixen of a Viscount

Beyond the Aristocracy

The Pleasure of a Pirate

Stella of Akrotiri

Origins

Deminon

Diana

CHAPTER 1

A VISIT TO THE TEMPLE

March 1817

Jeffrey Althorpe, Lord Sommers, stepped into the entry of the Temple of the Muses and took a deep breath. The odors of leather, vellum and wood as well as a hint of vanilla assaulted his nostrils. Exhaling with a good deal of satisfaction, he glanced around to discover only a few shoppers perusing the stacks of books that lined the back wall. Several employees stood behind the circular counter in the middle of the massive room whilst a few were off to the right unpacking what appeared to be that morning's delivery of the latest books.

Jeffrey smiled. Although it might have been more fashionable to shop for books at Hatchard's—its owner was said to be the bookseller to Queen Charlotte—Jeffrey rather liked James Lackington's approach to book sales. The Temple's original owner had painted "Cheapest Bookseller in the World" above the entrance to the place. For a man of Lord Sommers' modest means, the bookstore was sometimes his favorite place to spend a late morning.

Since most of the patrons of the store tended to shop later in the day or even at night, Jeffrey found he preferred the morning hours. No crowds to fight and less chance that another customer might be after the same new titles as he sought.

When his presence was noted by one of the shopkeepers,

Jeffrey nodded in the man's direction. "Good morning, Mr. Pritchard," he said as he made his way toward the open crates.

"And to you, my lord," the short man responded with a bow. "Your book arrived late yesterday. I've already seen to its placement on the third floor," Pritchard added with a wave toward the stairs. "New arrivals."

Jeffrey forced himself to take a few careful breaths before he dared respond. "Thank you," he managed to get out before a huge grin split his face as he nodded to the shopkeeper. "You will keep my name secret from anyone who asks?"

Mr. Pritchard nodded vigorously. "I shan't tell a soul."

Turning around, the baron made his way to the other end of the lobby. He ascended the stairs to the second level of the shop, passing by a lounging room and through a gallery featuring the most expensive titles on its rows of shelving, titles which were bound in leather and suitable for a gentleman's library. He climbed the stairs to the third level and paused by another lounging room, noticing a lady's maid snoozing in one of the upholstered chairs. At the end of the gallery of mid-priced books, Jeffrey glanced at an elderly couple studying the stacks, engaged in quiet conversation.

Near the stairs to the next level, a shelving unit jutted out from the wall—a shelving unit that held the latest titles. Removing his hat, he headed in its direction, intent on finding his newly released book.

*P*ulling off first one glove and then the other, Lady Evangeline Tennison gave the third level shelving unit a quick glance. She opened her reticule and stuffed the gloves inside, seemingly unconcerned that they would become hopelessly wrinkled in the process. Absently pushing an errant lock of blonde hair behind her ear, she spotted the book she'd been hoping to find on this visit to the Temple of the Muses.

The Story of a Baron.

She leaned her head to one side, studying the leather-bound book. The binding surprised her; many of the books on the third floor weren't bound in leather but sported covers made of dense card stock. Only after a book proved worthy to its owner did it receive a leather binding. The modest size of the spine suggested the book wasn't made up of more than a few hundred pages. What surprised her more was that it was only one volume. Due to the cost of paper and binding, most books were released in three volumes.

Reaching out with one finger, she pulled the book forward, leaning her head to the other side to read the title on the front. Sure it was *The Story of a Baron*, she pulled it completely from the shelf and opened it slowly. A small smile touched her lips. The subject of the book couldn't have much of a story if the book was only... she checked the last sheaf in the book to find the page number. *Two-hundred and sixty-two.* Arching an eyebrow, Lady Evangeline rested the bulk of the book on one velvet-clad forearm and used her other arm to keep the pages open whilst she quickly scanned the last page of print. When she found the very last sentence, she read it to herself.

Forever.

Evangeline looked up and glanced about, her heart pounding just a bit too fast.

Forever?

That was the last sentence of the book?

Well, it held promise, at least. And some degree of finality. But the simple word held absolutely no hint as to the quality of the rest of the book nor the author's writing skill—or lack thereof.

For once, she chided herself for always reading the last sentence of a book before she decided whether or not to buy it. Usually the last line gave away a bit more about a book's subject, a bit more about its characters, its tone, and whether or not it featured a happy ending.

But not this one.

Taking a deep breath, Evangeline did what she rarely did when considering a book—she shifted the pages so that the first page of the story was visible. Once again glancing about, hoping no one would notice, she found the very beginning of the story and read to herself.

Matthew Winters, Baron Ballantine, entered his favorite book-shop in search of a particular new title.

Evangeline inhaled sharply, realizing the subject of the book was doing exactly the same thing she was doing!

Success!

For if a character found pleasure in reading books, then certainly Evangeline could sympathize with him and his story.

Although other young women of her age might consider her a bluestocking—well, probably the entire *ton* considered her a bluestocking, although she had no evidence to support such a theory—Lady Evangeline didn't seem to mind. Given she was the younger sister of Lord Everly, an earl who spent most of his time exploring the world, she found it was far more satisfying to spend her days engrossed in the pages of a book than be sequestered in the parlor with her latest needlework and a hope that someone—anyone—would pay her a call.

Her brother was rarely in residence. His latest trip to southern India had commenced over six months ago, his mission to study the tropical fish that populated the waters off the coast. A missive from him, delivered just the day before, claimed he was scheduled to board a ship that would take him around Cape Horn and deliver him to England in a fortnight. *Him and a lined crate full of whatever he could catch*, she thought with a grin.

The library at Rosemount House already housed a large aquarium populated with exotic fish from warm southern waters. In need of a way to display his fish as well as to keep their water warm, the earl had employed an inventor, Henry Forster, Earl of Gisborn, to develop a tank and a heater. A combination of glass panes held together with steel strips and mounted inside a shallow metal pan, the aquarium was heated from below using the natural gas already being fed to the house for the purpose of lighting its interior. Despite Everly's extended absences, the fish seemed to thrive, most probably due to the footman who saw to their daily feeding.

Lord Everly's newest acquisitions would either join their brethren in the same tank or the earl would be setting up a new tank in the library. Evangeline allowed a smile. Some, like Lord

Norwick, found the colorful fish tedious and troublesome. The earl claimed that, upon his entrance into Rosemount House, a school of fish had deliberately swum about to set up a wave that cascaded over the top of the tank just as he passed by. The resulting water splash managed to land on his favorite riding coat, leaving a water stain his valet was apparently unable to remove.

Others, like her godfather, Milton Grandby, Earl of Torrington, loved watching the creatures as they moved about their environs, claiming they were a soothing sight. Torrington had occasion to visit the fish after especially challenging sessions of Parliament, claiming the little beasties had more sense than most of the lords.

Evangeline had no opinion of the creatures one way or the other. The fish had been in her brother's library for as long as she could remember, and although they always seemed pleased to see her, waving their translucent fins when she paused to greet them, she figured they probably felt more affection for the footman who fed them.

At least Evangeline could count on Lady Samantha Fitzsimmons and Lady Julia Harrington to keep her company on occasion. Sam, Lord Chamberlain's niece, was of the same age as Evangeline and in the same situation. Since their come-outs, neither girl had attracted a gentleman with the intention of marriage. And neither seemed particularly concerned by their lack of prospects. Julia, on the other hand, would probably be fending off suitors this season. She was younger and blessed with facial features men seemed to find most appealing.

Evangeline shook herself from her reverie and dared a glance at the second line of the book she held. She was about to read it when she became aware of someone standing nearby. Someone who smelled of sandalwood and citrus. Someone who was tall and lean. Someone who was apparently... well, he was shopping for a book, no doubt, she chided herself. Why else would he be standing on the other side of the shelving unit, apparently perusing the new titles just as she had done when the store opened? Or rather, a few minutes *before* the store opened. Mr. Pritchard was always kind enough to unlock the front door if she arrived prior to the official opening time. She was one of his best customers.

*L*ord Sommers took a quick glance over the three rows of shelving, determining almost immediately that the book he sought was not among the titles on display. He was about to search for Mr. Pritchard and ask as to the whereabouts of his book when he noticed there was a space between the books, a space through which he spied a young woman. Or at least portions of her. The space wasn't large enough for him to see all of her at one time.

She was lit by sunlight streaming in from a reading room window, the ethereal light making her appear as if she were an angel. The spine of a book rested on one forearm whilst she opened it with her other hand, apparently turning to the very last page of the book.

She was reading the last page!

After a moment, she turned to the front of the book and was apparently reading the first page!

It was then Jeffrey caught sight of the title page. A very brief sight, for the words, *The Story of a Baron*, flashed by in a blur.

She was reading the very book he sought! *My book!*

How *dare* she? Didn't she realize that by reading the end, she was spoiling it for herself? That by reading the beginning, she was... well, she was doing the very thing he'd seen at least a half dozen other people do whilst they shopped for books, so he couldn't fault her for that, he supposed. But she was reading *his* book!

Jeffrey stilled himself, once more realizing if he gave anymore thought to the woman's actions, he would make his presence known. He didn't wish to draw attention to himself. And upon further viewing, he found the young woman rather easy to watch.

He thought she might have blonde hair, although her bonnet hid far too much of it—and her features—for him to be sure. Fair of skin, with an oval face, she appeared young, but no longer young enough to be in the schoolroom. Her complexion was clear, her cheeks displaying a hint of color, no doubt due to having climbed the stairs to get to this level. Her pink lips were barely parted, the lower one a bit more plump than her upper one. Her lashes were so long, they hid her eyes whilst she read the book through a pair of gold wire spectacles that rested on the tip of her nose. And her left hand...

Jeffrey straightened. The woman's hand was *bare*, its long, slender fingers hardly grazing the surface of the page that held her attention. Fingers that were free of adornment. Free of any rings. Including the one that should have been on her fourth finger.

Tearing his gaze away from the young woman's fingers, afraid if he didn't he would begin imagining what they might feel like when held by his own, Jeffrey pretended to look at some books. Stealing another glance in her direction, he wondered who she might be.

Realizing the woman's attention was no longer on the first page of the book, Jeffrey quickly stopped his perusal of her and stared at the first book on which his eyes could focus. *Sense and Sensibility.* He sighed. *Well, here was a book for the masses,* he thought with an arched eyebrow.

He rather doubted there was such a trait among the *ton*.

*W*ondering if the man was watching her, Evangeline paused in her reading and glanced up. He stood motionless on the other side of the shelving unit, his face partially framed by the tops of the books and the bottom of the next shelf. The portion of him she could make out with her peripheral vision suggested he was at least twenty-five, perhaps thirty. His nose was definitely that of an aristocrat, which surprised her, given the early hour. Most men of the *ton* weren't up and about until well after ten. He sported rather long sideburns, their golden-brown coloring hinting the hair on his head might be the same.

She was tempted to bend her knees a bit and sneak a more direct peek, but she dared not call attention to herself. She did pretend to glance briefly at the books framing the vacant spot left by the book she held and was rewarded with a clear view of the lower half of the man's face.

Faith! His jaw was quite square. From what she could make of his mouth... Evangeline held her breath, barely able to suppress an audible gasp.

The man had lips that were positively enchanting. There could be no other word for them. They were perfectly shaped to form an easy smile. *Or a simple kiss*, Evangeline thought with a grin. She had to pinch her own lips together in an effort to keep her mouth closed or she would have looked like one of her brother's fish.

Lifting her free hand to her spectacles, she slowly removed them from her face but kept them close as she pretended to read the book. The end of one temple found its way to her lips, where it was promptly clasped in place by her teeth. Daring another quick glance in the gentleman's direction, she was relieved to see his attention was on something other than her. A twinge of... regret, perhaps, caught her off-guard. His profile showed a face with impressive cheekbones. The square jaw ended in a slightly rounded chin. Having seen all but his eyes, Evangeline thought perhaps he seemed familiar to her, but without a look at his entire face, she was at a loss as to where she might have met him.

And then, quite unexpectedly, he turned and stared at her.

CHAPTER 2

WORSHIPPING IN THE TEMPLE

*E*vangeline stared back at the man, remembering too late that she still held the end of her spectacles clamped between her teeth.

Unable to greet the man properly, Evangeline immediately looked away and completely removed the spectacles from her face.

Lord Sommers? *No, it couldn't be.* Lord Sommers was a baron. The man was probably still abed at this time of the morning.

She could feel a blush rising to color her throat and cheeks. *Damnation!* Why couldn't she have just ignored the man, whoever he was? He was, no doubt, ignoring her! And now that he had seen her, he was probably trying to remember if they had ever met before. If it was Lord Sommers... well, it just couldn't be. But it was.

The baron had been at Lord Weatherstone's ball—one of the few events she had ever attended where she actually had the opportunity to meet some of the male members of the *ton*. And the only reason she was able to attend that particular ball was because her older brother, Harry Tennison, Earl of Everly, was in London for a few months planning his next expedition. At some point during that short stay, he had managed to arrange for Evangeline to appear in front of the queen for her formal come-out, but he hadn't the time nor the inclination to host a come-out ball on her behalf. Lord Weatherstone's ball had acted in its stead, although no mention of her situation had been communicated to their hosts. She was quite sure if something had been said, Lord Weatherstone would have made an appropriate announcement upon her arrival, or at least saw to introductions to a few of the young bucks in attendance.

Not knowing many peers in London, Evangeline mingled with the few young ladies she recognized from her days at Warwick's Grammar and Finishing School, danced once with her brother, and otherwise enjoyed the spectacle that was a *ton* ball from the sidelines. And then Harry had made a rather peculiar comment about Lord Weatherstone's decorative plants.

At her brother's behest, she began keeping company with one of the rather exotic palms in the hope she could sneak a small frond for him to study. And she might have succeeded on her first try except that Lady Pettigrew was suddenly there on the arm of a baron, insisting Evangeline needed to meet him.

Well, they'd met—she had curtsied to his bow and given him her hand. He'd seemed quite intent on kissing the back of it until he realized her folded spectacles were clutched in her gloved fingers.

Damnable spectacles! It wasn't as if she required them to see clearly—she really only needed them for reading and doing embroidery—but given how much reading and stitchery she did in a day, she wore them almost all the time.

With a rather handsome young man holding onto her clutched fingers, Evangeline had been trying to transfer the spectacles to her other hand without interfering with the baron's elegant fingers. A pink blush covered her face when, of course, their fingers collided, sending the eyewear clattering to the floor.

The baron was quick to retrieve the glasses—quicker than she was—for their heads nearly collided as they both knelt down at the same time. Her nose did brush his hair a bit, a fraction of a second that allowed her to capture the scents of citrus and sandalwood before she had to forcibly exhale—her knees were suddenly in her chest, and her stays made their presence known with a sudden, uncomfortable squeeze.

But, for that moment of awkwardness, not once did she hear him curse her as her brother would have. Nor did he seem particularly inconvenienced as he reached for and retrieved the glasses from the ballroom floor.

When Lord Sommers straightened, one hand still clutching her gloved hand, whilst the other held her spectacles, he merely pulled her up with him and finally bestowed the kiss on the back of her hand as if nothing untoward had happened. "Your brother is the explorer," he said, not making it a question.

She nodded. "Yes. He's in London making arrangements for his next expedition," she replied. "To look for some kind of fish off the coast of India… or Africa."

Lord Sommers frowned. "Then, will you stay in London?" he asked, his question making it sound as if he were quite concerned about where she would be in her brother's absence.

Evangeline shook her head. "Shropshire. At our country estate."

Lady Pettigrew, one hand having covered her mouth for the entire incident with the dropped eye glasses, blinked several times before she seemed to recover her senses. "Well, then, Lady Evangeline. Do have a good evening."

And with that, the baron seemed to understand he was to leave her in the company of the palm tree and escort Lady Pettigrew back to her conclave of other older matrons.

That few moments had been unexpected and rather exciting, despite the incident with her glasses, for Lord Sommers had seemed ever so eager to meet her. But given the ball was nearly over and the other guests were already making their way to the exits, Evangeline couldn't help but feel she had left a poor first impression on the baron.

At least the evening hadn't been a complete waste of time. She had been able to retrieve a palm frond for her brother. And the small tree started from that acquisition was now growing in the orangery at Rosemount House. Should her brother ever host a ball in her late mother's ballroom, Evangeline figured that palm would join several others in providing a refuge for wallflowers and illicit romance.

• • •

*J*effrey shook his head. *Lady Evangeline?*

No, it couldn't be.

This was the comely woman who some claimed was a bluestocking. But she was also the sister of one of the men with whom he played cards at White's—at least, when the earl had enough sense to actually be in attendance at White's. The man spent entirely too much time away on his scientific expeditions.

This was the woman he had imagined as he wrote his book! He had envisioned his hero meeting her for the very first time in a bookstore, much like this one, instantly besotted by her beauty—much like what was happening right now.

Had his fictional story come to life?

Jeffrey gave a quick shake of his head, remembering this wasn't *his* first time meeting Lady Evangeline.

The first—and last time he had seen the girl—was a couple of Seasons ago. At a ball, he recalled, in the company of a rather elaborate plant. He didn't know her identity when he'd spotted her standing next to the potted palm, but he remembered feeling rather jealous of the tree. The damn thing had one frond touching her shoulder as if it had decided she was to be its next dance partner and wasn't about to allow any interlopers. And despite repeated pleas for someone—anyone—to introduce him to the tall, willowy blonde, it was well after the supper had been served before Lady Pettigrew took pity on him and made the introductions. By then, the quartet had finished playing, so there was no opportunity for him to dance with the earl's sister. She seemed shy but eager to speak with him, mentioning to him that her brother would be leaving the country to study fish somewhere off the coast of Africa whilst she would be at the family estate in Shropshire.

Sommers remembered thinking of her trapped in Everly's country estate, snowed in and wishing for companionship, whilst he was similarly trapped in Herefordshire with several bachelors and a deck of cards. If they'd been within ten miles of one another, Sommers would have gladly made the trek on foot through the deep snow to join her.

Wait... perhaps they *were* within ten miles of one another. *Damn!*

To think, they might have spent Christmas together, especially those days following the holiday when a near record amount of snow fell on the countryside. He could think of a dozen activities they could have engaged in to pass the time. He was, in fact, thinking of several when he realized the evidence of his thoughts was making itself known behind the placket of his breeches.

Biting the inside of his cheek, he took a deep breath and stepped out from behind the shelving unit. "Pardon, my lady, but are you Lady Evangeline?" he asked in a hushed voice.

Evangeline's eyes widened. "Why, yes. Yes, I am," she replied with a curtsy. When she straightened, she allowed recognition to show on her face. "And you are Lord Sommers, are you not?"

Jeffrey bowed. "I am," he replied, his face brightening at learning she recognized him. "And rather flattered that you would remember me from our brief introduction at Lord Weatherstone's ball."

Evangeline gave him a tentative smile. "As am I. I seem to recall I made quite a cake of it, though," she added as the memory of that night replayed itself in her head. Her smile faltered, but she kept her chin up, too embarrassed to do anything else.

"It was good cake, as I recall," Jeffrey replied lightly, one finger lightly scratching the outside corner of his eye. "And not enough of it."

Evangeline angled her head to one side. *Good cake?* Did the man think her actions were deliberate? Designed to wreak havoc that night? That she hadn't made enough of a cake of it by dropping her spectacles and nearly bumping heads with him? She certainly didn't do it deliberately. The spectacles might have broken!

Not enough of it?

Offended, and not quite sure how to respond to the odd comment, Evangeline swallowed hard. She remembered the book still opened on her right arm and quickly closed it, the resulting *thump* quite loud in the quiet shop. "Good day, Lord

Sommers," she said with a curt nod and barely a curtsy. She turned and moved to walk around the baron, quite certain his comment was meant to insult her.

Cake, indeed, she thought.

Knowing she was about to cry, Evangeline wanted to be sure she was well away from the baron long before the first tear could fall.

CHAPTER 3

A MAN AFTER HIS
OWN MUSE

*A*s he did nearly every Tuesday morning, Milton Grandby, Earl of Torrington, read the prior day's *The Times* as he sat in a reading lounge on the third floor of The Temple of the Muses. He would have read the paper in the comfort of his breakfast parlor at Worthington House, but when Harry Tennison, Earl of Everly, was away on one of his scientific expeditions, Milton felt it necessary to ensure the safety of the earl's sister, Evangeline, while she made her weekly trek to the bookshop. Although she was always in the company of her lady's maid, she was unmarried, and he thought it best to keep an eye on her. Not spy on her, exactly, but ensure she made it to the shop and home again without being accosted by some unscrupulous heathen.

Milton was her godfather, after all.

As the godfather of no fewer than one-and-twenty young ladies and at least a dozen young bucks varying in age from about eighteen to six-and-twenty, Grandby took his responsibility quite seriously, even if he was three sheets to the wind when he made his agreements to be their godfather back in the day.

Some of the goddaughters were married now. Lady Clarinda Anne Brotherton was the Countess of Norwick. Somehow the daughter of an earl had managed to tame the rake that was

David Fitzwilliam. The proprietor of one of the most exclusive brothels in London, the earl had waited until he was six-and-thirty before deciding to sell his businesses and court and marry Clarinda, all in less than a month's time.

The daughter of a rather successful businessman who was well-known in *ton* circles for helping peers of the realm make money, Olivia Waterford was married to one of her father's business partners. Michael Cunningham, the second son of Viscount Cunningham and a bare-knuckle fighter, was rather successful in his own business ventures. But he could be quite a dunderhead when it came to, well, everything else. It was a wonder he had managed to snag the lovely Olivia before it was too late.

Lady Elizabeth Carlington was now the Viscountess Bostwick, having proposed to George Bennett-Jones when all the *on-dit* suggested she would end up as the Countess of Trenton.

Her best friend, Lady Charlotte Bingham, had recently married and was now the Duchess of Chichester, a title everyone knew she would gain by marriage back when she was still in leading strings. The identity of her duke had changed, however, much to Milton's relief. He never much cared for the older son of John Wainwright. Having survived the fire that killed the rest of his family, the younger brother, Joshua Wainwright, had the title, and he now had Charlotte as his wife. *Now, that is a perfect union,* Milton thought with a good deal of satisfaction. He remembered how he had proposed to his own wife only the day before they paid witness to the ducal wedding in a small chapel in Plaistow.

Elizabeth's other best friend, Lady Hannah Slater, the daughter of the Marquess of Devonville, had married Henry Forster and was now the Countess of Gisborn as well as Milton's niece by marriage. According to his wife, Adele Slater Worthington Grandby, Hannah was enjoying life as a farmer's wife in Oxfordshire and doting on a son she'd delivered just six weeks ago. Apparently, her rather large Alpenmastiff was of the same mind, the dog having decided the babe's safety was his responsibility. As long as the baby didn't drown in the dog's slobber, Milton thought the arrangement most suitable.

He considered the next round of eligible goddaughters. Julia Harrington, certainly. Samantha Fitzsimmons at some point. And Evangeline Tennison.

Evangeline was the priority, if for no other reason than she was the oldest.

With her brother not due back from his latest expedition for at least a week, Milton was considering what could be done, short of bribery or deceit, to see to it Evangeline was betrothed and married before the man left again on another voyage.

So it was an overheard snippet of conversation that had Milton setting aside his newspaper in order to eavesdrop on Lady Evangeline and the young man who had apparently approached her just beyond the entry to the reading lounge.

Pardon, my lady, but are you Lady Evangeline?

Grandby listened intently, shaking his head when he heard the young buck say, *And rather flattered that you would remember me from our brief introduction at Lord Weatherstone's ball.* Then he rolled his eyes when the dunderhead said, *It was good cake, as I recall. And not enough of it.*

Milton frowned. *Faith!* Talk about making a cake of it! Lady Evangeline was probably halfway down the stairs by now, thoroughly offended and on a mission to locate a constable.

Reluctantly lifting himself from the comfortable chair, Milton moved to stand near the threshold. He peeked around the edge of the door frame and immediately recognized Jeffrey Althorpe. The baron was watching the back of Lady Evangeline as she took her leave of him, and probably of The Temple of Muses, if she had any sense.

Milton thought he really should follow the young woman to be sure she arrived at her next appointment unharmed. He didn't wish to make his presence known, though, and there was the issue of the baron still out in the hall. Having no wish to engage him in conversation nor make it known he was eavesdropping by scolding the fool for his offensive comment, Grandby leaned against the wall and waited until it was safe to leave the third floor.

CHAPTER 4

MAKING AMENDS FOR
MAKING A CAKE

Jeffrey Althorpe realized his mistake almost immediately.

It was good cake?

How could he have made such an awful comment? He wasn't supposed to have *agreed* with the lady's assessment of what had happened at Lord Weatherstone's ball. He should have informed her that she was *wrong* about what had happened. Well, not exactly *wrong*, but dropping her spectacles had merely been an accident. No harm had come to the eyewear, and although Jeffrey feared his breeches would split open in the rear as he dropped down to retrieve them, the unforgiving satin had held.

It was the moment when he stood up—that brief moment when she was still below him, looking up at him as he held onto her hand—it was that moment he remembered with such clarity. That moment when her face displayed a look of surprise, as if she hadn't expected him to make the move to pick up her glasses. He was sure her nose had touched his hair, the sensation not unlike a sensuous caress. He was quite sure his entire body had shivered in response. And when he gently tugged on the hand he still held to help her up, he had a passing thought that if Lady Pettigrew wasn't standing *right there*, he would have kissed the surprise right off of Lady Evangeline's lips before she'd had a chance to get her feet firmly under her.

Talk about making a cake of it!

But now Lady Evangeline had suddenly taken her leave of him—and the book with her!

Jeffrey hurried down the rows of books toward the stairs that would lead to the lower stories. A glimpse of the retreating hem of Lady Evangeline's gown caught his eye, though, and he slowed his steps. She had apparently gone into the lounging room, no doubt to begin reading the book.

My book!

He had made the trip to the Temple of the Muses for the sole purpose of acquiring one of the first printings of *The Story of a Baron*. He had even managed to arrive within a few moments of the store's opening, thinking he would be the only one in London with the sole errand of buying that particular book on its first day for sale in the store.

But someone else had his book.

Of course, he could simply ask Mr. Pritchard to order another copy on his behalf. *I can wait*, he told himself, rolling his eyes as he considered that he most certainly could *not* wait. He had to learn what the publisher had done with his tome.

My first book!

And who should end up with the first copy but the very young woman over whom he found himself feeling just a bit... *unsettled?*

Only because I am intrigued by her, he thought as he pulled up short of the doorway to the lounging room.

Damnation! Why would he think such a thing about Evangeline Tennison?

It wasn't because she had chosen his book to buy the very day it went on sale. He had been attracted to her that very first time he'd seen her at Lord Weatherstone's ball. Otherwise, why would he have embarrassed himself by begging *Lady Pettigrew* of all people to arrange an introduction? Lady Pettigrew—the only older woman whose bare breasts he had seen in their entirety and totally by accident—but that was a story for another day.

And now he had further embarrassed himself during their short interchange only a moment ago!

Talk about making a cake of it!

Learning there was only one copy of the book on the third floor had him curious, though. Did the Temple's book buyer think the work of fiction unworthy of space on their shelves? Did they think that a story about a baron wouldn't sell to London's readers?

Or was it too expensive? The publisher had said he would release it all in one volume instead of the usual three. That meant the book would be larger than most. More expensive than seven shillings, surely. Probably closer to twenty in cost. Even more with its leather binding.

Jeffrey hadn't had a chance to learn the exact price of the book. His publisher had never discussed the binding nor how many would be printed for its release. And the Temple of the Muses had a reputation for carrying books that were affordable. Perhaps after *The Story of a Baron* had been available for several months, the Temple would receive the remainders and sell those instead of first-run editions.

The excitement... no, the *pride* he'd felt on entering the bookshop that morning completely disappeared. All because Lady Evangeline had beaten him to his own book!

Or had she?

Perhaps he could talk her into allowing him to buy the first copy. Surely the woman could be reasonable. He would simply explain that he had written the book and wanted to buy the shop's first copy.

And then he would promise her the next one!

Jeffrey's new-found excitement was doused almost as quickly as it had been ignited. He couldn't tell Lady Evangeline he was the author! He didn't want the entire *ton* to know he had written a book that sometimes poked fun at the aristocracy. Nor did he wish to be known as its author, should someone take exception to its content. He'd been most careful in the names and descriptions he used for his cast of characters, changing them so that no one would be offended. But what if someone he hadn't used as inspiration accused him of slander? Or, worse, if he'd left said person out of the story when they wanted to be featured in it?

"Pardon me, my lady, but I wondered if I might have a word with you?" he ventured as he stood on the threshold of the lounging room. At first, he thought Lady Evangeline was the only person in the room, but a young woman, apparently her lady's maid, was standing in front of one of the chairs. He remembered her from when he had glanced into the room on his way to the *New Arrivals* section.

Lady Evangeline, still holding his closed book on her arm, was clearly startled as she turned to regard him. Her eyes were bright, as if she were about to cry. "So that I might make an even larger cake?" she responded, her query dripping with sarcasm.

Quite sure he had offended her with his comment about cake, Jeffrey stood staring at the young woman. "Truly, my lady, I meant no offense," he claimed as he shook his head. "In fact, I intended to inform you of your mistaken impression on the evening we met, but then I thought it would be wrong of me to do so. And so it is *I* who has made a cake of it." He paused a moment, hoping she was following his logic. "By not making myself clear," he added with a nod.

Lady Evangeline regarded the baron for a moment, still unnerved by his appearance in the lounging room. His tone was apologetic, his eyes suitably downcast, and his manner most sober. "So... no cakes?" she managed to get out before she had to suppress a sob by swallowing. Hard.

Jeffrey reached for her hand and leaned down to brush his lips over the back of it. "Only at tea, milady," he said, unaware he still held onto her bare fingers until he felt her gentle tug. "Oh, pardon," he added, a flush coloring his face as he released her hand.

The earl's sister nodded, noticing his embarrassment. Deciding not to add to it, she asked, "And what, pray tell, brought you to the Temple today?" she asked carefully, deciding it would be best to change the topic of conversation. All the talk of cake had her feeling hungry and wishing The Temple of the Muses offered a tea service.

Her question could not have been more perfect. "That book," Jeffrey replied as he pointed to the tome she held on her arm.

Her eyes widening, Evangeline glanced down at *The Story of a Baron*. "Oh?" she asked.

"I wish to buy it," he stated.

Straightening to her full five-foot, eight-inch height, Evangeline said, "As do I."

The room was suddenly rather warm.

Jeffrey frowned. "May I ask... why?"

Evangeline's eyes widened a fraction before she shrugged. "I thought to learn more about a baron, I suppose," she replied. As barons went, she was intrigued by the very man who stood before her. She had been ever since that night at Lord Weatherstone's ball. "And since it's written by Anonymous, I believe the author is probably a baron himself, so the story may be autobiographical."

Forcibly closing his mouth, Jeffrey swallowed. *How had she managed to come to the right conclusion?* Well, half right anyway. Most of what was in the book was what Jeffrey *hoped* would happen when it came to finding a wife. Ever since the Christmastime holiday, he had wondered what it might be like to have a wife with whom to hold on a cold winter night. Not that he could afford to take a wife, but if the book made him enough in royalties, he might be able to marry.

"As a baron, I thought to learn more about one of my brethren," Jeffrey responded after a moment. "Do you suppose you might allow me to buy it today? I would be sure to give it to you when I am finished," he offered, thinking the gift of a book wouldn't break one of Society's rules.

Evangeline stifled a gasp, but her lady's maid did not. "Really, Annabelle, it's not as if the gentleman has offered to buy me a gown or jewels," she scolded. Although, the thought of Lord Sommers buying her anything caused a fluttery sensation in her stomach. And one of annoyance. If he kept her much longer, she would miss her opportunity to call on Lady Samantha at eleven o'clock. For tea. With cake.

"I would be happy to buy you your own copy," Jeffrey

offered, pouncing on the alternative she offered. *Or almost anything you wanted*, he thought, realizing the young woman had him on the verge of frustration. Lust. And impatience.

One of her eyebrows arched up, and Evangeline decided she really didn't want to wait to read the tale. "Is there a reason you cannot wait until Mr. Pritchard can get *you* another copy?" she asked.

She had been sure to arrive at the store just before it opened for the sole purpose of acquiring the book. *If this... this brigand was so determined to get his hands on the same book, he should have arrived before I did!*

"My lady," the baron began with a hint of annoyance. "I could wait, I suppose, but is there any reason why *you* cannot wait?" he countered, his hands clasping behind his back in an effort to still them. He feared if he left them loose he might be tempted to strangle the girl. Or pull her very hard against the front of his body. He had never in his nine-and-twenty years been tempted to take the life of a woman and kiss her all at the same time, but at the moment, he thought he might actually be capable. Of both. At the same time.

Oh, why couldn't he have arrived just a few minutes earlier? Had he managed to wake up when he planned, he would have been at the front door when the shop opened! As it was, his valet had reminded him of the date when he opened the bedchamber drapes and added, "You said you wished to be on your way early this day."

Despite the valet's very best efforts, it still took the same amount of time it always did to shave and dress him. Jeffrey even left the house without having so much as a cup of coffee or a bit of breakfast. And with all this talk of cake, his stomach was reminding him of his oversight.

It was all going so wrong!

If only the bookshop offered a tea service!

Evangeline stared at the impertinent man, appalled he would suggest that she give up her claim to the new book simply because he couldn't wait to read it. Did other patrons of

The Temple of Muses have this problem when they wanted a new book? When they planned their morning with the express purpose of arriving upon the opening of the store to acquire said book?

She rather doubted it. But, given the baron's apparent zeal for the same book, she decided that he had probably planned his morning much the same as she had. He had probably arisen a bit earlier than usual, rushing through his morning toilette in an effort to be out of the house and at the storefront at precisely nine o'clock. Perhaps he had been delayed due to his valet, or his breakfast, or traffic. Perhaps it had been his intention to arrive *before* the store actually opened, much as she had. Did circumstances really dictate that *she* be the one to claim the book simply because she had arranged everything in advance and it had all worked out in her favor when it had not for this gentleman?

This gentleman.

This is Lord Sommers, she reminded herself. He had been the only gentleman to seek an introduction to her at Lord Weatherstone's ball. Perhaps she was looking at this all wrong.

"You intended to be here earlier, didn't you?" Evangeline finally answered, recognizing that the baron was staring at her with a look of expectation... and perhaps, something else.

"I did. I... My morning did not work out as I intended," he agreed, his sigh audible in the quiet surrounds. Jeffrey's gaze softened. If he imagined her without the ridiculous bonnet, he could almost see the honey blond, blue-eyed vision he'd spied, consorting with the potted palm that night at the ball. The willowy blonde he absolutely had to be introduced to before he took his leave of Lord Weatherstone's ball.

Here he had been thinking to strangle her, he thought with a guilty heart. "Forgive me, Lady Evangeline," he whispered, his head dropping into a bow. "I... I have been an absolute ass and..." He paused, realizing almost immediately what word had just come out of his mouth. Closing his eyes for a moment, he hoped beyond hope that he hadn't just spoken the inappropriate word loud enough so the lady could hear. "And worse," he added, his head shaking from side to side.

Evangeline stared at him a moment, her look of shock slowly replaced with one of contrition. "Lord Sommers?" she said with a hint of a question. "I... I apologize. I did not consider we might both find this book equally important," she said as a becoming blush colored her face.

Jeffrey sighed. His gaze took in her serviceable pelisse and a bonnet some would consider ridiculous. Despite her clothes, he found her delectable. Did her damned brother not give her an allowance for a decent modiste, though? The earl was off on one of his expeditions to discover who knew what—something about fish, Jeffrey remembered just then,—leaving his comely sister all alone and fending for herself in the largest city in the world. "It is I who should apologize," he countered, shaking his head in dismay. "About the cake. You must think me the worst kind of rake," he stated, his eyes rolling up and around to emphasize his plight.

"Of course not," Evangeline replied. "You're simply as desperate as I am," she reasoned. "We both wish to read the same book on the day of its release."

Jeffrey nodded. "And there is only the one copy."

Evangeline nodded in return. "There is." After a moment, she angled her head to one side. "Had you planned to spend the day reading it?" she asked, thinking that if he had not, she would offer to read it and then turn it over to him later. After all, how long would it take to read the book? It was the story of a baron.

His eyebrows rising to meet his hair, Jeffrey nodded. "The entire day," he agreed with a sigh.

Wondering if her lady's maid was still within earshot, Evangeline glanced around. "Me, too," she replied, deciding she didn't have to call on Lady Samantha at eleven o'clock. She considered their options. She could read it and then have it delivered to the baron's residence. Or she could allow him to read it first and have it delivered to Rosemount House. Or...

"Would you agree to reading it... together?" Evangeline offered with a raised eyebrow. "The weather is fine. We could find a bench in the square—"

"And read it side-by-side?" the baron asked, a shiver of

excitement racing up his spine. His voice was quiet, as if they were arranging a clandestine *affaire*.

Then he remembered what they would be reading.

His book. *The Story of a Baron.* A book he had written about a baron who was besotted by a certain young lady whom he had somewhat modeled after the very woman who stood before him.

Well, *modeled* might be too strong a word, he thought. He had simply borrowed some of the situations from her life and turned them around a bit. Created some opposites in the names of the settings. Invented a character that might have been any young lady in the *ton*. Surely Lady Evangeline wouldn't notice.

His heroine was really nothing like Evangeline, except that they could both benefit by employing a different modiste. Geraldine was brunette and petite. The description might suit half the young misses in London. Why, reading this book with Lady Evangeline might mean he could gauge her interest. Discover if she recognized any of the other aristocrats he had used as inspiration. Determine what she thought of his writing style.

So Jeffrey relaxed a bit and waited with bated breath for Evangeline to respond.

A shiver passed through Evangeline, the sensation leaving behind goose bumps on her arms and down her spine. "I think we shall have to read it side-by-side," she agreed. "Although I can read upside-down when circumstances require, I would not wish to do so when reading for pleasure."

Another shiver passed through Jeffrey. Pleasure. The woman read for pleasure. Probably because she had nothing else to do. He was considering several other pursuits she could do for pleasure, none of them involving books. All of them involving him. Naked, between the linens of his favorite bed in the family estate in Herefordshire. Or in his bedchamber in Sommers Place in Cavendish Square. "Of course," was all he could manage, hoping his arousal wasn't going to make itself evident.

"Then, it's settled," Evangeline stated with a curt nod.

Clutching the book in one arm, she led the way to the stairs, knowing her lady's maid would hurry to join them at any moment. Before she reached the bottom of all the flights, she had both gloves pulled onto her hands. When she passed by the circular desk, she merely nodded to one of the clerks, who acknowledged her with a quick nod and a receipt ready for her to sign.

By the time they reached the front door of the bookshop, Lord Sommers had hurried forward to open the door.

He stood aside as Lady Evangeline and her lady's maid took their leave of the store. When he noticed Mr. Pritchard staring at him with a look of shock, he gave the man a shrug. "Perhaps you can order me another copy?" he said *sotto voce*. He tossed a shilling in the man's direction. "Good day," he called out and hurried to catch up to Lady Evangeline.

CHAPTER 5

AFFAIRE IN THE SQUARE

A moment later, Milton, Earl of Torrington, descended the stairs into the lobby of the bookshop, his eyes darting about as if he expected books to come flying off the shelves. When he was noticed by the shopkeeper, he gave the man a nod and hurried up to him. "Did Lady Evangeline leave with Lord Sommers?" he asked *sotto voce.*

Harold Pritchard nodded and bowed deeply, wondering at the earl's lowered voice. "She did," he confirmed. "With his book," he added, one eyebrow cocked up. Then it furrowed. "I wasn't supposed to tell you that."

Milton frowned, wondering if the man meant that Lady Evangeline had run off with a book that belonged to the baron or if he meant the baron had written the book. If Lord Sommers was in pursuit, then Evangeline was at a disadvantage, given her heeled shoes. "Good day," he said quickly, donning his hat as he took his leave of the shop.

Why would his goddaughter have done such a thing as steal a baron's book?

He spotted the pair as they made their way into the center of Finsbury Square, rather relieved to see the baron wasn't chasing his goddaughter. In fact, from the way they walked side-by-side, Lady Evangeline's hand on Lord Sommers' arm, it didn't appear as if Lord Sommers was even in a hurry to retrieve his book. Evangeline's lady's maid followed behind, apparently unconcerned that her mistress was in the company of the baron.

Curious, the earl crossed the street and entered the square, deciding he needed to keep an eye on the situation.

The building that hosted The Temple of the Muses proved the perfect backdrop as Lord Sommers and Lady Evangeline settled themselves onto a park bench. The baron made sure to leave a few inches between them at first, but when Evangeline opened the book to the first page, she allowed him to pull the book in his direction so that one side of it rested on his right thigh while the other was held by her gloved hand, which she supported on her left thigh.

"Are you a fast reader?" Jeffrey asked as he allowed her to turn the front pages until the first page of Chapter One appeared. "I ask only because I am not," he clarified, not wanting to attempt to race her to the finish of each spread.

"Not particularly," Evangeline replied. "But if I get to the end of a page before you do, I shall wait until you have indicated you are ready for the next page before I turn it."

Jeffrey nodded and then wondered if he should feel a bit offended. Did the earl's daughter think him incapable of reading at the same speed as she? Although he usually didn't read quickly, he had written the book—he could probably skim the thing and be done in a few hours or so.

Except he had no idea what his publisher had done with the manuscript after their last meeting. An editor might have changed the story, or added a character, or God forbid, deleted a chapter. He might have changed Jeffrey's prose so that much of the life had been sucked out of his carefully constructed words, or perhaps the man had embellished the story to make it more flowery, or less comedic, or more dramatic, or completely ridiculous. *I'll have to read it completely*, he thought, giving Evangeline a nod when he saw she was waiting for a response.

"I am ready, my lady," he said with more certainty than he felt.

"As am I," Evangeline replied with a grin. She lowered her

spectacles so they rested on the end of her nose, and she began to read.

CHAPTER 6

OUR COUPLE READ IN
FINSBURY SQUARE

The Story of a Baron
A Novel in One Volume
Written by Anonymous

Chapter 1: In Another Time and Place
Matthew Winters, Baron Ballantine, entered his favorite bookshop in search of a particular new title. Having just returned from the family estate in Shropshire, a poorly maintained pile set against a hill and overlooking pastures dotted with sheep and a fishing pond, the baron found the library in his bachelor apartments just as depressing as when he'd left them the year before.

He had missed the fall sessions of Parliament in favor of helping with the harvest and seeing to repairs on several structures on Ballantine properties. Christmastime at Ballantine Park had been boring in the extreme—three days of drifting snow prevented him from leaving the estate, even to ride his horse. Once the snow had melted, it was time to arrange for seeding and sowing. Not particularly fond of farming and having tenants who could see to the lands, Matthew had decided it was time to return to Mayfair.

The Season was about to begin.

Despite the pleasant weather and a stack of invoices that

demanded his attention—and most of his bank account—Matthew was determined to spend the day ensconced in his library reading. Trouble was, he had read every book on the shelves.

Well, *read* was probably too strong a word.

The tome on farming had at least been opened and occasionally used for reference, and the two on parliamentary procedure had been excellent sleep aides, but Ballantine was in search of more satisfying fare. Nothing fictional, he had decided the night before, but instead something to help with a particular problem. Hence, his trip to his favorite bookshop, The Palace of Prose.

The baron made his way to the third story of the shop, figuring the book he sought, *In Pursuit of the Perfect Woman: A Gentleman's Guide to Finding a Wife*, would be mid-priced. At least, Thomas Christianson, Earl of Atherton, had assured him it was affordable. Atherton had also sworn by the book's recommendations, claiming to have used its advice not only to gain a loving wife, but one who came with a substantial dowry and a disposition that not only tolerated his mistress, but encouraged him to take another. "You never know when the first one will tire of you, dear," she had apparently said, "So it's best to have another waiting in the wings. Or between the sheets, I suppose."

Matthew wasn't sure if he believed his friend's recollection of Lady Atherton's position on mistresses, but the man did have money with which to gamble at Black's men's club. Although Matthew didn't gamble to excess—he couldn't afford to do so given his limited means—he thought it would be an improvement for his position in Society to stay at the gaming tables longer than half an hour once a week.

The baron stopped in his tracks as he reached the top of the stairs. Although it was too early for most shoppers of the famed bookseller, the third floor could claim at least one other on this pleasant day.

One of the female persuasion.

A female who was rather beautiful, in fact. Lit from above by a skylight and dressed entirely in pink, she appeared almost angelic as beams of light cascaded around her. Although her head was bent over an open book and somewhat shadowed by the brim of her pink bonnet, her profile suggested she was young, but at least of marriageable age.

As Matthew Winters regarded the petite gel at the end of the hallway, he thought she seemed familiar, but he couldn't place where he might have met her. In a ballroom, perhaps, or maybe she had been perched on a phaeton parked outside of Hunter's Tea Emporium.

The thought reminded him that he had promised his mother that he would escort her to Hunter's for an ice sometime that week. Given the fair weather, he decided he had best fulfill the obligation sooner than later. If it rained, he would be forced to enter the premises and endure introductions to every available unmarried daughter of the peerage.

Well, a number of them anyway.

The shop wasn't large enough to accommodate *all* of them.

The baron made his way past the shelves featuring books on botany and physiology and around a table on which was an artfully arranged display of books on keeping a household.

Convinced the woman was about to take her leave of the book shop, Matthew was determined to introduce himself before she did so.

Passing the sportsman's section, he paused to glance at a book on fly fishing. He was about to open the slim volume when he noticed the woman motioning toward one of the lounging rooms. He was nearly in greeting distance when her lady's maid appeared in the doorway.

Damnation!

The woman turned and regarded him for only a moment, recognition apparent in her eyes. "Lord Ballantine," the petite brunette said as she held out her hand in his direction. The lady's maid stepped back and pretended to study a book on art history.

Stunned, Matthew had to force his mouth to stay closed. Apparently, they had met in the past, but he couldn't put a name to the face. She was poised, not the least bit embarrassed about her lack of height, and was definitely not a milkwater maid. "My lady," he answered as he took her hand and kissed the back of the pink silk glove. "I fear you have me at a disadvantage," he admitted, deciding a bluff wouldn't work.

The woman, who sported a light pink pelisse and matching parasol, which, thankfully, remained closed, gave him a wavering smile. "Geraldine. We used to play together." When recognition didn't appear in his expression, she added, "In our youth, of course. We made mud pies. Skipped rocks. Hid in the folly." *Kissed in the barn.* She decided not to mention that last bit, if only because it would add to the list of indiscretions in which she had recently been accused of participating. After a slight pause, she added, "I recall hating you on occasion. You were best friends with my brother, Richard. Lord Afterly."

Matthew gave a quick shake of his head. "Of course!" He knew immediately why he didn't recognize the young lady. The last time he had seen Lady Geraldine Porterhouse, she was barely in the schoolroom! "I suppose no one gets away with calling you 'Jerry' these days," he commented in a teasing voice.

Her sea green eyes widening in delight, Geraldine raised a hand to cover her mouth. "You *do* remember! Although, I must admit, I wish you didn't," she replied with a wan smile. A pink flush colored her face before she could lower her head, although she might have appeared pink simply because she wore so much of the color. "I didn't really hate you."

The brim of her pink bonnet briefly hid her features from Matthew. *She's become a lovely creature,* he thought, rather heartened to hear her last words. Theirs had been a tumultuous relationship, but they had been mere children back then. Well, except for when he kissed her in the barn. They had been in their teen years at that point.

He wondered to whom she was married.

Her parents, the Marquess and Marchioness of Afterly, had both died when their carriage overturned on a trip in Spain. They had been on their Grand Tour of Europe, their trip nearly complete when they perished. Richard Porterhouse, still in his twenties, had inherited the marquessate. But his penchant for traveling—his avocation was archaeology—meant his older sister was left on her own for months at a time. At least the poor thing was a sociable creature; she managed to attend a variety of *ton* events despite not having an escort or a companion at her elbow. Even though he had only been back in London a few days, Matthew had already heard some gossip about her—everyone in the *ton* had heard about the supposed exploits of Lady Geraldine.

"It looks as if you were about to take your leave. May I escort you to your carriage?" Matthew offered, extending an elbow in her direction.

Geraldine glanced back to ensure her lady's maid still shadowed her. "Why, that's very kind of you, my lord," she replied, moving to rest her hand on his arm, as if she did it everyday. "I am actually on my way to shop in New Bond Street."

"Call me Ballantine," he replied quickly, daring a glance at Geraldine's jewel-bedecked hand on his arm. There were three rings, but none on her fourth finger.

"A barony seems to suit you, Ballantine," Geraldine commented as she allowed him to lead them down the stairs. "How long has it been?"

Matthew knew she referred to the death of his father, a rather unexpected event that had left his mother an almost helpless widow and a barony near receivership. "Coming up on four years now," he finally answered, chiding himself on how he had allowed the innocent question to result in a sudden fit of melancholy.

They made their way to the front of the bookstore, Geraldine's lady's maid following close behind. Not comfortable making small talk, Ballantine grasped for a topic he might bring up to keep the gel talking. "Forgive me, but I don't recall reading about your wedding," he ventured as a footman saw to the door. "Who is the lucky man, if I may ask?"

Turning her head to regard the baron as they passed through the front doors of the establishment, Geraldine had to resist the urge to snort. "You didn't read about a wedding involving me because there hasn't been one," she responded with a shake of her head and a quick wave of the hand decorated with gemstones. Or, perhaps they were paste. He couldn't really tell.

Matthew nearly stopped in his tracks. *Not married?* Geraldine Porterhouse was one of prettiest young women in the *ton!*

Her father had been a marquess. Her brother was now the Marquess of Afterly. How could she have avoided the bonds of marriage? "But you're... *betrothed*, certainly," Matthew insisted, glancing up and down the street in an attempt to determine which piece of equipage would be taking her to her next destination.

Geraldine allowed an audible sigh. "I am not, actually," she informed him archly. "A situation that will probably not change until my brother can see fit to spend more than a fortnight in London. Or a highwayman kidnaps me and takes me to Gretna Green," she added in an excited voice, as if she found the prospect of an elopement preferable to a more respectable betrothal.

"Is Afterly still in Greece?" Matthew guessed, a frown forming a vertical line between his brows.

"Rome now, I think," Geraldine replied. "But I've received word he will be returning soon. Which means he's about to run out of funding and needs to come home to beg for more," she said *sotto voce*. "I do hope he remembered his promise to bring me back a bauble or two from Italy. Seems the least he can do after leaving me alone for so long."

Matthew nodded his understanding. Richard Porterhouse spent months abroad on archeological expeditions, digging up bits of pottery and other remnants of societies long dead. "Does he truly leave you... *alone?*" Matthew asked with concern, a shiver of excitement racing down his spine as another part of him anticipated what he could be doing with the divine Lady Geraldine until her brother returned from the Continent. Kissing her, certainly. Divesting her of the pink gown she wore. Taking his time as he learned every inch of her with his tongue and teeth and the tips of his fingers. Burying himself inside her. Taking his pleasure until he was delirious. Giving her pleasure until she nearly fainted. And then doing it all over again the next day.

"Why, Lord Ballantine, you naughty boy!" Geraldine responded, her voice suggesting she wasn't teasing but had guessed exactly what he was thinking.

His face reddening at her comment, Matthew pondered if

he should agree with her assessment. He *was* thinking rather naughty thoughts of her just then.

Should he deny he had been thinking any such things? He could, but then he'd be telling a lie.

Ignore her comment, perhaps? Ignore it, and then say something completely unrelated so she would be forced to change the subject?

He was about to agree with her when the marquess' daughter stopped walking, forcing Matthew to spin to his right as her hand still clung to his arm. Geraldine's lady's maid, only a few steps behind them, nearly collided with her mistress.

Almost face-to-face, Matthew regarded Geraldine with a stunned look. "My lady?" he asked in alarm.

Geraldine's mouth opened as if she were about to speak, but no sound came out. Lowering her face, she sighed. "I apologize, my lord," she said in a small voice. "I... I cannot believe I could be so... *bold*. So brazen. You must think me awfully uncouth," she added in a most remorseful tone.

Matthew stared at the sorrowful woman. Her confident air had been replaced with one of contrition, her petite frame appearing even more shrunken as her shoulders slumped. He thought he saw her eyes brighten with unshed tears. And the thought that she might start to cry right there in the middle of New Bond Street had the baron in a state of near panic. "My lady, whatever you are thinking, let me assure you, there is no reason to believe that you have offended me, for you have not," he assured her. "And I... I do not think of you as particularly bold. Or brazen," he added for good measure.

Liar, he thought just as quickly. For, compared to other ladies of the *ton*, he surmised Lady Geraldine *was* rather bold. A bit too brazen. And the only woman on the planet with whom he could imagine enjoying the scandalous activities they could perform in his bedchamber.

Or hers.

I am going to hell.

Geraldine lifted her head, her eyes finally meeting his. One tear had escaped and was leaving a wet trail down her cheek. "I merely meant to tease you," she whispered, lifting her reticule in an attempt to find a handkerchief. Before she could get it open, though, Matthew had his own out of his pocket and was gently dabbing at her cheek.

He could admit he was guilty of the very crime she mentioned. He should own up to it. He should put her out of her misery and admit she was right. But he found he rather liked this version of Lady Geraldine. Teary-eyed damsel in distress. All woman. All soft and pliable. Angelic.

I could put her on a pedestal and worship her, he thought with a sigh.

But I'd rather worship her naked body with my bed as an altar, his baser side argued.

Faith! He hadn't realized how much he missed having a mistress until that very moment. If he spent two more minutes with the lady, she would be in grave danger of losing her maidenhead—if she even still possessed it, given the *on-dit* that suggested she had been intimate with at least three gentlemen. Matthew had a passing thought that her jewels might have been gifts from those gentlemen. His good mood turned sour.

Matthew glanced around, desperate to find an excuse to take his leave of her. "Let me assure my lady that you may tease me whenever you wish," he finally said, not realizing how his words could be misinterpreted.

Lady Geraldine's look of contrition was replaced with one of surprise. "You are too kind," she replied with a nod.

"I fear my appearance in The Palace of Prose may have kept you from your appointments this morning. What is your destination?" Matthew asked, thinking he would simply hire a hackney and see her on her way.

Geraldine cocked her head to one side, understanding that Lord Ballantine probably had errands other than hers planned for the day. Although her boldness hadn't seemed to offend the man, she had apparently taken up too much of his time. "Madame Diana's Emporium," she informed him, one hand pointing in the direction of the lady's shop across the street—a shop featuring corsets and night rails and all manner of undergarments for ladies.

Matthew's eyes followed the direction in which Geraldine

pointed, his eyes pausing on yet another large gemstone on her finger. His face once again displaying embarrassment, he bowed and lifted Geraldine's hand to his lips, giving the ring a thorough look. Although he wasn't positive, he was fairly sure the stone was paste. "Then I shall take my leave of you, my lady," he said with a nod. He kissed the back of her hand and gave a cursory bow before he hurried off in the direction from which they'd come.

A startled expression still on her face, Geraldine watched the baron's back as he made his way down New Bond Street. "Was it something I said?" she whispered to herself. "Or something he was about to do?" A shiver of delight raced through her body. She grinned, deciding she rather liked the grown up version of Matthew Winters.

Geraldine gave one more glance at the baron's departing back before making her way across the street to Madame Diana's Emporium.

As she was about to enter the shop, she dared another look up and down New Bond Street, hoping to spot the baron. There was no sign of him, though. Allowing a sigh of disappointment, she passed through the doors of the lady's establishment and disappeared from view.

Across the street, Matthew Winters watched from where he stood hidden in an alcove leading to a haberdashery. Although he thought about going back to The Palace of Prose to purchase the book, *In Pursuit of the Perfect Woman: A Gentleman's Guide to Finding a Wife,* he decided he might not require its assistance after all.

Although Geraldine Porterhouse wasn't the perfect woman, she might do in a pinch, he considered. And better someone he knew than someone he didn't—even if she did come with a bit too much scandal.

CHAPTER 7

ON SCANDALOUS
THOUGHTS ABOUT WOMEN

*B*ack in Finsbury Square
Jeffrey finished reading the last line, a sense of *déjà vu* settling over him at the same time he felt heat creeping up to color his throat and face with a hint of red. He had been correct in remembering the first chapter of his book featured the hero and heroine meeting in a bookshop. It was as if had foreseen his morning with Lady Evangeline and then documented the encounter. That is, if she had been more like Geraldine, and he had been more like Matthew, which, of course, neither of them were. Giving it another thought, he decided the two situations held little in common but the setting.

Curious as to what Evangeline thought, he turned his attention to her profile. "Well, what are your thoughts?"

Evangeline gave a sigh before she looked up from the book. "I am quite sure these two will end up together," she said with a good deal of satisfaction. "I look forward to learning how." She turned to regard Lord Sommers for a moment. "Even though they apparently knew one another when they were younger, Lady Geraldine seems a bit... well, a bit *bold* for Lord Ballantine's tastes." *For any man's tastes*, she almost said, but she knew so little of their sex, she thought it better she limit her comments.

Jeffrey gave her a sideways glance, his face still red with

embarrassment. The woman in the book was bold, yes, but the baron's thoughts were more so. The fact that they were written out so explicitly and that Lady Evangeline remained so calm as she read them had Jeffrey wondering if she were as bold as Geraldine.

He hadn't even considered his book might be read by women when he was writing it, especially not by women who were gently bred! How could Evangeline sit next to him and remain so... so *calm* as a male member of the *ton* thought such scandalous thoughts about what he might do with a woman? She hadn't made so much as a peep of protest whilst reading that part of the first chapter!

"Did you not find the story a bit... scandalous?" he enquired, keeping his voice down when he remembered her lady's maid was sitting on the other side of Evangeline.

Frowning, Evangeline thought for a moment. "No," she finally answered with a shake of her head. "Quite the contrary, given this is the story of a peer."

It was Jeffrey's turn to frown. "You expected it to be... to be *more* scandalous because a *peer* is involved?" he asked outright. *Faith!* What kind of books was Evangeline Tennison used to reading?

All kinds, a voice in the back of his head reminded him. What else did the poor girl have to do all day but read books, given her brother was away on his scientific expeditions most of the time? She had probably read every single book in the Rosemount House library!

Evangeline shrugged before she realized the baron probably wasn't used to reading fiction. He probably had to read books about farming and parliamentary procedures—books that would be better used to put a person to sleep. "Not scandalous, necessarily," she said with another shake of her head. "But it was, no doubt, written by a man who is familiar with life in the *ton*, and from what I gather from my brother's occasional comments on the matter, the men can be a bit... uncouth."

Jeffrey stared at the earl's sister for a moment. "Why do you think it was written by a man?" he asked, apparently no longer concerned about her feminine sensibilities.

Evangeline appeared somewhat surprised by the question. "Well...," she hedged a moment. "The description of Lord Ballantine is as I would expect a man to describe him. There is no mention as to whether or not he is handsome, nor anything about the color of his eyes or the shape of his nose. If he has a square jaw or a strong chin. If his lips are kissable." A slight blush crept up her face. "There's also no description of his clothing. The color. The cut. Whether or not it's made of quality fabrics. Does he wear boots or shoes? Are they shined?

"Had a woman written this, I am quite certain those attributes would have been described in great detail," Evangeline explained. "Of course, I could be wrong," she added, amused at the baron's quizzical expression as she gave him her list of reasons.

Straightening on the bench, Jeffrey regarded her for a moment. The lady wasn't wrong. He rather doubted she was often wrong about anything. "And the description of Miss Porterhouse?" he asked, eager to hear her take on the heroine of the story.

At his query, Evangeline seemed at a loss. "I have not met a woman quite like her whilst paying calls. Nor did I have any classmates who were like her in character," she answered carefully, her head shaking a bit.

"Classmates?" Jeffrey repeated, his brow furrowing.

Evangeline nodded. "I attended Warwick's Grammar and Finishing School," she said. "For three years. I would have had a governess like most daughters of earls, but with my parents having died and my brother away on his expeditions, it was better that I live at a boarding school. I had protection, of course," she added quickly, figuring he might balk at the idea of a young lady of the *ton* attending such a school.

"Ah," Jeffrey answered, folding his arms across his chest. The finishing school was favored by wealthy families who wished to have their daughters learn how to speak French, dance, draw and paint, sew, play piano-forté, and appreciate theatrical productions. "So, you probably attended with other young ladies of gentle breeding," he assumed, thinking the girls from Warwick's probably didn't plan practical jokes or pull pranks when they weren't in class. At least, not like the ones he'd been guilty of doing at Eton and Cambridge.

Nodding, Evangeline said, "Most of my classmates are married now. And my experience with Society events is still rather limited, so perhaps there are women like Miss Porterhouse, and I just haven't yet met them."

Jeffrey gave her a sideways glance. "Are you sure *you* are not like Miss Porterhouse?" he teased, wondering too late why he wished she were.

Evangeline's eyes widened in shock. "I most certainly am *nothing* like Geraldine," she said, her emphatic response causing Jeffrey to raise a brow. "Even if they were the best of friends when they were children, she was far too forward with Lord Ballantine, what with her comment about him being *naughty*," she argued. "Why, if she was a real person, I don't know how she would expect to find a suitable match when her reputation is already in question. Perhaps we'll learn if she truly is ruined, for I rather doubt this is her first time being so forward with a member of your sex."

His eyebrows furrowing so a fold of skin formed between them, Jeffrey shook his head. "What... what makes you say that?"

Evangeline lowered her voice before saying, "If she is so forward with Lord Ballantine—a man she has not seen in many years—she is no doubt that way with other gentlemen," she reasoned quickly. "Remember, Ballantine had heard gossip suggesting that she may have been intimate with as many as *three* gentlemen."

Jeffrey considered her words for a long time before he nodded, realizing any man who came into contact with a character like Geraldine Porterhouse would talk about her. "Men are the worst gossips," Jeffrey said in agreement.

It was Evangeline's turn to exhibit shock. "They are?" Lord Sommers obviously hadn't been in a Mayfair parlor at two o'clock in the afternoon!

Suppressing the urge to laugh at Evangeline, Jeffrey merely nodded. And then he watched as her expression changed from one of astonishment to one of concern. "What is it?" he asked.

Evangeline shook her head. "I was just wondering what was being said... about me, is all," she whispered, a flush of pink coloring her face. "If anything," she added quickly, not wanting to suggest there was any reason she might be a source of gossip.

Recognizing her look for what it was, Jeffrey leaned in and said, "I have not heard a single offensive word spoken about you." He could have claimed he hadn't heard a single word of *anything* about her, but that would be a bald-faced lie. Most of what he had heard had more to do with the pity people felt for her—pity because the poor thing was stuck with Lord Everly, her inattentive and mostly absent brother, as a protector. And there were those who referred to her as a bluestocking, but he didn't find the term particularly offensive. *What was wrong with a woman who was educated?* he often wondered. Wouldn't a man appreciate being able to speak on subjects other than the latest gossip and the fashions from France over breakfast with his wife?

I would, he thought with a sigh.

He glanced in Evangeline's direction, curious about the expression she showed. "What is it?" he asked.

"I find it very difficult to believe you," Evangeline stated, determined to make sure the baron understood he wasn't allowed to lie to her. "That is, unless you spend most of your time in your apartments and not out among the *ton*."

Jeffrey frowned, a bit offended that she thought he lived in housing meant for a bachelor rather than in the house in Cavendish Square he had inherited from his father. His frown deepened when he sorted she was accusing him. "Are you calling me a *liar*, Lady Evangeline?" he challenged, deciding he really was offended.

Evangeline's brows arched up and then settled back down to their normal placement. "Not exactly," she answered finally. "Yes," she said after another pause.

Jeffrey blinked. And then he burst out laughing. "I, my lady, do not find the term 'bluestocking' an offensive word when describing the attributes of a lady," he said in his own defense.

• • •

*B*luestocking!

There it was. The word she'd been dreading. The term she had suspected was being used to describe her. And his flippant statement hadn't made the word any less palatable.

Suddenly uncomfortable, Evangeline stared at the baron for a long time. She had known the *ton* had been saying things about her—about her tendency to read too much—and now the moniker of "bluestocking" had been applied to her. She would never be able to lose the label; even if she claimed to be spending her days doing embroidery—which is exactly what she did most days—or drawing silhouettes, or painting, or playing piano-forté—she would *never* be anything but a bluestocking to those in the *ton*.

The combination of frustration and anger had tears pricking the corners of her eyes, but determined not to allow them to fall, Evangeline blinked several times and took a deep breath.

*J*effrey remembered her comment about staying in his apartments and thought it best to clear up that matter right away. "I own a house in Cavendish Square, my lady. Although I spend my nights and mornings there, I spend far more time among my peers," he said gently.

Still miffed at the suggestion she was a bluestocking—even if he didn't mind a woman being a bluestocking—Evangeline let out the breath she'd been holding and straightened. "I must go," she said, not wanting to spend another minute with a member of the male sex.

"My lady?" Jeffrey replied, concern evident in his voice.

"I promised Lady Samantha I would pay a call on her this morning. At Fitzsimmons Manor," she said, unable to make eye contact with the baron.

"Of course." Jeffrey stood up and offered her his hand. Evangeline stared at it for a full second before placing her own gloved hand in his. She stood up, making sure the book ended up in the crook of her other arm. "Good day, Lord Sommers," she said as she gave him a curtsy.

Jeffrey felt a bit of panic. He wasn't about to allow her to take her leave of him, at least, not yet. He had more he wanted to discuss with her about the book. "May I escort you to Lady Samantha's?" he offered. "Fitzsimmons Manor is on my way," he lied. Actually, Lord Chamberlain's house was only on his way if he walked two extra miles and made at least three turns getting home from there.

Evangeline gave her lady's maid a glance. "I think not, Lord Sommers. I should hate to think of the gossip our jaunt would elicit."

Jeffrey had to suppress the urge to wince at her comment. She was right, of course. Even with her lady's maid following them, there would be someone who would claim there was something illicit going on between the two of them.

An affaire.

A sense of disappointment settled over the baron before he remembered the book. "Then, when can we next meet?" he asked, pointing to the book. "To read?"

A rather pleasant shiver traveled down Evangeline's spine as she considered Lord Sommers' question. He seemed so eager! "What about tomorrow? In the middle of Grosvenor Square?" she suggested. "If the weather is fine," she amended.

Jeffrey nodded. "Ten o'clock?" he offered.

Evangeline nodded. "Ten o'clock."

Jeffrey was about to allow her to leave when he considered the unpredictable British climate. "And if the weather is not fine?" he asked. "What then?"

Evangeline considered some options. Although it wasn't particularly proper for Lord Sommers to call on her at Rosemount House, the visit might generate just a hint of gossip that could work in her favor. Imagine the *on-dit* suggesting Lady Evangeline was being visited by a man whilst her brother was still abroad!

Perhaps she would no longer be labeled a bluestocking!

Excitement had her holding her breath lest Jeffrey hear her slight gasp. "The library at Rosemount House," she said with a curt nod, feeling rather bold just then. "We can have tea and biscuits whilst we read."

Jeffrey didn't hide his surprise at her suggestion. And he found himself hoping for inclement weather.

Days and days of it.

"Very good, my lady," he said as he reached for her hand. His lips brushed over her gloved knuckles before he straightened. "I look forward to tomorrow, and to Chapter Two," he added. "Promise me you won't read ahead," he ordered with a cocked eyebrow.

"I promise I will not," Evangeline replied before dipping a curtsy.

Giving her a deep bow in return, Jeffrey took his leave of Evangeline and her lady's maid and headed back toward the bookshop.

He intended to have a word with Mr. Pritchard about the limited availability of his book.

One copy, indeed!

CHAPTER 8

ON SCANDALOUS WOMEN
AND BOOKS

*E*vangeline watched the baron take his leave of the square before opening her parasol. She regarded her lady's maid for a moment. "Did I shock you, Annabelle?" she asked with amusement, not intending her question to be taken seriously by the lady's maid.

Annabelle regarded her mistress for a moment. "A bit, my lady," she admitted as she moved to walk alongside Evangeline. "But I've been thinking it was high time you did."

Evangeline spun around, a look of shock on her face. She was about to scold the lady's maid, but then caught the teasing gleam in Annabelle's eyes.

Having been her lady's maid since Evangeline was old enough to have a lady's maid, Annabelle was usually quite proper. A few years older than Evangeline, she often confessed she would have liked to spend more time dressing her mistress for *soirées* and balls and *musicales* rather than for paying calls on a few young matrons and unmarried ladies of the *ton* or for an occasional shopping trip. She had said just the week before that she thought Evangeline would be a married woman by now.

Perhaps it's time I shocked everyone, Evangeline considered.

Or, perhaps just some of my acquaintances.

Or maybe just Lord Sommers.

Evangeline bit her lip when she decided she might have a bit to learn from Geraldine Porterhouse. She quickened her step as she hurried from the square.

*J*effrey found the bookshop's manager sifting through a pile of books just inside the entrance to The Temple of the Muses. The man seemed surprised to see him back in the shop. "Lord Sommers?" he said with a quick bow. "I thought I saw you leave earlier—"

"I escorted Lady Evangeline into the square so that she might begin reading her copy of *The Story of a Baron*," he explained huffily. "Was that truly your *only* copy of the book?" he asked with such vehemence that Mr. Pritchard felt it necessary to take a step back.

"Well, it was the only copy that made it to the third floor this morning," Mr. Pritchard answered carefully. The manager waved toward a stack of books to his right. "Until just a few moments ago, I hadn't had a chance to unpack the rest of the shipment."

Jeffrey's eyes followed to where Mr. Pritchard's finger pointed. At least ten copies of *The Story of a Baron* were neatly stacked one atop another. Holding his breath a moment, at once feeling a great deal of pride before feeling a great deal of panic, Jeffrey shook his head. He could buy a copy, of course. Then he wouldn't have to read the book with Lady Evangeline.

A sense of immense disappointment settled over him. He *wanted* to read the book with her. Wanted her honest opinion. Wanted to have an excuse to sit next to her for a time. Every day, until they finished reading the book.

If he bought just the one copy, though, that would leave the remaining copies available for sale. Should Lady Evangeline learn someone else had the book, or if she discovered them on the shelves at the Temple of the Muses during her next visit, she might inform him and then rescind her offer of allowing him to read with her.

"I'll take all of them," Jeffrey said as reached into his waistcoat pocket for his purse. "And can you pack them up and deliver them to Sommers Place?" he added as he dumped a pile of silver from the purse into his hand and began counting.

"*All* of the them, my lord?" Mr. Pritchard asked, his brows furrowed in confusion. "But... But I thought you—"

"All of them, Mr. Pritchard," Jeffrey repeated. "And hide them. I shouldn't want anyone else getting a hold of a copy until... until next Tuesday at the earliest," he added as he considered how long it might take him and Evangeline to read the entire book, especially if they only read one or two chapters in a sitting.

Still stunned by the baron's request, Mr. Pritchard nodded and took the money from Jeffrey. "Very good, my lord," he agreed with a bow, resisting the urge to ask if the baron intended to single-handedly make his book a bestseller.

Having nearly emptied his purse to pay for all the books, Jeffrey felt a pang of panic. He had written the book with the intention of enriching his barony's coffers, and now he had just spent over three pounds buying up every copy the store had in stock!

He could only hope Mr. Pritchard would see fit to order more of the books for delivery next week. Many more.

CHAPTER 9

TEA FOR TWO, TEA FOR THREE

*H*aving walked the perimeter of Finsbury Square three times, Milton, Earl of Torrington, was about to begin a fourth revolution when he became aware that things had changed on the park bench that held Lady Evangeline and Lord Sommers.

The two had been quiet and motionless for nearly thirty minutes, their heads bent over the book they were apparently reading. And now, suddenly, Lord Sommers was up and on his way toward the Temple of the Muses, no doubt to buy another copy of the book, and Evangeline was up and making her way out of the square and off in the direction of Park Lane—with Lord Sommers' book!

Despite the two sitting rather close together on the park bench, Milton found their time together rather sedate. At no point had the baron attempted to take advantage of the earl's sister, and neither had Evangeline attempted to make a rake of Jeffrey Althorpe. Of course, Evangeline's older maid had been sitting next to her. The baron wouldn't have tried anything with the servant present.

Milton couldn't decide if he was relieved or disappointed. Then he chided himself. *Some godfather I am.*

He lifted an arm to wave at his driver, glad he'd had the black-lacquered coach remain in the square earlier that morning. Checking the time on his Breguet chronometer, he determined that if he left the square right away, he could be home in time to have tea with his wife. Still a newlywed—despite his age—the Earl of Torrington found the thought of having tea with Adele rather exciting.

And just a bit naughty.

As Evangeline made her way toward the Fitzsimmons' house, she couldn't help but wonder if Lord Sommers was anything like the baron described in the book. Matthew Winters seemed like an honorable man. Careful with his words, too, which probably explained why it seemed to take some time for him to come up with responses to Geraldine's remarks. His initial reaction to Geraldine was to be expected, she supposed, given the woman was described as beautiful. And with the heroine standing in a beam of light in the Palace of Prose, of course she would appear angelic.

Evangeline had half a mind to revisit the Temple of the Muses, climb to the top level of the shop, and stand under the skylight just to discover if she, too, could appear angelic. But if she did, whom would she query as to her appearance? She had to grin as she imagined her lady's maid rolling her eyes at the odd request. Perhaps if she stood there long enough, a man of Lord Ballantine's ilk would discover her, fall in love with her, and ask for her hand in marriage.

The thought brought a catch in her throat, and tears pricked the corners of her eyes. How many times had she hoped to be married by this time in her life? To have her own household? To be a wife? A mother? Probably every day for the past couple of years. If her brother didn't see to a suitable match when he returned to England later that week, or at least arrange for a sponsor or chaperone to accompany her to this Season's events, she would miss another opportunity to meet the eligible men of the *ton*—and be met by them. At her age, she simply couldn't afford another Season lost because she lacked an escort.

Feeling ever more distressed, Evangeline walked faster whilst Annabelle rushed to keep up. "My lady," the lady's maid managed to get out before her breath was gone. She inhaled sharply, wishing her mistress would slow down. A woman of her modest height didn't have a chance when chasing a woman of Lady Evangeline's height and long legs.

Slowing to allow Annabelle to catch up, Evangeline finally turned her attention to Annabelle. "I apologize. I don't know what came over me back there," she whispered hoarsely. She glanced about, impressed at the number of nurses and children who milled about, at the number of young matrons walking with their husbands, at the number of footmen who hurried through the square, no doubt running errands for their households.

Fumbling in her reticule, a difficult task given the book she held under her arm, Evangeline finally pulled out her timepiece. "I told Sam I would have tea with her and Lady Julia today," she said before stuffing the gold chronometer back into her reticule. "If we hurry, we can be there at eleven."

Still a bit breathless, Annabelle merely nodded her understanding. Lady Samantha would expect them, she knew. And while her mistress would be enjoying tea in the Fitzsimmons Manor parlor, Annabelle hoped she would be enjoying a few moments in the servant's hall having tea with a footman. A very handsome footman.

*S*eated in one of the floral upholstered chairs in the Fitzsimmons Manor parlor, Lady Samantha Fitzsimmons sighed as she removed several stitches from her latest attempt at embroidery. Usually after a few minutes or so of sewing, she attained a rhythm with the needle and thread that allowed her mind to wander without having to be too concerned about the size and placement of her next stitch. Today was apparently not a usual day.

Her best friend, Lady Julia Harrington, never seemed to have difficulty with the intricate sewing. She was also prolific. Julia managed to finish two or three samplers for every one Samantha completed. But the earl's daughter wasn't nearly as skilled at painting as Samantha. In fact, Julia had given up further attempts at that particular art when her last piece, a still life of a bowl of fruit, was misidentified by her father as a cairn in Devonshire.

"I wonder what's become of Eva," Samantha commented as she dared a glance at the mantle clock. She had expected Lady Evangeline to appear at ten o'clock on the dot. She was usually quite punctual.

Julia lifted her head from her embroidery hoop, absently pushing an errant golden blonde lock behind her ear. "Today is Tuesday," she remarked calmly. "New books at the Temple," she added with a lifted eyebrow.

Samantha relaxed. "Of course. How could I forget?" The brunette returned her attention to her stitching. "What topic do you suppose she'll choose this time?" she wondered, always surprised by the variety of books Evangeline managed to procure—and read in their entirety.

"Barons, in fact."

Both eliciting gasps of surprise, Julia and Samantha lifted their heads in unison to find Lady Evangeline on the threshold of the Fitzsimmons Manor parlor. "Barons?" Samantha repeated with a grin, setting aside her embroidery hoop and rising from her chair to greet her friend.

Julia did the same, hurrying over to kiss Evangeline on the cheek. "Oh, do tell," she urged as she took hold of the book from Evangeline's hand.

"*The Story of a Baron*?" Samantha read from the front cover. "Why, Eva, I had no idea you were interested in barons," she teased as she moved to ring the bell for tea.

Giggling, Julia rested the book on one arm and flipped it open with her free hand. She read the first line aloud. "Matthew Winters, Baron Ballantine, entered his favorite book-shop in search of a particular new title." She turned the first few pages, noting how they were already bent. "You've already started reading this," she accused as she flipped to the back page.

Evangeline nodded. "Indeed. And not by myself," she replied as she moved to take her usual place on the settee facing the fireplace. Although the navy striped velvet was worn, Evangeline found the settee the most comfortable piece of furniture in the parlor.

"Oh?" Samantha waved to a maid who was wheeling the tea cart into the room. "I'll serve, thank you," she told the servant as she leaned over to prepare the pot and pour the tea.

"Who was your companion then?" Julia asked, returning to her seat with the book still open to the last page. She read the last line. "Forever?" she added before looking up. "This is a work of fiction!" she exclaimed as she rifled through the pages. "Written by—" she flipped to the title page and furrowed her delicate eyebrows—"Anonymous."

Evangeline Tennison rarely read fiction; at least, if she did, she didn't tell her friends about the gothic novels. She instead regaled them with information she gleaned from books on philosophy, natural science, and history.

Evangeline accepted the cup of tea Samantha held out for her. "I was with Lord Sommers," she said as she added a lump of sugar and a bit of milk to the cup and stirred.

Samantha nearly spilled the tea she had just poured for Julia. "Who?" she asked, her own eyebrows furrowing.

"Jeffrey Althorpe," Julia answered, looking up from the book. "A baron. And a bachelor, no less," she teased, closing the book and setting it aside, apparently more interested in discussing possible gossip involving a member of the *ton* than learning any more about the book just then.

Taking a sip of tea, Evangeline wondered how to explain herself. "He was at the Temple of Muses, and he wanted to buy that book," she said as she pointed toward Julia. "But, since I was there first and had already decided to purchase it, we agreed to read it together. Just until Mr. Pritchard can get another copy for Lord Sommers." Rather proud she was able to distill her morning into such a simple statement, Evangeline helped herself to a lemon biscuit, sat back, and took another sip of her tea.

But Julia glanced over at Samantha, a look of shock on her face. "You're reading a book with a... with an *unmarried* man?" she whispered, blinking as if she might have something in her eye.

Samantha allowed a giggle. "Oh, Julia. It's not as if they

were reading it in *private*," she said with a wave of her hand. She turned to look at Evangeline. "You *were* reading it in public, were you not?" she asked then, secretly hoping that perhaps Lady Evangeline and Lord Sommers were involved in some sort of clandestine reading engagement that might lead to a more scandalous clandestine activity.

Finally! Some gossip that might involve Evangeline!

"Of course!" Evangeline responded, nearly spilling her tea. "We were... we were on a park bench in Finsbury Square," she explained, her face displaying a pink blush.

"*This* morning?" Julia asked, one finger pointing toward the floor.

"Yes. And... we're meeting tomorrow morning in Grosvenor Square to continue where we left off," Evangeline replied.

Barely able to contain her excitement, Samantha clapped her hands together. "So, you'll be sitting right next to him?" she asked with widened eyes. "Thigh to thigh?" she added, waggling her eyebrows suggestively.

"Sam!" Evangeline scolded, her blush returning to color her face a bright shade of pink. "We don't sit *that* close," she argued, not about to admit that they really had been sitting quite close. Scandalously close, truth be told.

Julia sighed. "But I'll bet the people who saw you thought you two were married," she whispered hoarsely, her eyes closing as she imagined the cozy scene in the square.

Evangeline regarded her friend for a moment, wondering why the thought didn't offend her. She wasn't sure how many people would have even noticed her and the baron sitting on the park bench, their heads bent over the book spread open on their laps.

A shiver passed through her when she remembered how snug Lord Sommers' breeches were, his muscular thighs straining the Nankeen fabric to near bursting. Her own thigh nearly touched his, although there were layers and layers of muslin and lawn and cambric between them. Their shoulders had touched a few times— how could they not, given how broad his were?—though neither of them seemed to mind enough to beg pardon or make mention of it.

But would a passerby merely think them a married couple rather than the two unrelated members of the *ton* they were? It would be an easy enough supposition to make. "Perhaps," she finally agreed with a shrug, trying her best to seem nonchalant. "And, anyway, what does it matter? We're merely reading a book," she said before taking another sip of her tea.

Samantha sighed, her head cocking to one side. "How romantic," she breathed in a quiet, teasing voice.

Evangeline frowned and set her cup and saucer on the low table in front of her. "Sam! We were reading," she insisted, a bit too forcefully.

"Ah, but you were sitting thigh to thigh, right out in public, for anyone to see," Samantha countered, her voice still soft as she lifted her brown eyes.

Daring a glance at Julia, who was doing her best to keep from giggling, Evangeline finally allowed a smile. "It was rather exciting at first," she acknowledged. "But nothing to write to my brother about," she added, her manner becoming more serious.

"And speaking of the wayward Everly, just when will he return to London?" Samantha asked, her interest piqued. Having been orphaned at a young age and raised by a much older aunt and uncle, Samantha relied on her friends to keep her informed of the latest *on-dit*. Given Evangeline's parents had perished on the Continent before she was old enough for her come-out, Samantha always felt a bit of kinship with her. And a fondness for her brother. Harry Tennison, Earl of Everly, may have spent most of his time away on expeditions, but when he was in London, he was the closest thing Samantha had to a brother.

Evangeline smiled, glad the topic had turned to something other than Lord Sommers. And thighs. "I expect him in a week at the most," she replied, helping herself to another lemon biscuit. "But I don't think he'll stay long. He's already decided on the destination of his next trip. He wants to go to some island off of Spain. Minorca, I think he said."

Samantha shook her head. "He cannot leave until you are

settled," she stated firmly, as if she would see to ensuring the earl did his duty.

"Oh? What's this?" Julia asked, lifting her eyes from the book.

Squirming on the settee, Evangeline shook her head. "I don't expect him to keep that promise," she replied, despite his vow that he would see to a husband for her before he departed on yet another expedition.

Evangeline wasn't sure she wanted him to find a suitable husband for her. What if he arranged for her to marry someone from his club? Some old fart of a lord who still needed an heir? Or some younger twit who needed her dowry to pay off gambling debts? Or one of his colleagues from the Royal Society, who was just as likely to spend his days away from London on expeditions? Or a bald, chinless widower? *Oh, the horrors!* It was bad enough she had only attended one *ton* ball and a few *soirées* the Season prior. Very few of the eligible bachelors even knew of her existence. Which made her wonder: How many aristocrats were left unmarried? Desirable ones, anyway?

Well, she knew of one, at least.

Lord Sommers.

The thought had her reeling for a moment. Jeffrey Althorpe, a baron, was unmarried. And probably not yet thirty. Handsome. With those muscular thighs and broad shoulders and long sideburns that gave him an air of authority, he was certainly desirable.

But did the man wish to marry any time soon?

Evangeline sighed. Perhaps she could find out whilst they read the book. Shoulder to shoulder and thigh to thigh.

A shiver racing down her spine, Evangeline had to hide her grin from her friends lest they begin teasing her all over again. Even if nothing ever came from her time reading with the baron, at least she was spending time in the company of an eligible bachelor.

CHAPTER 10

A LADY IN PINK

The following morning
Despite his wish for rain or snow or sleet or even hail so that he and Evangeline could read in the parlor at Rosemount House, the next day was sunny and bright when Jeffrey awoke an hour earlier than usual. His anticipation at seeing Lady Evangeline had him out of bed at half-past eight o'clock.

His valet, not used to Lord Sommers being up so early, rushed about with various coats and boots for his approval as Jeffrey prepared to join the lady in Grosvenor Square. In his haste to shave his master, Timmons nearly removed Jeffrey's sideburns on one side of his face, and then had to spend time evening out the one on the other side so it matched. Satisfied with the results, he saw to Jeffrey's stockings and doeskin breeches and then proudly displayed a pair of Hoby boots with a new shine. Although they were worn, the boots would have to do; arranging an appointment with the boot maker was nearly impossible this time of year.

At precisely ten o'clock, Jeffrey stepped off his phaeton and onto Brook Street. He tossed a coin to a young boy who would see to it the horse didn't walk off. Straightening his coat sleeves, Jeffrey made his way along one of the diagonal paths toward the center of the square, deciding it shouldn't be too difficult to find a lady of the *ton* with her lady's maid at this time of the morning. Most of the other ladies were still abed.

A flash of pink and black caught his eye, and he hurried past a large tree to discover Lady Evangeline making her way to a nearby park bench from another direction. Jeffrey allowed a smile to show; Evangeline was dressed entirely in pink, much like Geraldine Porterhouse had been in the first chapter of *The Story of a Baron*.

She even carried a pink parasol!

Although he had intended to show that Lady Geraldine didn't have very refined taste when it came to her gowns, the sight of Evangeline garbed entirely in pink had him thinking that perhaps he had erred in his choice of apparel for Geraldine. Evangeline was quite stunning in her ensemble.

Perhaps he had been unintentionally fashionably correct when he'd written about the lady's approach to dressing.

He slowed his gait, aiming to allow Evangeline a moment to choose their bench before he made his presence known. Her lady's maid, dressed entirely in black, settled onto an adjacent bench as he watched. She opened a small basket and took out what appeared to be knitting needles and a ball of yarn.

Evangeline was just about to take a seat when Jeffrey made his presence known with a shout and a wave. She smiled, an expression that seemed to make the morning sunshine even brighter than it was. Jeffrey caught his breath and took her hand. "Good morning, my lady," he said before kissing the back of her hand. "I trust you are well this morning? In all your pink glory?" he added in a teasing voice.

Her face pinking up to match her walking gown, Evangeline regarded the baron for a moment. "I have never worn an outfit such as this. With everything the same color," she amended quickly. "I thought I would give it a try. And make it easier for you to find me."

Jeffrey nodded, disappointed to learn that he *hadn't* quite guessed right when describing a lady's preference for monotone ensembles. "And found you, I did. And? Do you have a favorable opinion of Lady Geraldine's mode of dress?"

Evangeline gave him a shake of her head. "I have not. In

fact, I shall never wear this much pink ever again in my life," she said firmly.

Feeling a tad disappointed at the prospect of never seeing her in a color that was rather flattering next to her pale skin and honey blonde hair, Jeffrey frowned. "'Tis a pity," he said as he took a seat next to her on the bench. "Now, where were we when we finished yesterday?"

Evangeline had to stifle a gasp at hearing the baron's words. 'Tis a pity... because he liked the color pink? Or because he thought her pretty in pink? Or... When she realized he was giving her a look of expectation, Evangeline remembered his query. "Chapter Two," she answered, a bit breathless. She pulled the book onto her lap and opened it, offering one side to the baron. Jeffrey gave her a nod and held onto the side that rested on his thigh. Much like they had the day before, the two bent their heads and began to read.

CHAPTER 11

OUR COUPLE RESUME READING

The Story of a Baron
A Novel in One Volume
Written by Anonymous

Chapter 2: A Lady in New Bond Street

An hour after Matthew had taken his leave of Geraldine Porterhouse, he watched the lady as she exited the modiste's shop and made her way across New Bond Street. Her poor lady's maid followed behind, one arm wrapped around a box barely perched on one hip, whilst a hat box dangled from the other hand.

Thinking the two might be making their way to the Porterhouse residence on foot, he was about to wave them down and offer his town coach when he saw Geraldine hailing a hackney. Although one passed them by, apparently already carrying a fare, the one right behind it stopped. He watched as the two stepped up, the lady's maid waiting for Geraldine to climb in before she followed. Once the door was shut, the hackney was off and headed toward Piccadilly.

For a moment, Matthew imagined intercepting the hackney, imagined opening the door and insisting the two join him in his equipage rather than endure a hackney ride back to Rosehill Place. But had he done so, he knew he wouldn't be able to come up with suitable topics for conversation, nor would he be able to work up the courage to ask Geraldine to join him for a ride in Hyde Park during the fashionable hour. Truth be told, he'd rather take her on a ride when no one else was in the park, so they might have Rotten Row all to themselves.

Coward, he thought. He had deliberately stayed in New Bond Street, ducking in and out of stores whilst keeping an eye on Madame Diana's Emporium for the sole purpose of crossing paths with Geraldine again. And now he had allowed her to get away!

Well, until her brother returned from the Continent, Geraldine would remain unmarried. But once Richard Porterhouse, Marquess of Afterly, was back on British shores, Matthew expected the marquess would see to a betrothal for his sister before making arrangements for another archeological expedition. Surely Geraldine would be settled in the next few months.

But what if Geraldine had no prospects? Would she be satisfied with spinsterhood? Perhaps take a lover to alleviate lonely nights in London or at her family's estate home in Shropshire?

With a sigh, Matthew decided it was inevitable that Geraldine's brother had probably already lined up someone to marry his sister. But if he had, he hadn't informed any of the men at Black's.

And he hadn't informed Geraldine, either.

Snapping out of his reverie as he stared at the departing hackney, Matthew made his way to where his coachman had parked his town coach. He climbed in, taking a seat in the direction of travel.

Settling into the squabs, he pondered what to do about Geraldine. *Write her a note inviting her for a ride*, he reasoned, remembering Lord Barrick's invitation for a birthday picnic in the park the following day. What was the worst answer he could receive back from Geraldine?

Something along the lines of, *Thank you, but I'll be washing my hair.*

But if she agreed to a ride in the park? Well, he would have to overcome his nervousness and take her on the ride.

One thing was for certain. If he didn't capture and keep

Geraldine Porterhouse as his wife soon, he was going to have to find a mistress. For despite her gregarious manner and bold comments, he found the lady in pink had him in a state of discomfort.

Geraldine quickly took a seat in the hackney, facing against the direction of travel. Her lady's maid, Simpson, just about to settle herself into the same side of the hackney, instead took the seat in the direction of travel. "My lady?" she asked, surprised Miss Porterhouse would elect to ride backwards.

"I wish to look out this way, is all," Geraldine replied as she studied the throngs of shoppers through the dirty window. Finding Baron Ballantine in the crowd wasn't difficult. He was staring at her, or at least at the hackney, his gaze never wavering.

She had noticed him as they crossed New Bond Street, thinking he was merely looking for his carriage. Although she was tempted to wave in his direction, she hesitated and instead hailed the hackney. If the man spotted her and wished to help, she figured he would do so.

She *hoped* he would do so.

A shiver raced up her spine and through her breasts, forcing her to inhale sharply. Did the man have any idea what havoc he caused by staring at her so? She rather doubted it.

He hadn't seemed particularly happy to see her in the Palace of Prose. He hadn't even recognized her at first. And their conversation seemed stilted until his face had lit up when he realized she was Jerry.

But then, when he had the opportunity to say the words she usually heard from men who were interested in offering *carte blanche*—no man ever seemed interested in courting her—he didn't put voice to them. *Perhaps you will join me for a ride in the park?* Or, *might I interest you in joining me for dinner?* In fact, Lord Ballantine seemed most eager to see her on her way once they'd left the bookshop.

Geraldine sighed. *And then I had to go make a cake of it and accuse him of being naughty!* The man was probably incapable of forming a naughty thought, she reasoned. According to her brother, Ballantine had always been a bit on the proper side, but a man was still a man.

Perhaps he didn't find her attractive. Perhaps he preferred women who were more plain of face and dress.

Or perhaps he didn't prefer women at all!

A wave of panic washed through her before Geraldine managed to get her thoughts under control. Lord Ballantine couldn't be a molly. He *had* to prefer the company of women. Perhaps several of them all at once.

Geraldine shook her head.

Of course, he preferred women.

He had a mistress. Or, at least, he'd had one until her brother was last in town. She remembered him mentioning it over tea one afternoon. Why Richard would bring up a baron's mistress over tea had her questioning her brother's manners and his motives. But Richard had always been a bit jealous of Matthew, which probably accounted for his comment. *Seems I have myself a new mistress, since Lord Ballantine can't afford her.*

Geraldine had scolded Richard for bringing up the inappropriate topic, but she was secretly glad to hear the reason, if only to learn more about the baron.

Lord Ballantine can't afford her.

Because the mistress had insisted on expensive jewelry? Any kept woman would, Geraldine thought, even though she had no experience in the matter. She only knew that she appreciated a fine bauble when she saw them on the fingers of others. Around their necks or wrists. Dangling from their plump earlobes. Although Geraldine wore jewelry, none of the gemstones were real. They were all paste.

Perhaps the mistress wanted a larger townhouse or more servants. Any woman would, Geraldine imagined. The size of a townhouse was a measure of one's wealth. The more chimney pots on top, the more fireplaces inside, and therefore, more servants to see to it all.

Perhaps the mistress wanted to attend the theatre regularly and required her own box. Her own modiste. Her own coach-and-four. Her own pin money to spend when she traveled.

Any woman would want all of those things. *I want all of those things*, Geraldine thought. *But I want them with a husband.*

Geraldine watched Lord Ballantine as he continued to stare at her departing hackney, until various equipage and horses finally blocked him from view.

Lord Ballantine can't afford a mistress. Which probably meant he couldn't afford a wife.

Geraldine tamped down the sense of panic she felt, this panic so much different from what she'd felt only moments ago. What if Matthew Winters never courted her? Never considered her for marriage?

Now from where had that thought come from?

She'd only just renewed her acquaintance with the man earlier that morning! Although she had done so with the intention of determining if the man might be interested in her. And interesting. The few minutes she'd spent with him in the bookshop and on their walk to New Bond Street had proven he was a man of few words. He was apparently interested, if his staring at her hackney for such a long time could be construed as interest. She already knew he was still unmarried.

But what if Ballantine didn't make an offer?

What if she'd be forced to marry whomever her brother could find for her? Someone who would either tolerate her boldness or beat it out of her? Someone who would be proud to introduce her as his wife? Or leave her home night after night whilst he visited his mistress? Someone who would visit her bedchamber for a night of exquisite lovemaking? Or simply perform his duty in the form of a quick tumble?

A sense of despair settled over Geraldine as she continued to stare out the window for the entire trip to Rosehill House. Why, oh why did she behave in such bold and brazen ways when she should remain quiet and beautiful?

Nervousness, of course. Inappropriate words sometimes just popped out of her mouth at the least appropriate times.

She rather hoped Lord Ballantine hadn't noticed.

I accused him of being naughty.

Well, of that she was sure he had noticed.

CHAPTER 12

A TUMBLE TWEAKS A
THUMPER

*B*ack in Grovesnor Square

"Really, milady, are you quite sure you wish to continue with this?" Jeffrey asked as he raised his eyes from the book. *Faith! I had forgotten how inappropriate this language could be for a general audience,* he thought in horror. He could feel the front of his throat turning bright red. His cheeks would be next. At least he sported longer sideburns, although he remembered just then that Timmons had accidentally shaved them a bit shorter than normal, so they probably didn't provide as much coverage as he hoped.

The earl's sister continued reading as if she hadn't heard the baron. "Of course, my lord," she answered, never taking her eyes from the printed page.

Jeffrey dared a glance at her profile. *God, she is beautiful.* Even with her gold-rimmed spectacles perched on the end of her nose, Evangeline Tennison was a stunning woman. How could she not be betrothed to anyone? How could she still be unmarried at her age?

Well, the spectacles probably didn't help the situation, he had to admit. Then there was the matter of her absent brother. Anyone wishing to ask his permission to court his sister would have been unable to do so.

And she did have a reputation as a bluestocking. Which

meant there probably wouldn't be a competitor for her hand if he decided to marry her, he considered.

Marry her?

He wondered where that thought had come from. He had only considered how pleasant it might be to have a wife, especially on cold winter nights. He wasn't really in the market for a wife! Although, if one happened to fall into his lap, he had to admit he wouldn't necessarily turn her away. But...

Marriage?

The thought had a sober Jeffrey straightening on the bench, which caused the book to shift its position on his thigh, which caused Evangeline to absently reach for it in order to prevent it from tumbling from its precarious perch, which it continued to seem destined to do until she pounced on it, which meant she was no longer quite seated on the bench but leaning rather precariously in the direction of the baron. Which meant she had to reach out to steady herself with her other hand, which was suddenly pressed into his thigh whilst the other hand missed the edge of the book and ended up cupping his knee, which sent the book tumbling to the ground below.

Twisted about with her face almost touching his, Evangeline's eyes widened just as her spectacles slid from the end of her nose and tumbled into the folds of Jeffrey's cravat.

"Oh!"

Jeffrey held his breath, rather stunned by the very sudden turn of events of the past two seconds. Hadn't he *just then* decided he wouldn't turn away a potential wife if she fell into his lap? Especially this one, who was so close, he could bestow a kiss on her without so much as moving his head a mere inch or so?

Without thinking, except for knowing he needed to hold onto the young woman or risk having her tumble to the ground, much like the book and her spectacles had just done— her position was rather precarious—Jeffrey moved one hand so he could grasp one side of her waist whilst his other reached to her other side. Half his mind wanted to reposition her so she sat atop him whilst the other half—the half that had every rule of the *ton* drummed into it—thought to simply put her back onto the bench from whence she had come.

The proper half prevailed, mostly due to the assistance Evangeline provided by simply removing herself from him and the bench in a motion that any witness would claim was an elegant, graceful maneuver worthy of the very best ballrooms of Mayfair.

"Oh!" she said again, standing before him displaying a face so pink, it looked as if it had been designed as part of her gown and pelisse, which still swayed from her sudden movements of two seconds ago. "I... I don't know..."

Jeffrey blinked, disappointed by the sudden removal of Evangeline's body from his own. He'd practically had all of her pink parts pressed against him, the delicate scent of honeysuckle still tickling his nose, the honey blond hair that haloed her face caressing his cheek.

He had to close his eyes in an effort to burn the image of her just then onto the back of his eyelids. Had to hope he could remember how it felt to have her hand on his knee, another pressed into his thigh. And he had to do it quickly, or a certain member of his nether region was going to make itself very apparent.

"Thank you," he said simply, opening his eyes to find her still standing before him, her eyes wide.

The comment had her eyebrows arching. "For practically falling into your *lap?*" she whispered, stunned by his words.

Failing to suppress a smile, Jeffrey nodded. "For not screaming. For not..." He gestured to indicate the rest of the square, where a few people were out walking or lounging on the lawn or hiding behind trees. "For not hailing a Bow Street runner. For not threatening me with a visit from your *brother.*" He paused a moment, a brow furrowing in alarm. "You're not going to tell your brother, I hope?" he whispered hoarsely.

Evangeline quickly shook her head. "Of course not!" she replied.

What would she tell Harry? *Oh, by the way, I fell into Lord Sommers' lap whilst we read a book in Grosvenor Square.*

She couldn't even imagine how her brother would react.

Or perhaps she could.

In fact, she could hear him now. *That's nice, sister. Do you have any idea what Cook has planned for dinner this evening?*

Evangeline shook her head. "Although, he would probably thank you," she replied finally, lowering herself to retrieve the book from the ground.

A bit scuffed from its fall, the book's spine had held, and all the pages were still intact. She was about to pick it up, but Jeffrey was suddenly there, offering her the spectacles he'd retrieved from his cravat. For the second time in two days, he remembered the last time the two of them had been positioned like this, kneeling down to pick up something.

"This was entirely my fault," Jeffrey said as he stood up, holding onto Evangeline's hand much as he had at Lord Weatherstone's ball. "I wasn't holding onto the book as I should have, and... I would say I've made a cake of it, but..."

Not fond of hearing the comment about cake since their conversation in the Temple of the Muses the day before, Evangeline slowly rose to her feet and shook her head. "No cake," she replied simply.

Jeffrey nodded his understanding. "Should we—" he motioned to the book, "—continue reading?"

Embarrassed by what had happened, Evangeline glanced about. No one seemed to have taken notice of her almost-tumble onto the baron's lap. "I suppose," she agreed, returning to her seat.

Opening the book to where they had left off, Jeffrey made a point to hang onto his side of it. He hoped Lady Evangeline might have another occasion to fall into his lap, but he rather doubted it would be today.

CHAPTER 13

OUR COUPLE CONTINUE
READING

The Story of a Baron
A Novel in One Volume
Written by Anonymous

Chapter 3: A Marquess Returns to London

Richard Porterhouse, Marquess of Afterly, regarded his house in Bruton Street with a bit of dismay. Covered with a layer of soot that dulled its bright yellow coloring, the three-story Rosehill House looked as if it needed a thorough bath. One of the shutters hung a bit crooked, its fastening probably loosened during a wind storm. A piece of clapboard looked as if it was about to fall off. And one of the pickets was missing from the fence.

Having been gone for over six months, Richard had forgotten how much maintenance a house required. Apparently, his estate manager, Cuthbert, had as well, since he obviously hadn't seen fit to include the house in the list of duties he was to have overseen during the marquess' absence. Richard would have a word with the man once he located his sister and determined if anyone needed to be called out to meet him at Wimbledon Common.

Smithton, the butler, greeted him at the front door, opening it before Richard even had a chance to climb the two stairs to the house.

"Ah, at least *you* haven't changed," Richard remarked as he made his way across the threshold and into Rosehill House.

"I have not, my lord," Smithton replied, his bushy brows furrowing at the odd comment. "How was your trip, milord?"

The marquess gave his hat and coat to the butler. "Exhausting. Exhilarating. Expensive," he replied tersely. "Is my sister in residence?"

Smithton shook his head. "Not at this time, but I expect her shortly, milord."

Richard nodded and let out a loud sigh. "Shopping again?" he guessed as he moved beyond the vestibule and into the main hall. A silver salver featured a stack of white folded papers, only a few looking as if they might be invitations to the latest *ton* events. He would have to gird his loins before looking through the pile of invoices Cuthbert should have paid in his absence. *How much could a single woman spend in six month's time?* he wondered.

"The Palace of Prose, I believe," the butler said with a nod. "Her second time this week."

Having learned in a recent missive from his estate manager that several servants had taken their leave of Rosehill House, Richard knew there wasn't a groom nor a tiger who could have accompanied Geraldine had she taken the only carriage in the stables. He frowned. "How has she been getting about?" he asked.

Smithton glanced down at his shoes, their shine so clear he could see his reflection. "Hackney, my lord," he said in a quiet voice.

Richard screwed up his face, dismayed his sister would be so desperate as to hire a hackney when she probably could have walked to the most fashionable shopping areas. "Cuthbert is working on hiring a new groom," the marquess replied. "As well as a stable boy and another housekeeper." He paused a moment. "Did our departing servants give any *reason* for their leaving?" he asked, not sure he wanted to hear it.

The butler nodded. "Two of them were hired away by Lord

Abdington with the promise of more beef and less lobster at dinner," he stated simply.

Richard nodded, deciding he, too, would move to another household if it meant he didn't have to eat lobster four times a week. "And the third?"

At this query, the butler looked down at his shoes again. When he didn't give an immediate response, the marquess rolled his eyes, noting the paint on the ceiling needed a touch-up. Or a completely new coat of paint. "Out with it," he ordered.

Smithton sighed. "She said she couldn't continue to work in a household plagued by..." Here, the butler paused and took a deep breath, expecting he might be the next to take his leave of Rosehill House—and not of his own volition. "'A lady so prone to scandal, it's a wonder she doesn't work in a brothel.' Her words. Not mine," he added with a shake of his head.

The marquess stared at the butler for a very long time. *Good God! What has Geraldine been doing?* Richard had received one note explaining she'd been falsely identified as having been in the company of Lord Brotherly at Vauxhall Gardens wearing nothing more than her birthday suit. How had Geraldine put it in her letter?

"It could not have been me, brother, as I was home having my hair washed that night, and as you know, I do not go out in public with a wet head."

She had him there. The chit had so much hair, it took nearly a day for it to dry completely, or so she claimed.

As to the other incident he knew of, she could only claim her gown didn't fit her as well as it should have, and the top half of one of her nipples became—how had she put it? *loose from its moorings—* when Lord Atherton stepped on the hem of her gown whilst they were dancing at Lord Abdington's ball.

He recalled a similar incident when Lady Barrick had been at a dinner party and her bodice had suddenly lowered, leaving both of her nipples entirely exposed. The poor viscountess hadn't even been aware of what happened until all the conversation at the dining table had ceased and all eyes were suddenly on her. Or rather, on her nipples. Every bit the lady, the viscountess had merely readjusted her gown and continued her conversation with Lord Abdington, who probably hadn't heard a word she'd said before or after the incident.

What else could have happened? Richard had only been gone six months!

At the sound of horses in front of the house, Smithton excused himself and moved to open the front door. Lady Geraldine entered the vestibule, followed by her lady's maid, who bore the brunt of her lady's shopping excursion. "When you get a moment, have cook boil some water. After riding in a hackney, I always feel as if I need a bath," Geraldine complained. She was about to enter the hall when she stopped short. "Richard!" Dropping her reticule, she rushed to greet her brother.

Richard reluctantly hugged his sister, acknowledging her lady's maid's curtsy with a nod. "I've only just arrived," he said as they separated. He gave his sister a thorough look, determining almost immediately that she needed a new modiste. "You're terribly pink today," he said, not making the comment a compliment.

Geraldine shook her head. "It's too much, I know," she replied. "But Madame Eunice claims it's all the rage in France."

Richard raised an eyebrow, wondering which France condoned such dressing. Certainly not the one that included Paris.

Geraldine sighed. So her modiste's suggestion of dressing all in the same color apparently wasn't as fashionable as she had claimed. *How could I know?* Geraldine wondered, deciding immediately she should read *La Belle Assemblée* or some other fashion journal.

But fashion was the least of her worries now. At some point, she knew her brother would want a complete recounting of everything that had happened since his departure. And an accounting of her expenditures. She had no idea how she would explain the rumors about her and the men in whose company she was supposed to have been.

She hadn't even met two of them. As for the third, she wouldn't have necessarily minded being associated with Lord

Barrick, except that he'd been married to one of her best friends for the better part of three years.

Deciding she was in for a long evening, Geraldine excused herself and made her way to the parlor. Tea was sure to help make everything better, she thought. Tea and biscuits. And chocolate.

CHAPTER 14

ON SCANDALOUS
INCIDENTS

*B*ack on the park bench in Grosvenor Square
At this point in the story, Evangeline gasped, one hand moving to cover her mouth. "Oh, my," she whispered, glancing down at her monochromatic outfit. "This is truly the *last* time I wear such an ensemble," she vowed, mortified by her decision to dress like Lady Geraldine. She had thought perhaps the woman's choice of dress was truly fashionable—somewhere.

Jeffrey shook his head. "But you're lovely in pink, my lady," he countered, thinking his own cheeks were certainly that color given the descriptions of Geraldine's scandals. What had he been thinking to write such rubbish?

"Lady Barrick's incident at Lord Abdington's ball sounds exactly like what happened to Lady Pettigrew at Lord Torrington's dinner party last year," Evangeline commented, her brows furrowing. Although she hadn't been present at the dinner party, the incident had been reported in every parlor she visited the following week, and there was even a mention of it in *The Tattler*.

Jeffrey stiffened, remembering the incident at Worthington House quite well. Although he barely knew the Earl of Torrington, he'd been invited to attend the intimate gathering of about forty guests. Well, not so intimate, he decided, remembering how the dinner table had been so long, he couldn't see the ends from where he sat near the middle. He'd been placed directly to the right of Viscountess Pettigrew, where he had an up-close and personal view of the lady's charms when they unexpectedly went on display.

Which is why he had included just such an incident in the book.

Who could make up such a story?

"Now that you mention it, I do believe I heard something about that," he admitted, glad Evangeline wasn't in attendance at the dinner party to witness how *long* he had stared at the surprisingly pert plums on display. Surprising, because Lady Pettigrew was nearly old enough to be his mother.

"But I don't recall hearing anything about someone prancing about in their birthday suit at Vauxhall Gardens," Evangeline added with a shake of her head, sure that would have been a topic of conversation in someone's parlor.

That's because it was at Kensington Gardens, and no one was there to see Lady Bostwick in all her glory, Jeffrey thought to himself. *Well, except for her husband, George Bennett-Jones.* But since the viscount was the one to mention it during a fencing match, Jeffrey was fairly sure it was a true story.

Change the names, change the location, and *voila!* Titillating anecdote!

Aware Evangeline was staring at him, as if she expected him to either validate or repudiate the story, Jeffrey simply shook his head. "I'm sure I would have heard something," he said with shake of his head. And then he held his breath, worried she might decide he wasn't telling her the entire truth.

"You're not telling me the entire truth, are you?" Evangeline asked with a hint of disappointment.

Letting out the breath he'd been holding, Jeffrey shook his head. "Propriety, my lady, prohibits me from sharing what little I know of Lady Bostwick's adventure in Kensington Gardens."

Evangeline's eyes widened. And then a smile slowly appeared, lighting up her face in glorious amusement. "You needn't say anything more, my lord," she replied with a shake of her head. She might have missed most of the social events of a Season, but she did pay calls and was privy to most of the *on-dit* in Mayfair. Elizabeth Carlington Bennett-Jones was a rather bold woman when circumstances required it.

And even when circumstances didn't.

Jeffrey took a moment to consider the viscount's tale. He wondered if the man mentioned the incident as a means of embarrassing him, but then he thought perhaps it was a hint that Jeffrey could be enjoying a wife and a happier life should he leave bachelorhood behind. Bostwick had been a confirmed bachelor before meeting Lady Elizabeth. And now he seemed to be the happiest man in all of London.

Her head bent to one side, Evangeline regarded the baron. The man seemed lost in thought, as if he wished he were the viscount whose wife danced naked in the gardens. "We've finished another chapter. Do you wish to keep reading?" she asked as she turned the page to Chapter Four.

Jeffrey glanced at the sky, noticing how dark clouds were moving in from the south. He didn't want Evangeline to get caught with merely a parasol for cover. "I think not," he answered as he pointed toward the fast moving clouds. "Unfortunately, I expect it will rain," he said, thinking that to have two glorious days was at least one day too many, given the British climate. Rain was due. Past due. "Perhaps we should continue tomorrow," he offered, his disappointment apparent.

"Then you should come to Rosemount House. We can read in my brother's library," Evangeline offered. "Eleven o'clock?"

Despite hoping she would renew the invitation to read at her home, Jeffrey still had to suppress a look of shock. That is, until he remembered she would have her lady's maid there. And other servants, no doubt, including a butler who was probably two hundred pounds of pure muscle. "Eleven o'clock," he agreed. "May I escort you to your carriage?"

"I suppose," Evangeline replied, closing the book and tucking it into the crook of her arm. "I'm just down this path." She waved to her lady's maid, who got up from where she was lounging on the grass with a servant from another household. A rather handsome footman, she thought, who looked awfully familiar. The ball of yarn and knitting needles were nowhere to be seen.

The three strolled down the crushed granite path until they reached the Everly coach. As Jeffrey handed up Evangeline, he kissed the back of her gloved hand, promised her he would see her in the morning, and bade her farewell. Then he handed up Annabelle, performed a bow, and headed back the way he had come.

CHAPTER 15

THE SPIES HAVE IT

*M*eanwhile…

Lady Samantha watched as the baron passed by for a second time, hoping the man didn't dare glance to his left. She held a finger to her lips until Lord Sommers disappeared on the other side of the square, and then turned to Lady Julia and burst out laughing.

"You are *impossible*," Julia claimed, her own mirth barely contained. "However did you know they would sit on *that* particular bench?"

Samantha shrugged. "There aren't that many in the square, so I sorted they would choose the one in the middle," she answered, threading her arm through Julia's as they made their way out of the square toward her uncle's house.

Shortly after meeting that morning, the two had made their way to Grosvenor Square with the intent of spying on Evangeline and the baron. And spy, they had. But boredom had nearly gotten the best of them. Watching two people read a book was about as exciting as watching each other do embroidery in the Fitzsimmons Manor parlor.

Just as they were about to take their leave of the large tree trunk they used for cover in favor of a walk back to Fitzsimmons Manor, they paid witness as Lady Evangeline suddenly and inexplicably landed in Lord Sommers' lap.

Or almost landed in his lap.

They couldn't quite tell from their vantage point what had caused her to almost tip over and nearly end up atop the rather astonished Lord Sommers. And then Evangeline had performed some sort of maneuver akin to a pirouette, her body balanced on her tiptoes as she spun about.

"Oh!" they had both exclaimed in unison, their combined voices loud enough that they were quite sure Evangeline had overheard them. But her own "Oh!" had drowned out theirs, leaving them trying to suppress a sudden fit of the giggles. And then, when the baron and Evangeline had bent down to retrieve the book, which at some point had fallen off the bench, they watched with rapt attention as Lord Sommers lifted Evangeline's hand and slowly brought it to his lips and Evangeline to her feet.

Their long sighs, both in unison, caused another fit of giggles.

"How long, do you suppose?" Samantha asked, her gaze taking in the darkening skies above.

"How long for what?" Julia responded, not sure to what Samantha referred, but thinking she probably meant the impending storm. Neither had come prepared for rain.

"Before they're wed?"

Julia smiled and regarded her friend for a moment. "I'll bet they're married within a month," she said with a good deal of confidence.

Samantha nearly stopped in her tracks. "A *month?*" she repeated, looking ever so astonished. "Oh, all right. I guess I'll take that bet," she said with a sigh. "But I would have said three weeks."

It was Julia's turn to look astonished. And then even more shocked when the heavens suddenly opened up and rain began to pour down. With only their parasols for cover, the two were thoroughly drenched by the time they reached Fitzsimmons Manor.

· · ·

*A*s Evangeline settled into the town coach for the ride home from Grosvenor Square, she couldn't help but think of how much the description of Lord Afterly reminded her of her brother. The similarities in their avocations were striking, both requiring they be absent from the London social scene for months at a time, leaving an unmarried sister without protection or the means to meet eligible bachelors.

Meeting men seemed to come easily to Lady Geraldine. She had obviously done *something* to warrant her reputation for being fast—something beyond the events featuring Vauxhall Gardens or the ball—although the story hadn't yet mentioned just what that *something* might be.

Geraldine's behavior was bold, but that didn't necessarily deter Lord Ballantine from finding her intriguing. Indeed, Evangeline wondered at the baron's reaction to the marquess' sister. Was it just a man's attraction to a bold woman that seemed to have him already snared in Geraldine's net? Or did the man truly have feelings for her? Even if he was a few years older, they had known each other since childhood; certainly that had something to do with his fondness for the lady.

When the coach parked in front of Rosemount House, Evangeline stepped out and waited for Annabelle, opening her parasol as rain began to fall. Once her maid was out and on her way into the house, the footman closed the door and the driver pulled away, intending to park the coach in the carriage house off the alley.

Evangeline stood in the rain, staring at the departing coach, then studying the crest adorning the coach's door.

Everly.

Afterly.

Two aristocrats who spent months away from London pursuing their avocations. Two aristocrats who left behind sisters who were not married—not even betrothed.

If I can make the connection, certainly other readers will as well, she thought in dismay. A bit light-headed, Evangeline swayed as she stood on the front walk.

Her lady's maid, not yet in the house, noticed her distress.

"Milady?" Annabelle said with a bit of concern, her line of sight tracking Evangeline's so that she, too, was left watching the departing Everly coach.

Evangeline continued to stare at the gilded crest until it disappeared around the corner.

There could be no doubt.

Whoever had written *The Story of a Baron* had definitely used her brother as inspiration for the character of Lord Afterly.

Which had her wondering.

Who else had Anonymous used for inspiration?

CHAPTER 16

RAIN, RAIN, COME AGAIN
EVERY DAY

The following day
At precisely five minutes past eleven in the morning, Jeffrey Althorpe jumped down from his less-than sporty phaeton—it was black rather than the more coveted red in color —handed the reins to a stableboy who had hurried out from the carriage house, and climbed the steps to the front door of Rosemount House. Nervous, he straightened his waistcoat before lifting the lion-head knocker, and then, just as he was about to release it, the door opened.

A portly butler regarded him with a raised brow.

"Lord Sommers for Lady Evangeline," he said in an even tenor, hoping the nervousness in his voice couldn't be heard. Or the pounding of his heart against his rib cage. When the butler continued to regard him without stepping aside, he added, "I have a... a reading engagement with her ladyship."

Jones nodded and stepped back, opening the door wider as he did so. He took the baron's hat and placed it on a shelf in the vestibule before hanging Jeffrey's coat on a hook. He nodded again. "One moment whilst I announce you," he said, his deep baritone a bit intimidating.

The baron used his few moments alone in the entry to study the exquisite embroideries that decorated the silk-covered walls. He wondered who might have done them; they appeared too new to have been done by Evangeline's grandmother—or mother—and they weren't the typical samplers that hung in his late mother's parlor. A pair of the stitcheries featured single stems of plants with their leaves, as if they were botanical studies. Another pair of stitcheries looked as if it were part of the same series—they were similar in appearance but instead featured flowers, one of which Jeffrey recognized as some type of rose. Before he could study the second flower, the butler returned to the vestibule.

"Lady Evangeline has asked that I escort you to the library," Jones announced, apparently not too happy about the arrangement.

Jeffrey wondered at the butler's reticence as he followed the man and then remembered Lord Every hadn't yet returned from his travels. A man calling on an unmarried woman was rather unseemly, he supposed, causing another wave of nervousness to take hold.

He checked his reflection in a mirror as they passed through the great hall. At least he didn't appear too wind-blown from his quick drive from Cavendish Square, nor did it appear as if he'd been splashed by mud.

Despite knowing the Earl of Everly for several years, Jeffrey hadn't been in the house but one other time, and that was when the earl had unveiled his prized tank of tropical fish. The brightly colored beasties didn't seem particularly interested in the parade of humans that stopped to admire them, but Jeffrey remembered how they seemed to take particular exception to David Fitzwilliam, Earl of Norwick. Every time the tall man was near the tank, the fish would swim about until a wave of water would crest over the top edge and splash onto the earl. The resulting water stains ruined his favorite topcoat. *Those fish will be the death of me*, the earl was fond of saying, and not because he was fond of the fish.

Jones waved a hand into the double-wide doorway of the library. Jeffrey gave him a nod and turned his attention to the elegant room, but not before he noticed another pair of embroideries on the hall walls—embroideries so vivid, the subjects appeared real.

Jeffrey tore his gaze away and instead looked into the library. Aubusson carpet covered nearly the entire floor. Dark green upholstered furnishings carved from cherry wood were arranged for the specific purpose of reading. And shelves and shelves of books lined the walls, all the way up to the coffered ceiling. Two large windows provided most of the light in the room whilst a massive chandelier, hung directly over the seating area, gave off a warm glow. Although not lit, floor lamps were positioned next to nearly every chair in the room.

Jeffrey took a sniff and was rewarded with the scents of wood, leather and vanilla tinged with lemon. He inhaled and smiled, feeling at home in a room he had only been in one other time.

As Jeffrey quickly scanned the collection of books, he remembered thinking that Evangeline had probably read every one of them.

Poor girl!

"Good morning, Lord Sommers," Evangeline said from behind him. He turned to find her framed in the doorway, her blonde hair swept up in a simple chignon and her willowy frame ensconced in a light coral round gown. With her hands clasped together in front of her, she looked like an angel. Her curtsy was simple but deep.

Jeffrey hurried up to her, giving her a bow before taking her bare hand to kiss the back of it. He wished he could instead take her in his arms and kiss her on the lips. *What a pleasant way to start the day*, he thought as he reluctantly released her hand. "Good day, Lady Evangeline," he replied. "I trust you are well today," he said, noting how she seemed to glow under the gaslight of the chandelier.

"I am. And I do hope you weren't caught in the rain as you made your way here?" she replied as she entered the room. She moved to the only piece of furniture that would accommodate two people—a leather upholstered sofa fronted by a low table. *The Story of a Baron* lay open to the fourth chapter of the book.

Jeffrey glanced at one of the windows, where rivulets of water traced their way down the glass pane. "I was not," Jeffrey assured her as he moved to the sofa. Had he waited just one more minute to leave Sommers Place, he would have been as drenched as he was the day before when he took his leave of Grosvenor Square. Despite the soaking, he would do it all over again just for the opportunity to spend time with Evangeline.

"Jones, could you please see to tea and biscuits?" Evangeline called out, knowing the butler was hovering just outside the door. He had warned her he would do so when she told him of her plan to host the baron. *We'll only be reading*, she had said in her most proper manner, all the while wishing they could be doing something far more illicit. Like holding hands, or kissing. Or...

"Yes, milady," could be heard in the man's distinctive baritone.

Smiling coyly, Evangeline joined Jeffrey in front of the sofa and took a seat. He did the same, quick to flip his coattails behind him as he did so. For a brief moment, she was blessed with the sight of Jeffrey's rather well-sculpted bottom as it made its way down to sit next to hers. Delightful tingles shot through her entire body as he settled next to her.

Just as they had been on park benches for the past two days, his muscular thighs were next to hers, straining the leather of his doeskin breeches.

"Would milady like to wait for tea before we begin? Or shall we get started?" Jeffrey asked as he moved to reach for the book.

Evangeline had a passing thought of what else they could be starting. *A kiss, perhaps*. Giving her head a quick shake, as if to clear it of the inappropriate image, she replied, "Yes, let's. It may be a while before the tea tray arrives."

Nodding, Jeffrey pulled the open book onto their laps, positioning it much as it had been whilst they read in the park. Giving each other a quick glance, they began to read Chapter Four.

CHAPTER 17

OUR COUPLE READS IN THE LIBRARY

The Story of a Baron
A Novel in One Volume
Written by Anonymous

Chapter 4: Invitations Arrive

Her maid dispatched to put away her purchases, Lady Geraldine Porterhouse made her way to the parlor in Rosehill House and rang for tea. Her spirits still rather low, she was surprised when the butler arrived with a silver salver in one hand and a calling card in the other.

She helped herself to the only missive on the salver and stared at the masculine script. *Lady Geraldine Porterhouse.* Her brother's writing was nothing this neat, nor was she expecting news from him—he was already home. Curious, she broke the seal, scattering bits of wax in all directions.

> *Dear Lady Geraldine,*
>
> *May I request the honor of your presence on a ride in Hyde Park at two o'clock tomorrow afternoon? I have something of great importance I wish to discuss with you.*
>
> *Yours, Lord Barrick.*

Geraldine glanced up to find Smithton staring at her. He

still held the calling card, but finally offered it to her when he realized she wasn't going to ask for it. The card belonged to Harold Timmons, Viscount Barrick, which meant the viscount had delivered the missive himself. "How long ago was Lord Barrick here?" she asked as she set aside the note and read the card.

The butler glanced at the clock on the fireplace mantle. "No more than twenty minutes ago, my lady," he said with a shake of his head. "Will there be anything else?"

Glancing at the card again, Geraldine said, "No, thank you, Smithton." She continued to stare at the card until the butler had taken his leave of the parlor.

Damn the viscount!

What was the man thinking? Inviting her to go for a ride in the park, and not during the fashionable hour? Of course, Barrick shouldn't do such a thing no matter what the hour! He couldn't. The man was married!

What did he think to accomplish?

Geraldine took a breath and held it a moment. Did the man intend to ask that she be his mistress? What else could it be?

She thought a moment, her mind a jumble until she remembered she had attended finishing school with the viscount's wife.

Daisy McGowan had been a close friend during their last year at Warbuck's Finishing School. After classes, they spent their time shopping and reading *La Belle Assemblée* and dreaming of possible matches in the Marriage Mart. And before they had even completed that year, Daisy had an offer from Harold Timmons, Viscount Barrick. She was married six months later in St. George's and was pregnant before nightfall. Now, having already bestowed an heir and a spare on the viscountcy, perhaps Lady Barrick was enjoying someone else's bed and Lord Barrick was wont to do the same.

Or perhaps the man simply wanted some company during a ride.

Oh, the horrors! *Why me?* Geraldine wondered. She hardly knew the viscount. Knitting her eyebrows, she reread the note. He would be expecting an answer, she knew, but she couldn't exactly write one and have Smithton see to its delivery—the butler would suspect her of consorting with a married man! Unless...

She intended to respond with a firm, "No, I will not join you, and how dare you?" but gave her reply another thought.

Hurrying to the escritoire, she seated herself and opened an ink bottle. Pulling a sheet of her brother's stationery from the top drawer, she wrote her response.

> *Dear Lord Barrick,*
> *I cannot tell you how happy I was to receive your invitation. So happy, in fact, that I immediately penned a note to Daisy to let her know how excited I was to be joining the two of you on your ride to Hyde Park tomorrow. I'll expect you at two o'clock.*
> *Sincerely yours, Miss Geraldine Porterhouse.*

Sitting back for a moment, Geraldine regarded her carefully scripted letter, smiling as she considered how the viscount would react when he read it. *If only I could be a fly on the wall of the Timmons' dining room this evening,* she thought with a bit of spite.

Sprinkling some pounce on the parchment, she shook the sheet and curled it, dumping the pounce back into its glass container. With a great deal of satisfaction, she folded the note, dipped her sealing wax into the flame of the nearest lamp, and applied her 'GAP' seal into the shiny pool. She considered actually writing a note to Lady Barrick but thought better of it. No need to make poor Daisy more aware of what she probably already knew her husband was doing behind her back.

Geraldine was on her way to give the note to a footman to deliver when Smithton appeared with the silver salver again. He took the missive from her, one eyebrow cocked as if he found the folded paper repulsive. "Lord Barrick merely wondered what to buy for his wife. Her birthday is this week," Geraldine said with a wave of her hand, amazed she could lie so easily.

And then it dawned on her.

Daisy McGowan Timmons' birthday *was* this week.

Geraldine plucked the new missive from the salver, just as

Smithton left the parlor with her note, apparently in a hurry to see to its delivery. She studied the new missive, relieved to see the script was different from Lord Barrick's. Geraldine opened the note and read half of it when she realized something of great importance.

Lady Barrick's birthday was tomorrow.

As was the birthday party Lord Barrick was hosting on her behalf.

A surprise picnic.

In Hyde Park.

At three o'clock.

Geraldine threw her head back and stared at the coffered ceiling, wondering how long it had been since it had been dusted. *Faith!* The cobwebs looked positively ghoulish. Then she returned her attention to the note, scanning to the end to discover who had written the invitation.

She gasped, one hand going to her bosom. *Lord Ballantine.* Matthew Winters. The baron was requesting the honor of her company on a ride to Hyde Park for the surprise birthday party of Lady Barrick.

Although Lord Barrick said he will be delivering invitations this afternoon, I do not think he realizes his carriage will not accommodate everyone he intends to bring to the park. As one of Lady Barrick's friends, I expect you'll be in attendance. I would be happy to give you a ride to the park. The courtesy of your reply is requested.

Yours in service, Ballantine.

Ballantine.

Just *Ballantine.*

Not "Lord Ballantine" or his full name and title, Geraldine thought as she reviewed the signature.

She wondered when he'd had a chance to pen the note. Was it before their meeting earlier today? Or after she had watched him from the hackney as she and her maid left New Bond Street? The man looked... determined, perhaps. Or maybe resigned. Or... besotted?

Geraldine shook her head. *He was probably just woolgathering*, she reasoned. He may not even have known about the birthday party when he saw her in New Bond Street. Or... or perhaps he had known and had already dispatched the note and wondered why she didn't tell him in person her decision to accept his offer of a ride to the park.

But we hadn't yet renewed our acquaintance until this morning at the Palace of Prose, she remembered.

So he had to have written the note since their time in New Bond Street.

Well, no matter. She would simply reply to the missive as if she had just received the invitation this very moment. Which she had!

Hurrying back to the escritoire to write a reply to Ballantine's note, Geraldine remembered the awful missive she'd written to Lord Barrick. She had no desire to let the viscount think she was writing a missive to Lady Barrick, as if she were tattling on him. She rang the bell, thinking to catch Smithton before he dispatched a footman with her note.

The butler appeared so quickly, she wondered if he had been standing just outside the parlor door. "The note I just gave you? I'd like it back, please," she said, before returning her attention to the desktop.

Smithton's reaction was one of apparent discomfort. He began clearing his throat. "I... I haven't got it, my lady," he answered finally.

Geraldine looked up, stunned. "Well, where is it?" she asked, her pen poised to begin her reply to Lord Ballantine.

"I sent a footman with it as soon as I left the parlor. Foyles has no doubt delivered it by now," he said with a shake of his head.

Geraldine blinked. *Faith!* The Rosehill House footmen were certainly fast if they could deliver a note that quickly!

"Lord Barrick's house is just down the street," he added, as if he wanted to disabuse her of the idea that the footmen were fast on their feet.

Oh, damnation, Geraldine thought with a sigh. "Well, you'll need to send him back there to retrieve it, then," she replied, turning back to the desk to begin her response to Lord Ballantine. "And hope that Lord Barrick hasn't yet had an opportunity to read it." Which reminded her that she would have to pen yet *another* note to Viscount Barrick to decline his invitation for a ride. She had half a mind to simply walk down to the viscount's home and deliver the message in person, but if Lady Barrick was in residence and discovered she was there, Geraldine would probably have to stay and socialize with her. *Not today,* she thought with a shake of her head.

Smithton gave a nod to her back and hurried from the room, intent on finding a footman who might be faster on his feet than Foyles.

Geraldine regarded the blank sheet before her. *Lord Ballantine.* A shiver coursed through her entire body, not unlike the one she'd felt earlier when she'd watched the baron from the hackney. *Did the man have any inkling he could have her whenever he wished?*

She inhaled sharply.

Had she really just thought that? Had she really just imagined joining the baron in his bed, in the middle of the day, for a tumble and a spot of tea?

Shaking her head as if to clear it, Geraldine quickly put pen to paper and replied that she would be honored to join the baron for the trip to Hyde Park. She almost added, "And wherever else you wish to take me," but thought better of it. They would probably end up at the theater, or shopping in New Bond Street when she secretly hoped they would end up in his bed.

A girl was entitled to her fantasies.

Having proofread the note for the third time, Geraldine finally folded it. Dripping wax onto the seam, she pressed her seal into the red puddle. After waiting a moment, she pulled it away. Satisfied with her GAP, she took the missive to the butler and asked that it be delivered with all due haste.

Smithton regarded the white note for a long time before deciding it could wait an hour or so before being dispatched. After all, what if Miss Porterhouse changed her mind and wanted it back?

And so it was that Geraldine's reply to Matthew Winters' missive didn't arrive at Ballantine House until nearly eight o'clock that evening, just minutes *after* Lord Ballantine had taken his leave to play cards at Black's.

Twelve houses down the street from Rosehill House, Lord Barrick's butler regarded the breathless footman who stood at the back door. He recognized the livery the thin man wore—he'd seen it twice before in the past hour. "Yes?" he questioned with a good deal of trepidation.

"A message for Lord Barrick, sir," the footman said between gasps for air as he held out Lady Geraldine's amended response. "I'm told this will be the last time you see me this evening. Because this is the last missive from Rosehill House."

The butler sighed. He wasn't exactly sure what his master had written in the many notes he had penned earlier that day. And he wasn't sure why the man insisted on delivering them all himself. But given the number of notes that had arrived in return and the cook's sudden displeasure, it could not have been good. Not good at all.

CHAPTER 18

READING CONTINUES AFTER
THE TEA TRAY IS DELIVERED

The Story of a Baron
A Novel in One Volume
Written by Anonymous

Chapter 5: A Gentleman at His Club

Lord Ballantine regarded his cards before glancing up to catch Marquess of Brotherly pulling an ace from the end of his sleeve. The baron cleared his throat. "An ace up your sleeve, Brotherly?" he commented, one eyebrow arcing up.

Thomas Christianson, Earl of Atherton, straightened and turned an evil eye on the marquess. "Cheating, Brotherly?" he spoke in disbelief. "How dare you?"

The other two at the table, Harold Timmons, Viscount Barrick, and Vincent Fitzpatrick, Duke of Abdington, leaned over the felt-covered table. Both gave the marquess their very best murderous expressions. "Yes, indeed, how dare you?" Barrick repeated.

Lord Brotherly, looking not the least bit guilty, tossed the ace onto the table. "No more so than you, Barrick," he answered in his drawl. He reached over and plucked an ace from the viscount's sleeve. "Or you, Your Grace," he continued as he reached over and plucked another from the lace-edged sleeve of the duke.

Ballantine threw his cards face down onto the table. "Dammit! Are there any aces left in the deck?" he asked in dismay. "No wonder I can't win a single hand!"

"Now, now, Ballantine," the duke said quietly. "Let's put all the cards on the table and start this game over," he urged, crooking his index fingers as if he knew there were more cards hidden in the players' clothing.

Sighing, Barrick pulled another ace from his other sleeve, Brotherly flipped one from somewhere below the table—possibly from inside the placket of his breeches, but no one asked since none of them really wanted to know—and the duke pulled one from the folds of his snowy cravat.

"Dammit, Your Grace. You have *another* ace?" Ballantine accused, glancing around the table to see a number of aces displayed along with the cards they'd already been dealt. "These aren't even from the same deck!" he exclaimed as he picked up a pasteboard ace to examine the back of it. Indeed, the printing on the front didn't match the deck from which Atherton had dealt that round of whist.

Brotherly shrugged. "I can't help it if Black's uses a different brand of cards than Frank's Faro Parlor," he complained.

Atherton winced. "Frank's? You actually patronize that hell-hole?" he asked in disgust. "You really should have some self-respect."

The marquess shrugged, as if he didn't care where he lost his money...

CHAPTER 19

ON THE FIVE LORDS OF BAD BEHAVIOR

"My lady, I really wonder if you should be reading this particular chapter," Jeffrey said as he straightened on the floral settee and pulled the book entirely onto his lap. Although he could see any other aristocrat identifying with the antics of the Five Lords of Bad Behavior, he certainly didn't expect a young lady—a gently bred sister and daughter of an earl—to do so.

Evangeline shrugged. "Oh, it's fine, my lord," she answered, reaching over to pull the book back onto her thigh. She continued to read about the five card players as if she hadn't been interrupted.

When the baron didn't say anything in response, she tore her attention from the book and gave him a glance. "Has this happened to you?" she asked. "The reference to Black's is obviously meant to be White's, I would think," she said with a wave of one hand.

Although Jeffrey thought her reaction should have been one of far more... shock, he considered her comment and nodded. "I have been, and, yes, I agree. I do think Anonymous is referring to White's," he said reluctantly.

Damn! *I hadn't even considered this book might be read by a woman,* he once again thought in dismay. He hadn't given a thought to the curse words or swearing that occurred throughout the tale, or how coarse gentlemen could be when women weren't present. But not once had Lady Evangeline gasped or given any indication she found the text in the book objectionable. *Perhaps the finishing school she attended wasn't as proper as it should have been*, he thought absently. *Or maybe this book is tame compared to all the others she has read.*

The thought had him gazing at the hundreds of titles that lined the walls of the library, secretly happy that most were not fiction but rather books about scientific subjects.

"Are you finished with this page?" Evangeline asked as she raised her eyes to meet his. They darted over to the clock on the mantle. "I'm not expecting my guests for luncheon until one o'clock," she added.

"Luncheon?" he repeated.

"I invited Sam and Julia for luncheon today. It's my turn to host them for tea, you see, but I thought it would be better to offer a luncheon on such a gloomy day," she explained.

"That's very kind of you," Jeffrey replied, almost wishing he had been included in the invitation. The thought of having lunch with the Ladies Samantha and Julia had him reconsidering, though. They would probably tease him mercilessly once they learned what he and Evangeline had been doing these past few days.

"Thank you," Evangeline replied. She indicated the book with a tap of her finger on one of the pages. "Would you like to continue?"

Jeffrey blinked. "Oh, yes," he replied, quickly turning to the next page.

CHAPTER 20

RESUMING THE READING OF CHAPTER FIVE

The Story of a Baron
A Novel in One Volume
Written by Anonymous

Chapter 5: A Gentleman at His Club (continued)
"Come, gentleman, let's have them all," the Duke of Abdington said, his fingers still motioning to the other four card players around the table. When no additional cards appeared, the duke gave Ballantine a pointed look.

The baron sighed and pulled a king from his sleeve. The rest of the aristocrats at the table began to laugh. "A *king?*" they questioned in disbelief. "Is that the best you could do?"

Ballantine rolled his eyes. "Obviously, since you had all the aces," he countered, not the least bit embarrassed at having been caught with a king. Especially when everyone else had displayed far more aces than occurred in a single—or even double—deck of cards.

Viscount Barrick cleared his throat. "I do hope you all received my invitations for tomorrow's tête-à-tête in the park," he said, as if he'd been waiting for the perfect opportunity to bring it up. Except for Lord Ballantine, there were murmurs of, "No" and, "Haven't read my posts yet," and shaking of heads around the table. Undaunted, he added, "My wife's birthday is tomorrow. I'm surprising her with a small gathering," he explained proudly. "And a picnic."

The duke shuffled the cards and then dealt a round. "I have news from my wife," he stated as he picked up his cards and gave them a quick perusal.

"Oh?" Atherton remarked, giving his own cards far more attention than the duke did his.

"She is breeding again," Abdington announced proudly. "With any luck, she'll give me a spare, and I can be done with visits to her bedchamber."

Murmurs of agreement sounded from around the table, but Matthew looked up from his cards. "Is she... not agreeable in her bedchamber?" he asked, thinking he would certainly appreciate being able to visit a wife's bedchamber. He had no prospect of a wife yet, as the one woman he had been interested in, Lady Lydia, had agreed to marry Lord Farrington's youngest son—a son who wouldn't even have a title unless his six older brothers all expired from too much drink and whoring.

He briefly thought of Geraldine but tried to put her out of his mind. He hadn't heard from her, but he was sure his missive had been delivered shortly after her return to Rosehill House. He'd written it just moments after arriving at his own townhouse to discover Lord Barrick's note, and he had sent his note to Geraldine with a footman who boasted that he could run a mile in under five minutes.

"She's a *wife*." Abdington answered Matthew's query without a hint of humor. "Merely doing her duty as a good duchess should."

Matthew flinched at the duke's comment, thinking his preference would be to find a wife who would welcome him into their marriage bed. A wife who would know she was welcome to come to his should she desire.

Desire.

The word conjured images of Geraldine Porterhouse. Of her dressed in nothing more than his bed linens. Of her brunette hair splayed out on his pillow, making her appear angelic when any man with eyes could see she was the devil's temptress. Of her milky white skin flushing with his every caress, his every kiss. Of how she would return the favor, leaving a trail of kisses down his chest and belly, her breasts capturing his engorged manhood between their soft swells and delivering it, ever so slowly, to her sweet lips for a final hard and thorough kiss before she would beg him to take her. To make her his.

Dammit! Did the woman have any idea how truly naughty she could be? Of how naughty she could make a perfectly respectable man like him? She was worse than a mistress. Worse than a courtesan. Worse than a tavern doxy, or a lightskirt in Wapping.

Matthew straightened he realized the breeches he wore couldn't begin to accommodate the growing evidence of his arousal. He leaned back into his original position.

"Have you lined up a new lay?" Abdington asked, his attention on the baron.

Matthew feared the duke had somehow peeked beneath the card table and had seen the evidence of his arousal. But when he sorted the timing of Abdington's question was merely a coincidence, he wished the attention from around the table wasn't entirely on him. "I have not," he replied with a quick shake of his head.

The comment seemed to bother the duke. "Do we need to arrange an introduction to someone delectable?" he asked, a bushy eyebrow arcing up. "I am quite sure we can find the perfect bedmate for you," he offered, collecting the pasteboards into a neat pile so he could shuffle them.

Shaking his head, Matthew replied, "Thank you, but not at this time. Given the requirements on my time right now, I'm afraid I would neglect a mistress."

Atherton frowned as he regarded the baron. Then his face brightened. "Trouble in the barony?" he enquired, with perhaps a bit more glee than was warranted.

Matthew resisted the urge to flinch and instead gave a quick shake of his head. "Not at all. Just... busy is all," he mumbled. Busy trying to pay bills. Busy trying to balance books that could not be balanced given the current coffers. To add the cost of a mistress would simply bring him closer to receivership. The very last he wanted was for the entailed Ballantine properties to end up in the hands of the Crown.

So, what were his options? Debtor's prison? He could curse his father (and had many times), for the Fifth Baron of Ballantine had been the one to gamble away the assets of the barony and leave his only son with a trail of markers from here to Whitechapel to pay. Most of those hadn't made themselves apparent until long after his father's death, when weasels began appearing flanked by large, burly men with fists the size of ham hocks. He'd paid because he could—there were some monies back then—but when the bank accounts dwindled, he employed a solicitor to look into filing charges of extortion against the less-than-honorable collectors. That tactic had worked to get rid of the weasels. It didn't work for the monthly bills that continued to amass—bills for the ongoing expenses of a barony that didn't offer much in the way of industry or agriculture.

Matthew's only option, one that had come to him just that afternoon as his town coach carried him from New Bond Street to his small house in Mayfair, was to acquire a dowry. Which meant acquiring a wife with a dowry. Which meant getting married.

Geraldine Porterhouse, the daughter of a marquess, was purported to have a respectable dowry, along with a reputation that was not so respectable.

Having spent most of the card game imagining Lady Geraldine naked and acting every bit the devil's mistress, it was no surprise she had such a sullied reputation. Was it any wonder he lost nearly every hand of whist?

And what would be so wrong with marrying Geraldine? Matthew had known the girl since she was in leading strings. She had probably allowed him his first kiss, although a memory of her slapping him rather hard across the face flashed in his mind.

Funny how a man could conveniently forget such an event.

Perhaps she hadn't allowed the kiss. Or had she been the one to initiate it?

But now? Now that she was rumored to have shared her

favors with no less than three gentlemen, she would probably be a bit more tolerant of his attempt should he decide a kiss was necessary before the proposal.

Matthew briefly wondered who the three lucky gentlemen were. Had they promised marriage only to gain her favors? Or had her reputation for being fast given them reason to accost her? No one had ever mentioned names as they spread the *on-dit.*

So, he would have a wife with a bit of... *experience.* His nether region reacted again, making him shift in his chair.

What would it be like to have a wife who behaved as a mistress? The thought was simply too much for his breeches, and he was forced to turn his thoughts to more practical matters.

Geraldine Porterhouse was the daughter of marquess. A woman of the *ton.* It wasn't as if he had others in mind for his marriage bed.

But what benefit would she gain by marrying him? Besides his protection and the likelihood that the rumors would be curtailed or stopped altogether? That alone should be enough to persuade her to accept an offer, he considered. And then there was the title of baroness. Although it wasn't as lofty as duchess or marchioness or countess or viscountess, it was still a title she didn't currently possess. *She would be my baroness.* Lady Winters.

Matthew sighed, rather liking the idea of being married to Geraldine.

So, now he just had to court her. Starting tomorrow, he hoped.

Matthew sighed again. Well, that probably wasn't going to happen.

The woman hadn't even responded to his invitation for a ride to Lady Barrick's birthday picnic. Although, to be fair, his missive had been written rather hastily upon his return from New Bond Street.

He glanced at Barrick, silently thanking the man for being close-fisted enough not to employ a secretary to pen his correspondence. Having read the man's initial invitation for the picnic he planned—or perhaps it was his housekeeper, given the fact that Barrick was incapable of planning anything other than a trip to Black's—Matthew decided the man's ambitious plan to round up all of Lady Barrick's friends and bring them en masse to Hyde Park couldn't work. There wasn't a carriage large enough for such an endeavor.

Matthew thought to capitalize on an opportunity to spend a half-hour or so alone with Lady Geraldine by offering her a ride in his barouche. And even if her lady's maid had to tag along to act as a chaperone, Geraldine would probably prefer a private ride to having to endure being stuffed like a sausage into the Barrick barouche with twenty of her closest friends.

Having given up on the idea of courting Geraldine the following day, Matthew didn't think to check for messages when he returned home from Black's later that night. In fact, it wasn't until the next morning when his batman delivered the day's post during breakfast that he discovered Geraldine Porterhouse had indeed responded to his query.

Nervous, Matthew loosened the wax seal from the white parchment and unfolded the note. He read the feminine script three times before setting it aside.

It seemed he would indeed be escorting the marquess' sister for a ride to the picnic.

Well, two o'clock couldn't come soon enough, he decided as he regarded the remains of his breakfast. Best he get started on thinking up a way to inform Geraldine's brother. After all, he had no hope of gaining the woman's hand if he didn't have permission to court her.

CHAPTER 21

A LUNCHEON WITH THE LADIES

An hour later at Rosemount House

Evangeline entered the conservatory a moment after Jones had departed, wanting her guests to be seated before she made her entrance. "Good afternoon, ladies," she said brightly as she moved to take a seat at one of the white metal chairs that surrounded a matching garden table. Despite the wet, chilly air outside, the conservatory was warm and tropical, its greenery and bright flowers a welcome treat for those who didn't have a conservatory in their Park Lane homes.

"You've obviously been having one," Samantha said with an arched eyebrow. "And don't try to tell me your brother has returned, because I know he has not," she warned, thinking Evangeline would claim the baron was only at Rosemount House to see her brother.

Despite having been prepared for their teasing, Evangeline blushed. "Lord Sommers and I have just been reading the book, is all," she said with a shrug.

"Sitting side-by-side?" Julia countered, waggling both of her eyebrows. "Like you did in the square?" She had to suppress a cry of surprise when one of her shins sustained a kick to it. She turned to find Samantha's eyes wide and not very friendly. "In Finsbury Square, was it not?" she amended, just then understanding Samantha's warning. She had to be careful or Evangeline might guess that she and Samantha had been watching her and Lord Sommers read whilst in Grosvenor Square.

"We're quite proper about it," Evangeline replied, reaching for her glass of wine. A maid delivered plates of cut fruits and a tray of sliced cheese, giving her a reprieve from her guests' teasing for a moment. When she saw Julia's face fall, as if she was disappointed in her claim, Evangeline leaned forward. "Have I said something wrong?" she asked, glancing back and forth to study her friends' faces.

"We were hoping you were being naughty," Samantha said once the maid had left the room.

"But not being ruined," Julia added quickly, her head shaking from side to side.

Evangeline blinked, her mouth dropping open at their comments. "How could I be naughty without being ruined?" she asked, her brows furrowing. "How is that possible?"

Samantha shrugged, helping herself to a piece of the fruit. "Kiss without being caught," she answered before popping the berry into her mouth.

"Do anything without being caught," Julia countered, following Samantha's lead with the fruit. Her eyes widened. "Unless you *want* to be caught!"

Before Julia could accuse Evangeline of anything untoward, Evangeline raised a hand and held it palm side out. "And who says I wish to be naughty with the baron?" she asked. "Or *caught?*" she added with a mock look of horror on her face.

Samantha had moved on to the cheese plate and was regarding a slice before she pulled it apart between her fingers. "Are you denying that you find Jeffrey Althorpe utterly handsome and worthy of your affection?"

"Sam!" Evangeline said, having to keep her voice down since their soups hadn't yet been brought out. A footman might enter the conservatory at any moment and share their gossip with everyone else whose rooms were on the third floor. "Of course, I find him handsome," she agreed, not quite sure how much to admit. "I'm not yet sure about the *affection*, however," she admitted with a shake of her head.

"Oh," Julia replied, her disappointment apparent when her 'oh' sounded as if all the air had gone out of her.

"Attraction, then," Samantha stated before helping herself to another slice of cheese.

Evangeline glanced at her friends, not quite sure how much to admit. "Oh, of course, he's attractive."

"But are you attracted to him?" Samantha pressed.

Swallowing hard, and not because she'd eaten anything, Evangeline finally said, "Yes, I suppose."

Samantha and Julia squealed at the same time, the exact same time the footman arrived with the soup, which he nearly spilled upon hearing the high-pitched squealing.

Suppressing the urge to roll her eyes, Evangeline regarded her friends with a smile. "You two are incorrigible," she remarked as the footman set the soups before each young lady. She turned her attention to the servant. "Thank you, Simmons," she said. "We'll be ready for dessert whenever Cook has it ready," she added with a teasing grin. Which just made Samantha and Julia giggle again.

Raising a spoonful of soup to her lips, Evangeline wondered if the three of them would continue such luncheons once they were all married. The thought had her pausing, her spoon held in mid-air, as she realized she had never before thought of the three of them married.

If only it could be so, she thought with a sigh. *If only.*

"Will you let us know when you've finished the book?" Samantha asked.

"Or when Lord Sommers proposes?" Julia added, her delivery so deadpan both Samantha and Evangeline turned to stare at her.

Evangeline allowed a sound of disbelief. "I will be sure to inform you of any and all developments," she promised, her eyebrows waggling in a tease. "In the meantime, we really should decide what to do during the Torrington dinner party." In two night's time, the Earl and Countess of Torrington would be hosting a dinner party, and Julia's parents, the Earl and Countess of Mayfield, and Samantha's aunt and uncle, the Viscount and Viscountess Chamberlain, would be in attendance. If her brother returned to London by then, Harry would probably have an invitation as well, but Evangeline didn't think he would arrive in the capital until a few days past that. "Is there a play showing anywhere?"

"We should have a dinner party of our own," Samantha suggested, stirring her soup. "You, Julia, me, and Lord Sommers." She tried hard to keep a straight face, but a brilliant smile appeared to give away her.

"That's a wonderful idea," Julia said. "Maybe not the part about Lord Sommers, though. But we should host our own. Just for young ladies. No men allowed."

Evangeline wondered at the sense of disappointment she felt at hearing Julia's edict. There were a half-dozen young men who would probably appreciate the opportunity to attend a dinner party with a less-than-stuffy crowd. The matter of propriety could not be overlooked, however. Without her older brother as chaperone, the event would be a source of gossip for weeks. "We could have it here," Evangeline suggested. "Maybe invite some of the other daughters whose parents will be at Torrington House."

Although she should have been acting as her brother's hostess for any events he hosted at Rosemount House, Evangeline had little practice. He had held a reception the one time, mostly to introduce his tank of tropical fish to his colleagues from the Royal Society and a few aristocrats. Evangeline had seen to it the footmen delivered trays of hors d'oeuvres and kept champagne glasses filled—not exactly a very challenging event.

"It's too late to have invitations printed," Samantha said with a sigh.

"I could write them," Evangeline countered. "And have a footmen deliver them on the morrow. That is rather last-minute, but it will have to do."

"I can help with writing them," Julia offered. "What about a menu?"

Evangeline's eyes widened. "I should think I will need to work that out with the cook," she replied.

"And what will we do after the dinner?" Samantha asked.

Evangeline and Julia exchanged glances. "Parlor games. Charades. Maybe play cards," Julia suggested.

"Smoke cheroots and drink brandy," Samantha added, her face brightening when her friends displayed expressions of shock.

"We have claret and madeira," Evangeline countered. After a long pause, she grinned. "I think I shall enjoy doing this very much."

When the three finished their luncheon, they retired to the parlor where they went about penning invitations to their friends. They hoped that five out of the seven they were inviting could be in attendance. Then there would be the appropriate number for card games and charades.

Once Samantha and Julia had taken their leave of Rosemount House and two footmen had been dispatched with the invitations—it was nearly four o'clock in the afternoon—Evangeline met with the rather surprised cook to come up with a menu for eight.

By eight o'clock, when she was quietly eating dinner by herself in the dining room, Evangeline felt a combination of satisfaction and anticipation. Although neither Samantha nor Julia mentioned the coincidence, the cook certainly did. And she seemed determined to see to it the dinner party would be a rousing success if for no other reason than she thought it was time Evangeline have a bit of fun.

Evangeline's birthday was the same date as their planned dinner party.

CHAPTER 22

A LATE NIGHT READ

*L*ater that evening

Restless and still wide awake with excitement for the impending dinner party, Evangeline wandered through the rooms on the second floor of Rosemount House. The dim light from the lamp she carried wavered about, casting eerie shadows on the walls.

She thought of that morning when she and Lord Sommers read in the library. She thought of the few minutes they had stopped in the middle of Chapter Five so she could serve him tea and offer him a biscuit. Then she remembered her disappointment at having to send him on his way when she expected Samantha and Julia to arrive at any moment for their luncheon. He had been ever so understanding as they said their farewells in the vestibule, his hand holding onto hers just a bit too long.

Although she hadn't noticed, Jones certainly had, for the sound of his clearing throat had Jeffrey straightening and heading out the front door. He was up and onto his phaeton a moment later.

After he had disappeared down the street, Evangeline remembered they hadn't set a time for their next reading. With her friends arriving a few minutes later, she didn't have time to send a note. She decided if she didn't hear from him in the morning, she would send a missive to him.

Evangeline stepped into the mistress suite, inhaling deeply in the hope of capturing the scent of her late mother. A whiff of rosewater was all she could smell, though. At least the maids were diligent about keeping the room clean.

Setting the lamp on the dressing table, she took a seat and regarded the hinged box set in the middle. She thought about Geraldine Porterhouse and her desire for baubles as she allowed a string of her mother's pearls to slip over her fingers.

Had Eva Tennison requested her husband buy them for some ball or *soirée*? Or had he bought them as a gift for his beloved wife? Evangeline thought perhaps it was the latter. The little she could remember of her mother suggested the wisp of a woman was sweet-natured and easily satisfied—quite unlike the materialistic Geraldine.

Why would Anonymous have made his female character such a selfish woman? she wondered. There was no doubt Geraldine and Ballantine would end up married in the end. But what kind of union could they have if Geraldine was never satisfied with where she lived, or with what she wore, or with the baubles in her jewelry box? How long could the poor baron abide her endless demands?

Forever.

Remembering the last line of the book, Evangeline felt sorry for the baron.

Poor Ballantine.

Forever broke.

Picking through the gold and silver trinkets in the velvet-lined box, Evangeline paused as her finger hooked onto a gold ring. Adorned with a single large sapphire, the band glimmered in the candlelight. Evangeline held it up to the lamp, admiring the purplish-blue color. The engraving, a tiny script wrapped around the inside of the band, required she lift her glasses onto the end of her nose. "For my forever love, Eva. Your devoted Harold."

Evangeline straightened, stunned by the simple words. Tears pricked the corners of her eyes. *Forever.* Slipping the ring onto a finger, she held out her hand and admired the sapphire against her pale fingers. Had this ring been her mother's wedding band? Or a ring her father had bestowed on her for a special occasion?

Thinking she would ask her brother, Evangeline was about to examine the rest of the jewelry when the sound of a knock at the front door broke the silence. Startled, Evangeline wondered who might be paying a call so late. Her brother was still away— perhaps a friend of his thought him already back in London. Or perhaps it was a note from the earl, letting her know his ship had docked in Wapping. Or maybe a footman was already bringing an answer to one of the dinner invitations!

Curious, Evangeline descended the steps, hurrying toward the vestibule. She recognized the sound of Lord Sommers' hushed tones even before she spied him from the hall.

"Lord Everly isn't in residence, my lord," Jones said with a shake of his head. "Shall I leave word you called?"

The baron lowered his eyes and paused before replying. "I was actually calling on Lady Evangeline. I know it's late, but I—"

"Lord Sommers!" Evangeline interrupted before the butler could respond. "It's so very good to see you again. I hope all is well?"

Jeffrey's face brightened at the sight of Evangeline. "My lady," he said with a bow. "I apologize for calling so late—"

"Oh, do come in," Evangeline said, waving him into the hall. "Jones, could you please see that tea is delivered to the parlor? Oh, and have a footman bring up the book from the library, too?"

Before the butler had a chance to raise a protest, Evangeline had hooked an arm into Jeffrey's and was leading him up the stairs to the first floor parlor. "To what do I owe the honor of your presence this evening?" she asked, glad for the interruption and even more glad that he had come to pay a call on her and not on her brother.

"Curiosity, I'm afraid," the baron replied with a pained expression. "My lady, I have spent the entire day wondering about Lord Ballantine and Lady Geraldine," he admitted. "I simply cannot sleep until I know what has happened with their ride in the park."

Evangeline stared at Jeffrey, wondering if he'd been thinking the same things as she had. "I find myself in a similar quandary," she replied before moving to the sideboard. "Would you care for a brandy? Or something else stronger than tea, perhaps?" she offered, thinking he would usually be at White's this time of the night.

Jeffrey joined her at the sideboard. "You make an excellent hostess," he said quietly, reaching for a crystal decanter. "But allow me." He poured two fingers of brandy into one of the glasses and started to return the decanter to its salver. "Did you —" he paused—"want brandy? Or...?" He glanced about the sideboard and noticed several bottles. "Madeira or claret?"

Her face pinking up, Evangeline shook her head. "No, my lord. Tea will be fine for me." The sound of a throat clearing had her turning her attention to the door whilst she was sure Jeffrey took an entire step backwards.

The butler stood on the threshold with a tea service and an expression on his face that suggested he was none too pleased with Lord Sommers' presence in the parlor. "Tea, my lady," he said in his rich baritone. A footman hurried in with the open book. He placed it on the low table in front of the settee and quickly took his leave, as if he feared the butler's mood.

"Thank you, Jones. On the table in front of the settee is fine," Evangeline said. She moved to serve herself as the butler held his ground next to the table. Sensing his distrust, she said, "Lord Sommers and I are going to continue our reading," Evangeline explained in a quiet voice. "But we'll be no more than an hour," she added when she saw her words weren't changing Jones' reticence.

"Very well, my lady," he finally answered, reluctantly taking his leave of the parlor.

Evangeline watched him go, certain he would probably hover just outside the open door until Jeffrey left the house. Turning her attention back to the baron, she found him gazing at her in a most peculiar way. "What is it, Lord Sommers?" she asked as she lifted the tea pot and poured herself a cup.

He gave his head a shake, as if he thought better of what he was about to say. "I trust your luncheon went well?" he asked.

Her grin widened. "Very well. In fact, we have decided that we shall host a dinner party to coincide with Lord and Lady Torrington's dinner party. We've invited some of our friends— all young ladies, of course—those whose parents will be at the Torrington's. It's rather last minute, but even if it's only the three of us, we shall have a good time, I should think."

Arching an eyebrow, Jeffrey said, "Your dinner party sounds as if it will be far more enjoyable than Torrington's affair," he murmured. "I understand these events can take a great deal of planning. Am I taking you away from—?"

"Oh, it's all been taken care of," Evangeline said with a wave of her hand.

Jeffrey frowned. "Already?"

She nodded. "We wrote the invitations this afternoon and two footmen saw to their delivery. I met with the cook to go over the menu, and sometime tomorrow, a couple of footmen will see to rearranging this room so that we can play charades and cards. So, you see, it's all arranged."

"Is it for a special occasion?"

Evangeline allowed a shrug. "It is my birthday, I suppose, but I don't think I'll make mention of it."

Jeffrey's first thought was to ask what she might want for her birthday, but then he remembered he couldn't give her anything. It wouldn't be proper. "I just may have to crash that party," he teased.

"You wouldn't dare!"

"No, I wouldn't. I won't," he promised before he straightened. "I admit I was surprised to receive an invitation to the Torrington's."

Evangeline set the teapot on the tray and turned to regard him. "But, why would you be surprised?"

He angled his head, as if considering how to respond. "Politically, we're the same, but I've only ever been invited to one of his dinner parties before. From what I remember, most of those in attendance were married, which has me wondering if the countess has someone she intends for me to meet." This last was said with a roll of his eyes, as if he didn't wish any matchmaking efforts be done on his behalf.

"I haven't heard that the countess plays matchmaker," Evangeline replied. She tamped down the sense of disappointment she felt at learning someone might have a match in mind for him. "Are you on the hunt for a wife?"

Jeffrey stood holding his glass of brandy, not sure how to respond to her surprising query. On the one hand, it could have been considered rather bold of her to ask. But the manner in which she made the query seemed borne of simple curiosity. "You're nothing like Geraldine, are you?" he finally replied.

About to pour the milk into her tea cup, Evangeline paused to stare at the baron. "I... I should hope not," she replied, wondering why the comment sounded as if he had thought she was like the novel's heroine. Perhaps he had thought that before now. But why would he think her so shallow? So insecure that she would feel the need to do the brazen things Geraldine did in her attempts to land a husband?

Evangeline shook her head as if to clear it, deciding she didn't wish to dwell on the subject. Setting down the milk pitcher, she added a lump of sugar and nervously stirred her tea as she lowered herself onto the settee. With its back facing the door, the settee was positioned to allow light from a nearby window to illuminate it during the day.

Jeffrey moved to join her on the settee. *The Story of a Baron*, its pages already opened to where they had left off earlier that morning, lay on the low table in front of her. The page was marked with an elaborate bookmark. "That's a rather interesting piece of art," he remarked, hoping he hadn't offended the young lady with his earlier remark. She seemed so glad to see him this evening, and now she seemed lost in thought.

"Father made it for Mother when he was courting her," Evangeline explained. "But he didn't seem to realize that adding these gemstones would leave impressions in the pages if you actually closed the book with it inside," she added as she indicated the swirls of colored stones that created a floral pattern atop the flat metal strip. At the very apex of the metal, where the bookmark extended beyond the top of the pages, the gemstones were larger and made up the shape of a single tulip.

"It's beautiful," Jeffrey commented. "Was your father a

jeweler? When he wasn't performing the duties of an earl, I mean," he clarified, hoping she wouldn't think his question offensive to her father's position as a peer of the realm.

Evangeline nodded. "He was. Or rather, he would have been if he hadn't been the heir to the Everly earldom. He loved working with silver and gold."

Jeffrey frowned. "If your father was so interested in jewelry—"

"Metallurgy," Evangeline interrupted. "He was really more interested in metals and how they could be shaped and bent and curled. But Society is far more tolerant of a jeweler than a metallurgist," she said archly. "As was my mother, I suppose." This last was said with a wan smile.

Nodding his understanding, Jeffrey considered the late earl's hobby for a moment. "Then, from where did your brother inherit his fascination with flora and fauna and exploration?" he enquired, clearly curious.

Evangeline considered the question for a long time before she finally shrugged. "I have absolutely no idea," she admitted. "He's always been more comfortable out of doors," she added with a shake of her head. "Catching flutterbies, and fire flies, and snakes, and all manner of small animals. Made for a rather entertaining childhood for me, although I admit I did not care for the snakes."

"I should think not!" Jeffrey said quite firmly. "You could have been poisoned!" This last was said with such alarm that Evangeline moved a hand to her breast and leaned back a bit.

"Oh, I rather doubt it," she responded, hoping she hadn't underestimated the snakes her brother collected. "They were common snakes the gardeners would find whilst they scythed the lawn," she added with a grin. "But I appreciate your concern for my welfare."

Jeffrey nodded. At a loss for words, he pointed at the book. "I take it you are as curious as I am?" he asked with a quirked brow.

Evangeline grinned. "I cannot tell you how tempted I was to read ahead," she admitted.

"So, you didn't give into temptation?"

Smiling, Evangeline shook her head. "I have steadfastly avoided this book all day," she claimed as she leaned over to get the book. Using his left hand, Jeffrey caught the edge of the front cover and helped in lifting the tome onto his thigh.

"I do not care for snakes, so please believe me when I say that I shall never expose you to such an abomination," Jeffrey declared, for no other reason than to ensure she understood he meant her no harm. Ever.

Evangeline gave him a brilliant smile. "I believe you, my lord," she replied with a wink.

A wink!

Jeffrey stilled himself, goose bumps making their way over his entire body. Did the woman have any idea what her simple gesture had done to his sense of self? To his sense of well-being?

Perhaps she merely had something in her eye.

Or was she flirting?

God, I can only hope, he thought, before noticing Evangeline had already started reading.

Jeffrey quickly turned his attention to the page below and started reading the next chapter in *The Story of a Baron*.

Faith! Did I really write this drivel? he asked himself, remembering writing the scene in which the heroine, Geraldine Porterhouse, flirted with Lord Ballantine as he drove her to the birthday party for Viscountess Barrick. *She is shameless,* he thought. How could he have written a female character who would behave as Geraldine did—unlike any other gently bred woman? In real life, the chit would end up a spinster if she continued to act as she did, and yet, he knew first-hand that she would end up happily married to the baron.

She had to. He had written the scene in which she declared her undying love for Ballantine. Had written the scene in which they promised they would remain together forever.

Forever.

What was I thinking?

I was thinking of Lady Evangeline. Imagining how she would behave given her brother's extended absences from London, her freedom from his rebukes allowing her to entertain guests at all hours in her home and pay calls on any man who showed her the least bit of attention.

Jeffrey shook himself.

Lady Evangeline did no such thing! She was nothing like Geraldine. She would never pay calls on an unmarried man at midnight, even if he wanted her to. At the moment, he could think of no more welcome caller than Evangeline Tennison. At any time of the day or night.

"Are you finished with this page?" Evangeline whispered as her forefinger moved to turn to the next.

Not having read a single word of the pages spread below him, Jeffrey inhaled sharply. "Yes," he lied, and then watched as her slender finger lifted the paper and slowly flipped it to his side of the book so that the next spread lay before them.

A quick glance at the top line reminded him where they were in the story. *Faith!* At any moment, she would be reading about the baron's sexual fantasies regarding Geraldine! About how Ballantine imagined she looked without her walking gown covering her generous bosom. Of how she looked with her stays and her petticoats removed from her body. Of how she looked wearing only her stockings and her dance slippers, one leg slightly in front of the other in an attempt to hide the dark curls at the top of her thighs. Of her pert breasts swollen and ready for his tongue and teeth to claim her. Of how she would inhale sharply but allow him all the liberties Jeffrey had ever dreamed of taking with Lady Evangeline.

I am going to hell!

"I rather doubt that," Evangeline whispered, patting the hand that rested on the edge of the book.

Faith! Had he really just said that last bit out loud? He must have, for what other reason would Evangeline have to make such a comment?

"Thank you," he whispered, turning his head so his nose was just grazing her coiffure. The scent of lilies and honeysuckle had him inhaling slowly. Did she have any idea how good she smelled? Of how intoxicating her very presence could be?

When her head suddenly rested against his shoulder, his heart nearly stopped.

She knows!

Jeffrey allowed a grin and then dropped his head back until it rested on the edge of the settee. Given the silence in the parlor, he was acutely aware of the slightest sound coming from Evangeline. Her chest rose and fell with her even breaths, warmth emanating from where her body was pressed against his own.

Is she sleeping? How dare she?

He froze.

She was sleeping. She was sleeping with her head resting against his shoulder. How could she fall asleep in the part of the story when Geraldine determines she doesn't just want the lowly baron because she needs a husband but because she's decided she might be in love with him? *How could she not be enthralled enough to remain alert and awake to find out what happens next?*

How could she simply fall asleep?

Because she is tired, he chided himself. *Because she feels comfortable enough to do so? Because I am here, and she knows I won't take liberties with her?*

Jeffrey sighed, deciding he rather liked how Evangeline trusted him enough to simply fall asleep on his arm. Smiling, he leaned his head over so his cheek rested on top of her head. Inhaling slowly, he reveled in her floral scent and in the calming effect her very presence had on him.

Within moments, Jeffrey, too, was sound asleep.

CHAPTER 23

A BUTLER PAYS WITNESS
TO... WHAT?

Jones stood on the threshold of the parlor, his attention directed on the back of the settee. On the two heads that seemed to be resting, one on the other. On the silence that filled the Rosemount House parlor. He had already tamped down a sense of panic when he determined the two weren't kissing one another. And he had already decided not to storm the parlor in an effort to strike fear in the heart of the visiting baron so he might never darken the door of Rosemount House again. But he knew he could not simply stand on the threshold and do nothing as his master's sister sat with a male caller in the parlor. At twenty past nine o'clock at night!

Or, perhaps he could. Neither one of them seemed to be doing... anything. In fact, from the quiet in the room, he thought perhaps they were either very engrossed in the book they were supposed to be reading, or they were...

Asleep.

He watched as the baron's head slowly listed to his right until it rested atop Lady Evangeline's. After another moment, the telling sounds of a soft snore made their way to his hearing.

Faith!

Now what should he do? The two were sleeping together in the parlor!

Although, they were doing so rather innocently, he had to admit. Perhaps the book they were reading was boring. Perhaps they were both very tired and simply fell asleep. The parlor was rather cozy this time of night, the fire still crackling in the fireplace and the overhead chandelier illuminating only the settee, leaving most of the library in darkness.

Jones took note of the single chair that had been placed just inside the door. Duty required him to keep an eye on the lady and her visitor. He could do so if he took a seat in the very chair. If they did not wake up of their own accord within a half-hour, he would wake them and encourage the baron to take his leave of the house. Glancing down the hallway in both directions, Jones stepped into the parlor and took a seat.

Within minutes, he, too, was sound asleep.

*J*effrey was enjoying his rather vivid dream, one in which the love of his life had fallen asleep in his arms, when he became aware of an intruder.

A competitor for the hand of Lady Evangeline? he wondered, girding his loins for battle. *Or just an interloper?* Someone who took interest in the carnal activities of the *ton*, perhaps? *Or was it a servant?*

He concentrated on the sounds in the room, frowning when he recognized the oddest sound was one of snoring. *Could Lady Evangeline be capable of such a rumble?* He slowly opened his eyes. She was still leaning against him, although now her head was nestled into the crook of his shoulder. Her body barely moved with each breath she took, which meant she couldn't be the source of the violent sound of breathing that filled the room.

Someone else *was* in the parlor!

Certainly the fish couldn't make such a racket. He knew there was a tank somewhere in the house, but it wasn't in this room. The only fish he knew of in Rosemount House were in a tank in the library, and he rather doubted their snores could be heard up here in the parlor! *If fish even snored,* he considered for a moment before deciding the thought was simply ridiculous.

So, who could be sleeping with them?

My one opportunity to sleep with Lady Evangeline, and someone else has the audacity to join us!

He took a tentative look to his left, relieved when he saw that no one else was on the settee with them. There certainly wasn't room for another person on the petite couch. He made a careful glance to the right, ensuring no one was on the other side of Lady Evangeline. Closing his eyes, he concentrated on the source of the offending sound and determined it came from behind them.

Careful not to jostle Evangeline's head too much, he dared a glance behind him and frowned at the sight of the butler sitting just inside the parlor door.

Damnation! When had Jones joined them? And how long had he been asleep?

Perhaps his heart rate had increased, or perhaps he had moved too much, but Lady Evangeline stirred, one hand moving up his chest in the process. The delicate set of long, slender fingers came to rest in the folds of his cravat.

Jeffrey closed his eyes. A few more inches higher and they might have landed on his lips, where he would have drawn each one into his mouth and suckled them one by one in the order they appeared on her hand. The thought had his nether regions responding, his cock hardening until it strained against the placket of his breeches.

He forced himself to take a deep breath, which seemed to cause Evangeline's hand to fall from his cravat and onto the bulge in his breeches.

His sudden inhalation of breath had Evangeline's head angling up a bit.

Jeffrey dared a glance down. Evangeline's face lay against his shoulder, her lips slightly parted and her eyes still closed. Below, her hand rested on his manhood, apparently unaware of the pounding pulse her simple move had incited.

I could kiss her right now, he thought, his pulse nearly doubling in only a few seconds.

I cannot, he argued. *I cannot take advantage of her innocence.*

"Kiss me," he heard in a distant whisper.

Startled, Jeffrey stared down at Evangeline, wondering if she had been the one to invite a kiss.

"Are you sure, my lady?" he whispered.

"Of course," she replied.

He had never before been invited to kiss a woman. His one mistress didn't allow the intimacy—and from what he knew from his friends who employed mistresses, most didn't unless they were in love with the women. Having little in the way of experience meant he wasn't exactly sure how to proceed.

But Evangeline was waiting, the soft pillows of her lips just inches from his own. He took a deep breath before capturing her lips in a simple caress with his own.

Jeffrey closed his eyes, reveling in the feel of her pillow soft lips against his. *Like velvet and satin and my favorite brandy,* he thought before he finally released her willing mouth. Her head remained firmly pressed into the small of his shoulder, her faint smile apparently approving what he had done.

"Kiss me back," he whispered, wondering if she would even hear his plea. The hand that pressed against his swollen manhood was now squeezing gently through the fabric of the breeches, the fingers slightly curled around his hardening cock in a manner that would send him into ecstasy if she continued her erotic ministrations much longer.

Jeffrey allowed his head to rest on the back of the settee, his breaths coming faster as her fingers coaxed him closer to orgasm. Her lips suddenly captured his neck just above his cravat, nipping the skin in a gentle love bite that had him inhaling sharply. He moved his lips to hers, taking ownership of the firm, velvet flesh at the same time her fingers squeezed even harder around his erection. Not expecting the move, Jeffrey broke off the kiss when his manhood reacted, and he was forced to take a deep breath.

God, it had been ages since he'd had such a release, such a quiet, powerful and satisfying orgasm that left him blind but for the stars that seemed to appear behind his eyelids. He had to bite back the groan he was about to allow; somewhere, Jones was in the room, and he dare not let him know that Lady Evangeline had been the cause of his pleasure. *Jesus, did the woman even know what she had managed to accomplish in her sleep?* he thought as he barely opened one eye. She still seemed to be asleep against his shoulder, her lips still parted as if she expected he might kiss her again.

He did so, his light touch bringing her alive. His hand released its hold on the edge of the book and moved to her body, gliding up the soft sprigged muslin fabric until it reached the underside of one breast. Although the mound didn't completely fill his palm as it moved over the top of her bosom, the fact that he could hold it, press it, mold it, even give it a gentle squeeze through her stays had him so excited, so aroused, he thought he might come to completion again.

He moved his hand so his fingers could push her sleeve down her shoulder. Still covered by the bodice of her gown, her breast seemed to swell as his lips lowered onto her engorged nipple. When he pulled away, as much to take a breath as to ensure he hadn't yet been discovered by the servant, Jeffrey noticed the nipple's silhouette through the muslin. He couldn't help himself as he captured the bud between his teeth and gently bit it. Evangeline's slight hiss had him stilling his motions, had him pulling away just a bit.

"Please, don't stop," he heard, despite the pounding of his pulse in his ears.

Startled, Jeffrey raised his gaze to hers. Barely open, Evangeline's eyes seemed glazed and sleepy, their lashes forming an exotic curved curtain that barely hid her green irises. "Shh," he whispered, leaning in to kiss her gently. He thrilled at how her lips responded, at how her body arched so her breast filled his hand and her nipple moved to rest between two of his fingers. And then, suddenly, her breast was bare, her sleeve pulled down far enough that her nipple escaped the confines of her gown.

Pinching the ruched bud between his thumb and forefinger, Jeffrey deepened the kiss in the hopes that he could swallow any sounds she might make in response to his ministrations. He felt her gasp against his lips, felt her body arch up against him.

When he was sure she wouldn't cry out, he moved his mouth down to the nipple and closed his lips around it, his tongue laving over and around it until he was aware of her body shuddering beneath his, her hands clenching on his lapel and the bulge in his crotch. The sensation had him inhaling and then holding his breath in order to keep from calling out.

Evangeline settled against the front of his body, her face pressed into the space between his shoulder and neck as she exhaled what sounded like a very satisfied sigh.

Coming back to his senses, Jeffrey carefully raised her sleeve back to its place on her shoulder and adjusted her bodice as best he could.

Was that a moan of disappointment he heard as the fabric scraped over her breast? Or one of despair? Did the lady realize what had just happened? Was she already regretting the liberties he had taken with her?

Faith! I've taken advantage of a sleeping woman, he chided himself. A sleeping, gently bred woman who was the sister of one of his friends!

I am indeed going to hell!

When her lips found his again, Jeffrey's eyes widened. He barely had time to return the kiss before Evangeline pulled away. "Please, do not regret what has happened here," she whispered, her voice barely audible with her plea.

Jeffrey frowned. *Regret? Why in bloody hell would I ever regret these stolen moments of pure pleasure with Lady Evangeline?* he thought, as if he hadn't just been thinking of how guilty he felt only a moment ago.

And then he noticed the loud snoring had ceased. Remembering the book that was barely perched on his thigh, he moved one hand to steady it as Evangeline smoothed her skirts.

"I cannot believe Lord Ballantine is having difficulty finding a suitable match," Evangeline said, her voice filling the quiet library.

Jeffrey furrowed a brow. "Why ever not?" he countered, amazed she could say anything. His own brain was quite useless at the moment.

Evangeline bent her neck to one side. "Why then?"

"He's not exactly a prime candidate for the Marriage Mart."

"Why ever not?" Evangeline countered, her surprise at his response evident.

Jeffrey inhaled, reason finally returning to his addled brain. "The baron is... *broke*. I shouldn't think any lady would want to marry a man who only weds her for her dowry," he claimed, the words helping to calm his manhood.

Evangeline's mouth formed an "o" as she shook her head, thinking marriage like what he described happened all the time. Not necessarily because the woman *wanted* to wed, though, but because it suited her family. "But what if he also wished to marry her because he felt affection toward her?" she argued. "If he... if he confessed his affection for her and made it quite clear he wasn't marrying her just for the dowry?" she added quickly. "Not every woman is looking to marry a rich man." The words were barely out when she realized that perhaps most were looking for just such a match.

Geraldine certainly was.

Jeffrey regarded Evangeline for a long time before he nodded. Perhaps there was hope for him. "Thank you for... for sharing that information," he said in a whisper.

Nodding, Evangeline sighed. "I do believe this was a most satisfying chapter. Don't you agree?" she asked aloud, as if nothing of the last fifteen minutes had happened.

A most satisfying chapter... in the book? Or in their lives? "Very, milady," Jeffrey agreed with a slight nod, aware that the butler was still behind them and probably very awake. Or at least, very aware. "I do believe I should be taking my leave, though. It's quite late, and I didn't mean to keep you from your slumber." He moved the book onto the low table.

Evangeline suppressed a smile, figuring the baron had known she had fallen asleep at some point during the second or third page. "You have not, I assure you. I will show you out." Rising from the settee in one smooth movement, she caught the baron by surprise. Jeffrey stood up, though not with as much grace. A bit unsteady on his feet and hoping his waning erection wasn't too apparent, he offered his arm to Evangeline. "Thank you again for hosting me at such a late hour," he answered with a nod.

Evangeline led the baron past Jones and out of the parlor. She noticed how the butler was struggling to stand. "Oh, there's no need to get up, Jones. I'll see my guest to the door," Evangeline said as she and Jeffrey headed toward the vestibule. Tempted to ask him if he knew how long the butler had been in the parlor, Evangeline decided it was better she not know.

"Very good, milady," Jones replied, just as Evangeline walked past him with the baron in tow. He wondered how long he had been sleeping. Refreshed by his nap, he watched as Lady Evangeline escorted Lord Sommers to the front door and gave the man his hat. He watched as the baron leaned over her hand and kissed the back of it. He watched as she curtsied and gazed at Jeffrey Althorpe when he took his leave of Rosemount House. He watched as she closed the door and then leaned against it for several moments. Then he watched as she made her way up the stairs to her bedchamber.

Never in all his years as the Everly butler had he seen Lady Evangeline look so content as she did just then. Whatever had happened in the parlor that evening had happened without him paying witness to it. Perhaps the two had simply read the book as he was led to believe. Or perhaps they had engaged in inappropriate behavior, perhaps even kissed whilst he slept.

But he doubted it.

What was the likelihood that any member of the *ton* would find Lady Evangeline attractive enough to take advantage of her? *Her spectacles alone would deter most men*, he considered.

Jones went about his evening duties, stopping only for a moment when he remembered something.

Lady Evangeline hadn't been wearing her glasses when she was in the parlor. Nor had she been wearing them as she escorted Lord Sommers to the front door.

Jones sighed. *Damnation!*

Evangeline allowed Annabelle to remove all the pins from her hair and help her into her night rail before she dismissed her for the night. As she climbed onto her bed, the linens turned down to expose the white fabric, she felt the same shudder pass through her body as the one that Lord Sommers had incited in her earlier that evening.

How could she have allowed him the liberties she had?

How could I not?

She had awoken when her body was aware—suddenly alive–with the knowledge she was pressed against a man. Even now, his scent of amber and citrus and tobacco reminded her of how his hand had caressed her breast, of how his lips had felt pressed against her own. Of how they'd felt as they pressed against the soft skin of her breast. Of how his tongue and teeth had gently bit her engorged nipple and sent her into a rising tide of erotic shivers, each one more intense than the one before it, until she had thought she might faint from the sheer pleasure of his erotic touches. Even now, her entire body vibrated with the memory of it.

And then she remembered Jones had been in the parlor. She hadn't known the butler was seated behind them until she stood up and turned to escort Jeffrey to the front door. Surely Jeffrey knew, though, for if Jones hadn't been there, she could only imagine what might have happened. They might have experienced a few more minutes of pure pleasure!

I am as wicked as Geraldine, she decided, not nearly as scandalized by the thought as she probably should have been.

What a delightful night.

The thought had Evangeline smiling as she drifted off to sleep for the second time that night.

CHAPTER 24

A SUMMONED EARL
APPEARS

The following day

"I came as soon as I received your missive," Milton, Earl of Torrington, said as he stepped into Rosemount House, handing his hat to Jones.

The startled butler resisted the urge to say, "Obviously," since he had dispatched a footman with the note only the hour before—and the footman hadn't yet returned. "I remembered your orders that I should inform you should anyone... *unexpected*... pay a call on Lady Evangeline, my lord."

Still a bit breathless from his quick trip, the earl gave the butler a nod. "Is she here now?" he asked, keeping his voice low in the event the subject of their discussion was within earshot.

"She is not, my lord. She has gone to pay a call on Lady Pettigrew," Jones responded with a shake of his head. "She timed her departure so that she would arrive promptly at ten o'clock," he added with a lifted brow, as if he found her punctuality amusing. "May I ring for tea? Or perhaps you'd like something a bit stronger?" Jones asked, leading Lord Torrington to the parlor.

Milton gave the man a look of annoyance. "I don't suppose Everly keeps his brandy out where just anyone..." He stopped speaking as the butler moved to the sideboard and lifted a crystal decanter from a silver salver.

Jones poured a dollop of the dark liquid into a tumbler and offered it to the earl. "Lord Everly has sent word that he is on his way back to these shores. I expect him within the week, my lord," he explained.

Swirling the brandy in his glass before taking a careful sip, Milton regarded the butler for a moment. The man was rumored to be one of the best among the households of the *ton*, his no-nonsense manner and stern countenance tempered with fair treatment of the younger servants in the household. He was also the reason Lord Everly could spend so much time away from London—and his sister. With Everly's frequent and lengthy absences from London, others looked after the girl in his stead. The only reason Milton was involved in the girl's life was due to his position as her godfather.

During those few years when he had so willingly agreed to the requests to be someone's godfather, Milton was blissfully unaware of what he'd have to deal with once those godchildren were of marriageable age. *Twenty-one goddaughters,* he thought with a scowl. And all of them of marriageable age. At least six were now married, with two of those making up a ducal couple. With any luck, a few more would join their ranks before Parliament's recess for the Christmas holiday.

"So, who paid a call at the unfashionably late hour of nine o'clock?" Milton asked before taking another sip of the brandy. He rarely drank before noon, but for brandy as good as Lord Everly's, he made an exception.

"Lord Sommers, my lord," the butler replied, straightening to his full five-foot, seven-inch height as he stated the name.

Grandby gave a start. *Sommers?* "Did you... let him in?" he asked, wishing the butler would tell him everything without having to be prompted.

"I did," Jones admitted reluctantly, "but only because Lady Evangeline insisted I do so. She happened to be on the landing at the top of the stairs," he explained as he gestured toward the hall, "and heard his arrival."

Grandby's eyes opened wider. "And did you tell him Lord Everly was not in residence?"

The butler tried hard not to roll his eyes but failed and

nearly interrupted the earl with his reply. "Of course, my lord, but it seems he was here to see Lady Evangeline." This last he said in a whisper, as if he thought he might be overheard by another servant.

The earl inhaled and straightened. Lord Sommers had an occasion to call on Lady Evangeline at nine o'clock at *night?* "And?" he prompted, his head canting to one side. At this rate he would miss luncheon with his wife, a meal he especially enjoyed sharing with the former Lady Worthington because of what usually happened after the meal.

"They came in here and... they read a book," Jones said with a shrug. "The baron took his leave about ten o'clock, apologizing profusely for having come so late," he added.

"A book?" Milton repeated. At the butler's nod, the earl left the parlor, descended the stairs, and walked into the library. He glanced about, wondering if the two had been secretly reading one of Everly's many books on sexual congress. The man was said to have one of the most extensive collections on the topic, although some of the tomes apparently had to do with the mating rituals of creatures other than humans.

When he determined that all the books seemed to be in their places on the shelves, he remembered the book the two had been reading in Finsbury Square earlier that week. Milton went back up to the parlor and turned his attention to the furniture. On the low table in front of the settee, he found *The Story of a Baron*, its pages opened to the end of a chapter. *They're still reading the book,* he realized, surprised Evangeline hadn't purchased her own copy.

Or perhaps this was her copy and the baron hadn't purchased one of his own.

The Temple of the Muses might have been sold out since the day the book made its debut, but Hatchard's had them. He was sure that's where his wife had purchased her copy.

Hmph, he thought as he repositioned the book on the settee. Sommers was a baron, he considered as he studied the tome. Milton opened the front cover and read the title page, noting the date of publication. *A new release,* he confirmed. He shook his head when he saw the work was attributed to Anonymous.

That could be anyone. Someone who really was a baron or another member of the *ton* or... or not, he thought as he closed the book. The author could just be a hack making his living writing bad books.

Milton was about to return the book to its resting place when he noticed the indentations in the cushion of the settee. Two distinct impressions had been left, one deeper than the other, and the lighter one indicative of a woman's derriere. Had the two simply been reading the book as the butler claimed? Milton took up the book again and opened it to the first page of the first chapter. He read the first line.

Matthew Winters, Baron Ballantine, entered his favorite book-shop in search of a particular new title.

Milton lifted his head, wondering if Winters was really Sommers. He dared a glance at the very last line of the book.

Forever.

The earl slammed the book shut, the sound breaking the silence in the parlor. *What was the author thinking?* he thought with a great deal of annoyance. *That certainly didn't tell the reader very much.* But it was an ending that held promise, he had to admit. Which was saying a good deal if the story was truly about a baron. And apparently the baron and the sister of an earl were reading the story. Together.

What else might they being doing together? Milton wondered. There hadn't been a whiff of scandal surrounding Lady Evangeline—poor girl was lucky if she was ever able to step foot in a ballroom, given her brother's frequent trips. Everly never seemed to have someone lined up to chaperone his sister for events, trusting that she would spend her days calling on other young ladies of the *ton*, and...

Milton inhaled sharply. *And what?* Did anyone call on *her?* Did she ever go shopping in New Bond Street? Or have an ice at Gunter's whilst some young buck regarded her from the side of her carriage? Or take in a play in Drury Lane? Or visit a choco-late shop? He knew about her Tuesday morning treks to the bookshop and to Lady Samantha's and Lady Julia's for tea, for those trips coincided with his own morning strolls. But where else was she going besides the parlors of those on whom she paid calls?

Remembering he wasn't alone in the parlor, Milton turned to find the butler regarding him, one bushy eyebrow arched in question. "How often does Lady Evangeline leave the house after she pays calls?" Milton asked.

Jones looked to the coffered ceiling for a second before he replied, "Almost every day, my lord. She likes to go for walks." He dared another glance at the ceiling and made a mental note to speak with the housekeeper about the cobwebs that had attached themselves to the coffers.

Milton allowed his face to show his surprise. "Does anyone go *with* her?" he asked, aware the poor girl didn't have a chaperone. Although that was probably a good thing. Some chaperones would rather lock up their charges behind closed doors and never let them out than spend the time to introduce them into Society.

"Usually she is accompanied by her lady's maid. When Winslet is unable to go with her, the other maids take turns, my lord," Jones replied. "Some don't mind the walk whilst others are... less *enthusiastic* about the exercise," he added.

"And, at night? Does the lady... go out?" the earl asked, glad to hear that at least his goddaughter was getting some air everyday. Although, given the amount of soot in the winter, that wasn't necessarily a good thing, either.

"Not unless Lord Everly escorts her, my lord," Jones responded, "and that does not happen very often."

Milton inhaled, the scent of brandy still evident on his breath. There was really only one solution to the problem of Lady Evangeline. "'Bout time the girl was married, don't you suppose?" he asked rhetorically.

The butler clasped his hands behind his back, his gaze directed once more at the cobwebs decorating the ceiling. "I suppose," he answered quietly as he resisted the urge to inhale sharply. The cobwebs were positively ghoulish!

The earl gave Jones a quelling look. "As her godfather, I've a mind to find her a husband myself," he warned, unaware that most would find his threat a preferable alternative to Lord Everly taking on the task. At nearly thirty, the earl was still a bachelor, and he wasn't courting anyone... unless he had met someone on his most recent travels to the Indian Ocean and southern coast of Africa.

"Very good, my lord," Jones replied with a nod. "Shall I inform my master when he returns from his trip?"

Grandby regarded the butler for several moments before finally saying, "No. I'll see to it."

With one more glance around the parlor, the earl took his leave of Rosemount House, eager to have luncheon—and then dessert—with his wife.

CHAPTER 25

ON KISSES AND DOWRIES

*L*ater that day

"I don't suppose there is a single lady among the entire *ton* who tells a man to kiss her," Evangeline murmured, now mortified by what she had asked of Lord Sommers the evening prior. And a bit guilty that she had told Jones she was on her way to Lady Pettigrew's, when in fact she was planning to meet the baron in Grosvenor Square.

Jeffrey shrugged, not sure how to put Evangeline at ease. He hadn't minded being asked for a kiss in the least. He had been a bit shocked at his own reaction, though. Even knowing the butler was in the room, he hadn't declined her invitation—and if he had to do it over again, he still wouldn't. He had simply done her bidding and a bit more, but with her help.

What she had done to him... the memory of it now filled both his heads.

"Oh, dear," Evangeline sighed, her face pinking up even more. "Will you ever forgive me?" she asked in a quiet voice.

Jeffrey shook his head. "No, milady, for there is no need to apologize," he assured her. "So there is nothing to forgive. And, as for ladies asking for kisses, Lady Bostwick does it all the time with her George," he said, happy to reassure her.

Evangeline seemed overly concerned at having told him to kiss her, and although he had at first been shocked at the demand, he'd also felt... thrilled. Even more so when her hand had done such wonders for his manhood—literally and figuratively. Given her ready and positive response to his early morning missive about reading the book in Grosvenor Square if the fine weather held, he thought she was completely unaware of what she had done—apparently all in her sleep. "Or, so the *on-dit* would have it," he added with a nod, having to return his mental attention to George Bennett-Jones or risk a repeat of the night before. Right out in front of everyone in the square.

Evangeline straightened on the park bench. "Lady Bostwick?" she breathed. *That would be just like Elizabeth Carlington Bennett-Jones*, Evangeline thought. The founder of her own charity, Elizabeth was said to be very devoted to Viscount Bostwick. Devoted, no doubt, because George Bennett-Jones doted on her. Because he saw to it there was constant funding for her charity. And because he was said to leave little gifts for her to find throughout the house they shared in Park Lane—gifts he left for no other reason than he liked his lady to be happy.

The ladies of the *ton* knew such things because Elizabeth always spoke highly of her husband whilst in the parlors of Mayfair. "I should think Lord Bostwick would be the one demanding kisses, given how generous he is with Lady Bostwick," Evangeline commented.

Jeffrey regarded her with a grin. "Oh, not George," he said with a shake of his head. "The man has been in love with his wife since the first time he spotted her at a ball." He turned on the bench so he faced her. "She was dancing with Lord Trenton at the time," he said with a smirk. "Although, I often wonder if his affections were due to her starting her charity. One of his close friends was its first beneficiary."

Evangeline turned so she could regard the baron. "Indeed?" she replied.

"One day, we were in the middle of a session of Parliament when a footman arrived. He was searching for Bostwick. Seems his lady was feeling some discomfort—she was with child at the time—and requested his immediate presence at their home."

Suppressing a knowing smile, Evangeline wondered if Lord Sommers knew what George had done to help relieve his wife's pain. "Did he leave the chambers, then?" she asked with a waggling eyebrow, knowing in fact that he had.

"He did!" Jeffrey replied with widened eyes, obviously happy to share his tale. "And then he returned an hour-and-a-half later. Had a rather satisfied look on his face, too," he added with a hint of derision.

Evangeline angled her head to one side. "Would you do such a thing, do you suppose?"

Jeffrey regarded her with curiosity. "Whatever do you mean?"

Unable to prevent the blush she could feel coloring her face, Elizabeth lowered her head. "Would you hurry to your wife's side should she need sexual congress to relieve her back pain?" she asked in what she hoped sounded like a teasing tone.

Jeffrey Althorpe was acutely aware his mouth wasn't completely closed. And over the course of the nearly ten seconds it took him to consider how to answer Lady Evangeline's question, his jaw dropped even more, leaving his mouth wide open. "My lady," he struggled to get out, his words meant to scold when in fact they made him sound as if he were in awe. "I..." He stopped when he noted how Evangeline was waiting for his answer with bated breath, as if she weren't teasing him at all but was truly curious if he would do his wife's bidding. "I would, I suppose. If she thought it would... *help*," he struggled to get out.

Good God! Had Evangeline actually asked him if he would have sexual intercourse with her?

No. *No*, she most certainly had not.

She had merely asked if he would hurry to his wife's side. Well, if he would hurry to her side because she needed sexual intercourse, then of course he would *accommodate* her!

*E*vangeline took a breath, forced to do so when a pleasant little shiver shot down her spine and settled between her thighs. "I should think you will have a happy wife, then," she murmured with a nod, hoping the baron hadn't noticed her entire body vibrate just then.

"Happy wife, happy life," Jeffrey responded, the words

coming out before he'd had a chance to think where he had heard the expression before. At the gaming tables, no doubt. From one of his married friends. Lord Devonville, probably.

Evangeline giggled, the musical sound making Jeffrey smile. "What is it that has you so amused?" he asked, finding her happiness infectious.

"You, my lord," she answered, a smile still gracing her face. "How is it a man of your good humor and handsome appearance is still unmarried?" The words were out before Evangeline could censor them, before she realized they sounded exactly as if they had been spoken by Geraldine Porterhouse. "Oh, do forgive me, Lord Sommers," she added. "I do believe Lady Geraldine's behavior is having an ill effect on me."

Jeffrey stared at Evangeline for a moment, stunned by her question. *She finds me of good humor? And handsome?* His heart beating at twice its normal rate, Jeffrey found it hard to hear himself think.

What was the question?

How is it a man of your good humor and handsome appearance is unmarried?

"I am a baron," he answered simply, as if being a baron precluded him from being married. "A baron of a barony that seems to be lacking funds on a regular basis. And given my position in the *ton*, I find I cannot work and remain in good stead with other members of the *ton*," he continued. "Had I Michael Cunningham's head for business and ability with my fists, I might have taken his stance and simply aligned myself with a savvy businessman and earned some money through doing business in coal gas and smelting and taking the occasional bet in a bare-knuckle mill. The *ton* be damned!

"Or," he continued, apparently unaware he had cursed in the presence of a lady, "Had I known how little my father had in the way of a fortune, I could have taken Lord Norwick's position and built a fortune with a popular brothel and gaming hell, and then sold it after I inherited, so there would be plenty of working capital for the rest of my life," he explained with a wave of his hand. He stared at Evangeline for a full second before adding, "But I didn't. I didn't know how destitute he was. So, instead... I find myself with a continuous stream of bills and a slightly less continuous trickle of income."

With the last statement, Jeffrey settled back into the bench, crossed his arms, and took a deep breath, his eyes closing as if he regretted having spoken every word.

Lady Evangeline regarded the baron for a very long time. From the anger in his voice, she sensed the man wasn't looking for sympathy but rather a solution to his problem. And she had the distinct impression he would embrace it should she have a workable suggestion for him.

"I do believe you need to find a wife with a substantial dowry," she offered, not able to think of anything else she could say to assuage him.

Jeffrey stared at Evangeline for a very long time, amazed that she knew enough not to speak words of sympathy or suggest he set up a brothel and a gaming hell or contact Cunningham about how to go about setting up businesses based on coal gas and smelting.

Or learn how to fight.

Thank the gods!

"A wife?" he repeated.

"Yes," Evangeline replied with a nod.

Jeffrey stared at her for several seconds. "Given my position, who would marry *me?*"

Evangeline took a breath. "The daughter of a very rich tradesman," she offered, thinking that's what Michael Cunningham had done when he married his wife, Olivia. "Or the young widow of a coal baron," she continued, noting his brows furrowing in contemplation. "Or a daughter of an earl who hasn't yet found a suitable match," she finished, hoping he had enough sense to realize she meant her.

Jeffrey shook his head as if he'd been hit by one of Michael Cunningham's left hooks. "A young widow?" he repeated.

It was Evangeline's turn to close her eyes. "I don't know of one in particular," she said with a shake of her head. "The Marquess of Devonville married one," she said, thinking of

Cherice Dubois, the former Lady Winslow. The widow's mourning period had been over for exactly one day when William, Marquess of Devonville, made it clear to her and everyone else in the *ton* that she was to be his next marchioness.

Just as Jeffrey was about to consider unmarried daughters of the aristocracy, he realized the idiocy of their discussion. Lady Evangeline was just such a woman. Unmarried. The daughter of an earl. *And probably very able when it came to carnal matters*, he considered, remembering what her hands had been doing whilst she napped in the parlor the night before. Perhaps the boldness in how she spoke just then might be matched with her behavior in the marriage bed.

Like Geraldine, he thought in alarm.

Bold, brash Geraldine. Perhaps Evangeline *was* just like her in some ways. He had thought her much like his Geraldine when he wrote the character, only because he had conjured an image of Evangeline based on her living alone and unprotected. But she was perfect for him. He had practically ruined her in the parlor the night before. It only made sense he marry her.

The thought of Evangeline's brother forced him to sober a bit, though.

"When will your brother return to these shores?" he asked abruptly.

Evangeline lifted one shoulder. "I expect him in the next few days," she answered. "Why do you ask?"

The next few days?

Jeffrey bit his lip. Well, it wasn't as if he needed time to think about it. Perhaps Lady Evangeline would need some time. But why would she suggest "the unmarried daughter of an earl" if she wasn't referring to herself?

"I need to speak with him when he returns," Jeffrey replied.

Evangeline decided the baron would not be continuing any talk of a potential wife just then, which was just as well given her brother's continued absence. She indicated the book. "Shall we find out how Ballantine and Lady Geraldine fare on their ride in the park?" she asked, remembering she would need to read from wherever she was when she dozed off the night before.

Noting the book still lying open on his thigh, Jeffrey nodded. "Yes, let's," he replied, even though he would rather have spent their time together in conversation. But there was the book, and he was rather curious as to how much his publisher might have changed in this chapter.

He glanced at Evangeline, noting how she regarded him with a rather odd expression. He stared at her for a very long time, knowing he should say something—anything—but to do so right now wouldn't be proper. He needed to speak with her brother before he put voice to his plan.

The two slowly lowered their eyes to the book and began to read—both from the very beginning of the same chapter they had supposedly read the night before.

CHAPTER 26

OUR COUPLE READS IN GROSVENOR SQUARE

The Story of a Baron
A Novel in One Volume
Written by Anonymous

Chapter 6: Primping for a Party

Dressed in her new walking gown, Geraldine regarded her image in the cheval mirror critically. The drape of the fabric seemed of a more matronly style than she was accustomed to, and the bright green of the wool did nothing to enhance her brunette hair, nor her complexion. She leaned in closer to the mirror, studying her face, examining her neck, staring into eyes that stared back at her. The green irises seemed to bloom with bits of gold and then shrink as she continued to gaze at her reflection.

When she heard a sound, Geraldine turned to find her maid frowning. "What is it?" she asked.

Simpson hesitated before finally answering. "I do not think this is one of Madame Eunices' better creations," she said carefully. "I merely wondered if... perhaps she sent the wrong gown?"

Geraldine whirled around to study the gown in the mirror again. Of course, Simpson was right. The gown simply didn't fit.

The arms were too short and the bodice too snug and the color was…

"All wrong," Geraldine agreed with a nod. "Could you undo the fastenings? I'll have a footman return it to the shop right away. Perhaps whoever received my gown by accident will have returned it to her shop by now," she said. She could only hope there had been a mix-up in the modiste's shop and that this gown was meant for someone else. If not, she *would* have to find a new modiste.

In the meantime, she'd have to find something else to wear to the birthday picnic. And she couldn't wear the pink ensemble again.

"Would you like me to get out your blue carriage gown?" Simpson offered.

Geraldine sighed. At least two seasons out-of-date, with its ruffle-edged bodice and cuffs, the blue gown was really her only other option. Geraldine studied the gown. Still in good repair, it was far more appropriate for a younger woman newly out in Society. But if she could tuck the ruffles under the edges and find a suitable fichu, she could at least make it look more modern. "Yes, please," she murmured. "And bring some pins," she added as she removed the green walking gown. "It might be old, but there's no reason we can't make it work."

A half-hour later, Geraldine regarded her image in the mirror once again, one tooth buried in her lower lip. "Well, what do you think?" she asked of her maid.

Simpson smiled. "Removing the ruffles is an improvement," she said with a nod. "Given some time, I could have removed 'em proper and stitched up the neckline," she added, pinching some lint off the skirt. "I do hope the pins don't stick you through the fichu."

Geraldine sighed. She hoped not, either. There were at least twenty of them around the inside of the bodice anchoring the ruffles so they couldn't be seen. If she moved too much to one side or the other, she was sure to be stabbed by at least one pin. "I'll have you do that once I'm back from this ride," Geraldine agreed, trying to decide what to wear on her head.

"I'm thinking a hat instead of a bonnet," she murmured,

deciding the more mature look was appropriate. She was no longer a young *demoiselle*—it was time she started dressing like a young matron, even if she wasn't married.

Simpson hurried into the dressing room, returning with two different hats. Geraldine helped herself to the red one. Part of its brim was pinned up against the crown and decorated with a jaunty feather. She lifted it over her coiffure and regarded her reflection for a moment. "This will do," she said, nodding her head to see how the feather bobbed. *What will Lord Ballantine think of it?* she wondered. Would he find it striking, or attractive, or annoying?

Annoying, she decided.

Geraldine took off the hat and examined how the feather was attached. She asked Simpson for a pair of scissors and quickly clipped off the quill from where it was attached at the crown.

"Oh!" Simpson exclaimed as the feather floated to the floor. "But won't it be too plain?" she asked, watching as her mistress placed it on her head again.

"Not after we attach a small bow made of ribbon," Geraldine reasoned, reaching for a hat pin from the vanity. Within moments, she had a blue bow covering the spot where the feather had been attached. Pulling on blue gloves, Geraldine took one last look before taking her leave of her bedchamber. With any luck, Lord Ballantine would be impressed with her more mature look. With even more luck, he might ask her brother if he could court her.

Matthew Winters, Viscount Ballantine, halted his barouche in front of Rosehill House, chiding himself for the nervousness he felt. He was merely calling on Lady Geraldine. There was no reason to be so...

Whatever he was.

Matthew absently studied the reins he still held in his right hand. What was it about Geraldine Porterhouse? *Why does she have this kind of effect on me? She's a chit,* he thought with a bit of derision. And the only reason he was here today was to take her for a ride to the birthday picnic and attempt to make it clear to her that he was...

He was... *what?*

Her best chance at a suitable marriage. Yes, that's what he was. Her best chance.

What if she asked why?

I can say she has a reputation.

Reputation? A grimace appeared as he considered the word, for he didn't know anything first-hand. Everything he had heard about Geraldine had been voiced by someone who may or may not have been present when the scandalous events just seemed to have happened. Unfortunate things that made her...

Fast? He couldn't tell her that. Perhaps her overtures had merely been misunderstood.

Bold? She already knew that. She'd as much as told him she was.

Brazen? Well, yes, but in a way he found rather compelling. He couldn't exactly fault her for trying to get what she wanted.

Perhaps she wasn't willing to settle for the first man her brother might find on her behalf. Matthew couldn't blame her for that either, given some of Lord Afterly's friends. Although he could count himself among them, Afterly hadn't yet approached him about courting his sister. He wondered why. *Does he know I would be marrying her for her dowry?*

Well, not entirely, he had to admit.

He would do so to save her from a reputation that was nearly in ruin. To provide protection. To give her a home she could call her own.

To bed her.

Matthew squeezed his eyes shut, trying desperately to clear the image of her naked in his bed. Of her devilish dark hair splayed out on the goose down pillow. Of her parted lips ready to kiss his. Of her lush body welcoming him, embracing him with her petite legs and elegant arms, the secret place at the top of her thighs providing a warm, wet haven for his engorged manhood. He took a ragged breath.

Damnation!

His eyes opening slowly, Matthew caught sight of the bulge

behind the placket of his breeches. *Double damnation!* How was he supposed to escort Lady Geraldine on a ride in the park to the birthday party when all he wanted to do was ravish her?

Well, if he were married to her, he'd be able to do so whenever he pleased.

But would she want him to?

Waiting another moment to allow his ardor to cool, Matthew stepped down from the barouche and made his way to the front door of Rosehill House. Not of recent construction nor located in a particularly fashionable part of Westminster, the yellow house appeared as if it could use a bit of maintenance. The lawn was clipped and flowers displayed a riot of color along the front edge of the property, although one of the pickets was missing from the fence. As he was about to reach for the lion head's knocker, the door opened.

"Good day, sir. And who may I say is calling?" the butler asked.

A very frustrated, lustful baron, he thought to reply. Instead, he said, "Lord Ballantine. I'm here to collect Lady Geraldine."

From the raised eyebrows on the butler, Matthew decided his words were a surprise to the man.

"I'm right here, Smithton," he heard a feminine voice say from inside the house.

The butler disappeared, only to be replaced by the woman herself. Dressed in bright blue and sporting a conservative hat—it didn't even have a plethora of silk flowers or a feather arcing out of the top—Geraldine appeared as if she were already a married, respectable lady of the *ton*. Matthew felt disappointment, but it was soon replaced with awe. "My lady," he said in greeting, doing his best to keep his jaw from dropping. She looked positively... proper. And she was giving him a brilliant smile that had him forgetting what he was supposed to say.

He remembered what had happened the day before. How her brilliant smile had been replaced by a look that suggested she was embarrassed by her assertion that he'd been thinking naughty thoughts about her. That if she'd had the moment to do it over again, she might have allowed him more time to respond, to deny her assertion. Had she done that, though, Matthew didn't know if he would have been brave enough to send the note asking her to join him on this ride to Lady Barrick's birthday picnic.

The woman always had him so addled! And now... now he was supposed to be saying something.

"Good afternoon, Lord Ballantine," Geraldine said as she curtsied.

Matthew bowed and reached for her gloved hand. He brushed his lips over her knuckles, his mind blank. When he straightened, he found her gazing at him.

"Good afternoon, milady," he finally responded, remembering to offer his arm. Geraldine took it, just as she had yesterday morning when he had met her at the Palace of Prose. And just as if they'd known one another their entire lives—which they had, Matthew remembered just then—they set off down the front steps of Rosehill House for an afternoon ride.

CHAPTER 27

OF WANTS

"What do *you* want, Lady Evangeline?" Jeffrey asked, turning on the bench to regard Evangeline.

Evangeline gave a start. She'd been so engrossed in the story, she hadn't realized she was being addressed. "Want?" she repeated, thinking at first the tea tray had arrived and he was offering her biscuits, which was ridiculous since she would be the one to serve tea. And that was completely and utterly impossible because they were sitting in the middle of Grosvenor Square and there would be no tea served here. She gave her head a shake, attempting to bring herself back to the present.

"Yes," Jeffrey replied. "Are you fond of jewels, or gowns from France, or some other manner of frippery?" he clarified. The thought of finding a birthday present had been on his mind ever since he learned her birthday would be in a couple of days.

Evangeline reached for the bookmark. "My own home, I suppose," she finally answered. "Children, of course. A husband who is at least as fond of me as I am of him."

The baron's brows furrowed. "Is Rosemount House not your home?"

Before the blush could color her face, Evangeline turned away. "Rosemount House is my brother's house," she reminded him. "When he takes a wife, she will be its mistress."

Jeffrey shrugged. "Knowing your brother as I do, it may be a long time before he has a wife. Certainly, you'll stay at Rosemount House until then," he reasoned.

Melancholy settled over Evangeline just then. His words made it sound as if her brother would marry before she did. "Rosemount House certainly feels like home, but I'm quite sure whoever he marries will replace my mother's chipped china and worn furniture when she moves in," she said, sadly.

"Perhaps you can keep them then," Jeffrey replied, thinking the furnishings looked far more comfortable than most in Sommers Place in Cavendish Square.

Evangeline's face brightened at his suggestion. "Perhaps," she agreed, wondering where she would put the stuff-n-such when the new Lady Everly moved in.

"Your brother will not mind," Jeffrey said with a shake of his head. "Nor will your husband."

Evangeline's eyes widened at the comment. "You say that as if you already know who he will be."

Jeffrey had to tamp down the first thought that came to his mind. Of course, he knew. At least, he was pretty sure he knew. Trouble was, until he had a chance to discuss the matter with Lord Everly, he wasn't at liberty to say. "Well, I do not know who exactly, milady. Any man who could claim you as his wife would be a fool not to allow you to bring along the things that have meaning for you."

Evangeline regarded the baron for several moments, warmed by his words. "That would make for a small number of fools," she replied with a teary smile.

Just one, Jeffrey thought.

Hopefully.

"Shall we continue reading in the morning? Here? The weather appears as if it will stay fine," Jeffrey said, deciding he needed to change the subject.

"Yes, let's." Evangeline closed the book and put thoughts of marriage out of her mind.

CHAPTER 28

A GODFATHER AND HIS COUNTESS DISCUSS PROPRIETY

*M*eanwhile, at Torrington House

Having just enjoyed his second helping of dessert with his wife, Milton, Earl of Torrington, held his wife against the side of his naked body. Adele was nearly naked as well, save for the pearl necklace that graced her neck.

"I rather like this on you," Milton remarked as one of his fingers traced the row of cream-colored pearls.

Adele grinned. "You say that about all of my jewelry," she whispered. "Probably because you didn't have to buy it for me."

Milton pinched her bare bottom. "Careful, there, my love. When I'm good and ready, I'll bestow you with jewels that will put those to shame," he claimed as he settled his head into the feather pillow.

His wife lifted her head to regard her husband with a quizzical brow. "I truly don't need more baubles," she said quietly. She traced the blond curls that covered his chest, occasionally reaching down with her lips to kiss them.

"I had several callers this morning," she said, as if she had been waiting for the perfect time to share a concern with the earl.

"Don't you always have a houseful?" he asked, his eyes closed as he enjoyed her gentle touches. In all his early years, when he had employed mistresses rather than take a wife, and then later, when he preferred the company of widows, Milton thought never to marry. But after spending a Season escorting Adele Slater Worthington to every ball and acting as host for her annual *musicale*, he decided he couldn't abide living without her. They were married by special license a few months later.

"Hmm," Adele murmured. "We certainly will for tomorrow night's dinner party," she replied. "I thought I had invited forty, but we have one-and-forty who have sent acceptances."

"That's odd," Milton said, unaware of his pun. He turned to regard her, aware her expression of worry wasn't about the odd number of people coming to the dinner party. "But that's not what has you concerned right now, is it?"

"It wasn't this morning's callers so much as the gossip they shared. It seems Lady Evangeline is the current *on-dit*," Adele said, worry evident in her voice.

She was suddenly displaced from her position half atop her husband when he sat up and turned to stare down at her. "What are they saying?" he asked, urgently.

Pulling a bed linen over her bared breasts, as much for warmth as for modesty, Adele sighed. "Her neighbor claims a young man has been visiting the house—a couple of mornings this past week—and that Lord Everly isn't yet in residence. Is that true?"

Milton squeezed his eyes shut. "Did anyone say anything about last night?" he asked, one hand over his eyes. He split his fingers so he could peek at his obviously shocked wife whilst she considered his question. "No," she answered with a shake of her head. "What happened last night?" She propped herself up on one elbow.

Settling back into the mattress, Milton sighed. "Lord Sommers showed up at nine o'clock so they could read a book."

Adele stared at her husband for several seconds. "Lord Sommers?" she repeated. "Then, what have they been doing in the *mornings?*" she demanded, her brows furrowed.

"Reading a book," Grandby replied simply. "We *are* discussing Evangeline Tennison, remember," he said, with a hint of impatience.

Sighing, Adele also fell back into the mattress. "I'll have a word with her," she murmured, a half-smile touching her lips. She could pay her a call the following afternoon. Evangeline would probably be reading with Lord Sommers in the morning. "They must be reading *The Story of a Baron*."

Grandby opened his eyes again. "How did you know?" he asked in surprise.

"Oh, it's all the rage now, seeing as how it's sold out at the Temple. I managed to get the last copy Hatchard's had on their shelves," she told him with a good deal of pride.

Grandby stared at his wife, a grin forming. "*You* have a copy? Here at the house?" he asked, obviously pleased at the thought.

Adele giggled, wondering at his good humor. "Yes. And you can read it. We can even read it together, if you'd like," she suggested as she waggled her eyebrows, thinking they could read it whilst in bed. While they were naked.

"You minx!" her husband replied, moving to cover her body with his own. He kissed her thoroughly before resting his head on her shoulder. He was far too spent to make love to her again. "I'm too old for this," he whispered, before falling asleep in her arms.

Giggling, Adele wrapped her arms around his shoulders. "I don't mind a bit," she murmured and was soon sound asleep as well.

CHAPTER 29

OUR COUPLE RETURNS TO READ IN GROSVENOR SQUARE

The Story of a Baron
A Novel in One Volume
Written by Anonymous

Chapter 7: A Ride to a Picnic in the Park

Matthew Winters had his barouche merging with the traffic in Oxford Street as if he did it every day, which Geraldine thought he might very well do. She had no idea how the baron occupied himself, at least on the days when Parliament wasn't in session. "Tell me, Lord Ballantine. What would you being doing right now if you weren't on your way to Hyde Park for a birthday party?"

The baron glanced in Geraldine's direction, impressed by the question. He had thought they would be discussing the weather or the latest fashions from Paris. "I would probably be in my study seeing to the business of the barony," he replied easily.

With one hand hooked around his arm, Geraldine placed her other hand in her lap. "You don't employ a secretary to see to your barony?" she questioned, marveling at how he expertly avoided a child who darted out in front of them and then swerved when a costermonger looked as if he were trying to be run over by the older-model barouche.

Matthew considered how to respond. He would gladly

employ someone if he could afford to do so. "I do not," he responded as he took the turn onto Park Lane.

"Because you do not trust someone else to do it?" she half-questioned, her attention on the Abdington's mansion. "I've always thought that was the most beautiful house in this lane," she added as she openly admired the Palladian architecture, manicured lawn, and gardens in front.

"Indeed? I would have thought Lord Atheron's manor would suit you much better," Matthew countered, testing her to discover if she would stick to her original claim or change her opinion to match what he had just suggested.

Geraldine shook her head. "Although the Atherton pile is certainly impressive, it lacks... the modern look, I suppose," she replied carefully. "I'm just not very fond of Tudor architecture, I suppose."

His eyes widening, Matthew dared a glance in her direction. So the woman was versed in architecture. "Is Palladian your favorite then?" he asked, his attention turning to the mansion to their left, one he knew didn't belong to a member of the aristocracy but rather to a tradesman. A rather successful tradesman.

"I do love the Greek influence," Geraldine agreed. "In fashion as well as buildings," she added enthusiastically.

Matthew blinked. He had never seen Geraldine dressed in any gowns that took their cut from the Greek goddess dresses that had been so popular at the turn of the century. "And yet you do not wear such gowns," he noted.

Geraldine's eyes widened at the thought the baron was familiar with women's fashions. "True," she answered carefully. "Unfortunately, my modiste is quite set on styles that she claims are French but that my brother says are most certainly not. I am not exactly sure how *he* would know, though," she said thoughtfully.

Chuckling, Matthew patted the hand that wound around his arm. "Given his avocation, your brother is a worldly man, Jerry," he said, barely aware he had called her by her nickname. "He probably knows more about women's fashions than any modiste in New Bond Street, since he's managed to remove them from so many women." *And then had to help to put them back on*, he nearly added. The man would probably make an excellent lady's maid! Prior to his having earned a degree from Cambridge, Richard Porterhouse enjoyed the life of a randy member of the *ton*, his conquests ranging from young widows to willing maidservants to older women who were bored in their marriages.

Stunned by Ballantine's comment, Geraldine inhaled sharply, lifting one gloved hand to cover her open mouth. "Why, Matthew Winters, you take that back right now," she insisted, her manner suggesting she wasn't the least bit humored by his comment about her brother.

Matthew swallowed, shocked that he would put voice to such a thought, even if it was to Geraldine Porterhouse. "I apologize, my lady. I... I don't know what came over me just then," he said with a good deal of humility. "Just because we were fast friends in our youth does not give me the right to impugn your brother. Do forgive me."

Geraldine straightened in the squabs. "Are you testing me, Lord Ballantine?" she asked.

A quirk formed at the edge of the baron's mouth. "I am, indeed, Jerry," he responded, his face breaking into a wide smile. "I must admit that I feared you and your brother were no longer on speaking terms," he explained. "I did not wish to take sides, if that were the case, since you were both such good friends to me." He guided the barouche through the gates into the park.

Settling back into the squabs, Geraldine's face took on a serious expression. *Friends?* Was that all she would ever be to Matthew Winters? They had known each other since she was in leading strings. They had played in creeks, and made mud pies along the edge of the farm fields, and skipped rocks across the pond, and hid in the folly.

And kissed in the barn.

Even now, Geraldine felt a shiver of delight skitter down her spine. *When will I ever be kissed like that again?* she wondered. Despite all the rumors that had her kissing any man who would allow it, she hadn't kissed anyone since that night in the barn on the Ballantine farm. She couldn't remember if she had started it, or if Matthew had, but the two were suddenly lip-locked, their arms wrapped awkwardly around one another. As to who ended it, well, it didn't much matter since Matthew's father began bellowing the boy's name from somewhere behind the nearby house. "Go!" she had said, giving Matthew a gentle push, her eyes deliberately kept straight ahead, for she knew his arousal was apparent. Even now, she could remember how it felt to have it pressed against her belly as they held one another, how it had felt to imagine him lowering her to the straw below so he could lift her skirts and claim her as his own. She would have allowed it. Would allow it even now should he wish to claim her.

"If my father hadn't been looking for me, you would have lost your maidenhead that night," Matthew stated, his voice carrying a hint of warning.

Geraldine's eyes were wide as she turned to regard the baron. Had she said something aloud? Or could he read her mind?

Matthew held her gaze as if he dared her to look away before he did. He had to, though, when he realized the horse was veering off the road. Once he had the nag back on track, he returned his attention to Geraldine. "Would you have fought me off?" he asked, his voice almost a whisper.

Geraldine shook her head. "No." A vague memory of having slapped him across the face for the kiss he had stolen was there and gone in an instant.

Nodding once, Matthew turned his eyes back to the road.

Well, there was that, he supposed, wondering how different their lives would be if they had consummated their *affaire*, such as it was, all those years ago.

"I would never deny you what has always been yours."

The words were said so quietly, Matthew wasn't quite sure he'd heard them correctly. He led the horse to the side of the road and pulled back hard on the reins, his brows furrowing as he stared at Geraldine. Angrily, he asked, "Mine, and how many others?"

Geraldine inhaled sharply, the expression on her face turning from doe-eyed innocence to angry-eyed she-devil. Her blue gloved hand came out of nowhere and walloped Matthew hard across his right cheek, the strike so unexpected, the baron was nearly unseated. "How dare you!" she cried out, scooting across the seat until she was pressed against the other side of the barouche.

So startled was he by the chit's right hook—it was probably just a slap, but the baron wasn't about to believe that much pain could result from an open-handed hit—Matthew let go of the reins. The horse actually looked back at him, as if she might consider bolting. But then she would have to give up her snack of flowers.

Matthew gaped at Geraldine, and watched as tears pricked the corners of her eyes.

"I... I have *never* shared a bed with a man," she whispered harshly, her breathing so labored Matthew could hear her gasps for air from where he sat.

"Of course not," Matthew replied, his ire evident in the set of his shoulders. "Who needs a *bed* when there is a... hay bale or a table or a..." He was seeing stars as her reticule impacted his left cheek. He had a passing thought that everything she owned must have been in that reticule, for he was quite sure there would be a very large bruise covering half his face the following morning.

He shook his head, trying to clear the dancing stars that seemed to have replaced his usual clear-headed view of the world.

Tears flowing down her cheeks, Geraldine fumbled for the door catch, determined to take her leave of Lord Ballantine's barouche. They were already in the park; a short walk, and she would be able to join Lady Barrick and her band of surprise party-goers. She imagined casually strolling up to the group on foot, angling her head to one side and saying, "Surprise!" The alternative was to arrive on the arm of Lord Ballantine, who at the moment was regarding her with a look of surprise and... *was that admiration?*

Geraldine shook her head as she managed to get the door to open. "Thank you for the ride, my lord," she spat out. "I must inform you it will be the last I ever take with *you*." She stumbled out of the barouche, slamming the small door behind her before stomping off on a crushed granite path.

Embarrassed and belittled more than he felt when he

attempted to pay his monthly bills, Matthew watched Lady Geraldine take her leave of the barouche. He frowned when he sorted her determined steps were taking her in the wrong direction for the picnic.

"Lady Barrick's picnic is in the other direction, my lady," he managed to call out. He watched as Lady Geraldine's shoulders straightened. Although she didn't slow her pace nor immediately turn around, she made a wide arc so that her eventual direction was toward the grounds of the birthday party.

Dropping his head into his hands, Matthew Winters cursed himself. He cursed the horse. He cursed his mouth. He cursed Lord Afterly. And he cursed Lady Geraldine.

So, she wasn't the doxy the *ton* had made her out to be. She was merely the *ton's* current *on-dit,* a young lady who by circumstance of being beautiful suffered the wrath of a jealous aristocracy.

And he had just made it worse by allowing her to escape his protection.

When his breathing returned to normal, Matthew lifted the reins from the floor and urged his reluctant horse to return to the crushed granite path. He intended to make his way toward Lady Barrick's party. He had to find Geraldine. He couldn't allow her to show up unescorted!

In a few moments, the deep blue of her carriage gown appeared through the hedgerow that lined the lane. He hurried the nag on ahead and then parked the barouche at the edge of the lane. Getting out as quickly as he could, Matthew ran to the other side of the hedgerow and intercepted Geraldine... or at least a woman he thought was Geraldine. The startled matron, Lady Featherly, on a walk with no less than three smalls dogs, screamed at the sight of Matthew.

Faith! Could anything else go wrong today? Matthew gave her a deep bow, excused himself, and returned to his barouche, the yips and yaps of the dogs following in his wake.

Where could Geraldine be? Glancing back along the hedgerow, he was sure he could hear quiet sobs coming from behind a particularly thick area of vegetation. He worked his way around the hedgerow and found Geraldine in an indecorous heap next to her parasol. She was obviously unaware of his presence, and for a moment, Matthew allowed her to cry her eyes out. He knew they would be red-rimmed for the picnic, but perhaps a mention as to how happy she was to have her brother back in residence at Rosehill House would explain her crying.

Moving to her, Matthew lowered himself to the lawn and gathered her into his arms. "I am sorry, Jerry," he whispered, his heart heavy when he saw how hurt she was by his accusations. "I shouldn't have believed everything I've heard about you," he whispered as he held her against the front of his body. Despite her stylish hat, which lacked the usual feathers of some poor fowl, he was able to land a kiss on her temple just as he felt a pin prick into his chest. "Ouch," he murmured, pulling his chest away from hers.

"I hate you," Geraldine whispered, secretly glad one of the pins holding back the ruffles of her bodice had poked the baron.

Matthew shrugged. Having heard that particular comment from her more times than he could count, he didn't take it personally. "Of course, you do, my darling," he replied without a without a hint of humor. She had stuck him, and he couldn't quite figure out how she'd managed it.

"How could you?" she asked, which just started another round of tears.

"Because I'm a heartless heathen intent on seeing you as bereft as possible," he answered, again without humor.

Geraldine struggled from his grasp and turned to regard the beastly baron. "Damn you," she whispered harshly. "I was going to forgive you, but now... now you can just... *go to the devil.*"

Fighting the urge to smile at her indignation, Matthew cocked his head to one side. "There are some who would tell you I am already there," he said quietly.

Her eyes widening with fear, Geraldine pushed herself away from Matthew, ignoring the possibility of grass stains on her gown.

Matthew stood up and simply took the two steps required to stand over her. Reaching down, he grasped her beneath her arms and lifted her to her feet with little effort. Geraldine whimpered as he did so, and he had a passing thought that she might think he was going to take her virtue right there and then.

But Matthew now knew better than to allow thoughts of Geraldine in that way. If he did, it would be a long time before he could join the birthday party.

"I hate you," she said again, a tear rolling down her cheek.

"I know," he said with a nod. He held her against the front of his body, wondering if she would stick him with another pin. He was about to release his hold on her when it became apparent she needed him for support or she would simply return to the ground below in a graceful heap of broadcloth and lawn and muslin.

Hunting for a handkerchief with one hand as he held her up with his other arm, Matthew finally pulled a linen square from his waistcoat pocket and offered it to her.

"Thank you," she managed to get out as she used it to wipe the tears from her cheeks and blow her nose.

"You have a beautiful nose," Matthew commented before giving it a quick kiss.

"Oh?" she responded as she refolded the square of linen and offered it back to him.

"Hmm." When he was sure she could walk, he tucked her arm under his and led her out of the dense vegetation, just as a large party of...

Matthew held his breath and wondered if perhaps they should simply return to the cover of vegetation. The birthday party-goers were walking right past them.

"Why, Lady Geraldine," Daisy McGowan Timmons, Lady Barrick, greeted her. "You look..." The viscountess' eyes took a good look up and down Geraldine's grass-stained gown, her eyes stopping on several leaves that had adhered themselves to the wool so that the gown looked as if it had been crushed into the ground.

"Lady Barrick," Matthew interrupted as he reached for her hand and kissed the back of it. "Your arrival is most fortuitous. Lady Geraldine was set upon by a footpad only moments ago. I heard her cries and was able to chase the ruffian off, although I do believe Lady Geraldine was more effective when she hit him with her reticule," he said as he dared a glance in Geraldine's direction. "I do hope he didn't accost you as he made his escape," he added with a good deal of concern.

The viscountess turned her attention back to Geraldine. "*Faith!* Are you harmed?" Daisy asked in alarm, her gaze traveling over the marquess' sister and imagining a far different scenario than the delightfully scandalous one she had imagined only moments ago.

"Thanks to Lord Ballantine—and my reticule—I am unharmed," Geraldine replied, barely able to get the words out as she displayed her weighted reticule as evidence of her claims. "But let's not allow my unfortunate incident to ruin your celebration," she said as she turned, too late, to notice Lord Barrick shaking his head very quickly.

"Celebration?" Lady Barrick repeated.

Geraldine regarded the viscountess, understanding just then that Daisy Timmons still didn't know about the surprise party. She leaned in to whisper in Daisy's ear, "If I remember correctly, isn't today your birthday?"

Lady Barrick's eyes widened. "Why, yes, yes it is," she acknowledged with a nod. "But we're just going on a picnic," she countered, obviously unaware the picnic was in honor of her birthday. "Would you like to join us? I am quite sure there is enough food to feed the entire British Army," she claimed happily.

Geraldine exchanged glances with Matthew. "I... I would love to," she replied, giving the viscountess an uncertain smile.

"Oh, and you must join us, too, Lord Ballantine," Lady Barrick said, her eyes brightening as she turned to the baron.

Matthew dared a glance at Lord Barrick, who simply shrugged and seemed resigned to the fact that the picnic wouldn't be as much of a surprise as he had hoped. "I shall be honored, my lady," Matthew said as he took her gloved hand in his and kissed the back of it.

Lady Barrick blushed and turned to her husband and several other couples who stood watching her with a bit of uncertainty.

"It's settled, then. We're off to find a good picnic spot," she announced.

Stealing a glance in Lord Barrick's direction, Matthew hooked Geraldine's arm into his and escorted her alongside the other guests. "Thank you for playing along," he whispered when he was sure no one was looking in their direction.

Geraldine let out an unladylike snort. "Who said I was playing along?" she replied, her eyes aimed directly ahead and her manner suggesting she was most annoyed. "You footpad," she added with a raised brow.

Deciding it would be a long time before Geraldine would forgive him, Matthew allowed a sigh and girded himself for a long, uncomfortable afternoon.

CHAPTER 30

A COUNTESS PAYS A VISIT

ater that day
Adele, Countess of Torrington, ascended the steps of Rosemount House at precisely two o'clock in the afternoon. Her visit had not been preceded by a note nor a visit from a footman; she merely wished to pay a call on Lady Evangeline at a time reserved for such pleasantries.

Although this particular visit would probably not be very pleasant.

Jones opened the door at the sound of the knocker, bowing to Lady Torrington and stepping aside to wave her into the house. Garbed entirely in garments the color of red wine, she appeared every inch the countess she had become by marrying Milton Grandby the year before.

After hanging her pelisse and parasol in the vestibule, Jones led her up to the parlor and said tea would be but a moment. "Lady Evangeline has already ordered tea," Jones said in response to Lady Torrington's arched eyebrow.

"Is she expecting someone else this afternoon?" Adele enquired, thinking she might have to delay the talk she had planned with the young woman.

The butler shook his head. "Lady Evangeline plans for visitors at two of the clock every Monday, Wednesday and Friday, and she pays her calls Tuesdays and Thursdays," he explained.

"Other than Lady Samantha and Lady Julia, she rarely has a caller, however," he added with a slight nod. "I'll inform her of your arrival," he said before giving the countess a bow and taking his leave of the parlor.

Adele sighed. *Poor girl.* Besides being left behind by her adventurous brother, Evangeline suffered from not knowing very many unmarried girls her own age. And her reputation as a bluestocking didn't help in that regard, although it was the *other* reputation Adele was most concerned about just then.

"Good morning, Lady Torrington," Evangeline said happily as she breezed into the parlor and afforded the countess with a deep curtsy. A maid with a tea tray was right behind her, moving quickly to set down the tray on the table in front of the worn settee.

Acknowledging Evangeline's curtsy with a nod of her own, Adele was struck by just how pretty Evangeline seemed in the afternoon light, her blonde hair swept up in a tight bun atop her head and a series of ringlets at her temples. Her yellow round gown featured a print of tiny flowers and long sleeves and a neckline edged in lace. "Good morning, Evangeline," Adele replied with a smile. "You're looking rather chipper this afternoon," she added, wondering if the young lady's good humor was due to a certain baron's amorous attentions.

"Well, except for the rain that started this afternoon, it's a beautiful day. Please, have a seat and join me for tea," Evangeline said as she indicated the settee. "Will Lady Norwick be joining us?" she asked as she took the chair opposite and set about arranging the teacups.

Adele settled herself. Clarinda Fitzwilliam, Countess of Norwick, would normally join her on her morning calls, but considering the nature of the visit, Adele thought it best to come alone. Besides, she was sure Clarinda had been experiencing morning sickness, although the countess hadn't yet said anything about being with child. "Not today. She's been feeling a bit under the weather, I'm afraid."

"Oh, well, I suppose she would," Evangeline commented sadly.

Wondering how Evangeline knew why Lady Norwick was

feeling ill, the countess thought Lady Norwick and Evangeline might have met for tea in the past day or so. Perhaps the countess had shared news with Evangeline she hadn't yet shared with her.

"But I'm honored you have come," Evangeline added, interrupting Adele's reverie as she poured the hot water over the tea strainer. "Milk and two sugars?" she added, hoping her memory served her right. She had only been in a Mayfair parlor one other time when Lady Torrington was also present.

"Why, yes," Adele acknowledged with a nod, surprised Evangeline would know how she took her tea.

Evangeline finished pouring her own tea and added the milk and lumps of sugar into the cups. "And how does Lord Torrington fare?" she asked, handing a china saucer with a cup and a spoon to the countess.

Adele accepted the tea, impressed with Evangeline's ease at serving. She thought the poor girl wouldn't have had proper instruction given her mother had died when she was so young. "Your godfather is the same man he's been since the first day I met him," she responded with a quirked lip, not about to add that they had known one another since they were children. Her older brother had been friends with Milton. Adele took one of the cakes from the platter Evangeline held out. "Stubborn, handsome, far too serious and yet... one of the funniest men I know," she mused, her face lifting as she answered Evangeline's query.

Evangeline watched the countess as she recited the virtues of Milton, Earl of Torrington. "Have you told him he'll soon be a father?" she asked in a hushed voice.

Adele blinked, her expression suddenly one of shock. She dared a glance down to her lap and then back to Evangeline. "Why ever would you...?" Her eyes shifted to the left, as if she were trying to reason out how to answer the question.

"Oh," Evangeline managed as she straightened in her chair. "Oh, dear. That was an entirely inappropriate question, wasn't it?" she hastened to say. "I apologize. Oh, dear. I... I..." She set her cup and saucer on the low table and clutched her hands together in her lap, her shoulders slumping.

The countess stared at Evangeline for several seconds, her mind racing. Although she might have looked as if she had been eating a few too many cakes at tea, Adele hadn't thought it was due to being *pregnant*. Her husband had just been so insistent she eat more, claiming she seemed to have lost weight since their wedding the year before. But, now that she thought about it, she was late—quite late—with her monthly courses.

Taking in a calming breath, Adele angled her head to one side and regarded Evangeline with a smile. "No one yet knows," she offered, tempted to add, 'Not even me.' Her brows arched up to indicate that no one would know until she decided they needed to know. And that *she* would be the one to inform anyone when it was time for the news to spread through the parlors of Mayfair.

"I understand," Evangeline replied as she nodded quickly. "I won't say a word. I promise."

Adele gave her a wan smile. "I haven't confirmed it with a physician just yet," she offered, her heart racing. *What if I really am pregnant? What will Milton think?* They hadn't discussed heirs and spares and daughters as such. Her husband's latest attentions toward children were directed at those who were his godchildren. Most were grown now, although many hadn't yet married. "May I ask how it is you think I am? With child, I mean?" Adele asked. She almost asked about Clarinda, as well, since the girl seemed to know something about her condition, too.

Evangeline sighed, wishing she hadn't read quite so many books—especially the one about human reproduction. "Well, it's just that... you look as if you're glowing. Like you have a light inside. *Radiance*, it's called," she murmured. At the look of extreme interest on the countess' face, she continued, "And you look as if you might have eaten a few extra cakes at tea since last I saw you. Which is perfectly fine and to be expected since you are eating for two now," she added hastily, her face taking on a blush that colored her from the top of her bodice to the roots of her hair.

The countess gazed into her teacup for a moment, rather liking her reflection on the surface of the liquid. She smiled and then began to titter, one hand reaching up to her lips. "I do, don't I?" she acknowledged with a smile.

"Hmm. Would you like more tea?" Evangeline offered as she lifted the strainer and pot from the tea tray.

"I suppose I shall since I'll be having another one of these delicious cakes," Adele replied, with not the least hint of embarrassment.

Evangeline poured the water and settled back into her chair. "I'm feeling rather honored you would pay a call on me today," she said carefully, refilling her own cup more out of nervousness than because she wanted another cup just then. Lord Sommers would be along at three o'clock to read with her. Although they had read together that morning in Grosvenor Square, they decided to resume their reading that afternoon. The thought had her heart beating just a trifle faster, for she found she looked forward to the hour or so they would spend reading and in conversation about the book. This morning's reading had been especially enjoyable, if only because it was becoming apparent just how Geraldine and Matthew might end up with one another. Forever.

The countess set her saucer on the low table and gave a sigh. "I came because... well, it's about... it's about your late-night caller," she stammered.

Her face brightening, Evangeline straightened in her chair. Someone had noticed Lord Sommers' visit! She wondered if it was Lady Pettigrew or Lady Brougham who saw the baron. And had they noticed his arrival? Or his departure? A shiver shot through her body as she remembered the delicious sensations Jeffrey Althorpe had managed to invoke in her that night. The way he had kissed her lips, had stroked her skin with his long fingers, held her breast in his palm and used his tongue and lips... "Oh, Lord Sommers, you mean?" she managed to get out without sounding too breathy.

Adele didn't try to hide her surprise, stunned that Evangeline would so happily admit to receiving a man at such a late hour. "Why, yes."

Attempting an expression of contrition, Evangeline shrugged. "We've been reading, you see. The same book." She reached over to touch *The Story of a Baron*, the ornate bookmark poking out from the top of the pages. "I bought the last copy at the Temple of Muses at the same time the baron wanted to buy it. We had just completed a chapter that left us both wondering what would happen next, and neither of us could sleep, so..." She shrugged again, not sure what else to say in her own defense. Not that she really wanted to defend herself. There was actually a hint of scandal surrounding her!

Evangeline Tennison was a topic of gossip! And not because people thought her a bluestocking!

"May I inquire as to who... who paid witness to Lord Sommers' arrival?" Evangeline asked, hoping the countess would give up her source.

Adele shook her head. "A servant may have said something," she answered quickly. "Not Lady Pettigrew. Which is a relief, given your reputation was... *is* at stake," she added with a look of mock horror. She didn't miss Evangeline's look of disappointment, and sounded a gasp at the girl's behavior. "Evangeline Tennison! Are you *trying* to become the next subject of gossip?" she asked in shock.

Evangeline sighed and leaned back in her chair. "If no one saw the baron, then how is it you know...?" She broke off the question, her attention turning to the parlor door. The only other person who had been present during Lord Sommers' visit was Jones, the butler. *Damn him!* she thought, deciding just then that he probably had orders from her brother to report to Torrington should she do anything unexpected. Unladylike.

Scandalous.

Adele watched as Evangeline reasoned out the answer to her own question, rather impressed that the girl didn't need it all explained in sordid detail. "He's doing his job, Evangeline. Do not be angry with him," the countess said softly.

Shaking her head, Evangeline whispered, "I am not. I am just... disappointed."

The countess regarded the earl's sister for a moment before determining Evangeline's disappointment didn't stem from having been reported by the butler but by not having been discovered by a neighbor. "So... you really *are* trying to become a topic of gossip!" she accused, this time with more concern. "You should know then that you are. Someone has seen you in Lord Sommers' company, and they're speaking of it over tea."

Evangeline couldn't help but roll her eyes. She inhaled and let it out in a long sigh. "I have a reputation as a bluestocking. Anything I can do to alter that perception will be an improvement, I should think," she responded sadly.

"Oh, Evangeline," Adele replied as she shook her head from side to side. "A reputation as a bluestocking is far better than that of a *fallen woman*," she stated emphatically. She let the comment hang for several moments before asking, "Do you love him?"

Evangeline sighed. "I cannot yet say that I love him," she replied quietly. "I... I care for him. I... appreciate his opinions, even though I do not always agree with them. I am fond of him," she finally admitted.

Adele finished her cup of tea and considered taking another cake but thought better of it. "If he should offer for your hand, will you accept?"

Evangeline lifted her head, her nervousness apparent. "I should think that will be up to my brother," she answered with a shake of her head. "But, I've no reason to expect Lord Sommers will do such a thing."

The countess resisted the urge to sigh loudly and instead helped herself to another cake. "He will if he wants to. He will if he *has* to," she said with an arched eyebrow.

"Has to?" Evangeline repeated, a bit alarmed. "He's done nothing to ruin me," she lied. "And I don't want him to be *compelled* to offer for my hand if he doesn't... he doesn't *wish* to," she finished lamely.

Adele considered her words carefully. "I won't say anything to your godfather, but know this, young lady. If there's another hint of scandal involving you and the baron, Lord Sommers will be receiving a visit from my husband."

Evangeline's eyes widened as she listened to the countess' threat. "Yes, my lady," Evangeline answered with a nod, finding the words more of a comfort than a warning.

Her duty done, Adele took a bite of the cake and glanced

around the parlor, remembering she hadn't done so when she first entered the room. For a house occupied by an international explorer and a young woman who had been orphaned as a girl, the decor was surprisingly modern and very feminine. The peach watered silk walls and green Aubusson carpet made for a comfortable space, although the upholstery on the chairs was a bit worn, and the mahogany table was scratched in several places.

Noticing how the earl's wife was evaluating the decor in the parlor, Evangeline held her breath. "Please, don't look at the ceiling," she pleaded as she took the last cake.

Of course, the countess couldn't resist looking at the ceiling, angling her head to study the coffers above. "Why ever not?" she replied in surprise. "It's rather lovely," she offered, pretending not to have noticed the shifting threads of cobwebs strung from coffer to coffer. When she sorted Evangeline's discomfort over the lack of attentive housekeeping, she leaned forward. "Don't fret, dear. Worthington House has them, too," she added with a wan smile. Then the countess popped the last of her cake into her mouth and took her leave of Rosemount House just as more rain began to fall.

CHAPTER 31

LORD SOMMERS ARRIVES
FOR A READ

A few minutes later
Evangeline watched the Torrington coach as it left the semi-circular drive in front of Rosemount House, breathing a sigh of relief when it finally disappeared from view. Although she understood Lady Torrington's concern, she couldn't help but look forward to seeing Lord Sommers again.

No sooner had she thought about the baron than she was aware of Jones opening the front door. She glanced at the clock above the fireplace. Three o'clock. *The man is punctual,* she thought with a smile.

Before she had a chance to tidy up the tea tray, Jeffrey was standing on the threshold of the parlor, his dark hair glistening with rain drops. He bowed and said his greeting before hurrying to take her hand.

"Happy birthday. I almost came earlier," he said as he took her hand to kiss the back of it. His lips lingered a moment too long, but Evangeline wasn't about to scold him.

"Thank you, but it's good that you did not arrive any earlier, for I was hosting Lady Torrington for tea," she replied, one eyebrow arching up.

Jeffrey straightened, his good humor replaced with a more sober expression when he noticed hers. "Is anything the matter?" he asked carefully.

Evangeline shrugged one shoulder. "Apparently the butler told my godfather about your visit the other night," she replied. "And so his wife felt it necessary to remind me of propriety."

Alarmed, Jeffrey backed up a step. "I shall take my leave of you—"

"You will do no such thing," Evangeline replied with a shake of her head. "You will stay right here and read with me. For the rest of the day, should you like, although tonight is the dinner party. I'll be hosting some friends starting at seven o'clock."

His eyebrows furrowing, Jeffrey regarded Evangeline with new-found respect. She had apparently been counseled about her reputation and yet wasn't about to allow the countess' warning to prevent her from hosting him in her home. "Is your godfather... is he angry with me?"

Evangeline blinked. "Lord Torrington? I shouldn't think too much."

It was Jeffrey's turn to blink. "Torrington is your godfather?" he asked in disbelief.

Nodding, Evangeline said, "Do not be too—"

"I wonder if I have made a mistake in accepting the dinner party invitation at the Torrington's," Jeffrey interrupted, as the fingers of one hand speared his hair and slid over his head.

Evangeline felt a bit of sympathy on his behalf. "Since there are usually so many in attendance at their dinner parties, I shouldn't think you will be made the topic of discussion," she assured him. "Let's move to the library," she suggested, deciding they would be more comfortable in the leather couch than on the high-backed settee.

"Of course," Jeffrey agreed. Picking up the book whilst Evangeline saw to the tea tray, he followed her down to the library. A fire had already warmed the room, and Evangeline turned up the gas to the overhead chandelier so its golden light illuminated the couch and low table.

Once she was seated, Jeffrey joined her and accepted a cup of tea. Tempted to ask why she didn't pour one for herself, he instead pulled the book onto his lap, and they began to read.

CHAPTER 32

OUR COUPLE READS ON A
RAINY AFTERNOON

The Story of a Baron
A Novel in One Volume
Written by Anonymous

Chapter 8: A Birthday Picnic in the Park

The group of party participants settled onto the clipped lawn in Hyde Park, many remarking on how perfect a day it was to enjoy a picnic. Several footmen set about spreading large cloths over the lawn, erecting umbrellas to provide shade for the ladies, and then opened several baskets containing an array of foods—sliced meats, cheeses, clusters of ripe berries, sliced breads, cut fruits and tarts—and went about arranging them in colorful collections on each cloth. Several bottles of wine were uncorked and set upright inside one of the baskets. Two baskets remained unopened and off to the side, their contents unknown to all, save Lord Barrick. Matthew was tempted to take a peek, wondering what the viscount had for gifts for his beloved wife, but he reasoned their contents would be discovered soon enough.

And maybe sooner if the baskets didn't stop moving about.

"I do say, it's a beautiful day for such an outing," Matthew offered as he lay back in the grass and regarded the collection of white clouds overhead. Lady Geraldine, still rather incensed by the baron, gave a cursory glance at the sky and said, "I suppose."

Matthew sighed. If he didn't make things right with Geraldine—and soon—the afternoon would be ruined. He sat up and leaned over so only she could hear his words. "I am sorry, milady," he whispered. "I should have known better than to believe gossip about you," he added when he saw her furrowed brows.

Geraldine regarded him for a long time. "What... What is the gossip you've heard about me?" she asked quietly, her face taking on a bright pink blush.

Matthew considered how to respond. Didn't she already know? Or, perhaps she did know and wanted to discover if he had heard something different. He shrugged in an attempt to soften the news. "You've bedded three men, cavorted naked in a pleasure garden, and displayed your charms for any and all to see," he replied simply. "Although I believe the tale of you in a pleasure garden has been debunked enough that you are no longer thought to have been present," he added as he saw her look of astonishment.

"*Three men?*" she repeated in shock. She had heard the pleasure garden gossip. She knew first-hand about the ill-fitting bodice that had bared her breasts. "But... I have *never* been with a man in *that way*," she argued, attempting to keep her voice low. She shook her head from side to side. "You must believe me," she added, her voice taking on a hint of desperation.

Given her obvious surprise at hearing the gossip, Matthew felt immense relief. "I do," he replied with a nod. "But, Jerry, your reputation is ruined. Even if you didn't do a single thing the *on-dit* suggests, mere perception has you guilty as charged."

Tears pricked the corners of Geraldine's eyes. "What must I do?" she asked, her brows furrowing, her breathing quickening as if she were running. "If I deny the accusations, I am perceived as guilty. And I certainly have no intention of admitting they're true when they are not," she added with a shake of her head.

Even today, when Lord Ballantine had been so quick with his assertion that a footpad had been responsible for her grass-stained gown and disheveled appearance, several people in Lady Barrick's party had given her looks that suggested they had already come to their own conclusions about what had happened. Despite her innocence, Geraldine was, in most of the eyes of the *ton*, ruined.

Matthew regarded her for a very long time. He leaned in, his lips mere inches from her ear. "If you are married, all of the gossip will cease," he said quietly. "You'll be under a husband's protection."

Geraldine raised her eyes to his. Was the baron about to propose? If so, she knew she would have to agree to marry him. She had wanted nothing else since yesterday when they had renewed their acquaintance at the Palace of Prose. "I understand," she acknowledged with a nod. She held her breath, hoping Matthew would say the words that would save her.

"Come, everyone!" Lord Barrick called out. "It's time for a party game!"

Geraldine's eyes closed. Matthew rolled his eyes. And half of those in the party of twenty or more groaned so that the other half laughed at the simultaneous negative response. Those who laughed and some who had groaned stood up and joined the viscount for the game whilst the others remained where they were on the expanse of lawn.

Geraldine regarded Matthew for several moments, curious if he would offer for her hand. Instead, the man leaned over and kissed her temple. "I must speak with your brother," he said quietly. Then he pulled himself up from the ground and joined the others for the game.

Watching the baron as he took his leave of her, Geraldine frowned. "Bless you, Ballantine," she whispered. But the baron was already out of earshot. And it was nearly an hour before Lady Barrick understood the picnic was her birthday party, and only because her husband had her open the two remaining baskets. Daisy Timmons squealed in delight as two white puppies jumped out of the baskets and landed in her lap.

Geraldine tried very hard to be happy for the viscountess but found she could not share in her friend's delight. According to rumor and through no fault of her own, she was a ruined woman.

Such were the workings of the fickle *ton*.

CHAPTER 33

THE PLOT TWISTS

*E*vangeline looked up from the book. Her slight inhalation of breath had Jeffrey tensing. *She knows,* he thought, panic rising inside.

"I have thought this for some time," she started to say and then stopped, taking a steadying breath. "I find I am feeling very sorry for Geraldine."

"Sorry?" Jeffrey repeated. *This is unexpected.*

"She has a very similar history to my own," Evangeline murmured. "It's almost as if..." Although she left the sentence unfinished, from her expression, Jeffrey thought she might have concluded Geraldine's character was based on her.

And, yet, they were nothing alike.

In fact, now that he'd spent so many hours with Evangeline at his side, so much time in conversation, he had decided the two women couldn't be more different. Geraldine was proud of her station in life, vain about her beauty, and far too confident, he thought. *I wrote her that way.*

Now that he knew so much about Evangeline, he had grown fond of her. Although she was the same woman he had met at the Lord Weatherstone's ball, she wasn't who he had imagined once the introductions had been made and he had said his farewell. For the past couple of years, he had relived that night in his dreams over and over, each time changing something about their encounter so that now he questioned his memory of it.

What had really happened? And what had his imagination conjured?

He might have fallen in love with Evangeline that night. But the intervening years had him believing he and Evangeline could never be together. What daughter-of-an-earl would ever want to be married to a lowly baron? A poor, lowly baron? Perhaps imbuing Geraldine's character with the qualities he found unsavory in a woman was merely his way of dealing with his unrequited love for Evangeline.

He had been so attracted to Evangeline. And simply because she was the daughter and sister of an earl, he had imagined her to be like so many other women of the *ton*. Women who took on their fathers' or husbands' rank in the realm as if they themselves were the dukes or marquesses or earls or viscounts. Women who barely deigned to speak with him because he was a mere baron.

Jeffrey straightened, deciding now was not the time to admit he was the author. In fact, there was no reason for anyone other than his publisher to know.

"As if?" he prompted gently, giving his head a jerk in an attempt to escape his reverie.

*E*vangeline swallowed and wondered how to respond. The man sitting next to her didn't seem to make the connection. Perhaps she was reading too much into the description of the marquess and his sister. But how many aristocrats were absent for months on end for expeditions to the far corners of the planet? How many lived in houses which had the word 'rose' as part of their names? How many had inherited at a young age, having lost both parents to some tragedy during their Grand Tour?

And how many sisters of aristocrats had missed their come-outs and Season after Season of balls and *soirées* due to those aristocrats having left the country without first arranging a suitable companion or sponsor?

She only knew of one brother and sister who fit the description. Whoever had written the book knew her and Harry or knew their situation.

Shrugging, Evangeline sighed. "It's almost as if they know me. Or my brother," she amended, hoping she might be reading too much into the character of the sister.

Repositioning himself on the couch, Jeffrey knew exactly how to respond. "There are similarities to your brother, certainly," he stated with a nod. "So I can see where one might get the impression you were the model for Geraldine, but...." He shook his head, realizing he had to tread carefully. "We've already established that you are nothing like Geraldine."

Her eyes widening, Evangeline shook her head. "I should hope not," she replied, indignation evident in her voice. "Did you...?" She stopped, suddenly uncomfortable.

"Did I... what?" Jeffrey wondered, his curiosity piqued.

As her fingers nervously pleated her gown, Evangeline asked, "Before we started reading the book, did you think that I was? Like Geraldine, I mean?" How could anyone think she could be as vapid, as flippant, or as proud as Lady Geraldine?

Lowering his head, Jeffrey sighed. "I admit that I thought you might be." At Evangeline's inhalation of breath, he quickly added, "At first. But I know now that you are nothing like her. Lady Geraldine is *not* a reflection of you."

Evangeline dared a glance at the baron, hoping he spoke the truth. "Truly?" she asked, her eyes bright.

*J*effrey's eyes locked with hers, and for a brief moment, he felt a bit lost. *I could drown in those sea green eyes. Or I could just kiss her. Take her mind off the damned story. Promise her a happy ending.*

Forever.

The reminder of the last word of the book had him back in the moment. "Truly," he finally answered. "I assure you, I have seen no indication of pride, or... or vanity, or the brashness with which Lady Geraldine conducts herself in you," he said reassuringly. "In fact, I'm beginning to question if the baron is even aware of how ill-suited he is for the gel."

Comforted by Jeffrey's words, Evangeline relaxed. "I have wondered the same," she agreed. "In fact, I keep expecting a completely different woman to capture his fancy. I cannot imagine Geraldine is the woman he will marry, or he will not have a happy ending." Then she frowned, once again remembering the last word of the book.

Forever.

Jeffrey watched as Evangeline's expression changed once again. 'What is it?" he asked, worry showing in his features.

Evangeline shook her head. They were halfway through the book. "There isn't going to be another woman for him, is there?" she asked rhetorically.

Jeffrey appeared resigned. He already knew the baron would end up with Geraldine. Happily. "Perhaps... Perhaps the baron is fond of her for those very traits. Or... perhaps she'll change," he said hopefully. "Perhaps we'll see her character soften and become more like you, or perhaps she is merely play-acting and is already like you," he added with a nod. "Remember, she has had to live alone a very long time. It's made her self-reliant, but she's also had a string of bad luck. All the gossip, despite the fact that she truly hasn't done what she's accused of," he explained quickly. "Ballantine has already begun to realize it, if he hasn't already."

Evangeline watched Jeffrey's expression change from one of consternation to one of hope to one of happiness. She admired how his handsome features appeared as if they were lit by a dozen candles, especially when he said the words, "Already like you."

She could have kissed him at that moment. And she was about to do just that when the sound of a clearing throat startled her.

"Pardon the interruption, milady, milord," Jones began from where he stood on the threshold of the library. "This note was just delivered by a caddy," he continued in his impressive baritone. "I believe it is from Lord Everly, milady."

Evangeline stood up nearly as quickly as Jeffrey, her face coloring. Had Jones seen her just then? Had she really been just about to kiss Lord Sommers?

She was! And from the way he had been looking at her, she was quite sure he would have returned the kiss. As a series of what felt like pleasant flutterbies suddenly passed through her, she quickly moved a hand to press against her middle. The sensation, so unexpected and yet so pleasurable, almost had her giggling.

Evangeline stepped forward to retrieve the missive from Jones, thanking him as she did so. "Have the housekeeper see to my brother's bedchamber. Be sure it's aired out and the bed linens are fresh," she ordered. The butler nodded his understanding and quickly took his leave, but not before giving the baron a scowl. Turning her attention back to Jeffrey, Evangeline urged him to take his seat in the couch.

"Perhaps I should take my leave," Jeffrey suggested, having noted the look of loathing he'd seen on the butler's face.

"Oh no. Do stay," Evangeline implored him as she broke the wax seal and opened the folded note. She glanced at the signature, knowing before she even read the crooked script that it was her brother's. "It is from Harry," she said as she lowered herself to the couch.

Reluctantly, Jeffrey followed suit. "He is well, I hope?" he responded. He wondered how much longer it would be before the earl made an appearance at White's. There was a discussion he needed to have with the earl, and soon. Far better to have it at the club than here at Rosemount House.

"Yes. His ship has docked at Wapping, but he has some arrangements to make for his cargo before he'll come home."

Jeffrey regarded Evangeline as she continued to read the note. Had she been about to kiss him when the butler appeared? The servant had nearly scared him to death!

Perhaps that had been his intention.

"Cargo?" Jeffrey repeated, when he noticed Evangeline refolding the note.

"He always has specimens he has to see to before he can leave the ship," Evangeline explained matter-of-factly. "In this case, probably more fish," she said with a nod and a look of amusement.

"Oh, yes, the fish," he said, remembering their earlier conversations. When other Englishmen were on a fishing expedition, it was to catch fish for the sole purpose of eating them. "None are intended for the dinner plate, I take it?" he commented lightly.

"No," she replied with a shake of her head. "These will simply add to his collection. Besides, it would take a good many of them to make a meal," she added with a grin. "Although Lord Norwick often threatened to turn some of them into appetizers on occasion."

Jeffrey remembered Norwick's complaints about the fish. "Did you pay witness to the fish splashing him?" he asked in a hushed voice.

Evangeline's smile slowly faded. Sure her face was bright pink, she raised a hand to one cheek. Pointing toward the corner of the library where an upholstered chair and side table were positioned under a window, she said, "I was over there reading. I was... fifteen, maybe sixteen at the time, and Lady Clarinda asked if she could see the fish. My brother was so proud of them, and I think he might have been sweet on Lady Clarinda, so, of course, he insisted she take a look. And whilst she was watching them, they started wiggling their fins at her, as if they were waving at her. But she wasn't really paying them much attention because she had spied Lord Norwick through their tank." Evangeline paused, wondering how ridiculous the story must sound to the baron.

Jeffrey's eyes widened. "Go on," he insisted, intrigued by Evangeline's version of the tale.

Smiling, Evangeline blushed and said, "She fell in love with him." After a beat, she added, "Or it could have been his twin brother. I never could tell those two men apart," she murmured. "They were already betrothed." She was fairly sure Clarinda married the one she had met on the other side of the fish tank. "When he introduced himself to her, the fish splashed him.

Quite thoroughly," she said with a mischievous grin. "He'll never make peace with the little beasties."

Suppressing the urge to laugh, Jeffrey instead allowed a smile. "Do you suppose they would splash me?" he asked. *If I attempted to kiss you*, he almost added.

Evangeline regarded Jeffrey for a long time before she finally shook her head. "No," she replied. "They know better than to cross me."

Jeffrey nodded, hoping he understood her meaning. "I have to admit to feeling relief at hearing that," he murmured.

"Would you think me wanton if I kissed you?" Evangeline asked. Without allowing Jeffrey a moment to consider his answer, she leaned over and lowered her lashes until they nearly rested on the tops of her cheekbones. She reached up and kissed him on the corner of his mouth, one hand clutching his lapel.

Before Evangeline could pull away, Jeffrey angled his head and captured her lips with his. The kiss was quick and quite thorough, and Jeffrey would have allowed it until her guests showed up for their dinner, but he dared not linger in case the butler was still standing outside the library.

As he was about to sit up, Evangeline gripped his lapel harder, pulling him closer so her lips could touch his again in a kiss that was far more satisfying and far longer than his.

*T*he feel of his lips, warm and firm against her softer ones, was like nothing Evangeline had experienced before. He tasted of the tea they had shared, of the cake he had eaten between chapters. And his scents of sandalwood and citrus had her enveloped in a warm cloud. Sure she was purring, she reveled in the moment until she thought he really would consider her wanton if she didn't release him.

Reluctantly, she ended the kiss, but before she could straighten on the leather couch, Jeffrey had a hand wrapped around her shoulder. Pulling her against the front of his body, he whispered, "Thank you, my lady," and almost as quickly, let go his hold on her.

Evangeline regarded him with a small smile. "Shall we

continue reading?" she whispered back, thinking the sound of her heart beat was louder than her whispered plea.

He nodded. "Chapter Nine?" he murmured.

Her face still displaying a blush of pink, Evangeline nodded.

CHAPTER 34

OUR COUPLE CONTINUES READING IN THE LIBRARY

The Story of a Baron
A Novel in One Volume
Written by Anonymous

Chapter 9: Convent or Altar

Richard Porterhouse, Marquess of Afterly, was nursing a brandy in the card room at Black's when Matthew found him. There was talk the man was after funding for his next archaeological expedition and rumors the Scientific Society might back him.

"What's this I hear about you wanting to leave again so soon?" Matthew asked as he joined the marquess.

Richard clapped his friend on the back. "Good to see you again," he said. "And, yes, the rumors are true. It looks as if I'll be able to return to Italy," he acknowledged.

"Back to Rome?" Matthew asked. "Weren't you just there?" He recalled Geraldine mentioning it the morning they met at the Palace of Prose.

Richard didn't try to hide his surprise at Matthew's question. "I was. But I spent most of my time in Greece. Near Athens. What do you know of Rome?"

Nervous, Matthew shrugged. "I believe your sister

mentioned it when we ran into each other at a bookshop a few days ago," he replied, deciding the truth was easy enough.

The marquess nodded. "I passed through there on the way back here. The Coliseum was a mess. Trajan's Column is disintegrating. But most of the churches seem to be intact," he said, as if Matthew should have known what he was talking about. "I was there on a bit of a reconnaissance mission, if you will. There's some interesting work being done in one of the cathedrals there. Seems a fresco has gone missing," he said, his voice lowering, as if the missing fresco were a secret not meant to be shared.

Matthew merely nodded his understanding, even though his first thought had him curious as to how a fresco, presumedly a painting in plaster on a wall, could disappear. Unless the entire wall had disappeared. Which meant an entire building was probably gone as well. "I hope you're able to find it," Matthew said. He considered how to bring up the topic of Geraldine, but Richard did that for him.

"Tell me, Ballantine. What, pray tell, have you heard regarding Jerry?" the marquess asked, *sotto voce*.

Matthew had to resist the temptation to inhale sharply. "Heard?" he repeated. "I'm not sure what you mean."

The Marquess of Afterly rolled his eyes and moved closer to the baron. "*The gossip?*" he clarified. "Is it true she was parading about *au naturel* at Vauxhall Gardens?" he whispered with a hint of disgust.

Shaking his head, Matthew gave a sigh. "I believe you're referring to an incident involving Lord Atherton and his mistress," he explained. "Lady Geraldine was not in the gardens that evening," he added.

The look of relief on Richard's face passed quickly. "And I suppose you heard about the bare nipple. Apparently during a dance?"

Matthew swallowed. Hard. The thought of one of Lady Geraldine's nipples on display had another part of his body reacting in a way his tight leathern breeches could not abide. "I heard, although, from what Lord Abdington said, it was brief and entirely the fault of an ill-fitting gown," he responded carefully. "And the duke she was dancing with, of course, since he was the one to step on the hem of her gown." He paused a moment, wondering if a bit of advice might be welcomed by the marquess. "I do believe your sister would be better served by Madame Susanna in Oxford Street," he offered, remembering how Lady Atherton always gave credit to her modiste whenever anyone commented on her fashionable gowns.

Richard Porterhouse responded with a grunt. "Is that where your mistress goes for her gowns?" he asked, waggling an eyebrow.

Matthew shook his head. "If you recall, my mistress is now *your* mistress. I... I'm not currently employing one." And then remembered too late that his lack of a mistress would have the marquess curious. "I am afraid she would just be neglected," he added quickly.

The marquess eyed him with a bit of suspicion. "Because?"

Resigned to giving the man an explanation, Matthew shrugged and said, "The business of the barony has been taking so much of my time, I have none left for such endeavors as keeping a mistress happy."

Richard shook his head. "That's what estate managers are for," he chided before glancing about with his almost empty brandy glass raised in the air.

Acknowledging the comment with another shrug, Matthew said, "As long as they can be trusted." He arched an eyebrow to emphasize his point, hoping the marquess would drop the subject.

The Marquess of Afterly gave him a solemn nod. "I understand," he replied as he leaned in.

Relieved that he wouldn't have to admit his need for funds of his own, Matthew remembered the topic of Geraldine—the topic having to do with her lack of a betrothal—hadn't yet been addressed.

"Speaking of your sister," Matthew began before glancing around quickly. "Have you lined up a suitable match for her?"

Richard drained the brandy he'd been holding. "Given the amount of gossip about her, I'm thinking it was time I sent her to a convent," he replied, his tone suggesting he was rather proud of his solution.

Matthew was thunderstruck. "Are you... are you *serious?*" he asked. How could Afterly think a convent was an acceptable solution for Lady Geraldine?

"Of course. The chit is practically ruined," Richard replied with a devil-may-care shrug.

"But she is not," Matthew countered with a shake of his head.

The marquess leaned back, stunned at the baron's vehemence. "Who would marry her, given her reputation and all?" Richard asked, the question meant as a challenge.

Matthew stared at Afterly for several seconds before giving the man a nod. "I would," he replied firmly.

The marquess took a step backward as if he'd been punched in the gut. "*You?*" he replied.

"Yes, me," Matthew said, not hearing his simple response due to the sound of the blood pounding in his ears. *Good God, what am I doing?* But the thought of Geraldine Porterhouse living her life in a convent was simply not one he could begin to imagine.

The chit would look terrible in a habit.

And those legs, constantly bent and kneeling—he couldn't abide the thought that they wouldn't be bent and clasped about his thighs whilst they made love.

Afterly frowned. "Have you been bedding my sister?" he demanded, his voice raised so that anyone within fifty feet— which was pretty much the entire card room at Black's— could hear him.

"Yes," Matthew said as he scratched his chin. "I mean, *no,*" he managed to say with a shake of his head. "I haven't. Truly. But... But I would like to. Within the confines of marriage, of course."

Richard stared at the baron for a very long time, his brows furrowing into one long caterpillar across his forehead. "Do you... feel *affection* for her?" he asked, his voice quieter but containing a hint of disbelief.

Shrugging, Matthew considered the question. *Do I feel affec-*

tion for Jerry? He knew he felt lust for her. He had since the moment he had laid eyes on her at the Palace of Prose. The way she had been standing in the beams of light, angelic and slightly devilish all at the same time—he couldn't get that vision out of his head. "I... I can't answer that just yet," he finally replied. "As you know, I've known her since she was..." He held out his hand near his hip. "She was the first girl I ever kissed," he added.

"She slapped you so hard, you had a bruise for a week," Afterly countered with another raised eyebrow. He knew, because he remembered the bruise and Geraldine's explanation for how it got there.

Matthew grimaced, not quite sure how to respond to that comment since there had been more than just that one time. That one time had been the last, though. "But then she kissed my cheek. Said it would help it heal," he whispered, his cheeks reddening more than the day he had been slapped by Geraldine. "Haven't tried again since," he murmured, not adding that he had been tempted more times than he could count.

"Bollocks, Ballantine! You're in love," Richard accused with a hint of disgust in his voice. "You're doomed." The marquess regarded Matthew for a moment more, his gaze softening. "Remember when we used to play at the river's edge?"

Matthew's attention snapped back to Richard's eyes. "When we were boys?" he asked.

Richard nodded. "You had no fear of falling into the water. No fear of the eels or of creatures that might bite or sting," he said in a quiet voice, as if he were still in the past.

One of Matthew's eyebrows furrowed. "That's because I was probably too young and too stupid to be afraid," he replied with a snort. How old had they been back then? Ten? Twelve? "What is this about?" he asked, noting Afterly's expression was entirely too serious.

Shaking his head, Richard continued to stare at Matthew. "There are rumors that would suggest she is already ruined," he said, his voice very low, as if he thought a footman might overhear their conversation.

"Do you believe them?" Matthew asked, his voice just low.

"Do you?"

Matthew locked eyes with the marquess and didn't respond right away. She had vehemently denied bedding anyone. Did he believe her? Did it matter what he believed? *Faith*! Her brother obviously wanted to get the gel settled if for no other reason than to put some of the rumors to rest. Scandal could be managed, after all. Plenty of women in the *ton* had been the victims of gossip in the past, and many were married to peers who saw to it the gossip was squelched, even if it meant a trip to Wimbledon Common. He rather doubted he was up for a duel against anyone who put voice to rumors about Geraldine, but he could certainly shoot straight if need be.

Would he take a bullet for her, though?

"You just jumped in and rescued her," Richard said, his eyes once again glazed over. "Did you even think about the possibility you might have drowned in the process of saving her that day?"

All at once, Matthew remembered the incident on the River Clun. A ten-year-old Geraldine was humming, picking flowers that hung over the edge of the river as she tagged along behind her brother and Matthew as they made their way along the riverbank, barefoot, their trousers rolled up to their knees. Neither knew how Jerry ended up in the water—one minute she was hopping along the rocks and the next she was in the water, one arm waving above the surface as the rest of her disappeared below.

Matthew no longer had a memory of what he had done next, for he could only remember pulling her to the steep bank, his arms under hers as he dragged her along. There was a fleeting thought of how angry her mother would be when she saw Jerry's muddy dress. A thought of where Richard might be, although he appeared a moment later, breathless, as if he had run a great distance. And the curse he had uttered when he caught sight of his sister, at first afraid she was dead.

But after Matthew had hauled her another foot up the river-bank she started coughing. River water oozed out of her mouth and nose as she sputtered, her eyes squeezed shut as she started to cry. Her body shook, whether from shock or cold, he didn't know. Pounding on her back with an open hand, Matthew began yelling as loud he could, cursing her for having scared him so. And once she had her feet under her, Jerry had scampered away, tears leaving streaks through the dirt and mud that covered her cheeks.

He didn't see her again until the following summer. And none of them went near the river again.

Matthew lifted his gaze to Richard. "I didn't think about it, no," he finally answered. "But I suppose I would give up my life for her, if I had to," he added, looking away to hide his embarrassment.

"Whatever you decide with regard to my sister, you have my blessing," Richard offered then, one hand clasping Matthew's arm. "But whatever happens, don't drown."

Matthew nodded. He was drowning now, even though it was in debt and not some deep, slow-moving river. Geraldine could save him, though, he was sure of it.

Acknowledging Afterly's words with a nod, Matthew let out the breath he had been holding. "So, I take it I have permission to court her?" he asked, struggling to keep his voice from wavering. A few days ago, he was merely going to ask if there were any suitors for Geraldine. Tonight he discovered he was the one and only.

"Marry her within the month, and I'll double her dowry," Richard whispered quickly, his attention on the butler who was delivering his next brandy.

His eyes widening in alarm—and pound signs—Matthew nodded. "Very well," he said as he held out his right hand.

The marquess shook it and clapped him hard on the back with his left hand. "You still have to convince my sister, though," he warned. "In fact, I'll let you be the one to tell her."

Matthew balked. How much convincing would it take? It was him or a convent. Geraldine would certainly choose him. Wouldn't she?

The baron nodded to the marquess. "I understand."

CHAPTER 35

ENGROSSED IN THE STORY, THEY JUST KEEP READING

The Story of a Baron
A Novel in One Volume
Written by Anonymous

Chapter 10: Before the Ball

Matthew regarded his image in his shaving mirror, wondering what Lady Geraldine would think of his shorter sideburns and even shorter hair, now cut in the Titus style. His valet had finished the haircut only moments ago, and he gave a start when he first saw his reflection. He decided the change made him appear a bit younger—not a bad thing—and less stodgy.

Perhaps his time in Parliament had been too sobering these past few weeks. Attending a ball, if for no other reason than to have some fun, would be good for him.

It would be even better if Lady Geraldine was there as well. Matthew had no idea if she would attend. Although he had spoken with Richard, Marquess of Afterly, only the night before, the subject of the ball hadn't come up in conversation. But the subject of Geraldine had, if only briefly. Lord Afterly seemed more concerned about where he would secure funding for his next archeological expedition, a trip he intended to make in only a few months.

Matthew stared into the shaving mirror, still stunned by the proposition of the night before. *Faith!* He was about to go to Lord Tetherpound's ball where he could only hope he would find Geraldine so he could make his intentions known.

Marry her within the month, and I'll double the dowry.

It seemed he would be a married man very soon, but only if Geraldine accepted his offer. First, he had to discover if she was willing to be courted. *And if not?* There was always ruination, he supposed.

*G*eraldine regarded her image in the cheval mirror, wondering if Lord Ballantine, or anyone, for that matter, would appreciate the amount of time it had taken her maid to create the elaborate coiffure she sported. Would he notice the diamond drops she wore dangling from each ear and the one that rested in the hollow of her throat? Would he notice the delicate beads embroidered into the bodice of her gown, or the gold threads that decorated the silk skirt? She had considered dampening the silk so it might cling to her legs, but decided against it on the grounds that others besides Matthew Winters would notice. The baron wasn't always so perceptive. Or, if he was, he hid it well. She wondered how much of his behavior was an act or if he was truly unaware of what went on around him.

"You look lovely," Richard said from where he leaned against the bedchamber's door frame. "And who might be your target this night?" he asked.

Geraldine gave her brother a quelling glance and then noted that his evening clothes were especially fine for a run-of-the-mill *ton* ball. "I might ask you the same," she countered. "Hunting for a wife? Or your next mistress?" she added before reaching for her shawl. The length of silk was the same fabric as her skirt and felt sensuous against her bare shoulders. She quickly wrapped it around her arms.

"I could say touché, sister," the Marquess of Afterly replied as he pushed himself away from the door frame and stood on his own two feet. "But it's neither. I am after funding for my next adventure is all. Thought I'd better put my best foot forward for the duke," he said as he crossed his arms.

Threading the handle of her reticule over her wrist, Geraldine joined him at the door and placed a hand on his arm. "Then we should be taking our leave."

Richard frowned but led her down the hall, wondering at her sullen expression. "I know I was gone longer than expected, and I do apologize, but you really must tell me what is bothering you," he insisted, stopping at the top of the stairs.

Geraldine considered how to respond. Having received no word from him after his fourth month away, Geraldine had feared for her brother's life, sure he had perished at the hands of an unscrupulous competitor or in the jaws of a wild animal. So when a short missive arrived a few days before his return, she felt a mix of relief and anger.

How could he have so little regard for her when he was supposed to be her protector? And, had he died, what would become of her? Of his marquessate? Her godfather might have seen to a betrothal, but given his circle of associates, she might have ended up married to a man near death.

Of course, then she would end up a young widow—not necessarily a bad thing, she supposed.

Geraldine sighed before straightening to her full five-foot height. "Tell me truly, brother," she begged, "is there money for my dowry?"

Not once since his return from Greece had he asked if she'd had a gentleman caller. Not once had he asked after her prospects. Perhaps he hadn't been anxious for her to wed because he had no funds for her dowry. Or perhaps he thought she could have no prospects, given the rumors that featured her in a number of compromising situations. And positions.

Although she could imagine spending another year or two in spinsterhood, the thought of doing so for the rest of her life had her panicked.

Richard turned to face her. "Of course, there is," he replied. "Father saw to it years ago." He moved to take the first step down and then paused. "And I have not touched a penny of it, I promise."

Geraldine exhaled. "Thank you," she said quietly. "I didn't mean to accuse you—"

"I admit, I was tempted to raid it," Richard interrupted. "Last year, when Lord Warings pulled his share of the funding for my trip to India, I very nearly had to. But our estate manager assured me there were funds from the rents in Hertfordshire to cover the expedition," he explained quickly.

Geraldine's eyes widened. "But... don't those rents have to pay for the upkeep on...," she waved her hand around. "*This?*" she asked. "And the house and tenant cottages in Hertfordshire?" Her voice had taken on a hint of concern with the last question—the estate in Hertfordshire was where she spent more than half of her time.

Just her. And the servants, of course.

Richard clenched his jaw in an effort to hold back an angry retort. "Really, Jerry," he chided her. "You make it sound as if the Afterly marquessate is near receivership."

Geraldine continued to regard her brother with wide eyes. "It is not?" she asked in a quiet voice, a sense of relief obviously showing on her features.

"Christ, *no!*" Richard responded with a shake of his head. "Wherever would you get that idea?"

Geraldine lowered her head. She was sure the gossip she had overheard at Lady Howington's *musicale* was about her brother. About his losses at the gambling tables at Black's. About the massive amounts he spent on his archeological expeditions. And about how no income, other than an occasional fee from a speaking engagement, could come from such endeavors. *How does the man expect to afford a wife?* the elderly matron had asked her friend.

"Gossip, I'm afraid to say," Geraldine finally answered in a whisper, hoping there were no servants nearby to overhear what she was saying.

Richard's eyes narrowed. Gossip? About him? *This is unexpected.* He shook his head and raised his eyes to the ornate ceiling, silently noting that at least this ceiling was in good repair. "It seems I shall have to start some of my *own* gossip," he said *sotto voce.* He gestured towards the stairs. "We need to leave, or we'll be past fashionably late."

Geraldine agreed, relieved at hearing her brother's assurances. Within moments, they were in the town coach and on their way to the Tetherpound's ball.

"Have you been receiving gentlemen callers?"

Geraldine straightened in the squabs, surprised her brother would bring up the topic when he had shown no interest earlier. "Of course not!" she responded with annoyance.

"Jerry. I didn't mean it like that. Has anyone... has anyone been *courting* you?" he clarified. "When I left, I thought perhaps Norwood was going to pay a call." He thought about mentioning the baron, but decided to let Ballantine fend for himself.

Her attention on the window to her left, Geraldine shrugged. "He did. However, I found his impertinent behavior unacceptable and told him to leave."

Her brother leaned forward in his seat, closing the space between them. His imagination conjured scenarios that might require him to call out the viscount. "What the devil? What did he try to do?"

Geraldine sighed and turned her attention back to her brother. "Nothing that would require a trip to Wimbledon Common," she assured him. She couldn't imagine her brother would survive a duel with pistols at dawn. Or any other time of the day.

Richard frowned, not sure if he could believe his sister. "Just who are *you* trying to impress this evening?" he demanded abruptly. "You look as if you were vying for the role of the Duchess of Sumptershire."

Offended, Geraldine's jaw dropped. The Duke of Sumptershire was at least fifty years old and probably a molly, given the gossip she had heard at Lady Farthington's last *soirée*. "I will let a younger girl have at him," she responded curtly as she turned her attention to the gas-lit street beyond the window.

"And the coronet and other jewels associated with that dukedom?" he continued huffily. "I cannot imagine you turning down that many sapphires."

Pursing her lips, Geraldine held back a tart response regarding his lack of imagination in favor of a simple, "Just his."

Why did her brother think only of the jewels she might acquire when becoming a wife?

Richard settled back into the squabs. "If not a duke, then... what?" he persisted. "You're not getting any younger, Jerry. It's time we got you settled."

Bristling at his comment about her age, Geraldine knew she would need to give him an answer or he would simply persist in his questioning. "Merely a baron," she replied.

Afterly frowned. "Ballantine?" he guessed, barely remembering having had a conversation with the baron the night before. He must have drunk far too much brandy at Black's. Richard had known Matthew since they were children, even attended Oxford with him, although their disciplines didn't allow for them to share the same class schedules.

"The very same," she replied. "Seems he is... rather pleasant. Not at all what I expected," she admitted. "Although, I have no idea if he can afford a wife." She dared not add that the man had more than intrigued her, that Matthew Winters had an accepting quality about him that had her believing she would be allowed a good deal of freedom should she become Lady Ballantine. Whether or not she would exercise that freedom depended on the baron's feelings toward her— and his ability between the sheets.

And how often he visited his mistress.

If he has one, she considered. Did the man even have the means to afford one? What if the baron was merely interested in her for her dowry?

Intrigued by her comments, her brother asked, "What were you expecting?" The town coach came to a halt in front of the Tetherpound's Palladian mansion in Park Lane. Richard had the door open and was offering his arm to Geraldine just as the footman joined them.

Geraldine ignored the question. "Does Ballantine know about my dowry?" she asked instead.

Richard turned them toward the flagstone path leading to the front door. "I can't say it's ever been a discussion at our card games," he commented coyly, not mentioning their conversation the night before. They hadn't been playing cards at the time. "Why do you ask?"

Pulling her silk wrap more tightly around her shoulders, Geraldine paused before answering. "I should like to think a man might wish to marry me for something other than my dowry."

The marquess gave a grunt in response. "And if it's half and half?" he responded. His sister's sudden inhalation of breath had Richard stopping in his tracks. "Is that not enough, sister?" he asked, his manner brusque.

Hurt by his query, Geraldine stared at her brother. If a man merely wanted her for her dowry, then of course she would turn down his offer. If a man wanted her despite her bold and sometimes brash behavior, then of course she would accept his offer.

But if his reasons were a bit of both?

Could she abide a man who simply would put up with her because he received twenty-five thousand pounds in compensation for taking her?

"I do not think so," she finally replied.

Heaving a sigh of disappointment, Richard resumed leading them down the flags to the front door. "If you are not settled by the time I leave for Italy, you will return to Hertfordshire when the Season ends," he stated. He decided not to mention the convent just then.

Geraldine's eyes widened. Another summer and winter spent in Hertfordshire in a barely staffed house and a sorry excuse for a library? She had read every book in the house! "I cannot," she replied with shake of her head. "I'll find a companion. I'll *become* someone's companion," she said firmly. "But I will not go back to Afterly Park for another winter by myself."

Richard allowed another couple to move ahead of them at the front door. "We can discuss this later. If it's still an issue," he added, patting the hand that rested on his arm. "In the meantime, do try to enjoy the ball. Perhaps I'll catch you kissing Ballantine in the gardens, and he'll have to marry you," he gently teased.

Horrified, Geraldine stared at her brother. "You wouldn't

dare!" she countered. How had her brother guessed that she planned to meet the baron in the gardens at midnight?

Just because the baron didn't know of her plan...

"I am having a bit of fun at your expense," Richard hastily assured her. He handed his hat to one of the footmen in the vestibule whilst Geraldine gave her wrap to another.

Given the number of people still divesting themselves of their coats in the grand entry, Richard decided the Tetherpound's ball was going to be a crush. "Besides, it sounds as if you've already set your cap on him," he reasoned as he handed her a dance card.

"And who have you set your cap on?" she asked, allowing him to tie the card's ribbon around her wrist along with the charcoal pencil. They had worked their way to the butler who would announce them.

"No one, as yet," he replied, lowering his head to speak to the man who would call out their names as they descended to the ballroom. "Lady Geraldine and Lord Afterly," he said before turning his attention back to his sister. "Perhaps when I am one-and-thirty," he said with a shrug.

One-and-thirty?

That would be two years from now!

Geraldine had hoped her brother might decide to marry this year, giving her a sister with whom she could spend the long months whilst he was away on another expedition. "Have you truly no one in mind? What if something were to happen to you? You have no heirs," she reminded him as they descended the wide stairs.

Richard shrugged, his eyes scanning the crowd below in search of the Duke of Sumptershire. "Marquessate goes back to the Crown."

Geraldine glared at her brother for a long time before she was aware of young matrons greeting her and young bucks meeting her brother and bent heads whispering to one another, no doubt sharing gossip featuring her. She could present herself as an innocent falsely accused—she was when it came to the story about Vauxhall Gardens—or she could simply pretend she really was capable of prancing about in her birthday suit and act every bit as bold as she was rumored to be.

Pasting on a brilliant smile, she turned her attention to those around them and concentrated on finding dance partners to fill her card.

CHAPTER 36

THE FEAR OF SCANDAL

"Oh, dear," Evangeline whispered as she finished reading the last page of Chapter Ten.

"What is it?" Jeffrey raised his head from the book, rather pleased the chapter read as well as it did. Not having had a wife or sisters, he could only describe Geraldine's preparation for the ball as he remembered his mother doing it when he was a small boy.

He would watch as she attached earbobs to each earlobe, wrap a shawl about her shoulders, and slide her dainty feet into dance slippers, all the while wishing he could attend the fancy balls with her and his father. Although some of his current associates eschewed Society events, he found he enjoyed them—the pomp, the pageantry, the beautiful clothes, the beautiful women—all because they reminded him of those evenings when he could spend some time with his mother.

"I fear Lady Geraldine will misbehave at the ball," Evangeline replied, just as a maid carried a fresh tea tray into the library. "I'll serve the tea, thank you," she said to the maid, who curtsied and left the room, her shock at seeing Lady Evangeline in the company of a man apparent on her face. The poor girl had nearly dropped the tray as she moved to set it down!

Evangeline wondered who among the servants had passed along word of Lord Sommers' calls to the servants of the households on either side of Rosemount House. After this morning's visit by Lady Torrington, Evangeline thought her wish to add some scandal to her life might be a bit selfish. Should Lord Torrington make good on his wife's threat, it meant a man would be forced to ask for her hand in marriage.

Allowing a wan smile, Evangeline leaned forward. "I meant to ask you earlier. How do you take your tea, Lord Sommers?" She had still been so addled by Lady Torrington's visit, she hadn't noticed if the baron added any milk or sugar to his tea after she had handed him a cup.

"With just a bit of milk," Jeffrey replied. "And, please, call me Sommers." On seeing her expression of surprise, he shrugged and added, "Since we're spending so much time together reading this book,"—*and kissing*—"it only seems appropriate."

Evangeline nodded, adding milk to his tea before offering the cup and saucer to him. "Very well, Sommers." She turned and filled a cup for herself, slowly stirring milk and sugar into it.

"Why do you suppose Lady Geraldine will misbehave?" Jeffrey enquired.

Evangeline took a sip of tea. "She seems of two minds, as if part of her wants to be prim and proper whilst another wants to shock and surprise people," she remarked. She could have been describing herself just moments ago.

"I think most people are like that," Jeffrey replied.

"You do?"

Jeffrey nodded. "We tend to show Society our proper selves, I suppose, whilst sometimes wishing we could behave with a little less propriety," he explained, deciding the words could certainly be applied to him. Especially at that moment, in fact. He wished he could be kissing the earl's sister instead of reading the book.

But he didn't dare tell Evangeline what he was wishing.

Evangeline nodded in agreement. For some reason, she found the baron's words a comfort. Just that morning, she had wondered if others sometimes wanted to do things that were out of character. Now that the baron had admitted as much, she felt relief.

"Lord Norwick is like that I suppose," Jeffrey said, his brow furrowed.

"What do you mean?"

The baron inhaled and seemed to hold his breath a moment. "At one time, the earl owned..." Here he stopped, aware he couldn't really tell a gently bred woman about the man's businesses.

"A brothel and a gaming hell?" Evangeline finished for him, the manner in the way she said the words suggesting she wasn't the least bit offended by them.

"Why, yes," Jeffrey replied. He paused a moment. As with Geraldine, no topic of discussion seemed off-limits with Evangeline. "He had to sell his businesses because he wanted to marry Lady Clarinda."

"She demanded it of him," Evangeline agreed, already familiar with the story of how Clarinda had managed to land the earl as her husband. "I've always thought it showed good judgement on his part to give up the businesses," she added, "especially since earls aren't really supposed to work in trade for their income. And Clarinda wouldn't have married him otherwise."

Jeffrey stilled at Evangeline's comment. Writing a book could be considered work. What would she think of him if she ever found out he was the author of the very book they were reading? "I rather doubt Norwick actually did any *work* when it came to his businesses," he murmured.

"I suppose not, since his brother saw to the books," she agreed.

His brows rising in surprise, Jeffrey regarded Evangeline for a moment. "How is it you know all this?"

Evangeline almost declined to answer. Perhaps men didn't realize just how much their women knew. "I paid a call on Lady Pettigrew on a day when she was hosting the countess and Lady Torrington," she explained. "They spoke about how Clarinda ended up married to Lord Norwick, so the topic of his businesses came up." She paused a moment. "And my brother used to—" the blush returned, only brighter in color this time—

"patronize one of the businesses," she finished, wishing she hadn't brought up the topic.

Jeffrey knew immediately to what she referred. Even he had spent a night in Norwick's brothel, but only the one night—he couldn't begin to afford any of the women who plied their trade in the exclusive brothel. Harry Tennison, on the other hand, had employed a particular favorite among the high-priced harlots, one who kept a rather large snake in bed with her.

But Jeffrey wasn't about to share that information with Evangeline.

Or did she already know about the snake?

"Chapter Eleven?" Evangeline asked as she indicated the book. "I believe we have enough time before my friends arrive." She still had to change into dinner clothes, too, but she thought to do that with Samantha and Julia's help. She hadn't yet decided what gown to wear.

"Are you quite sure?" he asked. He still had to change into dinner clothes for the Torrington dinner party. "Pray tell, how many are you expecting this evening?"

"Just six of us," she replied with a shrug. "Not optimal for playing cards, but we will make the best of it."

"I hear there will be one-and-forty at the Torrington's dinner party," Jefferey remarked. "Which means the countess won't be playing matchmaker on my behalf."

"You seem pleased," Evangeline guessed, hoping he was.

"Relieved, actually." Jeffrey quickly finished his tea. "So let's read Chapter Eleven."

CHAPTER 37

ONE MORE CHAPTER BEFORE
THE DINNER PARTIES

The Story of a Baron
A Novel in One Volume
Written by Anonymous

Chapter 11: The Tetherpound Ball

"Ah, Lord Ballantine!" Lady Geraldine glided toward the baron. "Just the gentleman I've been looking for," she declared, giving Matthew Winters a deep curtsy and a brilliant smile.

Caught off-guard, Matthew could barely get a bow in before the marquess' daughter had her hand extended in his direction. "Lady Geraldine, you have me most curious. Happily so," he said before he kissed the gloved knuckles. A ring with a very large green gemstone, probably paste, but he couldn't be sure, nearly collided with his nose. "I am at your service, of course," he offered, curious as to why the most beautiful woman in the ballroom would be searching for him. Especially when she still seemed rather miffed at him when he had returned her to Rosehill House following Lady Barrick's birthday picnic.

Perhaps she had decided he was not her enemy.

Or perhaps her brother had shared their conversation from the night before.

Geraldine held out her other hand. A dance card and pencil

dangled from her wrist. "One more, and it will be full," she hinted, angling her head to one side.

His eyebrows cocking up in surprise, Matthew found the open space on the card and wrote "Ballantine" on the single empty line. "A cotillion, I see," he commented, disappointed the waltz was already taken. He wondered who had managed to secure the only waltz of the evening.

And how could Lady Tetherpound only offer one waltz? Surely the evening's hostess must know men would leave the card room for a waltz? He was about to check the dance card when Geraldine, distracted by the curly haired Earl of Wurthingham, pulled her hand away in order to touch the man's sleeve, apparently in an attempt to gain his attention.

Matthew watched as the expression on the face of the blond, blue-eyed earl brightened at the sight of Lady Geraldine. *Bastard*, he thought in annoyance. The newly-minted earl seemed to have it all—and was apparently spending it as if he did, according to reports from around London. *At least Geraldine still has her other hand on my sleeve*, Matthew considered, rather enjoying having a woman on his arm. Unfortunately, she soon gave up her tenuous hold on him as the crush in the ballroom increased. Geraldine shot him an apologetic glance as she disappeared into the crowd.

Matthew turned his attention to the entrance as another wave of aristocrats descended the stairs into the brightly lit ballroom. Lady Tetherpound would have to be feeling quite proud at how many had chosen to attend her ball instead of paying homage at Nonmack's. Lady York, one of the patronesses of the dance hall, was apparently giving out vouchers to all the young ladies—vouchers that allowed them to waltz—as enticements to attend that evening's fête. With nothing stronger than weak lemonade and equally bad food, Nonmack's was a destination for the *ton* in the rare event something better wasn't offered.

Lady Tetherpound's ball was definitely better.

Not having signed any dance cards for the first few sets, Matthew made his way to the card room. Despite the early hour, several tables were already full. He spotted Lord Brotherly waving in his direction, and so made his way among the groups to join the three who were in need of a fourth player.

Lord Barrick watched as the baron took his seat. "Not dancing this evening?" he asked as he finished shuffling a deck of cards.

"Just a cotillion with Lady Geraldine at this point," Matthew informed them as he watched the viscount deal the cards.

"Ah, Lady Geraldine," Lord Atherton commented as he took a peek at his cards. "Beautiful chit. And a big bosom, I must say."

"Agreed," Lord Brotherly responded quickly, picking up his cards and grimacing before he could put a suitable poker face into place.

"Doesn't matter. She'll never wed, and she probably won't take a lover until she's past five-and-twenty," Lord Barrick declared as he examined his cards.

Angered at the comments he was hearing, Matthew sighed. At least he wouldn't have competition for Geraldine's affections from any of these gentlemen. They were all married, although Lord Atherton was famous for taking mistresses, usually more than one at a time. *He must be awfully flush*, Matthew thought as he arranged his cards. How else could the man afford the rents on all the townhouses as well as pin money for multiple mistresses?

As he studied his cards, Matthew determined he had a full house, which was usually enough to win a hand with only four players. He declined the offer of a different card.

"You all seem to forget her brother will not allow it," Lord Brotherly went on, exchanging two of his cards. No one could miss his disappointment over his new cards.

"And what kind of sway will he hold over Jerry?" Atherton asked, taking three cards.

Matthew winced at the marquess' use of Lady Geraldine's childhood nickname. The girl was a woman now; self-assured, beautiful, and even if she wasn't looking to get married right away, perhaps he could entice her to do so. Given her dowry, he was sure he could afford her. *Marry her within the month, and*

I'll double the dowry, her brother had said. Rumor had it, Geraldine had developed a taste for fine furnishings, finer clothing and the finest jewelry.

Just rumors, Matthew thought. *Hopefully.*

"We should begin a wager, gentlemen," Brotherly suggested as he regarded his cards. "I'll open." He tossed some coins so they landed in the middle of the table.

"What kind of wager?" Barrick asked. "I'll fold," he added as the man tossed his cards onto the table.

"I wager Lady Geraldine never marries because her brother is never in town to see to a suitable match," Brotherly responded, leaning back in his chair and crossing his arms.

Atherton laughed, tossing some coins into the middle. "You do realize that no one will be able to collect on your bet for the rest of our lives. The chit might get married once Afterly meets his Maker."

"To whom? She'll be an old crone," Barrick complained.

Matthew thought to suggest himself as a groom, but he held his tongue on that point and instead informed them, "The marquess is, in fact, back in town. I spoke with him at Black's just last night." He straightened in his chair and tossed his coins into the center of the table as the others around digested his comment. "I call," Matthew said, hoping his full house would hold.

"Back for how long, though?" Brotherly tossed in his cards, apparently no longer interested in playing.

"A few months," Matthew replied as he watched Atherton add some coins to the pile. "And then he'll be off to Italy."

The earl spread out his cards. Two pairs and an ace. Matthew followed suit with his full house and then pulled the coins toward him. If he stopped playing right now, he would have enough money to see him through to the end of the month. "Thank you, gentleman." He pretended to listen to the music. "I must take my leave of you. I've promised someone the next dance."

Ignoring the jibes and cries of cheating from the gentlemen, Matthew made his way back to the ballroom.

He needed to think. He was considering matrimony. He

was actually thinking of asking Geraldine Porterhouse for her hand in marriage!

Independent. Beautiful. Self-confident. Goodness, she had practically asked him to dance with her hint of having one dance left on her card! And he had gladly signed on the one remaining line.

A *cotillion*, he remembered. Well, it would be starting soon. He made his way into the ballroom in search of Lady Geraldine.

CHAPTER 38

A BARON'S BUTTON

Jeffrey glanced sideways, thinking Evangeline had her attention on something other than the pages they were supposed to be reading.

"Are you finished?" he whispered. She hadn't moved to turn the page when more than the usual amount of time had passed since the last turn.

"Hmm," she murmured, apparently lost in thought.

Following her line of sight, Jeffrey realized Evangeline was staring at the cuff of his sleeve. At the empty buttonhole where there *should* have been a cuff link. Or a button.

He sighed.

The button was in his pocket; it had come loose almost as soon as he'd stepped onto the phaeton to make his way to Rosemount House, and rather than take the chance that it would be lost, he had simply jerked it off his cuff and stuffed it into a waistcoat pocket.

Embarrassed, he gently raised his shoulder so his arm slid farther into his coat sleeve. The offending cuff nearly disappeared, but not before Evangeline straightened and returned her attention to the book.

"I have the button," Jeffrey claimed, deciding she was probably curious as to the fate of the carved wood button.

Evangeline turned to stare at his wrist again. "Does your valet know?" she asked, concern in her voice. If the poor servant didn't know his master had the button, he was probably at this moment searching for a replacement in one of the men's shops in New Bond Street.

Jeffrey frowned. "Well, not yet," he answered, moving his other hand to pull his coat sleeve down so the cuff was completely hidden. Since he had named one of the characters in the book—Viscount Barrick—after Timmons, Jeffrey was careful not to mention his valet by name.

Evangeline was suddenly off the couch, the book pushed off to one side. Not having expected her to leave his company so quickly, Jeffrey was slow to stand up. He watched as Evangeline made her way to a basket near the fireplace. She bent down and reached into it, pulling out a needle and a length of white thread.

"What are you doing?" he asked as he watched her thread the needle as if she did it every day.

She probably does. He remembered the exquisite stitcheries that graced the vestibule and hall walls.

Evangeline held out a hand. "The button, please," she said with an air of authority that had Jeffrey rooting around for the wooden circle in his waistcoat pocket. He passed it to her. "Remove your coat, please," she said as she threaded the needle through the loop of the button.

Jeffrey remained where he stood, trying to decide if he was going to comply with her request. He dared a glance toward the library doors. Was the butler still guarding them? Not seeing the stout man, he considered what he wore beneath his topcoat. His shirt was clean enough—this was the first day he had worn it since his valet had laundered it. His waistcoat was in good repair —it had all its buttons, at least. And his cravat was neatly folded. He dared a glance down into the folds, hoping none of them held any remnants of his breakfast. When he was sure it was clean, he undid the topcoat's buttons and took it off, folding it once before placing it over the top of a nearby chair.

Evangeline was already in front of him, her needle and

thread ready to reattach the button to its cuff. "Wouldn't it be easier if we were sitting down?" he asked as she took the first stitch.

She shook her head, already starting the next stitch. Jeffrey watched as her deft fingers maneuvered the needle under the fabric, though the button's loop, and back under the fabric. She repeated the steps as he watched with rapt attention.

Having never observed the art of sewing performed at such close hand, Jeffrey was mesmerized. He studied her long fingers, marveled at their perfectly manicured nails, at their shape and the tiny wrinkles at each knuckle, and before he could move his eyes to her delicate wrists, she was tying off the thread.

"One more moment," she said before she headed back to the sewing basket. She returned with a tiny pair of scissors and clipped off the remaining thread. "All done," she announced as she made her way back to the basket.

Jeffrey watched her lower herself to put away the needle and thread. Sewing on his button had taken her but a few minutes, whereas it would have taken his valet far longer. As he studied her handiwork up close, he decided she had done a far better job than Timmons would have. He hurried to join her at the fireplace, reaching down to take her hand and help her to stand.

"Thank you," he whispered. Bringing her hand to his lips, he kissed the back of it, leaving his lips on her knuckles far longer than was appropriate.

Evangeline watched as Jeffrey kissed her hand, her breath held until he finally released her. "You're welcome," she whispered. At the moment, if the baron had dared a kiss, she would have obliged him, for she was quite sure she was about to kiss him. Again.

"Pardon, my lady, but the Ladies Samantha and Julia have arrived to help prepare for the dinner party," Jones' deep voice announced from the library's threshold.

Jeffrey bristled at the interruption. He was just about to kiss Evangeline. Again. "You have guests," he said before he composed himself. "I should take my leave then," he said as he bowed and moved to put on his topcoat.

Evangeline regarded the butler, none too pleased at the

inconvenient timing. Or, perhaps... she glanced over at the baron, who was buttoning his topcoat. If he left now, he would have to pass her friends on his way to the front door. "Escort them to the dining room, please. We'll be reviewing our plans in there," she directed, suppressing the naughty grin she was about to display.

"Tomorrow morning, then?" she said to Jeffrey, rather liking the idea of reading every morning for an hour or so with him.

"Eleven o'clock?" he offered. "Here?"

Evangeline nodded. "That will be grand."

Jeffrey nodded and gave her a bow before taking his leave of the library, determining too late that he would have to pass her dinner party co-hostesses as they were being escorted to the dining room.

Had Evangeline deliberately planned his departure to coincide with the arrival of the two young ladies?

Jeffrey didn't have time to consider the question, for Lady Samantha and Lady Julia were directly in front of him. He bowed, said his greetings and kissed the backs of their hands just as if he'd been the master of the house. And before he reached the Rosemount House vestibule, he had to smile as he heard them burst into a fit of giggles.

He was nearly at his phaeton when he remembered the gift he had for Evangeline. Reaching into his topcoat pocket, he pulled out the flat pasteboard box and considered what to do. With a determination he hadn't felt in a very long time, he turned around and marched back into Rosemount House, ignoring the shocked look on Jones' face as he passed the butler.

Just about to enter the dining room, Evangeline stopped and regarded him in surprise. "Is something...?"

Before she could finish the sentence, Jeffrey had one arm around the back of her waist and his lips on hers. The kiss, hard and demanding and ever so wonderful, had Evangeline falling against the front of his body. After a moment, she returned the kiss, even allowing a slight moan in an attempt to encourage him to continue.

When Jeffrey finally pulled away, he left his forehead pressed against hers. "Happy birthday, my lady," he whispered. He pressed the box into one of her hands, took a step backwards, gave a bow, turned around, and marched past the even more startled butler.

By the time he was on his phaeton, his grin had grown into a brilliant smile.

CHAPTER 39

PREPARING FOR A DINNER PARTY

A moment later
A bit light-headed, Evangeline turned to enter the dining room and found she could not. Both Samantha and Julia were standing on the threshold, their faces a testament to disbelief.

"What is it?" Evangeline asked, deciding it best she pretend the kiss had never happened.

Both girls blinked twice before Samantha asked, "What was it like? I wish to know every detail. Every sensation. Was it your first? Why, how is it you're still standing? I think I would have swooned."

Julia turned to regard Samantha in disbelief. "You've never fainted a day in your life," she accused.

"I could if I was kissed like that," Samantha countered.

Evangeline rolled her eyes. "Join me in my bedchamber if you would. I need help choosing a gown." From the delicious odors wafting from the kitchens, she knew the cook had the dinner courses well in hand. Besides, she didn't want to have a conversation about kissing within hearing distance of the butler. He was probably about to send a footman to Torrington House at any moment to report the baron's behavior. And hers.

At least the earl wouldn't be paying a call on her this evening to scold her. He had his own dinner party to host, after all.

Which only reminded her that Lord Sommers would be in attendance at that dinner party. What if Milton, Earl of Torrington, confronted the baron in front of all his guests? Publicly humiliated Jeffrey Sommers for having kissed her? Why, she might never again see him! Or she would see him every single day for the rest of her life when the earl demanded the baron marry her.

Well, that last thought didn't seem so very awful. In fact, a rather pleasant frisson passed through her entire body as she thought of what it might be like to spend time with the baron every day. They could eat breakfast together. Surely his house in Cavendish Square had a breakfast parlor. Perhaps they could share a luncheon or tea. They could read books together. They would have dinner in the dining room, of course. Share a bed on occasion…

Evangeline gave her head a shake when she noticed her friends staring at her. She turned her attention back to the butler, deciding it best she prevent anything untoward from happening that night.

Adopting the very same determination she had witnessed in the baron just a few minutes earlier, Evangeline marched up to the servant, stood as tall as she could, and said, "You will *not* send a footman to Torrington House this evening. You will not inform my godfather of what you saw. Nor will you tell my brother when he returns."

Jones blinked. He blinked again. "Yes, my lady," he mumbled, leaning backwards—Evangeline was thumping his chest with a small pasteboard box as she made her demands— until he ended up pressed against the hall wall.

Evangeline took a deep breath. "*I* shall be the one to inform them," she announced. With that she turned and headed for the stairs.

Her friends followed her, Julia managing to glance in the butler's direction. Given his size, she had expected him to do *something* to Lord Sommers. Perhaps plant a fist in the baron's face, or a make a demand for an apology to Evangeline. But after Evangeline's uncharacteristic behavior, the servant appeared as if he wanted to disappear into the wall he was leaning against.

Once they were inside her bedchamber, Evangeline shut the door. "First, I beg you forgive me as the baron and I spent far too long reading this afternoon."

"You're forgiven," Julia said as she opened Evangeline's wardrobe and began rifling through the gowns hung inside. Meanwhile, Samantha had begun undoing the laces down the back of Evangeline's gown. "But only if you tell us *everything*."

Evangeline ignored Julia as she regarded the white pasteboard box the baron had pressed into her hand. She had almost forgotten it—it was so light it might have been empty—until she was using it to emphasize her directives to Jones.

"What's that?" Samantha asked as she pulled down the day gown so Evangeline could step out of it.

Evangeline continued to stare at the box. "A birthday present," she murmured.

Julia and Samantha exchanged quick glances. "Open it," Julia encouraged as she brought over a confection of coral silk and taffeta with gros grain ribbons made into rosettes trimming the seam where the ruffle was attached.

Absently, Evangeline stepped into the gown as she pulled the lid from the flat box. She pushed back a layer of tissue. Beneath lay an embroidered square of linen, the letter "E" in script surrounded by tiny flowers. A border of blond lace surrounded the entire square. She pulled it out and unfolded it, barely aware of Samantha taking the box from her hands before she did up the fastenings on the back of the gown.

"It's beautiful," Julia breathed. "Lord Sommers has very good taste."

Evangeline nodded before she lifted her head. "We've only been reading a book together," she murmured. "And then discussing it between chapters," she added with a shrug.

"How did he know it was your birthday?"

Her eyes widening, Evangeline grinned. "We talked about the dinner party. He is attending the one at Torrington House this evening, and I said we would be hosting one here for the daughters who weren't invited." She pressed the hanky to her chest and allowed a sigh.

"He kissed you," Samantha whispered. "Quite thoroughly, from the looks of it. And he's given you a gift—"

"Not an inappropriate one, though," Evangeline interrupted with a shake of her head. She thought of *The Story of a Baron* and of the Viscountess Barrick's birthday picnic in the park. "I could have ended up with a basket of puppies."

The other two frowned. "What?"

Evangeline grinned. "In the book, *The Story of a Baron,* Lady Barrick ends up with puppies for her birthday," she explained. "Although I might one day like a dog, I am quite satisfied with this hanky."

"Are you *sure* you've just been reading a book together?" Julia prodded.

"Quite," Evangeline replied, just as sounds from below reminded her it was time for guests to be arriving. "Let's go see to our party, shall we?"

Samantha exchanged another glance with Julia. "We weren't going to tell you until later, but perhaps it would be best you know that—"

"Don't give it away!" Julia interrupted.

"This is a surprise party. For your birthday. So… just act surprised," Samantha continued. "Don't worry. Your cook knows. We already told her."

Julia rolled her eyes. "Now everyone in the household knows," she said with a huff. Then she brightened. "Happy birthday."

Tears collected in the corners of Evangeline's eyes at the thought that her friends would remember her birthday. "Thank you both," she murmured.

For the rest of the evening, she and her guests entertained one another with stories as they ate dinner and then giggled when they employed their theatrical skills playing charades. It was nearly one o'clock in the morning when Evangeline saw Samantha and Julia to their carriage. "I cannot thank you enough for the party," she said as she gave them each a hug. "And thank you for the book."

"We thought you should have your own copy of *The Story of a Baron* so you could give the other to Lord Sommers," Samantha explained.

"That was rather thoughtful of you. But, tell me, wherever did you find a copy?" Evangeline asked. "The Temple of the Muses only had the one."

"Hatchard's, of course," Julia replied. "They had at least five copies when I was there."

Evangeline blinked. "Oh," she managed. She certainly hoped Lord Sommers wasn't aware, for if he acquired a copy of his own, he might no longer continue to read with her! The thought had some of the evening's delight fading a bit faster than it should, until she remembered the new hanky in her pocket. And that she and the baron would be reading Chapter Twelve tomorrow morning.

*M*eanwhile, at Torrington House, Jeffrey Sommers was about to take his leave when his hostess approached. Although he barely knew the former Lady Worthington, he had come to adore her during that night's dinner. She positively glowed, her happiness infecting everyone else in attendance so no one spoke of serious matters or put voice to complaints. Besides having spent the evening smiling, the Countess Torrington looked splendid in a gold gown accented with her sapphire jewelry. Jeffrey was sure her ensemble was worth more than his income from the past five years.

"So good of you to join us this evening, Lord Sommers," Adele said as she offered her hand.

"I was honored to be invited, my lady," he said before kissing the back of her hand. "And may I say how lovely you look this evening? "

Adele angled her head. "Thank you for saying so. I do hope you didn't mind that I didn't try to even out the guest list with a... with a widow or a spinster for you," she said in a quiet voice.

"Oh, I didn't even notice," he lied. After a moment, he added, "May I ask, though, why not?"

The countess gave a slight shrug. "Oh, I think we both know the answer to that, Lord Sommers." Then she winked at him. "Have a good evening."

Jeffrey blinked and stared at the retreating back of the Countess of Torrington, just then remembering she had paid a call on Lady Evangeline the day before. *Evangeline, I could kiss you*, he thought with a grin.

His grin widened when he remembered he already had.

CHAPTER 40

A RIDE TO NOWHERE

*M*eanwhile, outside of Rosemount House

"What are you thinking?" Julia wondered as she took a seat in the Harrington town coach, a footman holding the door for her whilst she held up her skirts to take the steps.

"About Lord Sommers?" Samantha asked. "Or Evangeline?"

Julia gave a smirk. "He is rather handsome, which makes me wonder why I haven't noticed him before," she commented, taking a seat in the coach. Samantha settled in next to her, the two facing the direction of travel. Although Julia wasn't always allowed to take the town coach on her occasional visits to Rosemount House—Harrington House was only a few streets south in Park Lane, and she could have easily walked—she had done so tonight so she could collect Lady Samantha from her uncle's house just a half-mile farther down Park Lane.

"He is, but..." Samantha paused and let out a sigh. "He's only a baron," she said with a teasing grin, making it evident that she would have no qualms about considering a baron for a husband. Given her tenuous place in the *ton*—her uncle was an earl and her mother had been the daughter of an earl, but her father had never been a titled gentleman—Samantha never thought to marry above her station. Given Matthew Fitzsimmons' advanced age, it was likely his nephew, Charles Fitzsimmons, Viscount Reardon, would inherit the earldom. Once that happened, and if she wasn't yet married, Samantha wondered what might happen to her. She and Reardon were cordial with one another, but Samantha had no reason to expect him to house her, let alone provide an allowance to pay for her gowns and such. She would be at the mercy of whatever plans her uncle might have made with respect to his estate.

Julia nodded, understanding her friend's comment about Lord Sommers being a baron. "I would like to believe I'll be open to advances from men of any title, but I often wonder if my mother would allow me to marry a man who was less than an earl's son."

Samantha smiled. "I cannot imagine a match less than a marquess for you," she commented playfully.

"Oh, please no," Julia countered, thinking the higher rank would require far more decorum than she was willing to exhibit. No, the title of countess would be just fine.

"So, is Lord Sommers good enough for our Evangeline?" Samantha asked, getting back to the matter at hand.

Julia took a breath and sighed. "I find myself hoping so. Do you think he'll propose marriage?"

"They've been seen in public, although apparently not by anyone who thought it scandalous, or we would have heard something by now. Which means he doesn't *have* to ask for her hand, out of a sense of honor or anything," Samantha replied.

"But, *we* saw them," Julia argued. "Kissing. Couldn't *we* insist he do the honorable thing?" she asked, thinking they could force the baron to propose by sending the man a note claiming he had been spotted kissing an unmarried lady.

Samantha snorted. "Be careful, Julia. You sound as if you want to create a scandal where none exists."

"Well, if it gets Evangeline an offer of marriage—"

"And Lord Everly hasn't yet returned from his trip," Samantha continued, interrupting her friend. "Any honorable gentleman would ask permission of her protector before courting a woman."

Julia didn't bring up the obvious—what if Lord Sommers wasn't an honorable man? What if his sole reason for spending time with Evangeline in the guise of reading the book was to steal a kiss or two? He had certainly kissed her. What if he had already compromised Evangeline?

Perhaps the two had already done more scandalous things with one another!

The thought had her wishing that were the case—for Evangeline to finally have a suitor would mean hope for the two of them. "We'll be next," Julia said, turning to regard Samantha with a look that suggested she was either panicked or relieved.

"Whatever do you mean?"

"To marry," Julia replied, as if it were obvious. "Our godfather takes an interest in these matters, you must know, even if our own fathers—*uncles*," she corrected herself, "Don't seem to."

Samantha straightened in the squabs. "I don't think my uncle has taken an interest because I haven't exactly given him a reason to," she argued. She never discussed possible suitors in the presence of Lord Chamberlain, nor did she mention anyone she had danced with at balls if she happened to attend when Lord and Lady Chamberlain did not. "And your father won't because he doesn't want to have to come up with your dowry." This last was said with a teasing chuckle.

"It's not funny, Sam," Julia said with a look of annoyance.

"I apologize," Samantha offered. "Even though I know I speak the truth."

Julia was still thinking of their mutual friend. "Do you think Evangeline wants to wed Lord Sommers?" she asked, returning to the subject at hand. "She kept referring to the book they were reading, as if that were the only reason they were spending time together. Can that be all there is to it?"

"Maybe. But I do believe she wants to wed the man. They are well suited. He's a friend of Everly's. And he's certainly tall enough for her," she added mischievously.

Julia resisted the urge to snort. "So, if it looks as if our Evangeline needs a bit of help in the scandal department—in order to ensure a proposal—what will we do?" she asked, her expression suggesting she was already plotting scenarios that could force a gentleman to propose.

"Nothing!" Samantha replied, her eyes widening. "Or, at

least, very little." She quieted as she thought about her own scenarios to ensure Lady Evangeline received an offer of marriage.

Smiling, Julia finally turned her attention to the coach window. "Oh, dear," she murmured. "We're not moving."

It was Samantha's turn to giggle. "That's because you never told the driver where to take us," she whispered. Reaching up with her parasol, Samantha knocked on the trap door above. When the driver opened the door and peered down, she said, "Back to Fitzsimmons Manor, please."

The driver nodded and closed the door.

In a moment, the Harrington coach pulled away from the Rosemount House drive, its occupants deep in thought about courting, scandalous liaisons, and possibly randy barons.

CHAPTER 41

GRAY SKIES, RAIN AND TEA

The following morning
With the gray skies and pouring rain, Evangeline feared Lord Sommers would forego their morning read, but just a few minutes after the appointed hour for their sixth day of reading *The Story of a Baron*, the baron appeared in the Rosemount House vestibule. His cape coat was drenched, as was his beaver, but his smile upon his arrival at the threshold of the library had Evangeline's heart skipping a beat.

"You came!" she said with a brilliant smile, unable to keep the surprise out of her voice. "You might have caught your death in this downpour," she added, worry showing with her furrowed eyebrows.

Jeffrey returned the smile, heartened to hear her concern for his welfare. He was also happy to see Evangeline dressed in a bright apple-green gown, her smile chasing away the gloom. "Of course, my lady," he replied as he took a bow and hurried to kiss the back of her hand.

"Would you like tea? Or something stronger, perhaps?" she offered, trying to ignore the shiver that passed through her body as the baron's lips touched her skin.

"Tea, please, as I find myself a bit chilled. I cannot recall having two springs in a row where it's been this cold," he commented as they moved to the leather couch. He was surprised to find the tea service already on the low table. "Did you have a caller this morning?" he asked, glad they were meeting in the library instead of the parlor.

Evangeline shook her head. "No, but I wanted to be sure the tea was ready to serve if you did come, since it's so cold and wet out there," she remarked. She took her usual seat in the couch and leaned over to pour tea. "And it's warmer here in the library."

Jeffrey joined her on the couch then, touched that she thought to have a warm drink ready for him. "Thank you," he said as he leaned over and kissed her cheek.

Evangeline dared a quick glance in his direction as she finished pouring a cup of tea for herself and finally gave him a nod. Unable to hide her blush, she allowed a grin. "You're welcome. And thank you for the hanky. It was very thoughtful of you."

"But not inappropriate, I hope," he replied.

"Not at all," she assured him. "Did you enjoy the Torrington's dinner party?"

"I did. Lady Torrington was a gracious hostess. She saw to it everyone had a very pleasant evening. I cannot quite explain how she did it though, but her happiness prevented everyone from putting voice to a single complaint," Jeffrey commented.

Evangeline's eyes widened when she remembered why the countess would be so happy. She leaned over and whispered, "You cannot tell anyone, but she is with child."

Jeffrey blinked. He turned to stare at her with a combination of shock and amusement. "Does the earl know, I wonder?"

Lifting one shoulder, Evangeline replied, "Did he seem just as happy?"

His brows furrowing, Jeffrey tried to remember if he had even seen the Earl of Torrington the night before. Jeffrey had been seated at the opposite end of the very long dining table from the earl's carver. "I can't say that I noticed."

She sighed. "Probably not, then. Shall we begin?"

Tempted to kiss her again, Jeffrey realized he could not— the damned butler was watching them from the library door, his scowl firmly in place. "Yes, let's," he agreed.

CHAPTER 42

READING ON A RAINY DAY

The Story of a Baron
A Novel in One Volume
Written by Anonymous

Chapter 12: The Business of Being a Baron
With a good deal of trepidation, Matthew stood before the largest piece of furniture in the library. The mahogany behemoth had been a gift to his father from his mother. The baroness had arranged for its construction with the words, "It must have a large surface and enough drawers to hold the business of being a baron."

Well, the furniture maker had not disappointed. With ten drawers and a smooth surface nearly the size of the library door, the desk had been the sixth baron's pride but not joy. The lack of joy, of course, was due to the lack of funds associated with the barony. Now that he had inherited the desk—and everything else in Ballantine Place—Matthew understood his father's take on the mahogany monstrosity.

Despite the library being his favorite room in the entire house, this one piece of furniture nearly ruined it for him. And all because several invoices had multiplied into too many—so many, in fact, that there was little space left on the desktop.

Now that he had his winnings from the card game at the ball, Matthew decided it was time to see to some payments.

He ran his fingers through his hair before taking the large chair on the other side of the desk. If he could have afforded the expense upon inheriting the barony, he would have hired a secretary to do the monthly bills. Seeing to the financial requirements was his least favorite responsibility of being a baron, for it reminded him of how very close he was to insolvency. The sooner he married and secured a dowry, the sooner the barony would be safe.

Marry her within the month, and I'll double the dowry.

He would speak with Geraldine on the morrow, he decided.

CHAPTER 43

A DEATH IN THE TON

"Is it like this for your barony?" Evangeline asked, her brows furrowed with concern. "I know last year was particularly difficult for the entire country," she added as she turned to regard Jeffrey, referring to the Year Without a Summer. The incessant rain and cold temperatures meant little in the way of crops, near famine for part of the country, and a huge loss in livestock.

Jeffrey considered how to respond. His barony was in a far better financial situation than the one he had described in the book, but if the coming summer was as bad as last year, the Sommers barony would be on the brink of insolvency. "It was," he agreed. "For those who depended on agriculture for their livelihood," he added. "However, I have the benefit of owning a coal mine and a farm with a herd of sheep that survived the year," he explained. "And a contract for the wool, of course." He spoke without considering Evangeline might be ignorant of the textile business in England.

Evangeline nodded her understanding. "I've no idea what my brother's investments involve," she said, her attention on the library's windows. "I suppose I should ask, since he'll probably arrange another expedition just as soon as he's home."

Jeffrey suppressed the urge to react. "Do you think he'll

arrive today?" he asked, trying his best to keep his tone conversational.

"Today, perhaps tomorrow".

Jeffrey felt a bit of panic set in. "My lady," he started to say.

"You really should call me Evangeline," the mistress of the house replied, one of her hands brushing his coat sleeve. "I insist."

Jeffrey swallowed. "Then you should call me Jeffrey," he countered, his breaths still short. "So... Everly could walk in on us at any moment."

Evangeline shook her head but then reconsidered. Harry Tennison really could arrive at any moment. "I suppose," she replied simply.

"Milady?" a deep voice sounded from the doorway.

Evangeline turned to find Jones standing on the threshold.

"Yes, Jones?" She stood so that she could turn to regard the butler. Jeffrey stood as well, curious as to the reason for the butler's interruption. He was quite sure the man had been standing just outside the door the entire time Jeffrey had been in the library.

"A caddy just delivered word that Lord Norwick has perished."

Evangeline stared at the butler for several seconds, his words penetrating her brain but not quite making sense.

Seeing her distress and feeling some on his own behalf, Jeffrey reached for one of her hands. "Did the caddy say what happened?" he asked of the butler, stunned at the news that David Fitzwilliam had died. The man was in his mid-forties, true, but *dead?* "How... how did he die?" he asked, knowing Evangeline wouldn't put voice to her own curiosity.

The butler afforded him the courtesy of a nod. "The caddy said he witnessed the accident in Oxford Street. Apparently, Lord Norwick was thrown from his horse and broke his neck when he hit the pavement below," Jones explained, uncomfortable when Lady Evangeline clamped a hand over her mouth, her shock quite evident in her widened eyes.

Jeffrey wrapped an arm around her shoulders and pulled her

to his chest. "But he was an expert horseman!" he declared, addressing his comment to the butler.

Evangeline sucked in an unsteady breath. "Lady Norwick," Evangeline whispered in despair. "She'll be heartbroken." Tears filled her eyes. *She's with child.*

Jeffrey turned his attention to Evangeline, saddened at the sight of her tears. He pulled a handkerchief from his waistcoat pocket. "Evangeline," he whispered, offering the square of fabric.

Instead of taking the proffered handkerchief, Evangeline shook her head before burying it in the small of his shoulder. The scent of honeysuckle wafted past Jeffrey's nostrils, reminding him of the last time he had held her so intimately in the parlor. She was acquainted with the earl's wife, he remembered from their discussion the day before.

Lady Norwick was now a widow.

Faith! Norwick was one of the few in the *ton* who actually loved his wife, who had given up his ownership of a celebrated brothel, given up who knew how many mistresses, and given up any hint of a scandalous life in order to marry Lady Clarinda Brotherton.

The woman would be inconsolable.

Since she hadn't yet given birth to an heir, he could only hope she was with child. Although, if she was not, Norwick did have a twin brother, Daniel Fitzwilliam, who could step in and assume the earldom.

Jones cleared his throat, obviously distressed at seeing the baron holding the earl's sister as if they were betrothed. Jeffrey let go his hold, although Evangeline remained with her head against his shoulder. "Lilies," she said. "Jones, please see to a delivery of lilies to Norwick House," she ordered. She raised her head to regard the baron. "I need to pay a call on Lady Clarinda tomorrow morning," she said. "Perhaps we can meet to read the day after?" she requested, her voice quiet.

Given the news they'd just heard, Jeffrey was surprised Evangeline wished to continue their morning reading session at all. "I look forward to it," he said quietly, not wanting the butler to overhear him.

"As do I," Evangeline admitted in a whisper. Her entire day was arranged around when she could sit with the baron and read the book. What would she do with herself when they finished it? Melancholy settled over her as she left her head resting against his shoulder.

Jeffrey felt excitement at her words. His entire schedule was built around when he and Lady Evangeline could meet to read the damned book. But there were only a few chapters left—what would he do when they were finished? He couldn't imagine a day without Evangeline in it.

Faith! If the damned butler hadn't been standing there staring at them, Jeffrey thought he would have kissed her right then and there, kissed her and perhaps even proposed marriage —on the condition that her brother would allow him to, of course.

In the meantime, he knew he really should take his leave of Rosemount House before the butler had him bodily removed—or worse. "I will call upon you the day after tomorrow," he said, raising his voice so Jones could hear. He lifted one of her hands to his lips and kissed the back of it. "Please, give Lady Norwick my condolences and your brother my greetings."

Evangeline looked crestfallen as she watched the baron bow and leave the library. Having lost her ability to stand on her own, she settled back onto the leather couch, dropped her head into her hands, and wept.

CHAPTER 44

THE EARL OF EVERLY
RETURNS

The following day
Harry Tennison, Earl of Everly, stepped down from the hackney and glanced up and down Park Lane before he regarded Rosemount House. Despite being gone for nearly six months, he felt satisfaction as he took in the clean, white exterior. The glass in the neat row of windows across the front gleamed as if it had been cleaned only that morning. The two columns holding up the portico above the front door were straight and appeared free of soot. The front door, a deep garnet, sported a polished lion's head knocker.

The gardener appeared to have been busy. Flower pots on either side of the front door steps displayed a riot of colors, although when he leaned down to take a sniff, he discovered the flowers were made of silk. The colder-than-normal spring was obviously to blame for the lack of real flowers in the pots. At least the front lawn was beginning to display green shades.

Taking a deep breath, which didn't smell as bad as he might have expected, Harry climbed the steps of Rosemount House. The front door opened before he reached it. Jones stood to one side, giving him a short bow as he stepped aside. "Welcome home, milord," the butler said as he took the earl's top hat and cane.

"Good to be home, Jones," Harry replied as he gave the

vestibule a cursory glance. He stopped to study the pair of embroideries of plants. Evangeline's intricate stitches had captured every detail of the *Pteridophyta* and *Metroxylon sagu*, and Harry had to allow a grin. "I see Evangeline has been keeping busy," he murmured as he peered through his spectacles. Who knew she had an interest in ferns and palms?

Having set his master's hat on the shelf and seen to his cane, the butler sobered. "She has, milord, although..." He paused, not quite sure how to inform the scientist that his sister had also been consorting with a baron.

Harry turned his attention from the embroideries to a nearby mirror. Shocked at how tanned his face had become during his weeks spent on the Indian Ocean, he frowned. Probably just as well, he decided, given he intended to visit an island off the coast of Spain on his next expedition. He was about to turn his attention back to the butler when two footmen entered with one of his trunks. "That can be taken to my study," he instructed, "and the other to my bedchamber." The earl turned to regard Jones. "Although... what?" he queried.

Jones regarded the earl with newfound respect. There were times the man didn't seem to be aware of his surroundings or acted as if he hadn't heard a single word spoken to him, but now was obviously not one of those times. "She has recently bought a book and has been reading it—"

"Harry!" Evangeline called out from the top of the stairs. His sister grabbed a handful of her skirts and rushed down the stairs, wrapping her arms around his shoulders as she nearly knocked him off his feet.

"Eva," he replied with a grin, ignoring Jones to return his sister's hug. "I see you've taken good care of things in my absence," he commented, noting his sister seemed another inch taller than when he had last seen her.

"It's kind of you to say so, although I think you have Jones to thank for the general condition of the house," she responded as she turned and walked with him toward the library. She knew he would want to check on his fish before seeing to anything else. "A colorman was just here last week matching paint for the front door, and two days later, it was painted."

Harry stepped aside to allow his sister to enter the library before him. "Any trouble while I was away?" he asked as he followed her in. He rushed over to the large glass tank that held his prized collection of tropical fish.

"Lord Norwick died."

The earl peered through the glass, one finger touching it as he seemed to count the number of fish as they swam about. He straightened and turned to regard his sister. "Here?" he asked, his brows furrowed in concern.

Evangeline shook her head, curious as to why her brother would think the earl had even been at Rosemount House. Everyone in the *ton* knew David Fitzwilliam despised her brother's fish. "No. Yesterday, in Oxford Street. A caddy said he'd been thrown from his horse."

Harry frowned. "But... Lord Norwick is an expert horseman," he replied as he shook his head, his eyes glazing over. "Poor Clare," he whispered as he considered the widowed countess. The woman was still so young, and she had not yet borne a child. "Have you arranged for flowers to be sent?" he asked, thinking that David's brother, Daniel, was probably already making plans to return to London from the Norwick estate home in Sussex.

"Lilies, of course," Evangeline answered with a nod. "I paid a call on Lady Clarinda earlier. To pay my respects."

The earl nodded, his manner still most sober. "He always said my fish would be the death of him," he murmured, glancing back at the tank. "I must admit, I'm quite relieved to see they've all seemed to survive my absence."

Evangeline moved to stand next to the tank. "Mosby does an excellent job caring for them," she told him, referring to the footman who fed them. "He captures rain water and adds a hint of salt to it before pouring it into the tank," she explained, watching intently as one of the angel fish swam by. "But I know he's concerned at the dwindling supply of food. I do hope you've brought some back with you."

Harry nodded. "Food as well as more fish," he answered, his mood still grim. "Their crate should have arrived here yesterday."

Her eyes wide, Evangeline shook her head. "Oh, dear. I do hope it was brought indoors. It was chilly last night," she said.

Finally allowing a smile, Harry shook his head. "The cold would not have been a problem," he replied. "As long as it didn't freeze," he amended.

"No. Not for over a month," his sister informed him. "Do you suppose we'll have a summer this year?" she asked, thinking it was still far too chilly for March.

Her brother nodded. "It will most certainly be warmer than last year. Amazing what volcanoes can do to our weather," he said absently, referring to a series of eruptions that had wreaked havoc on the climate of the North American continent as well as Northern Europe the year before. "All that rain helped clear the air. Sunlight can get through now."

He regarded his sister for a moment, surprised to find she was at home in the middle of the day. Perhaps she didn't pay calls everyday, or she was expecting someone to visit her this day. "I trust you've been behaving," he commented with a grin.

Having missed the glint of humor in his eyes, Evangeline's face reddened. "What have you heard?" she demanded, her eyes wide.

Curious about his sister's reaction to his simple tease, Harry blinked. "I've been away for six months. And I just returned to these shores yesterday," he replied. "I haven't heard a thing." A look of suspicion crossed his face, though. "Is there something you need to tell me, Eva?" he asked.

Realizing she had overreacted, Evangeline shook her head. "No, there's nothing."

Harry nodded, although he took note of her blush. Was there something his sister wasn't telling him? If there was, he would surely hear about it at White's. After a shower bath and a change of clothes, he would be paying a visit to the venerable men's club. One evening there, and he would be caught up on all the latest *on-dit* of London.

CHAPTER 45

THE GENTLEMEN AT WHITE'S

Later that night
The Everly town coach pulled up to White's, stopping for only a moment to allow its single occupant to step out before pulling away to park farther down St. James Street.

Harry Tennison gazed up at the men's club. He wasn't surprised to see that absolutely nothing of the exterior had changed during his absence from London. The men's club did on occasion accept a new member, though, and the betting book changed on a daily basis.

He took a deep breath before stepping over the threshold. A butler greeted him in the foyer, taking his hat and cane. "Your usual card game has been set up in the front room," he said as he gave a bow. "A brandy for you, milord?"

Harry was pleased the butler not only remembered his drink of choice but could act as if he hadn't been absent for half a year. "That would be splendid," Harry replied as he made his way out of the foyer and into the club. Several members acknowledged him with greetings. Some stopped and spoke with him. And when he finally arrived at the table where he played cards when he was in town, there were his usual opponents, all sitting in their usual chairs.

"Now here is a sorry sight," William Slater, Marquess of Devonville, said with amusement as he shuffled the cards.

Viscount Barrings acknowledged Everly with a nod and a wave toward his empty chair. Sir Richard Waggoner stood to shake his hand. And Lord Sommers gave him a nod and a look that suggested he might not be as pleased to see him as the others.

"Gentlemen," the earl said as he took his place at the table. "I am back from the Indian Ocean and the Cape. It seems another Season has begun. I believe I am in need of an update."

As Lord Devonville dealt the cards, he said, "It's about time you returned. I do believe there was talk that you must have drowned so your earldom was going back to the Crown," he teased gently.

Harry colored. "I was gone longer than I had planned, but I did send word. And my sister was obviously receiving my letters since she wrote in response to each one," he said in his own defense.

The marquess completed the deal and moved to pick up the pile in front of him. "You've no doubt heard about Norwick," he said carefully. "Terrible shame. Good thing he had his own spare. His brother, Daniel, will take his place in Parliament."

"And at Norwick House, no doubt," one of the gentlemen said as he waggled his eyebrows. Barrings could be uncouth at the worst times.

Harry frowned, not appreciating the insinuation that Daniel Norwick would be taking his brother's place in Lady Clarinda's bed. Harry had secretly held a candle for the gel for years, as had probably half the men in White's. But it was true that Daniel would be Clarinda's protector now. He had courted her before David suddenly stepped in and insisted he was going to marry her.

"Anything else happen while I was away?" Harry asked, wanting to change the subject to less serious matters.

Lord Barrings shrugged. "There is a book causing a bit of a stir."

Jeffrey Althorpe straightened in his chair. "Oh? And what

book might that be?" he asked as he pretended to rearrange his cards.

"My wife is reading it," Sir Richard offered. "Some drivel about a baron lusting for an earl's sister."

Jeffrey paled. From where had Sir Richard's wife, Mary, purchased her copy of the book?

"And the sister is fast," Devonville chimed in. When the others gave him an incredulous look, he added, "I found a copy in the parlor last night after Lady Devonville went to bed. *The Story of a Baron.* Read three chapters before I retired for the evening," he admitted.

Harry's attention was suddenly on the marquess. "My sister is reading that book," he commented before tossing a chip onto the ante. "I'll open. I noticed it was open in the library. I do hope the tale isn't too inappropriate for a lady," he commented absently. Although he knew Evangeline had read nearly every book in his library, he wanted to promote the appearance that she hadn't. Especially those detailing every possible position for sexual congress—with colorful illustrations.

Jeffrey felt a flush of heat color his face and took a quick sip of brandy in an attempt to hide it. At least his book didn't have colorful illustrations!

Barrings turned to Jeffrey. "You'll have to read it and let us know how true it is," he teased. "Since you're the only baron among us."

"Lady Geraldine is not fast," Sir Richard countered, ignoring Barrings' comment. "She's merely the victim of malicious gossip."

"But the baron doesn't seem to care, so what does it matter?" Barrings countered. "They'll end up married, he'll get double her dowry, and all will be well." The viscount turned his attention to his cards.

Harry glanced about, entertained by the conversation. "I suppose I am saved from having to read it, then," he remarked as he patiently waited for the Marquess of Devonville to bid.

The marquess tossed his cards into the middle. "I fold," Devonville said, although he didn't seem too upset by having to do so. "And isn't that how it's supposed to be? Out of the five of us here, what? Three of us are leg-shackled. I know I originally did so to get a dowry," he admitted without shame —or regret. "Although I suppose I also did so because it was my duty. The whole 'siring an heir' requirement," he said *sotto voce.*

Sir Richard shrugged. "I did, too, but I married my lady because I was rather fond of her," he stated. "And, truth be told, I still am."

Having purchased every copy of *The Story of a Baron* from the Temple of the Muses, Jeffrey dared to ask, "Where might I obtain this book, *The Story of a Baron?*"

Sir Richard continued the bidding and threw some chips into the center of the table. "Hatchard's, probably," he replied.

Jeffrey held his breath. How could he have overlooked Hatchard's? More aristocrats probably shopped there than at the Temple of the Muses.

When he realized the players were giving him a look of expectation, he tossed a bunch of chips into the middle. "I'm in."

"My wife only gets her books at Hatchard's, so I expect that's where she bought her copy," Sir Richard commented, his attention on his cards. "And I'll raise you ten."

"I fold," Barrings said as he tossed his cards down.

Jeffrey finally focused on his cards, stunned to see a full house. He moved a stack of chips to the middle. "Call," he announced. "Are you enjoying the book?" he asked carefully.

Sir Richard showed his two aces and two kings. "Enjoying?" he repeated, as he watched Jeffrey carefully lay out his full house. "The parallels to real life are rather entertaining."

Harry tossed his cards onto the felt tabletop. "Damn. It's my first night back. The least you could do is let me win the first hand," he said with humor.

Jeffrey reached for the pile of chips in the middle of the table. "Thank you, gentlemen," he said with a good deal of relief. Although his take wasn't particularly large, it would cover his expenses for a few weeks.

"The settings in the book are familiar," Devonville offered. "The men's club is called Black's—obviously a nod to White's.

And Nonmack's is Almack's. Same bad lobster patties," he commented with a grin.

Barrings nodded, but his brows furrowed. "There is an archeologist—a marquess—who seems to be away from London frequently," he mentioned as he gathered up the cards.

Stiffening, Jeffrey held his breath.

"The chit's brother," Devonville offered in Jeffrey's direction.

"And she wouldn't have her sullied reputation if her damned brother would bother to stay in London during the Season," Sir Richard stated in disgust. "The man is off on archeological expeditions for months at a time and leaves the poor girl without so much as a..." The baronet suddenly paused, his mouth open as he stared at Harry.

The Earl of Everly stared back at Sir Richard. He shook his head. "What?" he asked when he noticed Barrings had stopped shuffling the cards. Suddenly, everyone but Lord Sommers was staring at him. Harry straightened in his chair, his expression darkening. "Now, see here—"

"I do not believe Sir Richard meant any offense to you," Jeffrey offered as he turned to regard the earl. "The Marquess of Afterly is nothing like you," he said with a shake of his head.

"Of course, not," Sir Richard agreed, his head shaking a bit. He blinked and turned his attention on Jeffrey. "What do you know of the Marquess of Afterly?" he asked, his brows furrowed into a single bushy line across his forehead. "I thought you said you hadn't read the book."

Jeffrey groaned, realizing he had given away too much. "You said Afterly was an archeologist," he accused quickly, hoping he could erase any suspicion his comment might have generated among the rest of the card players. "I hardly think anyone would equate what Everly does with archeology."

Barrings resumed shuffling the deck. "But you have to admit, Everly, you do leave Lady Evangeline alone for months at a time," he said to the earl.

Sighing, Harry regarded the viscount and nodded. "I do. However, she always has a lady's maid with her when she's out and about, and I arranged it so she has someone seeing to her welfare on a daily basis."

Jeffrey froze. He had spent hours with the young lady every day for nearly a week, and at no time had anyone appeared to check on her. No one except for the butler, of course, but Jones could hardly be expected to follow Evangeline when she was out making calls or meeting him to read in the square.

Or could he?

He certainly would have noticed if the butler had followed Evangeline to Grosvenor Square! Jeffrey was still pondering where Jones might have hidden when Barrings began dealing the cards.

"Good evening, gentlemen."

All eyes turned to Milton, Earl of Torrington, as he stood with his hands in his pockets, regarding them with a mischievous grin.

"Good evening, brother," William Slater, Marquess of Devonville, replied. The best of friends since they were young boys, he and Milton were now brothers-in-law. A chorus of greetings were exchanged by the others at the table.

"Welcome back to civilization," Milton said to Harry.

The Earl of Everly nodded. "Thank you. And your appearance is most timely, as I was just telling everyone here that my sister is well looked after during my lengthy absences," he said.

Milton's eyes narrowed in annoyance. It wasn't as if Harry Tennison had ever actually *asked* him to look after Lady Evangeline; Milton had simply done so out of a sense of duty to his goddaughter. "She is," he acknowledged. His gaze drifted to Jeffrey Althorpe, who seemed to straighten up when their eyes met. "She is, indeed," Milton added with a grin. He turned his attention back to Harry. "Before you leave on your next trip, I expect someone else will be seeing to her welfare on a daily basis." With that, he gave a nod to the table in general. "I'm off for home to have dinner with my countess. Don't stay out too late," he said, his eyebrows waggling as if he knew they all probably would.

It was obvious from the earl's statement that Torrington had overheard Lord Everly's original comment about someone watching over Evangeline. And, on top of that, no one at the table missed the earl's meaning regarding Evangeline's future, including Harry.

The Earl of Everly stared after the older earl, watching him as a footman saw to his coat and hat. Torrington expected him to have Evangeline settled in a marriage before he left for his next expedition.

Jeffrey watched as the Earl of Torrington took his leave of White's, curious if the earl had been aware that he and Lady Evangeline had been meeting to read the book. He had never actually seen Torrington whilst he was with Evangeline, but, truth be told, he hadn't been aware of anyone else when he was with her. It was as if the rest of the world didn't exist when they were sitting side-by-side.

At least he could be assured that Torrington hadn't paid witness to the indiscretions that had taken place that one night in the parlor, a night he had replayed in his mind every night and every morning since. During lunch and whilst he ate dinner, as well. Even now, the thought of Lady Evangeline had his cock at attention. And his heart feeling rather glad.

Well, if Torrington intended for his goddaughter to be married before Everly left on his next trip, Jeffrey realized he had better see to it he was the only one allowed to court her. For the idea of Evangeline with another man caused him to experience an emotion with which he was completely unfamiliar.

Jealousy.

CHAPTER 46

A GODFATHER AND HIS WIFE

The following morning Adele, Countess of Torrington, hurried into Worthington House. She divested herself of her umbrella and coat, their surfaces dampened by the thick morning fog. Had anyone else but Clarinda Fitzwilliam, Countess of Norwick, asked for her company on a walk in the park on such an inhospitable day, Adele would have politely declined. But Clare was her best friend and a widow for barely two days. If the day had remained sunny and bright, the poor woman wouldn't have been allowed the outing.

Milton appeared from the breakfast parlor. "There you are," he said, glancing beyond her to see their butler hanging up her wet coat. "What were you doing out in this horrible weather?" he asked, hurrying up to plant a kiss on the corner of her mouth.

Because of her late husband's hesitance to show the least bit of affection, other than behind bedchamber doors, and sometimes not even then, Adele welcomed her new husband's amorous attentions.

"Clare sent word she wanted to take a walk," Adele replied. "It was a beautiful day just a couple of hours ago."

"It was cold," Milton countered.

Adele shrugged, as if the weather hadn't really mattered.

"And then, after I left Clare at her coach, the fog suddenly rolled in."

The earl nodded, a look of sadness crossing his face as he thought about the new widow. "How is she?" he whispered, taking Adele's hand and tucking it into the crook of his arm. He headed them toward the breakfast parlor.

"She's... heartbroken and... frightened," Adele offered carefully, deciding not to tell her husband that the widow was also with child. As was she—Lady Evangeline's observations had proven true—but she hadn't yet decided how to tell Milton that bit of news.

"Frightened?" he repeated, his brows joining together to form a salt-and-pepper caterpillar across his forehead.

"Of David's brother, Daniel. Seems they had an awful row a few years ago. She's afraid the man will evict her from Norwick House."

Milton allowed his wife to precede him into the breakfast parlor. "Daniel won't evict her," he asserted with a shake of his head. He pulled a chair out from the table and saw to it Adele was seated before a footman hurried into the room. "Coffee, tea, toast..." He turned to his wife and raised a brow. "Cake?"

Adele regarded her husband with a wan smile. "Yes, cake," she agreed, deciding she could indulge. She was eating for two and already looking as if she were. At some point, she would have to have her modiste create a new wardrobe. "And what makes you say that?" she asked.

"Daniel loves Clare. He has since before David courted her," Milton replied as he took his seat across the small table. At his wife's look of disbelief, the earl shrugged. "They're identical twins. She didn't know which one she was marrying."

Adele gave a snort of disbelief. "How can that be?" She was sure Clarinda would be able to tell the difference between the two men. Twins usually had a feature or two that were a bit different.

"Haven't met Daniel yet, have you?" Milton asked. "Clare probably spent... maybe... an hour all told being courted by those two. David hardly had to court her—they had been betrothed for years. So he let his brother do all the courting, including the proposal. Then he moved in, got the girl, and the rest, they say, is history."

Frowning at her husband's claim, Adele shook her head. "*His story*, you mean," she said with a huff just as a maid delivered a tray with the tea service. A footman followed with a tray of toast, biscuits, and cake.

"Good one, my lady, but I stand by my story." He helped himself to a Dutch biscuit. "Clare will still be Lady Norwick a year from now," he claimed. "She'll just be married to the other twin."

Pouring a cup of coffee for her husband and a cup of tea for herself, Adele decided she had done the right thing by recommending Clare give her brother-in-law the benefit of the doubt. Although she didn't necessarily believe the countess would end up with the brother as a husband, she hoped they could at least be friends. "It was good of you to be the one to inform Clare," she said quietly.

"I never want to have to tell another goddaughter that her husband has died," he said with a shake of his head. He'd been the one summoned to confirm the identity of the fatally injured man. And once he'd done so, he had ridden straight to Norwick House to inform Clarinda that David had died. He rather doubted he would ever again be welcomed in her home after bringing such tragic news. But he would see her again in a couple of days at the funeral, no doubt.

Having been in Lady Norwick's shoes only a few years ago, Adele understood some of what Clarinda was going through, somewhat only because she and Samuel Worthington were never in love. One of the early entrepreneurs in the business of building steam ships, her first husband had made a fortune—a fortune she had inherited upon his untimely death at the age of only forty. Then there had been one engagement prior to her renewing her acquaintance with Milton. James Weston had apparently been counting the days until she was out of mourning, beginning a courtship she found she welcomed because the man seemed so sincere in his attentions toward her. Once she learned Weston's true intentions, however—he needed her fortune to pay off gambling debts and, presumably, to allow him to continue to gamble— she ended the engagement.

When Milton chose to escort her to all the society events last year, she was thrilled by the attentions of a man who usually chose much younger widows for the honor. At the end of the Season, she expected him to end their liaison much as he had done with every other widow he had ever escorted during an entire Season—with an expensive bauble and a parting kiss. Instead, Milton Grandby had asked for her hand in marriage and bestowed a rather large sapphire ring on her finger at the same time he was bestowing a rather long and luscious kiss on her open mouth.

Faith! That kiss had shaken her to her toes.

How could she say no? The man had his own fortune, and although he occasionally gambled, he didn't do so to excess. Now that she had been married to him for nearly six months, she couldn't imagine a life without him. Which reminded her of Lady Evangeline and her lack of a husband. "Has Lord Everly returned to these shores?" she asked.

Milton straightened in his chair. "A couple of days ago," he replied with a nod. "He was at White's last night, in fact."

"Arranging a match for Evangeline, I hope?" Adele hinted.

The earl blinked. Even if Adele hadn't brought up the subject, he would have at some point.

Although Evangeline's brother should have been seeing to a suitable match for her, he didn't seem to have been match-making the night before. "I think I may be able to arrange it on his behalf," the earl hedged, his attention on something beyond Adele's shoulder.

"It's past time the poor girl was settled," Adele said as she leaned forward and helped herself to another cake. She refilled her teacup and offered more coffee to Milton. He shook his head but took another biscuit.

Allowing a grin, he considered how he was going to go about putting the final pieces of his plan into place without offending the Earl of Everly. "Tell me, are you still reading that book? *The Story of a Baron?*" he asked.

Adele had to suppress a grin. "I'm only about halfway through it, but—"

"Who's the baron?" Milton asked as he leaned forward, his elbows on the table.

Blinking a few times, Adele sighed. "You mean Matthew Winters?" she responded after a bit of hesitation. "Lord Ballantine."

"In real life," her husband clarified. "Who do you believe the book is *really* about?"

Adele gave her husband's question a good deal of thought. She had no reason to think the book was anything but a work of fiction. She thought Lord Afterly seemed similar to Lord Everly, but as for the other members of the aristocracy, she hadn't really noticed any veiled identities.

Was Lord Ballantine supposed to be based on a real baron?

Milton sighed. "Maybe I was just reading too much into it, but doesn't Matthew Winters seem an awful lot like Lord Sommers?" he asked.

Adele frowned. "When did you have a chance to read the book?" she asked in surprise.

Her husband rolled his eyes. "Only the first few chapters," he said, not adding that he had done so whilst in Hatchard's. He had no intention of spending any money on another copy.

The countess grinned, but considered his question. Yes, Lord Ballantine did seem a bit like Jeffrey Althorpe. "But Afterly's sister, Geraldine, isn't anything like Evangeline," she asserted.

"Of course not," Milton agreed. "Anonymous didn't know her. Or know her well enough when he used her as the model for Geraldine," he said with some authority.

Staring at her husband, Adele shook her head. "Why would you think Evangeline was the model for Geraldine? They're... they are nothing alike," she argued, wishing she had managed to read more of the book.

"Orphaned at a young age, alone all the time?" he replied quickly. "I think Anonymous is rather fond of our Lady Evangeline," he added with a quirked eyebrow.

"Evangeline Tennison would *never* do the things Anonymous has Geraldine doing in that book," Adele said. "Or, at least accused of doing."

Milton regarded his wife for a long time before he replied. "Not yet, anyway."

Although he was pretty sure he knew the true identity of Lord Ballantine, he had some work to do before he could confirm his suspicions about Anonymous. Depending on just who that someone was, that someone just might be asking Lady Evangeline for her hand in marriage.

When, without warning, Adele stood up from the table, Milton gave a start. "What's wrong?"

"Nothing, but now you have me so curious, I'm going to read more of that book. Right now. I'm up to Chapter 13." And with that, Adele marched out of the breakfast parlor.

"I'm coming with you," Milton said as he joined her, pretending he didn't notice the cake she held cupped in one hand as she took her leave.

CHAPTER 47

TWO COUPLES ARE READING
THE SAME CHAPTER

The Story of a Baron
A Novel in One Volume
Written by Anonymous

Chapter 13: A Farewell Kiss

Geraldine leaned over and took Matthew's mouth with hers.

The kiss was scorching in its intensity. Her lips had been made for this, their tender flesh fitting perfectly to his. Before he could think to pull away, memories of their brief encounter all those years ago came flooding back again, filling him with the same sense of urgency, of need, he had felt that night they declared their feelings for one another. Not even the threat of a slap across his face would keep him from returning Geraldine's kiss.

When the baron had shown up on the steps of Rosehill House at precisely seven o'clock in the evening, Geraldine had thought he was there to call on her brother, or to provide a ride to Black's, since a new groom and tiger hadn't yet been hired.

"I am not here for your brother," Matthew had whispered. He stood with his back to the front door, clutching his hat in one hand.

Geraldine had stared at him for several seconds, her heart pounding so hard she was sure he could hear it.

"You're not?" she managed to say in response. His lips were suddenly on hers, the kiss soft and tender and ever so sweet. She was sure she had allowed a squeak of disappointment to escape when he slowly pulled away.

That's when Geraldine leaned over and kissed him, kissed Matthew as if it would be their last kiss. For as far as she knew, it would be.

When she pulled away, apparently to take a breath, Matthew was left slightly dazed. "What is it?" he whispered, noting how a tear had escaped the corner of one eye.

"I leave for Montbury Abbey in the morning," she whispered, her lips quivering as if she were about to really cry. At the baron's furrowed brows, Geraldine sniffled. "Richard has made good on his threat and has arranged for me to live at a convent," she continued, a sob interrupting her words.

"No," Matthew replied, his head shaking back and forth. "No. You cannot go," he replied, mentally cursing Richard Porterhouse. He was sure the man had only mentioned sending his sister to an abbey as a warning, as a means of forcing Geraldine to behave in a more ladylike manner. He didn't think the man truly meant his words!

Tears now streamed down Geraldine's face. "I do not have a choice. My coach leaves at nine o'clock in the morning." With that, she gave the baron a curtsy, turned and hurried from the vestibule.

She was sure she would never again see Matthew Winters.

CHAPTER 48
ANONYMOUS REVEALED

*M*eanwhile, *at Rosemount House*

Evangeline dared a glance at the baron, wondering at his sudden reaction of surprise to the page they just finished reading. "What is it?" she asked with concern. They were back in the library, the baron having arrived at precisely eleven o'clock to continue where they had left off in *The Story of a Baron*. Apparently, he had secured permission from Harry to continue reading the book with Evangeline.

Jeffrey sat shaking his head, his own brows creased in concern. "This... This is all *wrong*. This didn't happen!" he exclaimed as he continued to shake his head. "The marquess gave his permission. In fact, he practically begged Ballantine to marry his sister," he said, his eyes still on the open book before them.

Glancing between Jeffrey and the book, Evangeline whispered, "What... what are you referring to? Did you... did you read ahead?" she accused, thinking perhaps the baron already knew—or thought he knew—what was supposed to happen next.

"No," he replied, still shaking his head back and forth. Jeffrey looked up at the ceiling, one brow arching up when he caught the telltale signs of cobwebs in the coffers. *Just like the library in Rosehill House*, he thought absently, rather proud that he had managed to get *that* particular detail correct. There were probably cobwebs in the coffers of every house in Park Lane, though. And then his mind was somewhere else, trying desperately to remember the original details of the particular scene he had just read.

As he remembered writing it, Ballantine had paid a call on the Marquess of Afterly, intending to ask Richard Porterhouse for his sister's hand in marriage. The way he had written the scene, the marquess granted permission for Ballantine and Geraldine to wed, although he had done so somewhat reluctantly—not because he didn't want to get his sister settled with the baron,—but rather because he didn't want his friend left with the responsibility of having to look after a young lady who was the subject of so much gossip. Ballantine argued that marrying Geraldine would help alleviate further gossip. Given the whims of the fickle *ton*, the incidents involving Geraldine would be forgotten in a fortnight, or about the length of time they would be gone on their wedding trip.

Now the story apparently had Afterly turning away Ballantine, telling the baron that he was saving him from the scandal associated with Geraldine by sending her off to a convent—after telling him he would give him double the dowry if he married her within the month back in Chapter Nine!

Continuity issue!

Evangeline continued to watch Jeffrey, seeing the baron's apparent distress, his wrinkled brow aging him by ten years or more. Wanting desperately to smooth away his concern, she lifted a hand to his face and drew her thumb across the wrinkle. Her gentle touch seemed to bring Jeffrey back from his reverie, for the baron's eyes cleared as he regarded her.

"I promise you, they end up together. They have to. I wrote it that way," he said as he took her hand and kissed the back of her fingers.

Evangeline inhaled at the feel of his lips on her bare skin, at the warmth of his hand as it held hers. Her entire body vibrated at the sensation, a pleasant shiver radiating from her hand to her toes and finally to the space at the top of her thighs. She was quite sure he was going to kiss her, quite sure she would kiss him if he didn't make the effort this very moment. And then, at very the moment his lips were about to touch hers, his words permeated her brain.

I wrote it that way.

Evangeline jerked away, pulling her hand from Jeffrey's grasp as she inhaled sharply. Moving quickly to the other end of the couch, Evangeline sat staring at Jeffrey with a look of horror on her face. "What... What did you say?" she asked, her mouth open in an oval.

Realizing too late what he had said, Jeffrey swallowed. He considered how to respond. "They'll end up together, I promise," he said lamely. "They have to," he added, his words coming faster. "They'll be together. Forever."

Forever.

The word repeated itself in Evangeline's thoughts, but the other words drowned it out. The words he had said that were the reason so many elements of the book were familiar.

I wrote it that way.

Jeffrey wrote the book they were reading.

Jeffrey Althorpe was Anonymous.

So it was true—Lord Afterly was meant to be her brother.

Rosehill House was Rosemount House.

She was Geraldine!

Evangeline dared a glance at the ceiling. Cobwebs, their feathery threads strung across the coffers, waved about with each change in the air currents.

Had they been there the first time Jeffrey Althorpe visited the house, for the unveiling of her brother's fish tank? Why else would they have been mentioned in the book?

"Sommers Place has them in nearly every ceiling," Jeffrey whispered, as if he could read her thoughts.

Evangeline ignored his comment. There were too many other horrors to consider just then.

Such as Geraldine Porterhouse.

The female protagonist had no doubt been based on her, Evangeline believed, although she was quite sure any *on-dit* about her didn't include naked nipples, or trysts with three different men, or even a compromised reputation.

Or did it?

Panic gripped her.

She had practically invited gossip by meeting Lord Sommers in Grosvenor Square. And having him join her at Rosemount House on the rainy days when they couldn't be out-of-doors. Perhaps it had been Lady Pettigrew who said something to Lady Torrington rather than Jones; why else would her godfather's wife pay a call on her and ask about her late-night visitor?

Her breaths coming in short gasps, Evangeline felt tears prick the corners of her eyes—tears as much from anger as from panic and the hurt she felt at what she considered a betrayal.

How could Lord Sommers use her as his model for Geraldine? A vain and petty woman whom the poor, dear Lord Ballantine would be stuck with forever?

Is this what Jeffrey Althorpe thought of her? That *he* would be stuck with her for the rest of his life?

Leg-shackled to me?

Well, that was just ridiculous. The baron hadn't asked for her hand in marriage, let alone asked to court her, which only made the lump forming in her throat that much more painful.

Jeffrey watched Evangeline's face as she continued to sort out the implications of his admission. She was a smart girl, clever enough that she would be able to figure out on whom each and every character in the book was based if he allowed her a few more minutes. But he didn't want to wait a minute more to apologize for what he was sure she would see as an offense.

When he had written the character of Geraldine, he'd had no idea of Evangeline's manner, no idea how she behaved, of how refined and intelligent she was. "Evangeline, I'm..."

A sharp pain suddenly radiated from his left cheek, forcing his eyes to squeeze shut. Despite the pain—no, the *surprise* at the rather hard slap Evangeline's bare hand had managed to impart on his unsuspecting person—Jeffrey managed to put voice to the rest of what he wanted to say. "I am sorry. I meant no offense, my lady, truly. Just the opposite, in fact," he managed to get out.

Evangeline was already off the couch and moving to the door, though. "Jones will see you out, I'm... I'm sure," she managed between sobs that seemed to take away her remaining breath. "Good day." She even managed a curtsy before she took her leave of the library and a very sorry Lord Sommers.

CHAPTER 49

THE AFTERMATH OF A REVEAL

As she hurried toward the staircase, Evangeline wished she had never met the baron in the Temple of Muses. Seven days. They'd spent part of nearly every day for just over a week together reading the damned book.

She should have allowed him to buy the only copy. Then they could have been on their way, and she never would have known there was a book featuring her and her brother and whomever else the baron had used for inspiration.

Despite the tears that spilled down her cheeks, Evangeline made her way up the marble steps and into her bedchamber, shoving the door so it made a satisfying *slam* as it closed behind her. She rushed to her bed, throwing herself onto the peach velvet counterpane in a manner she imagined Geraldine would have done when she was overcome with anger and grief.

How could he?

How could Lord Sommers write a book about her and her brother and not foresee there would be repercussions? He had to know someone would recognize the barely veiled characters. If she recognized the description of her brother in Lord Afterly, so would someone else. Anyone else who knew of her brother's avocation, which meant just about everyone in the *ton*.

From there, it followed that they would think she was Geraldine. The baron? Why Jeffrey had to be Matthew Winters.

Winters. Sommers.

Evangeline moaned in despair, her heart pounding so hard, she could hear her pulse in her ears. She sighed, dropping her head onto the counterpane and shaking it. Pins escaped her coiffure, and locks of honey blonde hair spilled past her cheeks.

So, he had written an autobiography of sorts, she decided, another sob forcing her to gasp for air.

Or was it what he hoped his life might become?

But Jeffrey Althorpe hadn't known Evangeline since childhood.

They had only met at Lord Weatherstone's ball. She thought of the other characters, of the other four that made up the Five Lords of Bad Behavior. Lord Abdington, a duke. She couldn't reconcile him as any duke who made his residence in London. But Lord Barrick had to be Lord Barrings, a viscount. His viscountess, not nearly as dim as Daisy McGowan Barrick, occasionally complained about her husband's late nights at White's and his poor card playing skills when she paid calls at Worthington House. Poor playing skills meant losses at the whist and *vingt-et-un* tables. She hoped the viscountcy could withstand his gambling.

Thomas Christianson, Earl of Atherton, might have been Sir Richard if the man cared for his wife as much as Sir Richard cared for his wife, Mary.

The marquess, Lord Brotherly, was undoubtedly William, Marquess of Devonfield. The man had married a widow just the year before.

She thought of the butlers. *Was Smithton anything like Jones?* Butlers were all of a kind, it seemed. If they weren't a foot taller and three decades older than everyone else in the house, they were short and stout and crabby.

Evangeline sighed and pushed herself off the bed. She moved to the window seat. Settling onto it, she stared out at the dreary gray of the Mayfair skies. Rivulets of rain traced down the window glass, obscuring her view of the gardens below. This early in the spring, very few flowers had bloomed, but unlike the year before, at least their leaves were turning green. Now she found she didn't care if they ever bloomed again.

When a knock sounded at her door, Evangeline gave a start. She didn't know how long she had sat gazing at the scenery below, only that she was feeling the chill as it seeped through the window glass. Shivering, she called out, "Come in," and lifted herself from the window seat.

Her lady's maid, Annabelle, peeked in around the door. "My lady?" she said tentatively.

"Yes?" Evangeline replied, moving closer to the door. Annabelle stared at her in alarm.

"What has happened, my lady?" Annabelle asked as she quickly moved into the room and closed the door behind her.

Evangeline was about to reply with, "Nothing," but thought better of it when she caught her reflection in the cheval mirror. *Faith!* She looked as if she'd been tumbled! Which couldn't be good since Lord Sommers had been in her company only... well, sometime earlier that hour. She had no idea how much time had passed whilst she sat in the window. "I had a bit of a shock, is all," she murmured.

Annabelle's shoulders seem to sag. "Oh," she replied sadly. "I don't suppose it has anything to do with Lord Sommers?" she ventured carefully. "Since he's down in the library. And you're not." She seemed to be taking stock of her mistress, noting the red-rimmed eyes and locks that had fallen from their pins. And the pins scattered about the counterpane.

"He's still *here?*" Evangeline responded, her eyes widening in shock. "How dare he!"

"Hmm," Annabelle nodded. "He's reading. And he's not very happy, if you ask me," she added.

She herded Evangeline to the dressing table and pulled out the chair. Evangeline sat down, no longer able to hold herself up. "I heard a curse word or two as I passed by the library," the lady's maid murmured.

"That makes two of us," Evangeline answered with a huff, watching as Annabelle expertly gathered up the hair that had fallen and rearranged it into a rather elaborate hair style.

"You will be rejoining him in the library, I hope," Annabelle said, not making it a question.

Evangeline stared at her maid's reflection in the looking

glass. "I will not. I cannot believe he has the... the gall... to stay in there and continue reading that... that *damned* book," she managed to get out, not the least bit apologetic at having used a curse word.

Her lady's maid stepped back and regarded her mistress in the mirror, her face screwed up into one of confusion. And then her face split into a huge smile. "Oh, this is a lovers' quarrel, is all," she said happily. "We'll have you looking presentable in no time," she promised as she tried to move Evangeline's head so it rested on the back of the chair.

"Lovers' quarrel?" Evangeline repeated, shocked at Annabelle's assertion. "It most certainly is not!" she countered, her ire evident in how her cheeks reddened.

"Oh, that's good, my lady. The color is coming back to your cheeks. Now, we just have to get your eyes..."

Evangeline stood up, not about to allow her lady's maid to think for one moment that she and Lord Sommers were lovers. Or even *acquaintances* at this point.

Annabelle stepped back, her hands on her hips. "Every lady's maid three houses down and across the street is of the opinion that you and Lord Sommers are having an illicit *affaire*," she stated with a good deal of authority. "Which means that by now, every lady in those houses is probably thinking the very same thing." She regarded Evangeline with an arched eyebrow, as if she dared the woman to counter her claim. "And if they haven't already, they'll be sharing their news when they next pay calls on their mutual friends in Mayfair."

Evangeline inhaled, stunned by the words. Of course, Annabelle was right. That was the way gossip worked in the aristocracy. She quickly sat down, afraid if she stood for one more minute, she would faint for the first time in her life.

Lady Torrington had been right—Evangeline's ploy to become the victim of gossip had apparently worked, and far too well. And if Lord Sommers was still in the parlor, that meant his conveyance was probably still parked at the curb, or, with any luck, one of the stable boys had seen to moving it to the mews behind the house.

"Did ye say something to offend the man?" Annabelle asked in a quiet voice, her hands wringing together.

Sighing, Evangeline said, "No." She shook her head to reinforce the answer. Then she dropped her head into her hands, the right one still sore from when she had slapped the baron. "I hit him, though," she whispered.

Annabelle frowned, trying to imagine her mistress hitting the baron. "As, in his shoulder?" she ventured carefully, pantomiming a punch to Evangeline's upper arm.

Evangeline sighed again, her manner becoming indignant. "No. I slapped him across the face," she said. "About broke my hand," she complained as she shook out her right hand. She hadn't even noticed the pain when she had actually hit the man, but now her palm felt as if she had held it too long over a lit candle.

The lady's maid nodded. "Well, then I expect you owe him an apology," she said helpfully.

"An apology?" Evangeline countered in disbelief. "I think not! He used me as a character in his book."

Annabelle planted both of her fists on her hips and regarded her mistress with a sigh. "If you're speaking of *The Story of a Baron*, then let me be the first to assure you that you're nothing like Lady Geraldine, nor would anyone in Mayfair think such a thing."

Evangeline blinked, as much to clear tears from her eyes as in surprise at hearing Annabelle's words. "You know about the book?"

The lady's maid shrugged. "Housekeeper's been reading it to us every night after tea this past week. Amusing piece of fiction it is, but the author did get the cobwebs right. Housemaid will see to them in the morning when the groom brings in a ladder to help clear them away."

Sniffling, Evangeline considered the comment.

Feeling the tears prick her eyes again, Evangeline lowered her face into her hands. "Oh, Annabelle—"

"Oh, no, no you don't," the lady's maid said as she pulled Evangeline back up against the chair so her head was upright. "You're going to march right down those steps, enter that parlor, sit down next to that handsome lord, and act as if nothing happened."

Her mouth opened in shock, Evangeline stared at her maid. "I will do no such thing!" she countered.

"Then, I'll send Lord Sommers up here. Tell 'im to ravish you so he has to get a special license and marry you on the morrow."

Her eyes wide, Evangeline shook her head. "You wouldn't *dare*!" she replied, outraged at the lady's maid's odd behavior.

Annabelle's eyes narrowed into slits. She planted her hands on her hips again before turning and stomping to the door. The lady's maid took her leave of the bedchamber without so much as a curtsy in Evangeline's direction.

Evangeline waited a moment, thinking Annabelle was bluffing. But when she heard the woman's feet padding down the marble stairs, she realized the maid meant what she'd said.

Hurrying to the half-opened door, Evangeline opened it wide to find Lord Sommers standing in the hall, not one foot from the door.

"Oh!" she managed to get out in alarm, stepping back as she did so.

Jeffrey, looking every bit as chagrined as he should have, reached down. He took her hand in his, lifting it to his lips so he could kiss her knuckles. His eyes closed so the tips of his lashes brushed against her skin. A shiver of excitement caused Evangeline's entire body to give a start, and Jeffrey released her hand. "You left the parlor before I could finish my apology," he said quietly. "I would have come sooner, but I thought for the sake of my life that I had better give you some time to... to calm yourself." He saw fire in her eyes and added, "Or arrange for my untimely death and funeral."

Thinking the man would be seen by other servants if she didn't get him into the bedchamber, Evangeline grabbed the hand that had just held onto hers and pulled him hard. She could see Annabelle's smiling face at the top of the stairs, and she was about to give the lady's maid a scowl, but Annabelle turned and hurried away.

"My lady," Jeffrey said with a shake of his head. He looked

as if he was about to turn around and leave the bedchamber, but instead stood and regarded Evangeline with a look of sadness. He sighed, his shoulders sagging. "I am so sorry I did not admit to being Anonymous when we first met at the bookshop," he said quietly, as if he thought they might be overheard.

Evangeline had an image in her head of a dozen servants standing outside her door, their ears all pressed to the carved wood. She thought about opening it quickly so she could watch them all tumble into the room. After another second, she decided to try it. She pulled the startled baron farther into the room, carefully placed her still-stinging hand on the door handle, pressed down on it, and quickly pulled the door open. No servants fell into the room, though, and a quick look out into the hall showed there were no servants about. Surprised, Evangeline stepped back into the room and closed the door.

"What was that all about?" Jeffrey asked, his brows furrowing in that way that made him look older than he was.

"I didn't wish for our conversation to be overheard by every servant in the house." She took a deep breath before crossing her arms over her chest. "You owe me an explanation," she whispered hoarsely.

Jeffrey nodded. "Indeed. I… I do." He paused and glanced around the bedchamber. "May we sit?"

"No." Evangeline held her ground as she regarded him with an expression of annoyance.

His body jerking as if he'd been hit with a roundhouse blow to his middle, Jeffrey looked suitably chagrined. "That night at Lord Weatherstone's ball? When Lady Pettigrew took pity on me and introduced us?" he began. "I asked for the introduction because I had spent the entire evening admiring you from the other side of the ballroom." At Evangeline's sound of disbelief, he added, "I've known your brother for years and cursed him for not having introduced you when you had your come-out."

"That night *was* my come-out," she countered, her chin rising. Not a very successful one, but then her brother hadn't hosted a ball in their home, nor had he even danced with her that night.

"Still, I was honored, and then I spent the next year imagining what it might be like to have someone like you…" He dipped his head. "I invented Geraldine as your… your exact opposite. In fact, almost everything in *The Story of a Baron* is the opposite of what it truly is."

Evangeline inhaled sharply. "How can you say that? My brother—"

"Is almost exactly as I depicted Afterly," Jeffery interrupted. "Deliberately. I admit, I have been… incensed—nay, *angry*—with Everly's indifference to you. Leaving you as he does for months at a time. Without protection. Without having arranged a betrothal." He sighed. "Depicting him as he truly is was my way of… shaming him, I suppose."

Evangeline furrowed a brow. "But in making him so obviously my brother, I am being thought of as Geraldine," she argued.

"Never! Anyone in the *ton* who knows you—"

"All ten of them?" she interrupted, tears pricking the corners of her eyes. "I hardly know *anyone* these days, Jeffrey. If it weren't for Sam and Julia, *I* would have put myself in a convent," she claimed just before she swallowed a sob.

Wincing at her words, Jeffrey attempted to gather her into his arms and hold her, but Evangeline stepped back and crossed her arms.

"I didn't think of that," he whispered. "I am so sorry, Evangeline—"

"It's *Lady* Evangeline," she said sharply.

Jeffrey swallowed, realizing it was going to be more difficult than he feared to regain her trust. "I never wanted to hurt you, or offend you, or God forbid, have you hate me—"

"I don't *hate* you," Evangeline murmured, remembering the moment when Geraldine had said she hated Matthew. She certainly didn't want to sound like the character. Didn't want to reinforce any similarities she might share with Geraldine. "Dislike intensely, perhaps," she added on a sob.

Jeffrey allowed a nod. "This past week has been the best week of my entire life," he murmured. "All because of you. If it hadn't been for that damned book…" He squeezed his eyes shut when he realized he had cursed, his eyebrows knitting together.

Evangeline reached up with a thumb and smoothed away the wrinkle. Jeffrey closed his eyes at her gentle touch. "I love you, Evangeline," he whispered, his eyes opening to find her staring up at him.

"You do?" Evangeline blinked her disbelief.

"I have since that night I met you. And then I made a cake of it and thought you would never want to have anything to do with me. But I didn't stop thinking about you…"

Before he could finish his thought, her lips were on his. Although she couldn't claim much experience in the matter, Jeffrey thought her kiss the sweetest he had ever had the pleasure of receiving from a woman. And considering it was only his fifth or sixth and Evangeline had been the first and only one to ever kiss him—other than his mother, of course,—he felt rather blessed at that moment.

When Evangeline finally lowered herself so her heels once more touched the ground, she gazed up at Jeffrey's face. "The neighbors all think we're having an illicit *affaire*," she said quietly.

"Oh?" he replied, not too surprised by the news. He had never been the topic of gossip before, though. And he supposed he couldn't blame the neighbors. He had been a visitor at Rosemount House six times in the past eight days. And not once had Lord Everly been in residence during his visits. In fact, even after Everly had returned to London, he seemed conspicuously absent from the house, as if he was doing everything he could to avoid Jeffrey. "Are we… are we attempting to make true their gossip?" Jeffrey asked, perhaps a bit too eagerly.

Evangeline gave him a quelling glance, her head coming to rest against his shoulder. "Although I am tempted—that is, if you are—I don't dare do anything more than we already have done in this house," she replied quietly. "What we've already done is far more than I could have imagined doing before marriage." Should Jeffrey ask for her hand, she rather hoped they could continue what they had started but in the comfort of Sommers Place.

Jeffrey wrapped both his arms around her shoulders, pulling her hard against his body. "More than you can ever know," he replied, matching the tone of her voice. "But until I can speak with your brother... I... will not," he said with great difficulty. He continued to hold her, though, his cheek resting on the side of her head.

"Did you finish reading the book?" Evangeline asked then, her head tilted up from where it rested against his shoulder.

"No," he said with a shake of his head. "I'll be paying a call on my publisher tomorrow, though," he said with a sigh. "Since he made changes to the story that I cannot abide." Until he finished reading the book, he had no idea how the couple would reconcile to end up together.

"Hmm," Evangeline responded, wondering if there were more changes than those they had stumbled on earlier that day.

"Would you have told me?" Evangeline asked. "That you were Anonymous?"

Jeffrey shrugged. "Eventually, I suppose. I never really intended to keep it from you," he claimed. "I just thought it would be good to get the opinion of a lady, seeing as how I completely neglected to think a woman would ever read such a book when I was writing it," he said by way of an excuse.

"Why did you write it?" she asked.

Jeffrey lowered his head and cleared his throat. "When I started the book, I needed a way to earn money without being obvious about it," he explained. "My father left the Sommers barony near receivership when he died. But I've made careful investments, and the sheep are fine, so all is not as dire as it once was." He paused a moment. "But the real reason was so that I could consider taking a wife."

Nodding, Evangeline regarded him another moment before asking, "And why did you write a story about a baron?"

Jeffrey had to resist the urge to snort. "It's what I know," he replied. "And I couldn't think of anything else to write about."

"And Geraldine?" she pressed.

His shoulders slumping in resignation, Jeffrey took a deep breath. "Like almost everything else in the book, she is a direct opposite of her inspiration," he admitted. He straightened then. "But you have to admit, there are women in the *ton* who are just like her," he challenged.

Evangeline gave a shrug. "I really cannot say with certainty as I know so few," she said on a sigh. Then she frowned, realizing that perhaps she did know of some matrons who were materialistic and vain.

Jeffrey pulled her head to his shoulder and kissed her forehead. "I'll be sure to escort you to every event of the Season to which we're invited," he promised before moving his lips farther down to kiss her once more. "I shall never tire of kissing you."

Sighing as she allowed a wan smile, Evangeline reached up and kissed the corner of his mouth. "Although my reputation is probably beyond repair, I suppose you really should take your leave," she whispered.

Jeffrey nodded, his hold not lessening on her. "Tomorrow, then?" he said as he gave her a squeeze and finally let go his hold. "Finsbury Square? You'll bring your lady's maid, of course."

Evangeline's smile widened, thinking she might pay a visit to The Temple of the Muses much like she would on any Tuesday morning. "Ten o'clock?" she suggested, thinking she might still make it to tea with Samantha and Julia.

Jeffrey nodded. "I'll see you there. Bring the book, and we'll finish it." With that, he turned and opened the door, much as Evangeline had done only moments earlier. A half-dozen servants fell into the room, their startled faces and exclamations of surprise sending Evangeline into a fit of giggles and Jeffrey into uproarious laughter.

Stepping between their sprawled bodies, he gave Evangeline one last smile and took his leave of her bedchamber and of Rosemount House.

CHAPTER 50

A PROMISE IN THE SQUARE

The following day
The next morning brought sunshine and a happy Evangeline to Finsbury Square. Annabelle, asleep in the Everly town coach, no doubt because she had been up entirely too late spreading gossip among the other servants in the neighborhood, would probably join her once she awoke and realized Evangeline had taken her leave of the coach in favor of shopping at The Temple of the Muses.

After seeing the shelf on which ten copies of *The Story of a Baron* were displayed quite prominently, Evangeline selected a small volume, *The Young Lady's Guide to Managing a Household*, and took her leave of the bookshop.

When she saw that Annabelle was still asleep in the coach, Evangeline made her way to the very same park bench on which she and Jeffrey had sat the week before. She allowed a contented sigh as she watched the nurses and children at play, the couples walking arm in arm, the servants rushing about on their errands. The scene was familiar because it was the same as it had been a week ago.

Only one week!
When Jeffrey appeared, his dark blue top coat and red waistcoat a nice contrast to his Nankeen breeches, he carried a small bouquet of roses. He bowed and offered her the flowers, taking

one of her hands with his free one. Leaning over, he kissed her cheek instead of her hand. "I have given this a great deal of thought. I rather doubt they will equate me with Lord Ballantine," Jeffrey insisted. "And no one would ever mistake you for Lady Geraldine."

Evangeline gazed at the baron, knowing his words were only half true. Ballantine was perhaps more clever than Lord Sommers, and his manner more guarded, but given the *on-dit*, Evangeline was looking more and more like Geraldine when it came to scandalous behavior. At least she didn't share Geraldine's desire for jewels and clothes and... *things*.

Jeffrey took his seat next to Evangeline and reached over to wrap her hand about his arm. "Which is quite refreshing, really. Because, you see, in my experience, nearly all the other women in the *ton* seem to be like her."

Evangeline considered the baron's comment as she buried her nose in the roses and took a deep breath. She found she had to agree with his assessment. Geraldine could have been almost any of the unmarried young ladies or young matrons she came across when she paid calls in the early afternoon. They could be so proud, so cutting, when speaking of others. *They're bitter*, she thought, which had her curious as to why. Why, when some, like Lady Bostwick, seemed so content. So happy.

And then she remembered some of what they talked about in the parlors of Mayfair.

"Perhaps because they are married to men who have no regard for them. Or because they are seen as a means to fatten a man's purse, or as a source of funds to pay off gambling debts." She turned to find Jeffrey regarding her, his mouth a bit slack, as if he was just then realizing something very important. "Walk with me," she said, gathering the book into the crook of her arm before standing.

Jeffrey was quick to do her bidding, rising and reaching over to take the book from her. He placed it under one arm and then offered the other one to Evangeline.

Gripping her parasol in one hand, Evangeline rested the hand that held the roses on Jeffrey's arm and allowed him to lead the way. "Just now, you looked as if you were thinking of something very important," she said when they were on a crushed granite path.

Jeffrey nodded, his manner most sober. "I do not believe I could marry a woman only to gain her dowry," he finally said in a quiet voice. "Although I can certainly understand the temptation to do so," he added, thinking of the limited funds in his account at Barings Bank. "And, in the end, it's all about my doing my duty."

Evangeline gave a small shake of her head. "And what duty might that be?" she enquired.

Jeffrey shrugged. "To take a wife. We have to be married in order to father legitimate heirs," he reminded her, as if Evangeline wasn't part of the realm and already well-versed in the requirements placed on a lord. "Whether we wish to be or not."

Evangeline gave him a small smile. "Are you one of those who would rather *not* be married?" she asked. A sense of dread settled deep within her.

His face darkening, Jeffrey shook his head. "Nothing could be further from the truth, milady," he stated emphatically. "I want nothing more than to *be* married."

Evangeline straightened and nearly stopped walking. Using the hand that held her parasol, she indicated the book. "But not to... not to someone like Geraldine?" she half-asked.

"Oh, of course not!" Jeffrey assured her. "Well, at least, not *now*. I suppose when we started writing this..." He grabbed the edge of the book and shook it once. "I thought she was the one because I thought most young women were like her," he said with a huff. "But I cannot afford a woman who wants everything. I don't *want* a woman who wants everything."

Holding her breath, Evangeline stared at the baron. "*We?*" she repeated. "Did you write this book with someone else?"

Jeffrey frowned and rolled his eyes. "My publisher and me, I should say. I spoke with him this morning," he said, his voice filled with disappointment. Unable to sleep due to the events of the night before, he had been on the doorstep of the man's office when it opened at nine o'clock.

Evangeline nodded her understanding. "Did he say why he changed your story?"

Angling his head to one side, Jeffrey said, "My story needed more *conflict*, it seems. Adding the chapter about Geraldine going to a convent turned out to be a wise choice." At Evangeline's look of surprise, he added, "I have not read any further, I assure you. But I must agree, it does give the book a bit of drama near the end."

Evangeline nodded her understanding. "It does at that. We still don't know how they will end up together if she's to go to a convent in the morning, though," she said with worry.

The baron regarded her for a moment. "It has a happy ending, I assure you." He wondered if his own story would end so well. "As I explained yesterday, I thought if I could earn enough money writing books—anonymously, of course—then I would be able to afford a wife. That I would be seen as a good catch by some young lady. But because I thought most women in the *ton* were like Geraldine," he continued, his words coming quickly, "I sorted that if I could simply find one with a decent dowry, one whom I could at least be fond of and who might... who might be fond of me, I might not *have* to write the books."

"And, now?" Evangeline prompted, aware from his gaze that he watched for her reaction to his words. A look of awe settled on her features. She was sure she blushed under his gaze and looked away.

"I'm quite in love with you, Evangeline. Dowry or not."

When her eyes finally met his, Jeffrey leaned over and captured her lips in a kiss, so soft and so brief, she barely had time to reach for his lapel to steady herself. Perhaps he heard her whimper when the kiss ended too quickly, for he kissed her cheek and quickly placed his lips on hers again for another kiss. When he pulled away, he left his forehead resting against hers.

"I promise you, should your brother allow it, I will ask for your hand in marriage," he whispered.

Evangeline nodded, knowing it might be some time before he could do so. "And I promise I will accept," she murmured, a smile lighting her face.

Aware of several people staring at them, including a young boy in short pants, the embarrassed couple straightened and hurried back to the park bench. Taking their usual positions, they opened the book and spread it over their laps.

"Chapter Fourteen?" Evangeline asked, as if nothing of the last fifteen minutes had happened.

"Indeed," Jeffrey responded. "I am most eager to learn how my publisher arranged for Geraldine's eviction from the convent."

CHAPTER 51

OUR COUPLE READS IN
FINSBURY SQUARE

The Story of a Baron
A Novel in One Volume
Written by Anonymous

Chapter 14: A Baron Gets His Bride
At exactly eight-forty-five the following morning, a black-lacquered coach pulled into the semi-circular drive in front of Rosehill House. The driver jumped down and moved to steady the lead horses. Several footmen brought trunks out of the house, securing them to the back of the coach. The coach door was opened, and the steps were lowered by another footman.

Geraldine Porterhouse, dressed entirely in black and wearing a black bonnet with a veil covering her tear-stained face, passed through the front door and made her way to the coach. She allowed the footman to assist her, thanking him as he shut the door and waved to the driver. With a lurch, the coach took its leave of Rosehill House.

When Geraldine finally lost sight of the only home she had ever known, she turned and faced the front of the coach interior, frowning when she determined she wasn't in the Afterly coach. Glancing about, she marveled at the supple leather that made up the squabs, at the rich carpet beneath her feet, at the exquisite coach lights with their cut crystal covers.

This isn't a hackney, she thought with a start. And the coach hadn't driven much more than a mile when it turned into the semi-circular drive in front of a Palladian mansion across from the park. She rather doubted the beautiful structure was a convent, although it could boast a variety of blooms along the crushed granite driveway that looked as if they were tended by servants of God. The countless pots of flowers along the front near the portico and the close-clipped lawn meant a gardener had been quite busy.

When the coach halted and a footman opened the door, she carefully stepped down whilst keeping her attention on the house. Perhaps living at a convent wouldn't be so bad after all, she considered as she stared at the white stuccoed house.

She made her way up the marble steps, marveling at the Ionic columns she passed to get to the double doors. Before she could reach for the brass knocker, the door opened. A rather stout butler, balding and looking ever-so-serious, opened the door and stepped aside.

"Welcome to Convent House, milady," he said with a bow.

Geraldine gasped as she glanced about the elegant vestibule, nearly forgetting to remove her pelisse. Handing her parasol to the butler, she continued her perusal of the house, moving to the grand hall just beyond the entry. A huge floral arrangement, rather ornate and regal, graced a round table in the center of the hall. A pair of matched curved staircases, looking as if they were made entirely of Italian marble, led to the upper floors. At the place where the staircases met at the top stood a man. A rather handsome, well-dressed man.

Not a person she would expect in a convent, but then, there was a butler.

"Who died?" the man asked before he turned and leisurely made his way down one of the staircases.

Geraldine's mouth fell open as she recognized the voice, recognized the man who was at this very moment walking toward her with the most amazing expression on his face.

"Ballantine," she breathed.

"Matthew," he countered, reaching for her black-gloved hand and kissing the back of it. He gave her a deep bow. "Welcome to your new home."

Shaking her head back and forth, Geraldine thought she might still be at Rosehill House, in her bed, dreaming. "*My* home?" she repeated in awe. "I hadn't realized nuns lived quite so... *well*," she whispered, keeping her voice low so she wouldn't wake herself from the glorious dream. At that moment, she thought to look up, astounded by the beautifully painted ceiling and a crystal chandelier at least as large as the mahogany table below it.

Matthew smiled and allowed a chuckle. "Do you like it?" he asked, reaching for her other hand. He was nervous, his eyes shifting about in an effort to decide what to show her first.

He had only thought to get her to the house before the hackney that was supposed to take her to the convent arrived at Rosehill House. Having already dispatched a note to Lord Afterly demanding the payment of double her dowry within the week, Matthew was determined to marry the young lady before noon that day. Since he had already secured a special license, a quick trip to a bishop was in order. And he needed the dowry to pay for the house. And the town coach. And all the furniture he had managed to have delivered over the past week.

He'd had no idea how much went into setting up a household for a woman who wanted everything, but he was determined she have it. Her dowry allowed him to do so.

Geraldine, looking as if she might swoon, continued to gaze at him. "It's everything I ever dreamed of. You're... *you* are everything I've ever dreamed of," she whispered. She rushed into his arms, bestowing a kiss on the corner of his mouth.

Sighing, Matthew wrapped his arms around her shoulders and pulled her hard against the front of his body. "Jerry, marry me. Today. Now," he whispered into her ear.

Sprinkling kisses along his jaw and then finally on his lips, Geraldine nodded. "Yes, of course, today," she replied, her head bobbing up and down.

Closing his eyes for a moment, Matthew took a deep breath, intoxicated by the scents of lemon and honeysuckle.

"Where are the nuns?" Geraldine whispered, not surprised by how quiet the house was, but nevertheless, she expected one or two to be about.

"At the nunnery, no doubt," Matthew replied with a teasing grin.

Geraldine pushed away from him so that she could better see his face. "So this... this isn't a convent?" she asked in confusion.

"No," he replied, the teasing grin returning to his lips. "It's just named Convent House," he explained with a shrug, not adding that he had given it the moniker just the day before, thanks to Richard Porterhouse and his claim that he was sending Geraldine to one.

The man was probably just now discovering his sister hadn't been taken to the nunnery he had in mind for her.

"Oh," Geraldine replied. "And, *we're* to live here?" she asked in awe.

"Indeed. It's your house—our house, I suppose. At least, it will be after we're married," he remarked, still watching how impressed she seemed by her new home.

"Today?" Geraldine asked, a smile finally lighting up he face.

Matthew nodded. "Today. And tomorrow, and the day after that, and—"

"Forever," she whispered.

Smiling, Matthew nodded again.

Forever.

*E*vangeline allowed a sigh and turned to gaze at Jeffrey. "Well, that was rather clever of Lord Ballantine," she said with a smile. "And Geraldine didn't even have to escape from the nunnery."

Jeffrey nodded. "It was clever. I rather wish I'd thought of it," he murmured, disappointment settling over him.

"What is it?" Evangeline asked in a whisper. "What's wrong?"

"Well, now that we've finished the book, I'm wondering

how I'm going to have an excuse to see you every day until we can marry," he replied.

Her face lighting up in delight, she said, "Well, that's easy. We can buy another book."

Jeffrey allowed a chuckle before he sobered. "Until I am allowed to ask for your hand, my lady, I fear we cannot…" He paused to indicate the bench on which they sat. "…we cannot continue to do this, or your reputation will be in tatters." Evangeline's expression of disappointment had him adding, "I do hope you'll still agree to be my bride."

A slow smile spread over Evangeline's face as she regarded him. "I look forward to your proposal," she whispered.

CHAPTER 52

HAPPY BIRTHDAY

The following day
Jeffrey Althorpe regarded his image in the looking glass in his bedchamber. *Happy birthday,* he thought, his mood somber and perhaps even morose. The past years hadn't been kind to his visage. There were tiny lines on either side of his eyes and mouth, his nose appeared to have extended at least an eighth of an inch, and there were what could only be described as worry lines across his forehead.

When did this happen? he wondered. The late nights at White's had probably taken their toll to some degree, and he found the days spent in Parliament didn't help when issues important to him weighed heavily long after their fate had been decided.

Indeed, the only light in his life had been Lady Evangeline.

Had it just been eight days since the two had argued over who would take possession of *The Story of a Baron?*

Eight days.

And now that they had finished reading it, he no longer had an excuse to see her every day.

God, how he missed her!

For a reason he had yet to discover, Harry Tennison had been rather effective at avoiding him. Until he secured permission from the Earl of Everly, he dared not court Evangeline, nor could he formerly propose to the lady.

To the love of his life.

He let out a heavy sigh, turning when the bedchamber door opened to admit his valet. "Ah, Timmons," he murmured. He watched as the young man hurried about, retrieving breeches, a waistcoat and a topcoat from the clothes press to present to him for his approval. "Fine," he nodded at the valet's choices. "I'm thinking I'll ride later, perhaps during the fashionable hour," he added. He was feeling restless.

A knock at the door preceded his butler's unexpected appearance. "A note just arrived for you, my lord," the older man intoned, his voice several octaves deeper than one would expect from such a small man.

Jeffrey nodded as he took the note from the silver salver, turning it over to see the Earl of Torrington's seal in the dark red wax. "Thank you," he murmured, breaking the seal and unfolding the white parchment. The handwriting was obviously masculine, and knowing the earl as he did, he figured the man had penned it himself rather than have his secretary write it.

I am paying you a call at precisely eleven o'clock this morning. Be dressed and ready. Torrington.

"Faith," Jeffrey whispered. Milton Grandby never called on him! In fact, Jeffrey was rather surprised the earl even knew who he was, although he had been invited to the man's house those two times for dinner. "What time is it?" he asked, not addressing his question to either the butler or his valet.

Timmons glanced at the mantle clock above the fireplace. "Ten-forty, my lord," he answered.

"No bath today. But I need a shave," Sommers ordered, moving to take a seat before the mirror in his bathing chamber. "And make it quick. I must be in my study at ten-fifty-five," he added, his stomach churning. *The one morning I don't get up early and this happens.* Indeed, had he arranged to read another book with Evangeline, he would already be on his way to meet her, which made him wonder what Lord Torrington would have done when he found him already gone from Sommers Place.

*T*rue to his short missive, Milton, Earl of Torrington, appeared on the doorstep of Sommers Place at exactly eleven o'clock. He was led directly to Jeffrey's study, where he found the baron at his desk, looking as if he'd been there for several hours reviewing the books for his estate.

Milton knew better, though.

"Sommers," he said by way of a greeting, acknowledging the baron's short bow with one of his own. "I see thirty minutes was enough to get you ready this morning."

The baron regarded the earl with a frown. "It usually is," he replied. There was no reason to admit he had been abed until ten-thirty, although it was a bit later than he usually slept. *Another effect of aging*, he thought. "Would you like coffee? Or tea, perhaps?" he asked, remembering his mother's lessons in hospitality.

"Coffee, please," Milton answered with a slow grin, settling into the chair across from the desk.

Jeffrey made a motion to the servant who had followed the earl into the study. "And to what do I owe the honor of a visit from you? Did you come to wish me happy?"

The earl cocked a dark eyebrow. "Did you already ask for her hand?" Milton asked, his grin turning to a frown.

The question had Jeffrey blinking. *Ask for her hand?*

Faith!

Torrington wasn't here about his birthday. "No," he replied carefully. "It's my birthday," he said after a pause.

Milton took a quick look at the ceiling before returning his attention to the baron. "And how many years have you been on this damned planet?" he asked, the question tinged with anger. From the looks of the man who sat before him, he would guess Jeffrey Althorpe was in his early to-mid thirties. If he ever left White's at an earlier hour of the morning, he might actually look younger than he was.

"Thirty," Jeffrey replied hesitantly.

Grandby gave a noncommittal grunt. "It's time you were married," he stated firmly.

"I agree," Sommers replied with a firm nod.

"Time you gave up your bachelor ways, and your late nights, and your whoring, and..." He paused a moment, one bushy eyebrow cocked up. "Wait. What did you say?"

Jeffrey sighed. He supposed he should have taken offense at the earl for making his state of matrimony his business, but he found he couldn't. He'd had the vague idea of marriage on his mind since late December. Since the weekend after Christmas, when the massive snowstorm had buried most of England in the cold, white stuff. While most men of the *ton* were ensconced in their bedchambers with their wives, seeing to the creation of the next generation of the peerage, Jeffrey had been holed up at his country estate with several friends—all bachelors—and a deck of cards.

It was the worst holiday of his life.

"I agree," he repeated. "And, as for the whoring, I haven't indulged in quite some time. I've an aversion to venereal disease," he added. *And a lack of funds to pay for a mistress.* But he didn't put voice to his thoughts, thinking his financial state was really none of the earl's business.

Milton regarded the baron for a long moment. "Do you have someone in mind to be your baroness?" he asked then, the one already arched eyebrow lifting nearly into his hairline.

Jeffrey took a deep breath and finally nodded. "I do."

When he didn't offer a name, Grandby's other eyebrow joined the first in elevation. "Does the future Lady Sommers have a *name?*" he finally asked, his eyebrows finally settling into their normal location.

Jeffrey was tempted to put voice to his annoyance, but he decided the earl could be of some help. "Lady Evangeline," Jeffrey offered, his voice barely audible. "I believe she'll have me," he added, dipping his head before meeting Milton's gaze. She had said she would. Promised him she would. But they both knew it wouldn't matter if her brother didn't agree to the betrothal.

"*Have* you?" Milton repeated. "Of course, she'll have you.

I'll tell her to *have* you. She's three-and-twenty and not getting any younger," he claimed, one hand waving in the air as if to reinforce his point.

The door opened and a maid appeared with the coffee service. She set the tray on the corner of the desk before pouring two cups for the gentlemen.

Glad for the interruption, Jeffrey swallowed and considered Grandby's words. He was curious as to why the earl had taken such an interest in Lord Everly's sister. Lord knew, Lord Everly certainly didn't. The two times Jeffrey had tried to bring up the topic of courting Lady Evangeline had left him frustrated and impatient with the explorer. The man might be a genius when it came to some scientific topics, but he was a dunce when it came to the matter of marriage for his sister.

The maid curtsied and left the study. Milton continued to regard Jeffrey with an expression that required some kind of response.

"I kissed her," Jeffrey stated, straightening in his chair as he made the claim. He thought it better not to mention how many times. Or that she had initiated a few herself.

"Proud of yourself for that?" Milton asked rhetorically, and then wondered why the baron would admit to having kissed Evangeline Tennison if not to reinforce some kind of claim on the young lady.

Jeffrey shrugged. "Not *proud*, exactly," he replied. After a pause, he added, "It was necessary. I... I was about to take my leave of her, and I knew it might be some time before I could see her again, and... I did not wish to part as mere... friends."

Milton regarded Lord Sommers with what appeared to be respect. "Did she... *welcome* your advance?" he asked, thinking Lady Evangeline might have put up a fight if she didn't. *And if she didn't, the fish in that damned glass aquarium would.*

"Of course she did. Do you think me capable of forcing my advances on an unwilling lady?" Jeffrey answered, obviously annoyed.

Angling his head to one side, Milton gave a huff. "What are your plans for her?"

Jeffrey was about to respond with something along the lines

of, "It's none of your concern," but thought better of it. The Earl of Torrington was a powerful man and well-liked among his colleagues. "I plan to send a note and ask if she'll join me on a drive in the park this afternoon," Jeffrey suggested, hoping that would be enough to get Torrington out of his study and on his way.

"Agreed," Milton stated before taking a drink of his coffee. "Given her age, I think you can forgo a chaperone, but if she insists, recommend she bring her lady's maid," he suggested quickly. "Maids are more willing to go if they don't have to walk. By the end of the drive in the park, ask if you can court her, and then, when you get back to Everly's house, ask for her hand."

Jeffrey blinked once. He blinked again. "All in... all in one *day?*"

Milton's eyes widened. "Yes, in one day! Today!" he responded, his patience at an end. "Get a special license and marry her next week. You're thirty, for God's sake. It's time you were leg-shackled," the earl nearly shouted. "With luck, she'll be with child by the end of the month, and you'll have an heir at Christmas."

Jeffrey Althorpe regarded the earl for several moments. "You're quite serious," he finally responded. "Will you... will *you* be explaining all this to Lord Everly? Despite my requests for an audience with her brother, the man hasn't made time to meet with me."

Milton regarded the baron for a moment, only somewhat surprised to learn that Sommers really had been considering Lady Evangeline for his baroness. "Leave it to me," the earl replied with a nod. "Never let it be said I don't see to my goddaughters' welfare—"

"Goddaughter?" Jeffrey repeated in disbelief. *No wonder he's so concerned!*

"Since a week after she was born," Milton said with some pride. He rose from his chair. "By the way, Lady Torrington is expecting, you might have heard."

The baron gave a start. "Congratulations," he said with as much reverence as he could muster. "You must be—"

"Scared to death. Thrilled. Happy. Humbled. Excited," Milton interrupted with several nods. "I am. Stedman is thrilled, too. I've made him a very rich man," he added, his head still bobbing up and down. "Bought three necklaces for my wife last night."

At the mention of jewelry, Jeffrey remembered he would need a ring. He wondered how he would be able to work a trip to Ludgate Hill into his already busy schedule for the day. "Is this Stedman... is his shop open late?" Jeffrey asked as he got to his feet.

The Earl of Torrington drained his coffee. "Probably until ten, but I wouldn't wait that long. You'll want time to choose wisely. This is Evangeline we're talking about. Skip the diamonds and go straight to the sapphires. No need to be cheap about it."

And with that, Milton Grandby took his leave of Jeffrey's study.

CHAPTER 53

ARRANGING A RIDE IN
THE PARK

*A*fter Milton Grandby took his leave of Jeffrey, the younger man sat down at his desk and considered what he was about to do. *I'm going to propose*, he thought, his breaths coming a bit quicker the more he thought about it. Well, if he was going to propose today, as the Earl of Torrington insisted, then he had much to accomplish.

Pulling a sheet of parchment from a drawer, he dipped a quill into the ink bottle and began writing a note.

> *Dear Lady Evangeline,*
> *I wish to request the pleasure of your company for a drive in the park this afternoon at four o'clock.*

Jeffrey paused, wondering if the time would be too soon. The fashionable hour in Hyde Park was five o'clock. But traffic would be a crush at five o'clock.

> *I look forward to your reply,*
> *Sincerely, Sommers*

Jeffrey quickly folded the note, deciding he needed to see to its delivery before he thought about it too much. Lighting the sealing wax, he dripped a red puddle onto the space where the seams met and stamped his 'JDS' seal into the middle.

Once the wax was dry, he dispatched one of his footmen to Lord Everly's house with the note. And the footman returned forty-five minutes later, bearing a note written in a beautiful, feminine hand with the simple words, "I await your arrival, Eva."

Eva.

Jeffrey Althorpe closed his eyes for a moment after reading the simple missive.

To hell with waiting until the fashionable hour.

Eva was waiting for him.

CHAPTER 54

A PROPOSAL

Two o'clock in the afternoon
Lady Evangeline sat by herself drinking a cup of tea in the parlor of Rosemount House. Ever since she and Lord Sommers had finished reading *The Story of a Baron*, she felt at loose ends. She hadn't realized how much she had looked forward to the time she spent with the baron, even if it was to simply read a book.

Harry Tennison, Earl of Everly, had taken his leave some time ago, shortly after requesting that his carriage be brought around. Curious, Evangeline thought to ask if she might join him on his errand, intending to use the time to tell him she had accepted Lord Sommers' offer of a ride in the park. But Harry's attention was entirely on a book he had open and was apparently reading as he made his way to the vestibule. And Evangeline was quite sure the book was *The Story of a Baron*.

Sighing audibly in the hopes he might hear her, Evangeline resigned herself to another early afternoon spent alone at Rosemount House.

She was about to pour herself another cup of tea when Jones cleared his throat. "Do I have a caller?" Evangeline asked, excitement in her voice even before the butler could announce anything. She was nearly to her feet, hoping some lady of the *ton* had remembered she was sequestered in her brother's house for the Season and had taken pity on her by paying a call.

Jones held his hands together behind his back, his disapproval apparent. "Lord Sommers has asked if he might have a word," he intoned, obviously still bothered by the impropriety of a gentleman calling on an unmarried woman without a companion or chaperone present. Having already reported Lord Sommers' recent late-night appearance to the Earl of Torrington, he had decided that a visit by the baron was maybe not an unacceptable situation, but his own morals prevented him from feeling entirely comfortable with the visit.

Evangeline was sure her suddenly thundering heartbeats could be heard from across the room.

He is here.

Already.

She dared a glance at the mantel clock, surprised to see it was only two o'clock. "Well, do see him in, Jones," she responded. "He is here to see Lord Everly, I suppose," she added as she nervously smoothed her skirts. Before last week, an eligible bachelor such as Jeffrey Althorpe was not a man she would expect to have calling on her, but one could always hope. His earlier missive had been such a surprise, she had immediately written a reply. "He only asked if your ladyship was in residence and apologizes for arriving earlier than his note indicated."

The thundering heartbeats nearly deafened her to Jones' last words—until she heard the part about an apology. Perhaps the baron had changed his mind and was withdrawing his offer of a ride in the park. Or perhaps he thought they could start reading another book. "Do send him in, then. I shouldn't like to keep a baron waiting."

The butler took a breath and looked as if he was about to argue. He must have seen the flush that colored Evangeline's face, though. "Right away, my lady," he replied, turning on his heels and leaving the parlor.

Evangeline stood where she was until Lord Sommers appeared on the threshold. She struggled to withhold a gasp, for he was quite imposing, dressed for a ride in a smart, perfectly tailored scarlet jacket and buckskin breeches that hugged his muscular thighs. His black Hessians were polished to a high shine, and he held a riding crop in one black kid-gloved hand. She supposed she should have wondered why he hadn't given it to the butler when he gave up his hat, but it seemed to give him an air of superiority. A shiver shot through her when she imagined him wielding it. What awful deed might she commit that would have him threatening her with it? Her cheeks blushed a bright pink at what she was imagining.

Blinking in an effort to pull her thoughts from those better left in a bedchamber, Evangeline forced herself to concentrate on Lord Sommers' other attributes.

Bowing deeply before saying a word of greeting, Jeffrey's eyes seemed to caress her. "Lady Evangeline, please do pardon my interruption," he said, his voice almost a plea.

Evangeline, her lips slightly parted, afforded him a deep curtsy. Even before she had returned to a standing position, Jeffrey had moved into the room and reached for her hand, lifting it to his lips so that he could bestow a kiss on her bare knuckles. His lips didn't just brush over her skin as she expected they might, but rather took purchase and kissed her as he did the times he had kissed her lips. A tremor shook her body, the shock of his touch so unexpected and so pleasurable, she had to suppress another gasp. "Of course, Lord Sommers. You are most welcome at Rosemount whenever you should wish to call," she replied, keeping a small smile in place. She felt almost giddy that Jeffrey would kiss the back of her hand as he had done. Indeed, he hadn't yet let go of her hand. And, at the moment, she didn't really care if she ever took it back. As far as she was concerned, he could keep it.

Jeffrey seemed relieved to hear her response, his expression otherwise one of indecision. "My lady, I..." He glanced back at the open door, wondering if the butler hovered somewhere beyond. "I know this may seem... untoward," he stammered, "but I was wondering if we might go for a ride in the park a bit earlier than I indicated in my note? It's not the fashionable hour,

I know, but by that time this afternoon, I am rather hoping I will have completed courting you and have an affirmative response to my request for your hand in marriage. So that I might find myself on the morrow at Doctors' Commons in pursuit of a special license so that we might marry in a few days." The words came tumbling out, with no hint of embarrassment or self-doubt or regard for propriety.

Lady Evangeline gazed at Jeffrey Althorpe for a moment, blinking before a brilliant smile appeared. "You're not being the least bit untoward, Lord Sommers," she replied with a slight shake of her head. Just as he had promised, Jeffrey intended to ask for her hand! Which meant he must have spoken with her brother.

"Jeffrey," he stated, his hand moving to hold hers more tightly. "Remember, you should call me *Jeffrey*," he added, taking a step closer to her.

"And you should call me Evangeline. Or Eva, if you prefer," she countered, realizing her heart had settled into a rhythm that, although still entirely too fast, was at least quiet enough that she could hear her own words.

"Eva," Sommers breathed, his lips hovering over hers.

Evangeline closed her eyes as his lips settled onto hers, as the hand that held the riding crop moved to the back of her shoulder to pull her body closer. She took a step forward so that her entire body collided with the front of his.

Her free hand reached up to rest on his shoulder and then moved to the back of his neck as his lips opened against hers. She allowed her lips to follow suit, aware that the tip of his tongue was brushing over her teeth.

At some point, a moan or a mewl escaped her, which only encouraged Jeffrey to deepen the kiss. The hand that held hers released it and came to rest on the back of her waist, pulling her body harder against his. The hardening bulge behind the fall of his breeches pressed into her soft belly through the fabric of her gown. He rather wished there was less fabric separating them. Far less. None, in fact, but there would be more appropriate places for what he wanted to be doing with her just then.

Evangeline thrilled at the thought that she had caused his

arousal, not for a moment frightened by what could happen next. Jeffrey was going to propose!

"Eva," he whispered, his lips pulling away from hers so they could leave soft kisses along her jawline. Jeffrey wrapped one arm around Evangeline and used his free hand to keep her body pressed against his. "Eva," he whispered again, loving the sound of her shortened name. He would call her that when they shared a marriage bed, he thought. And in the breakfast parlor, when they shared their morning meal.

"Jeffrey," she whispered back, her hand sliding through the waves of his silken brown hair. She was sure she felt a shiver pass through him as his lips moved to her earlobe. In a moment, his teeth were teasing the soft flesh, sending shivers through Evangeline, much like the ones his caresses along her bare skin had caused the one night when she had asked for a kiss.

The hand behind her waist moved up and around so it rested on the side of one breast, the thumb caressing her hardening nipple. Evangeline couldn't stifle the small shriek that erupted from her throat.

Jeffrey's lips moved to cover hers, kissing her as he repeated the stroke over her nipple. "Marry me, Eva," he whispered, his lips moving to cover hers before she could reply.

Evangeline nodded against his lips. When he finally pulled away to take a breath, she said simply, "Yes." She was aware of the hand next to her breast moving to somewhere inside his coat, so that he had to pull his body away from hers for a moment. Then her left hand was held in his and a ring was sliding onto her finger.

"It's not the real one, of course," he murmured, his forehead coming to rest on hers. "But I'll have one far better by tomorrow," he promised, his whisper urgent.

Evangeline dared a glance at her left hand, stunned to see his opal signet ring wrapped around her middle finger.

"You have made me a very happy man, Eva," he whispered, his lips saying the words against hers.

"And you have made me a very happy woman, Jeffrey," she replied with a sigh. "Perhaps... perhaps we could just skip the ride and continue what we're doing instead?" she suggested, her words coming out in little breaths. Had she taken a moment to consider what she had just said, she might have been shocked at how much like Geraldine she was behaving at this very moment. She might even have begged forgiveness for her impropriety. But the look on Jeffrey's face indicated he would be most disappointed if she did such a thing.

"As my lady wishes," he replied with an enthusiastic nod. "Although, I do believe I need to sit down. You have left me quite unable to stand of my own volition."

Eva giggled, leading him to a large wing chair. Even as he sat down, he pulled her atop him, settling her so her bottom rested on one of his thighs and her head settled against his shoulder. "My brother said nothing," she whispered, irate that Everly didn't share the good news of her impending betrothal to Lord Sommers before he left the house.

Jeffrey let out a snort. "That's because I haven't yet asked his permission to court you," he replied, his arms wrapping around her body so his hands were clasped together as they rested on her hip.

"Oh?" Evangeline replied quietly, wondering if she should be disappointed that he hadn't followed protocol. "I do not think he'll object," she murmured, reaching out with her lips to kiss his jaw.

"He had better not, or the Earl of Torrington will have his hide," Jeffrey stated, his own lips moving to cover hers for a quick kiss.

Evangeline straightened on his lap, eliciting an inhalation of breath from Jeffrey as her hip pressed harder against his manhood. "What does my godfather have to do with this?" she asked, her brows furrowing together.

Jeffrey had to suppress a chuckle. "Your brother may be blind to love, my lady, but Torrington is not. He's a rather convincing matchmaker when he puts his mind to it."

Evangeline regarded Jeffrey for a moment. "You didn't ask for my hand because he *ordered* you to do so, did you?" she asked, suddenly doubtful of the baron's intentions.

Jeffrey tilted his head to one side. "No, of course not," he replied carefully. "Although, I will admit I am asking a bit sooner than I expected to be allowed to, only because he said he would see to your brother on my behalf."

His future baroness seemed satisfied with his answer, for she settled her head back onto his shoulder. "Would it be all right if we had a small, quiet wedding?" she whispered, her lashes resting on the tops of her cheekbones as if she might take a nap in a moment or two. Despite the excitement of the proposal, there was something rather restful about being held in the arms of her betrothed.

A chuckled erupted from Jeffrey just then. "I would prefer it, but I want you to have the wedding of your dreams," he murmured sleepily.

"Mmm," she purred, her eyes still closed.

Jeffrey gave a sigh of his own as he closed his eyes and concentrated on the scent of honeysuckle that wafted around her honey blonde bun and ringlets.

Not only had Lady Evangeline given him the kind of response he could only fantasize about and write in a book, she had been everything Jeffrey had hoped for in the woman he would one day marry. A day that was just a few days hence.

Instead of following the Earl of Torrington's instructions, he had managed to accomplish an entire afternoon of courting in just a few moments. Of course, most of the courting had happened the week before as they read the book.

And an even greater miracle was that, despite the fact that the butler hovered just outside the parlor door, the man never once interrupted them to take issue with him over the impropriety of how he held her or how she was positioned rather suggestively against most of his body. He was just deciding he was going to enjoy being leg-shackled when the sound of a carriage caused Evangeline to give a start and open her eyes.

"Good afternoon, my beautiful," Jeffrey whispered with a teasing grin.

There was a moment when Evangeline thought she had simply moved from one dream to the next, for to open her eyes and be in the arms of a man as handsome as Jeffrey Althorpe wasn't something she thought to do again—especially after the one night in the parlor. But the light press of his lips against her forehead brought her back to reality and she smiled. "Are you quite sure you can abide a wife who would fall asleep in the arms of her intended?" she whispered, her furrowed brows suggesting she was quite serious.

Jeffrey grinned. "Absolutely," he replied with a nod. He kissed her then, most thoroughly, just as the sound of the front door closing reached his ears.

Evangeline was quite sure she had never moved so quickly in her life, especially when it wasn't of her own doing. For one moment she was nestled against the front of her betrothed, and the next she was sitting quite primly on the settee and Jeffrey was back in the wing chair with a cup of tea covering the bulge in his crotch, regarding her as if none of the previous thirty minutes had happened.

Her brother's entrance into the parlor might have been a bit on the violent side, he no doubt having been briefed by Jones regarding the presence of Jeffrey. But when Harry found his sister regarding him with an arched eyebrow and Jeffrey quite properly seated across from her, he relaxed. "Is it... is it done then?" he asked, his attention going back and forth between the two.

Jeffrey Althorpe stood and gave Evangeline's brother a nod, wondering if Lord Torrington had just spoken to the man. "I have asked for your sister's hand, and she has accepted," he replied with another nod. "And, as Lady Evangeline would prefer a small ceremony, I will see to a special license so that we might marry—"

"Did you ruin her?" the earl interrupted, his attention darting from Evangeline to the baron. "It seems my sister is the current *on-dit,* and not for her propensity to read too much."

"Harry!" Evangeline cried out in surprise, her fists clenching at her sides. "How dare you?"

Jeffrey held his hand out in front of Evangeline, as if he meant to protect her from her brother. "I admit, I kissed her," he countered, his chin raised in defiance. Jeffrey gave Evangeline a passing glance and turned his attention back to Lord Everly. "I kissed her. Several times," he stated proudly. "And I'll kiss her whenever she wants me to, I'll have you know."

Evangeline gave a huff. "*I'm* the one that asked to be kissed!" she argued, turning to her brother to poke a finger into his chest. "And I am *not* ruined," she added before turning to Jeffrey to poke the same finger into his chest, just then remembering what he had said about when he would kiss her. "And I'll kiss you whenever you want me to," she continued, her voice lowering to a whisper.

Jeffrey's eyes darted to Harry before he said, "Agreed."

Harry Tennison regarded the two people who stood before him. "So, when's the wedding?" he asked.

"Next week," the two replied simultaneously. They both blinked and turned to regard one another. "That would be lovely," Evangeline whispered, giving her husband-to-be a tentative smile and a nod.

"Ah, something we can all agree on, I see," Lord Everly said with a much larger smile. "If you are in need of her services, Lady Torrington has offered her help in arranging the nuptials." The earl shrugged and gave the two each a nod. "What a relief. I was in fear I might have to arrange for Evangeline to move to a nunnery."

Evangeline inhaled. "You wouldn't dare!" she cried, her protest drowning out Jeffrey's sound of disbelief.

Her brother shrugged and then grinned. "That was my favorite part of the book," he whispered in Jeffrey's direction, his comment eliciting a pair of dropped jaws and expressions of disbelief. "Instead, I can get on with arranging my next trip. I was beginning to think I'd be stuck in England looking for someone to marry my sister."

Before either Evangeline or his future brother-in-law could respond, he added, "If you need me for anything, sister, I shall be at the Royal Society." He turned his attention to Jeffrey. "And I shall see you later at White's."

Jeffrey shook his head. "Now see here, Everly. You owe me an explanation." At the earl's look of confusion, he added, "You've been avoiding me ever since your return to London."

Harry frowned but finally allowed a nod. "I have, I admit," he agreed, reaching into his waistcoat pocket. "I still owe you money from our last bet, but I didn't have any English currency when I arrived back in town." He pulled out a guinea and tossed it to the baron. "Had to visit the bank this morning."

Frowning, Jeffrey regarded the guinea before turning his attention to his future brother-in-law. "You were avoiding me over… over *money?*" he asked in disbelief.

The earl allowed a shrug. "You've done the same with me," he countered. He gave a shrug and then said, "Good day to you both." Then he took his leave of Rosemount House.

Jeffrey turned slowly toward Evangeline, his look of astonishment slowly changing to a smile. "That went well," he said, reaching out to wrap his arms around her shoulders. He pulled her against the front of his body and kissed her on the forehead.

"When do you suppose he had time to read the book?" she asked.

"Probably stayed up all night," Jeffrey murmured. "I wish I'd had some way to learn more about you *before* I wrote the book," he whispered into her hair. "But given the circumstances, I am not sure how I could have managed it."

Sighing in reply, Evangeline allowed a wan smile. "You could have asked me to read a book with you," she suggested with mischief.

Jeffrey smiled. He never would have thought to use that tactic. "As opposed to asking you to join me on a ride in the park?" he countered.

Evangeline's eyes widened. "I think not. My skirts would be covered in grass stains," she accused, one eyebrow dancing.

"You minx!" he cried out in mock horror. "If only I'd known, I could have simply ruined you, and we could have avoided reading the book!"

Evangeline started to giggle, but the sound of a throat clearing brought them both back to standing on their own accord, their attention on the door to the parlor.

Jones stood in the hall, his dour face suggesting he was none too pleased to pay witness to their hug.

"I must take my leave of you," Jeffrey announced loudly enough for the butler to hear. "But I shall return to take you for a ride in the park as promised. Good day, my lovely fiancée." He bowed over her hand and planted a rather indecorous kiss on her knuckles as Evangeline gave him a curtsy.

"And to you, my love."

Jeffrey took his leave of Rosemount House, a happy man. And Evangeline watched him go, thinking if there was to be a wedding the following week, she had best get started with some planning.

CHAPTER 55
POST PROPOSAL

Four o'clock in the afternoon

As promised, Jeffrey returned later that afternoon to take Evangeline for a ride in the park. When he saw his way to the parlor, he found his betrothed regarding the settee, one of her hands skimming over the top of the carved wood frame whilst her face took on a look of sadness. When she realized he stood on the threshold, however, a brilliant smile appeared. "Jeffrey!" she said as she hurried to him.

The baron met her halfway, wrapping his arms around her and kissing her head. "You act as if you didn't expect me to return," he accused with a grin. When he pulled away, he noted her melancholy. "What is wrong?"

Evangeline angled her head, giving it a shake as she considered how to respond. "I was just saying good-bye, I suppose," she murmured, one hand waving at the furnishings.

Jeffrey remembered Evangeline's comments about her mother's things, about what the next Countess of Everly might do with them once she was mistress of the house. "I would be most obliged if you would bring along any household items your brother will allow to Sommers Place," he said in a soft voice.

Evangeline's eyes widened in surprise. "Do you really want me to?" she asked, remembering her comments about the worn furnishings whilst they read in the parlor.

Jeffrey nodded. "I believe Sommers Place could do with more charm, my lady. And I want you to be surrounded by all the things that are important to you."

Even before he finished speaking, Evangeline wrapped her arms around his shoulders and kissed him on the cheek. "Thank you," she said, about to give up her hold on him but finding his arms were locked around her waist. She left her arms where they were, angling her head as she regarded him.

Holding her tightly, Jeffrey closed his eyes when he saw hers were bright with unshed tears. "You really are satisfied with the simplest things, aren't you?" he whispered on a sigh. When he finally opened his eyes, he found Evangeline's cheek resting on his shoulder.

"Would you have me any other way?" Evangeline replied as she smiled, a blush of pink coloring her face.

Jeffrey took a deep breath and lifted a hand to cup her cheek. "As a matter of fact, yes, I would," he said with a firm nod. When Evangeline's eyebrows arched up, he added, "But I admit to a special fondness for this one."

He barely had the words out before Evangeline's lips were pressed against his. He had to suppress the sudden urge to chuckle at her response, and then his manner sobered as he opened his mouth and allowed her to deepen the kiss, allowed her tongue to explore his mouth and tangle with his own tongue, allowed a moan to escape when he thought for a moment she was about to end the kiss. Pulling her harder against the front of his body and turning her so her back was to the door, he was the one who finally had to end the kiss, if for no other reason than he was aware they weren't alone.

The sound of a throat being cleared had Evangeline's eyes opening wide. With her back to the door, she had no idea who was witnessing her tête-à-tête with the baron. She was about to jerk away from Jeffrey to find out, but his hold on her had tightened, his hand moving from her cheek to around her shoulder in a protective hold.

"I admit to a great deal of relief in learning first-hand you're marrying my sister because you feel affection for her and not because you're in need of her dowry," Harry Tennison stated as he leaned a shoulder against the parlor door jamb. He held the bowl of a pipe in one hand as the other rested on his hip. "Or because Torrington told you to."

Jeffrey considered the earl's words before finally giving the man a nod. "Had you been in London these past two weeks or allowed me the opportunity to ask permission, I could have assured you first-hand, and Torrington wouldn't have felt it necessary to be involved at all," he countered, his manner most serious.

The Earl of Everly nodded. "Touché," he replied. He took a puff from the pipe and straightened, his manner suggesting he was bored. "As for household items, Eva..." At the mention of her name, Evangeline finally looked over her shoulder at her brother. "You're free to take anything you wish. Except for the fish and books, of course," he said. "I expect whoever has the unenviable task of being my wife will want to replace almost everything anyway." This last was said with sadness, as if the earl didn't expect to marry someone who felt affection for him—or have an appreciation for Rosemount's older furnishings and accessories.

"Oh, but she won't," Evangeline said with a shake of her head. Still in her fiancé's arms, she turned her body to better face her brother. "She'll be delighted to live here when she's not gallivanting all around the earth with you," she added, thinking Lady Samantha would welcome the opportunity to travel, even if it meant living out-of-doors or without the comforts found in a typical house.

One of Harry's eyebrows arched at his sister's claim. "From your words, it's apparent you already know who she is," he said in bewilderment.

Evangeline allowed a smile. "Well, I think I know who it should be," she replied with a coy smile. She turned her attention to Jeffrey, who sported a look of confusion. "She'll make a delightful sister," she added, as if that would clear up any confusion.

At the sound of her brother's sputtering, either because the pipe had grown too hot to hold or because he was surprised to hear there was a willing candidate to be his wife, Evangeline winked at her husband-to-be. "He is a smart man. I should think he will figure it out in due time." With that, she took hold of Jeffrey's hands and led him out of the parlor.

"Where are we off to?" Jeffrey asked, giving the earl a shrug as he passed him.

Evangeline smiled. "You asked me for a ride in the park. It's nearly the fashionable hour," she replied happily.

Jeffrey chuckled as he checked his chronometer. "Indeed, my lady." With that, they took their leave of Rosemount House for their ride.

*L*ater that night at White's, when he sat at a card table with Lord Barrings, Sir Richard, and Lord Everly, Jeffrey Althorpe couldn't help but notice the Earl of Torrington sitting in a wingback chair nearby. In a voice he intended the Earl of Torrington to overhear, Jeffrey mentioned having had a rather memorable thirtieth birthday. "I have asked for the hand of a woman I have wanted to marry for some time, and she has agreed to be my wife," he said proudly.

Two of the other gentlemen regarded him with looks of surprise. "You? *Married?*" Lord Barrings replied, his astonishment apparent in the way his eyebrows lifted.

"You make it sound as if you *want* to be leg-shackled," Sir Richard stated, his own bushy eyebrows raised in astonishment.

"Who's the unlucky chit?" Lord Barrings asked.

"Pray tell," Sir Richard encouraged.

Jeffrey sighed and shook his head. "Her identity, gentlemen, is—"

"My sister, Lady Evangeline," Harry interrupted. "Gave my blessing this afternoon."

Lording Barrings and Sir Richard both blinked. "The *on-dit* was true?" Sir Richard asked. "I didn't believe it."

"Nor I," Barrings agreed. "If I had, I would have placed a bet."

"I did," Harry said proudly. "Made back the guinea I lost to him—" he pointed to Jeffrey—"When I said Torrington's countess wouldn't be giving him an heir."

Jeffrey frowned. "I'm quite sure I don't know what you're talking about," he replied, well aware Torrington could hear every word they said. He threw in his cards. "I'm reminded I need to purchase a bauble in Ludgate Hill," he said to the surprised men at the table. With that, he left to pay a visit to Stedman and Vardon.

Still seated in the wingback chair nearby, the Earl of Torrington smiled.

CHAPTER 56

A BROTHER'S FAREWELL

Five days later

Jeffrey Althorpe regarded his new brother-in-law with a curious expression. "I was surprised when you told the sharps at White's that it was Evangeline who I was to marry," he said, keeping his voice low amid the crowd of guests enjoying the wedding breakfast. The festively decorated backyard of Sommers Place was filled with a dozen tables surrounded by chairs filled with merry makers. Far more had been at St. George's that morning, the spectacle of a *ton* wedding too promising to miss, especially one so quickly planned.

Harry gave a careless shrug. "It would have been far better for the news to come from Torrington," he replied, giving a curt nod in the direction of Lord and Lady Torrington as they passed by, arm-in-arm. "He's been an especially attentive godfather to my sister," he remarked.

"But, Eva's your sister. Shouldn't the announcement have been made by you?" Jeffrey asked. Just because the earl preferred spending his time in pursuit of flora and fauna far from England's shores didn't give him the right to shun his responsibilities as a brother.

"Even better that it come from you, Sommers," Harry said quietly. "It's your story, after all," he added before giving the baron a nod. "Or should I say, the story of Anonymous?" Everly paused a moment. "Take good care of her, Sommers, or you'll have to answer to Torrington," he warned with a teasing grin. Giving the baron a nod, the Earl of Everly took his leave of the festivities.

Jeffrey Althorpe watched as the earl made his way to the front of the house and disappeared, chagrined that Harry knew he had written the book.

Before Jeffrey had a chance to rejoin the growing crowd around the breakfast tables, Evangeline moved to wrap her arm around his. "You look as if you've seen a ghost," she murmured, her eyes bright with amusement. "Or my brother. He just gave me his farewell," she added, her manner becoming more sober.

"Me, too," Jeffrey replied with a nod. He leaned over and kissed her temple, secretly glad her hat's brim was so small. "He knows I wrote the book. How do you suppose he sorted it?" he asked in a quiet voice.

Evangeline dipped her head. "He didn't. I told him," she admitted. "He said he has the perfect title for your next book."

Jeffrey blinked. "Oh?"

His wife grinned. "'The Story of an Earl'," she said with delight.

CHAPTER 57

WEDDING DAY WONDERS

*L*ater *that afternoon*

"I was beginning to think they would never leave," Jeffrey murmured as he took Evangeline's hand and pulled her into his arms, a rather bold thing to do even if he was in his own home. Evangeline returned the hug, tempted to leave her head resting on his shoulder. Despite the clock having just chimed three, she felt as if she'd been up since dawn.

The wedding breakfast had been more a luncheon; by the time most of the wedding guests had made the trip from St. George's to Sommers Place, it was past noon.

The servants had outdone themselves, having seen to the arrangement of several long tables and trestles on the back lawn, their white linen coverings the perfect backdrop for the colorful hot house flowers that decorated them. Although Sommers Place could boast dinner settings to serve fifty guests, the day's festivities required another twenty sets be brought over from Rosemount House. Crystal stemware and silver flatware reflected the brilliant rays of the sun, a welcome sight considering rain had been predicted by nearly everyone in attendance. And rightly so—after their guests enjoyed a leisurely breakfast of ham, eggs, kippers, rolls and toast, chocolate and a generous serving of the sugar-frosted wedding fruit cake and what seemed an endless supply of champagne, the clouds moved overhead and soon the heavens opened up. At the sight of the dark clouds, most guests took their leave. The rest departed under the protection of umbrellas and parasols, hurrying to their coaches with cries of congratulations and best wishes.

But before Ladies Julia and Samantha took their leave with Lord and Lady Chamberlain, Evangeline pulled them aside and slipped them each a sliver of the wedding cake wrapped in a napkin. "You know what to do," she whispered with a grin.

Julia shook her head. "Something about sleeping with it under a pillow and dreaming of the man you'll marry?" she asked, not yet having had the opportunity to actually put the superstition into practice.

Samantha took the linen package in her gloved hands and gave a slight shake of her head. "I'll put it under my pillow, of course, but I rather doubt I shall dream of a groom-to-be," she replied in a quiet voice. "The only gentleman I ever seem to have visions of whilst I sleep is your brother," she added with a roll of her eyes, as if dreaming of the earl was somehow an annoyance.

Evangeline allowed a slow grin to form. "I could not ask for a finer sister," she said.

Until her dying day, Evangeline would never forget the look on Samantha's face as the girl considered her words. "Oh," she breathed, as if she had never considered Harry Tennison anything more than her best friend's brother. And then, arm-in-arm with Julia, Samantha had followed her aunt and uncle to their ancient town coach, the expression on her face one of amusement.

When Evangeline surveyed the grand hall, she saw that everyone but the servants and her husband had left the house. "Rain certainly has a way of driving people to their homes," she remarked, a mischievous smile appearing as she regarded her new husband.

A parade of maids appeared from the backyard carrying urns and vases filled with the flowers that had decorated the tables. Each took them to a different room, distributing the fresh flowers so that Sommers Place was soon filled with their floral scents. Evangeline took a deep breath and closed her eyes.

Before she opened them, Jeffrey moved to kiss her lips. "I could not help myself," he whispered when Evangeline opened her eyes.

"I wouldn't want you to." She lowered her head. "I know it is early, but..." She sighed and angled her head. "Do you suppose we might—?"

"Go to bed?" he finished for her, his words sounding breathless. They would be leaving on their wedding trip to Devonshire in the morning, opting to remain at Sommers Place until then.

Evangeline nodded. "I don't wish to seem... wanton, but..." She took a breath, her heart pounding so hard she was sure Jeffery could hear it.

"Oh, you can seem wanton whenever you wish," Jeffrey replied "Well, except if I'm not in the room, and then you cannot," he stated, deciding to make the rule quite clear right then and there.

"I cannot imagine feeling wanton if you are not present," Evangeline countered. "Unless, of course, you're here and then suddenly you've taken your leave of me to go to White's or somewhere else—"

"I shan't," he replied. "Especially right now," he added as he took her hand and led her up the steps to his bedchamber. "I know this is probably not how you imagined your wedding night," he said as he pulled her into his room and shut the door behind them, turning the key in the lock. His lips found hers, fitting over her mouth until they seemed to lock into place, the resulting kiss as much a continuation of what they had started below as part of the promise they had made to each other during the wedding ceremony only hours earlier.

"Oh, it's very close," Evangeline managed to get out before his lips captured hers again. Her back was to the door, his lips were traveling across her jaw and down her neck and into the hollow of her throat. "Except I didn't imagine we'd get up the stairs," she whispered, her breaths coming in short gasps.

Jeffrey paused in his ministrations, briefly lifting his head to regard her for a moment. "Where, then?" he asked, before revisiting her throat. Once he'd drawn the tip of his tongue across the hollow and felt her steady pulse, he moved his lips along the edge of her bodice.

Evangeline's hands finally landed on either side of Jeffrey's head, her fingers raking through his dark silken hair. "I thought maybe you'd take me in the library," she whispered, a gasp ending her comment as Jeffrey's teeth nipped at one of her swollen breasts.

"Library?" he repeated, one hand moving to pull down a sleeve of her shoulder.

"Mmm. It seemed appropriate," she murmured, her own lips finally taking purchase on the top of his head, her fingernails barely scraping his scalp so that he jerked and lifted his lips from the top of her breasts.

"Tomorrow," he whispered. "Before we leave," he murmured, finally freeing one of her breasts from the confines of her stays before quickly suckling it. "It will take us some time to work through the upper rooms," he said before freeing her other breast and seeing to it the nipple was thoroughly teased and kissed and suckled.

Evangeline couldn't bite back the giggle at hearing his words. "You intend us to make love in every room of the house?" she asked between gasps. She reached down between them, sliding her hand down his front until it covered the bulge behind the placket of his satin breeches.

His breath hitched and he let go of her nipple. "Yes," he said, sounding rather clear-headed. "No," he added. "Not the cellar. I shouldn't want you on the dirt floor," he whispered before turning his attention back to her breasts.

"Oh," Evangeline answered, not sure she was capable of saying anything else. But why would he think *she* would be the one on the floor of the cellar?

"You could be the one on the floor whilst I ride atop you," she whispered, not quite sure why she encouraged lovemaking in the cellar, of all places.

Reluctantly, Jeffrey pulled away so that he could look her in the eyes. "Eva!" he admonished her. "Riding St. George? I thought you were a virgin!" he gasped, the glaze over his eyes clearing for a moment.

Evangeline stared back at him, stunned by his accusation. "I am," she responded, but she took the opportunity to cup his arousal a bit harder.

Jeffrey jerked and pulled away. "You minx," he accused as he seemed to come up for air. "You've read every book on sexual congress in your brother's library, haven't you?" he accused in a hoarse whisper, his voice so husky he barely recognized it as his own.

Her eyes widening until she could appear as demure as possible, Evangeline gave a slight shrug. "Maybe."

His eyes forming slits in an attempt to seem predatory, Jeffrey lowered his head and returned his lips to her breasts.

Despite having read every book about sexual intercourse in her brother's library, and having studied the illustrations in those not written in English or French, she was discovering they all lacked the language to describe the sensations that gripped her body just then. She was reminded of the dream she'd had the night they'd been reading in the parlor, when she'd asked Jeffrey to kiss her.

She had dreamt of placing her hand over the back of his, of bringing it up to her breast, of helping him in taking down the sleeve of her gown so that he could more freely kiss her collar bone, the curve of her shoulder, the slight swell of her breast. The dream had been so vivid, she had imagined him kissing her nipple, drawing the pearled bud into his mouth as his lips took possession of her. Her entire body had shivered then, pleasant tingles darting from her breast to her very core. An intense sensation had her stilling, her nerve endings strung so tight she thought they might snap and leave her void of feeling.

But something Jeffrey had done with his lips and tongue had released that tension. And that release had been the most amazing sensation she had ever experienced. So it was no wonder she had opened her eyes, suddenly so awake and so alive, she thought she might never sleep again. The sight of Jeffrey, eyes glazed over as if he, too, had been sleeping, brought her back to the parlor and to the sounds of the butler snoring somewhere nearby.

The very same sensations she had felt that night were

assaulting her again, only now, in the privacy of Jeffrey's bedchamber, she felt comfortable enough to allow her breaths to sound out as gasps. "Jeffrey," she whispered, a shiver darting through her breast. "Please undo the buttons," she whispered, turning her body around.

Jeffrey's lips had to let go of his prey, although one hand cupped the breast as she turned in his arms. He had to give up his hold on her to unbutton the gown, though. "I suppose I should have allowed you a few moments with your lady's maid," he whispered hoarsely, suppressing the urge to curse the fastenings. His fingers wanted to be doing other things—naughty things—and so they didn't seem to work as well as they should. When he finally had enough buttons undone so that her gown slipped off her shoulders, Evangeline turned in his arms.

Jeffrey shook his head and pulled her gown down until it fell past her hips and ended in a puddle of satin and tulle at her feet. He motioned with his finger for her to turn back around. "As much as I love looking at you in just—" he motioned down the front of her to indicate her chemise, corset and stockings "—these, I do believe you'll be more comfortable out of them."

Evangeline giggled, reaching for the knot of his cravat. "And you will be more comfortable out of everything you're wearing," she countered, flipping the undone ends of his cravat around his neck until it was completely unwound. Her fingers moved to the buttons of his waistcoat, deftly undoing each until she could push the offending garment off his shoulders and toss it onto a nearby chair.

"My valet will be furious with me," he whispered, his hands sliding along her silk-covered arms until he reached the little bow that held the chemise closed between her breasts. Tugging, he released the tie and then slid his hands around her waist and felt for the tie of her stays.

"I'll beg his forgiveness," Evangeline whispered, her hands moving to pull his shirt from his breeches. Once it was free, she pulled it up, forcing him to give up his attempt at undoing her stays.

Behind the curtain of white lawn that briefly covered his face, Jeffrey gazed at the woman he had just taken as a wife.

With her hair still up in its pins and her lips swollen from his kisses, she looked every bit the proper English miss ruined, or a randy mistress in a hurry for a tumble. That is, except for the gleam in her eyes. "Are you enjoying this?" he asked, his voice husky.

Evangeline stilled her movements, which left his shirt only half off of his head and shoulders. "I am," she admitted, her head lifting up as if to emphasize her answer. She finished pulling off the shirt and then tossed it in the direction of the chair. The billowing fabric had it completely missing its mark. "Oops," she whispered.

A shiver of excitement coursed through Jeffrey. He hadn't considered his wife might find the time they spent in a bedchamber as enjoyable as he knew he would. "I'm going to like being married to you, aren't I?" he said, jerking when he discovered Evangeline's attentions were now on the buttons of his breeches. Her nimble fingers were undoing each one in turn until she had the palm of her hand pressed against his hardened cock.

"I should hope so," she replied with widened eyes.

"I love you," he said as he quickly moved to the chair and sat down to remove his boots and stockings.

Still leaning against the door, Evangeline took a deep breath and nodded. Letting it out in a long sigh, she said, "I know, and I love you, too," she said as she pulled down the stays, shimmying her hips until the offending garment was past her thighs and could join the puddle of fabric below.

"Oh," Jeffrey complained. "I was going to do that," he said as he rejoined her at the door, stepping out of the breeches and tossing them so they joined the shirt. His manhood was so engorged, it poked nearly straight out from his smalls.

"You can do it tomorrow night," Evangeline promised, arching her back when his hands moved to claim her breasts through the silk of her chemise.

"Promise?" he responded, his lips moving to capture one of her nipples.

Evangeline had to steady herself by placing her hands on either side of his head. "My lady's maid will not mind," she whispered, her eyes closing as the now-familiar sensations returned to her breasts, to her very core. The heat between her thighs had become nearly unbearable, the moistness at the top of her thighs so hot she thought she might be burned. Slipping her hands beneath the edge of his smalls, she slid them down until they could go no further, his manhood preventing their descent.

"Just... tug," he murmured as he moved his attention to her other nipple.

Evangeline had to suppress a smile as she did as she was told. Freed from their mooring, the smalls fell to the floor. Free from the confines of the smalls, his manhood was suddenly pressed into her soft belly. Jeffrey straightened, flattening his body against the front of hers as he gathered up the hem of her chemise and slowly worked it up her body. His hands, warm and firm against her skin, pushed the garment up and over her head. Once it was free of her body, it joined the rest of the puddle of fabric below.

Jeffrey took a quick glance at her as she leaned against the door. Clad only in her stockings and slippers, and with one leg slightly bent, she looked positively erotic. She was everything he imagined and more since that night he had nearly ruined her in the Rosemount House parlor.

One of his hands skimmed over her silken skin, rosy from his ministrations and warmer than should be possible. Although not nearly as well-endowed as the mistress he had briefly employed years ago, Evangeline's breasts were firm and slightly mounded, their ruched nipples perfectly placed. They wouldn't slide to her sides when he was atop her, a thought that had him wanting her on her back right then.

As Jeffrey seemed to drink in the sight of her nakedness, Evangeline did the same of him, her gaze moving from the lean muscles of his arms to the light dusting of hair on his chest, to the line of crisp curls that led down to where his manhood pressed into her. One of her hands slid down from his silken hair to his neck and over the long line of his shoulder and down his chest, her fingertips barely brushing over the nipple there.

She moved her hand across the front of his chest to the

other one, one finger circling the bud. At his slight inhalation of breath, Evangeline lowered her face so that she could reach it with the tip of her tongue. She grinned at Jeffrey's sudden jerk and gasp until he lowered his head to do the same to her nipple.

In only a moment, it seemed as if he had her entire breast in his mouth, his tongue doing delicious things to her nipple and skin. A wave of pleasure coursed through her, and she was cast adrift, no longer anchored to the floor. Unable to hold herself up, Evangeline started to slide down the door. She had a passing thought that she might faint, but the next thought, that she would miss out on whatever came next if she did, slowed her breathing.

Jeffrey pulled his attention away from her breast and lifted her into his arms. "I believe we'll be more comfortable on the bed," he murmured, secretly glad the housekeeper had seen to turning down the dark velvet counterpane that usually covered it.

The servants probably hadn't thought the newly wed couple would retire so soon, but he couldn't imagine having to wait until nightfall to claim his wife. He—and his body—had been pining for her since that day they had started reading his damned book.

"You forgot to carry me over the threshold," Evangeline managed to say, although she didn't know from where the thought had come. She wrapped her arms around his shoulders and kissed his neck, his collarbone, the top of his arm.

"This, my love, is the threshold," he said as he placed her as near to the middle of the bed as he could given the height of the mattress. The bed linens, cool and smooth, enveloped him as he joined her on the downy bed. He slid his body alongside hers until he could reach her earlobes with his lips.

"Oh," Evangeline sighed. "Is the bed in the mistress suite as comfortable as this one?" she asked, trying not to stare too much at Jeffrey's naked body next to hers.

Jeffrey stilled his kisses. "You'll only find out if I'm there with you," he warned.

Evangeline gave him a smile as she reached down and wrapped one hand around his manhood. Reveling at how he jerked and moaned in response, she began sliding her hand up and down the silken shaft, her thumb occasionally brushing over the top before sliding back down to where his balls rested against his thighs.

"For one who has only read books, you're rather good at this," Jeffrey murmured in appreciation.

"I did wonder if I was doing this right," Evangeline whispered, her hold on him tightening.

Groaning his pleasure, Jeffrey thought she might bring him to completion, much as she had that night in the parlor, except he hadn't expected her ministrations then and had been unprepared. Tonight, he was determined to wait until he was deep inside her before releasing his seed.

As one of his hands slid down her body and moved to part her thighs, he lifted himself so he was nearly atop her. The hot wetness against his hand made him pause and stare down at her. "I love you," he said before moving his body between her spreading legs. "I don't want to hurt you, but I hear—"

"Ssh!" Evangeline managed as she lifted her thighs and pressed them against the side of his hips. Reaching down with one hand, she found the tip of his manhood and positioned it near her opening, not exactly sure of what she was doing.

"Jesus, Eva," he moaned as he found her silken opening and slid in. He paused a moment, his eyes opening to find hers, aware that her hands had taken purchase on the sides of his body and had moved down until they were firmly pressed into his buttocks, pulling him into her. If she felt any pain, he didn't see it in her eyes as he watched her until he had to close his own. Her tight sheath, warm and wet and pulsing as he began to pull out of her, gripped him. He had to slow his movements even as Evangeline tried to pull him back into her, a quiet whimper making him stop.

"Don't stop," she whispered, pulling hard on him.

He gave into her plea, thrusting deep into her so that she inhaled sharply, her entire torso rising from the bed as her head sunk deeper into the pillow. One of her breasts was instantly within reach of his mouth, so Jeffrey lowered his lips to its nipple, kissing it and suckling it until he felt a shiver pass through her body. He slowly pulled himself out, nearly to her opening, and then he thrust in again, his own moan nearly drowning the sound of her gasp. When she said his name in a whisper, he thrust one more time and allowed his own release. Burying his head into her shoulder, his groan of pleasure filled the bedchamber.

His strength drained, his settled onto her body as he felt her arms wrap around his shoulders.

"I... I couldn't..." Had he really just taken his own pleasure before seeing to hers? he thought in disgust.

Evangeline placed a finger against his lips. "Shh," she whispered with a shake of her head.

Jeffrey relaxed as sleep took hold, his entire body satiated and warm and comfortable.

Smiling in the growing darkness of the room, Evangeline held her husband against the top of her body. Had the mattress not been as soft as this one was, she might have felt squished or trapped by him. But the comfortable cloud enveloped her, keeping her warm everywhere Jeffrey's body didn't cover her. She slowly allowed her legs to slide down the sides of his legs. She thought she could still feel his manhood inside of her, but soon, it slipped out, leaving her feeling bereft.

As she lay staring up at the coffered ceiling, the last thing she noticed before falling asleep were the cobwebs strung across the coffers.

CHAPTER 58
THE FINALE

L *ater that night*
"Did my brother see to getting you my dowry?" Evangeline asked when she knew Jeffrey was awake. He had rolled onto his back, but his arms had wrapped around her shoulders so that part of her body ended up atop his. "He has already departed for Wapping," she added, disappointed the earl would take his leave of London so soon after arriving. At least this trip to the island of Minorca would be short. Harry mentioned wanting to study some monolithic stone structures and collect butterflies, a task he thought might take a month.

Jeffrey nodded. "He did," he replied carefully. "Although he didn't have to, I hope you know."

Evangeline lifted her head from his shoulder, intrigued by his words. "So... you are not as broke as Lord Ballantine?" she ventured, hoping she hadn't offended her groom with talk of her dowry.

Shaking his head from side to side, Jeffrey grinned. "My coffers will no longer be as empty as Matthew's," he said with a hint of pride. "Seems *The Story of a Baron* is selling quite well. My publisher has even asked for a second book, which I have yet to start writing," he added with a sigh.

Evangeline's eyes widened. "That's... that's wonderful," she said. "Will you? Write the book, I mean?" she asked before planting a kiss on his cheek.

Jeffrey shrugged. "What would I write next?" he mused, not at all sure he was interested in pursuing the craft of writing. His success with his first book might be a fluke; what if his second proved a total failure? He thought he should just quit while he was ahead.

"*The Story of an Earl,*" his new wife reminded him. "Lord Afterly returns from his latest trip to court Lady Geraldine's best friend."

Frowning, Jeffrey wondered to whom she referred. "But, Geraldine doesn't have a best friend, other than Daisy," he said with a roll of his eyes. "And she is already married to Lord Brotherly, the viscount," he added, hoping he had the details right. He might have written the story and even read it just the week before, but for some reason, certain details didn't come easily to him.

Evangeline shrugged. "You'll have to create her, of course," she responded. "Brown-hair, blue-eyes, orphaned at a young age and being raised by her aunt and uncle. Her uncle is an earl, of course," she told him, one hand in the air as if she were drawing the character for him to envision.

Jeffrey regarded his wife for a moment. "That sounds an awful lot like Lady Samantha," he murmured, wondering if Evangeline was merely teasing him.

"Exactly!" she replied with a nod. "And she's secretly been in the love with Earl Afterly, but he has no clue about her feelings for him," she went on, as if he hadn't interrupted her.

"Does the earl have feelings for this Lady... *Lady Georgina?*" he guessed, thinking up the name that would have been bestowed on a baby expected to be a male heir.

Evangeline's eyes widened. "Oh, of course. But he doesn't know it yet," she replied.

Jeffrey frowned. "He doesn't?"

"No. They never do."

Jeffrey's brows furrowed so that a fold of skin appeared between them. "Well. How am I supposed to get the earl to fall in love with Lady Georgina?" he demanded, his face showing concern. At the rate they were going and with some plot points and a bit of conflict, he could have an entire book written in a month's time!

Evangeline stared at him for a moment. "Well, I don't know," she replied with a shake of her head. "You're the writer. I'm sure you can invent something that will make the earl fall heels over head in love with her," she said with a wave of her hand. "You did with me, didn't you?" She regarded him as he lay with his head deep in the feather pillow. "In fact, why *did* you fall in love with me?" she asked, lifting herself up from his shoulder with her elbow.

Jeffrey stared at his wife for a moment. "Well, it wouldn't be the same in this book," he said.

"Why ever not?"

"Because... because I was jealous when I realized I was in love with you," he replied then, sounding ever so annoyed. At Evangeline's look of confusion, he went on. "I couldn't abide the palm tree attempting to ensnare you with its greasy frond," he explained. "Damn thing looked as if it wanted a private dance with you. And if anyone was going to have a dance with you, it was going to be *me*, but the damned ball was over. The orchestra was already finished for the night, so there was nothing I could do, short of chopping down the damned palm tree and whisking you off in my carriage to ravish you... "

Evangeline snorted, her sudden giggles suppressed by a hand over her mouth. When her husband displayed his annoyance, she tried to appear sober but couldn't. "I suppose now is not the time to tell you I took that palm frond home with me that night," she said as tears from her laughter streamed down her cheeks. "My brother asked me to get it for him," she added when she saw his look of horror.

Jeffrey blinked. "Whatever for?" he replied, sitting up in the bed. He could imagine it now. Him, in Wimbledon Common, having challenged the palm to a duel. He imagined they would have to use swords since he rather doubted the tree could pull the trigger on a dueling pistol. His second would be Everly, of course, but who would be the palm tree's second? Another palm from the Weatherstone's ballroom? A few whacks with his sword, and the tree would be kindling!

He came out of his reverie to find Evangeline gazing at him, an amused expression on her face. "Where *were* you just then?" she whispered, her smile full of teasing. "Writing another book?"

"In a duel with the damned palm tree, I'll have you know," he replied. "I vanquished it, though," he proudly added. "It's kindling. Probably already burned up."

Evangeline rolled onto her back, her honey blonde locks spilling over the pillow as she began to giggle.

Chuckling out loud, Jeffrey pulled his wife back into a hug before he considered the story she proposed.

Maybe he could figure out a way to see to it the earl married Lady Georgina. Perhaps he would be on an archeological expedition, and Lady Georgina would just happen upon his dig and be involved in some kind of intrigue involving stolen artifacts from a nearby ruin and require his help in solving the mystery of who stole the crystal crowns!

"Promise me you'll be my muse forever," he whispered, nipping one of her ears with his tongue and teeth.

Evangeline inhaled at the sensation. "Of course, I will," she whispered, once again settling her head into his shoulder and wrapping one of her legs over his.

"Forever?" he murmured, just as he finally drifted off to sleep.

Evangeline smiled, remembering the last line of *The Story of a Baron*. "Yes, my love. Forever."

EXCERPT

Read on for an excerpt from Linda Rae Sande's
Book 2 in The Sisters of the Aristocracy series
The Passion of a Marquess

Anyone living in London was probably denied the scene that greeted Lady Samantha as she made her way up from her cabin on *The Fairweather*. A sky full of brilliant stars drifted overhead, their lights winking like diamonds on black velvet. The ship rocked so gently, she could imagine she was still on dry land.

Her aunt, Lady Chamberlain, was probably wishing they were. The poor woman was below deck with a case of seasickness she claimed prevented her from joining her niece on her nightly walk on the deck.

"You would feel better if you took the air," Samantha said as she offered her aunt another damp cloth.

Caroline Fitzsimmons, Viscountess Chamberlain, regarded her charge with a shrug. "Probably," she agreed. "But the mere idea of climbing those stairs is not the least bit appealing. You go on ahead," she urged Samantha. "It's not as if you'll be accosted by anyone at this time of the night."

Samantha considered the older woman's words. Her aunt did have a point. The ship's captain had assured the ladies his men would be below deck after dark most nights, although one was always behind the wheel if he wasn't.

Still ruminating on her aunt's words, Samantha didn't realize she'd been joined by another of the ship's passengers until he cleared his throat. "A pleasant night for a stroll," he remarked as his gaze swept the heavens above. The clear sky was a rare sight for those used to London's usual fog and smoke-shrouded skies.

Samantha regarded the intruder for a moment. If the Marquess of Plymouth could somehow parlay his handsome good looks with his disagreeable manner, he might be a tolerable guest at dinner. Why the man sported a continuous scowl every moment of this trip—or at least those moments she had been in his company—was beyond Samantha's comprehension. Any aristocrat who could claim a title and lands as rich and varied as his should be displaying a permanent smile, she thought.

Samantha turned from where she had paused at the rail, her attention caught by the sky's sudden change in color as the effects of the sun disappeared completely. Wondering if the marquess expected a response, Samantha turned to face him. "The fair weather has been a blessing on this trip," she agreed. Suddenly nervous at being alone on the deck with a man, she added, "I trust you're faring better than the viscountess. She is still overcome by seasickness." Fighting the urge to roll her eyes at the image her not so pleasant comment created in her mind's eye, Samantha turned to make her way to the stairs and her cabin below.

"I apologize if I disturbed you," the marquess replied, taking a step in the direction she was heading, as if he intended to intercept her.

Pausing in her retreat, Samantha blinked. *Had the man actually apologized?* And without any evidence of the sour face he had worn for the four days they had been on the open seas?

At some point, *The Fairweather* would dock near Rome, and she and her aunt would embark on an abbreviated version of the Grand Tour. Not having gained the attention of any marriage-minded men during the past Season, and realizing her best friend's brother wasn't yet ready to propose, Samantha had announced her desire to travel. Eager to be out of London during the summer months, Caroline Fitzsimmons had wholeheartedly agreed. "Perhaps we'll find you a suitable count in Italy. Or a Russian prince on his travels in Greece," her aunt enthused.

Samantha had merely nodded. If she hadn't been able to land a husband after five seasons in London, she rather doubted a foreign aristocrat would show any interest in her. If Harold Tennison, Earl of Everly, didn't propose in the next year, she would be officially declared on the shelf.

The prospect wasn't as daunting as it should have been, she decided. Other unmarried women tended to exploit their independence to their advantage, taking lovers and traveling on a whim. But Samantha found herself wanting a husband. Wanting children. Wanting a life beyond the one she had at Fitzsimmons Manor with her aunt and uncle.

"Oh, you didn't disturb me," Samantha claimed as she stilled herself and decided she really didn't want to go back to the cabin. The warm night, occasionally cooled by a slight breeze, seemed almost magical. Moving to the opposite rail, she gripped the worn wood and gazed out over the ocean.

"It must have been quite a shock to learn your maid was Trenton's sister," the man said then. A brief, bright light split the darkness as he scratched a match. The blaze grew larger as he lit a cheroot and inhaled.

What a rake! Samantha thought as she regarded the marquess. *He dares to smoke in the presence of a lady!* Despite feeling a bit spiteful, she managed to keep her voice light when she responded. "A very happy one, indeed."

For a moment, Ethan Range, Marquess of Plymouth, seemed surprised. His face returned to its passive expression of boredom almost immediately. So quickly, in fact, Samantha was left wondering if he had displayed any reaction at all or if she merely imagined her simple words had done the trick.

The bastard! Lily Harkness had been her lady's maid since before her come-out. There had never been any scandal surrounding the girl, nor any suggestion she was other than what—or who—everyone thought she was. And then, just last year, Gabriel Wellingham, Earl of Trenton, appeared at Fitzsimmons Manor and announced Lily was his illegitimate sister. He was there to see to it Lily enjoyed the life and comforts of being an earl's daughter.

Samantha had seen to Lily's come-out, such as it was, at Lord Mayfield's ball. Although Lily had been nervous, she soon realized her new sister-in-law, Sarah Cumberbatch Wellingham, had far more reason to be nervous. The manager of a coaching inn in Staffordshire, Sarah had captured the earl's attention—and heart—and was now the Countess of Trenton. Lily, her short blonde curls the *au currant* in coiffures, had spent the evening dancing with every young buck at the ball, and offers of marriage were made every week until the end of the Season. At least Lily had enough sense to declare she was still too young to marry just then, thinking to wait until the end of this past Season to make a decision. *Perhaps she is considering an offer this very moment.*

Samantha couldn't feel a bit of jealously, however. She had shepherded the girls's education in the ways of the *ton* and seen to it she was able to attend the very best balls and soirées.

"I hear she's already betrothed," Lord Plymouth said before taking a long draw on his cheroot.

Smiling so her straight and perfect teeth shone in the twilight, Samantha nodded. "I have heard the same." She hadn't, really, but given the number of gentleman callers in the past few months, she wouldn't be surprised if Lily had finally made a decision to accept an offer.

The marquess frowned. "You seem... pleased," he said in a quiet voice. He dropped the cheroot to the planks at his feet and moved a boot-shod foot over the dying embers. A simple twist of his boot had the lights snuffed.

"I am. I was her sponsor," Samantha replied, her chin rising just a fraction. *I might not have made an impression on the men of the* ton, *but at least I could see to it Lily had two successful Seasons,* she figured.

"Rather sporting of you," the marquess commented. He turned suddenly, his attention on something to the west.

Curious, Samantha turned to peer in the direction of his

gaze, spanning the horizon. The breeze, suddenly blustery, picked up in intensity. "What is it?" she asked as she tried to make out what had captured the attention of the marquess. Glancing up, she realized she couldn't see a single star in the sky. The ship, until then seeming to float on its course, suddenly rose as a swell passed beneath it.

"We need to get below deck," Lord Plymouth announced suddenly, tearing his gaze from whatever had him spellbound only the moment before.

"What is it?" Samantha asked as she continued to stare to the west. The ship lifted again, this time higher, so that the main mast wavered above them. She had to take a step to the right to keep her balance, even though the marquess had taken her upper arm in a grip that would surely leave a bruise.

The sky to the west lit up with blue-white intensity as a lightning bolt seemed to strike the ocean.

Nearly to the stairs, Samantha was about to descend when a wave crashed over the rail and sent seawater washing over the deck. Several barrels suddenly lost their footing as the water lifted them and sent some over the side of the ship. When the wave of water hit the wheelhouse, it rolled back over the deck, grabbing Samantha and nearly upending her. Seawater poured down the stairwell as the ship suddenly tilted.

Lord Plymouth kept his hold on Samantha, jerking her away from the stairs just as the water would have caught her and probably sent her head-first through the opening.

"Hang on!" he managed to get out as he gripped a railing.

Samantha reached for anything to grab onto, one gloved hand grasping the marquess' lapel while the other tried to hang onto the railing.

"Christ!"

The curse had Samantha following the Lord Plymouth's startled gaze.

Damnation!

Although she was fairly sure she didn't put voice to her own curse, Samantha Fitzsimmons would remember it for all the days of her life. For directly in front of them, a wave of monumental proportions descended on the ship. The roar was deafening. The force of the water was far more than her tenuous grip on the railing could withstand. Within a fraction of a second, she was forced to let go and move her hand to the only body she could hang onto.

That of the Marquess of Plymouth.

In the cold, black, swirling water in which she suddenly found herself, Samantha held her breath and hung on for dear life. Years of spending summers in the Isis River had her kicking with all her might, her half-boots fighting the water's drag on her skirts, on her petticoats, on her lungs as she struggled not to take the breath she desperately needed to take.

Just when she was quite sure her lungs were about to explode, her head cleared the top of the water and she gulped air. And just as quickly, she was below the surface again. Her entire body seemed to go numb all at once, the cold water permeating her very being. The desire to simply let go and allow the water to take her down was almost more than she could fight.

But then an arm wrapped around her waist and she kicked as hard as she could. For what seemed an eternity, she tread water has best she could given her half-boots and sodden gown and undergarments. At some point, the marquess had disappeared below the water and she was suddenly aware of his arms around her thighs, of a hand grasping at fabric, of her petticoat ties coming undone. A moment later, her efforts at staying above the water's edge suddenly seemed easier.

Good grief, she realized as her teeth began chattering. The marquess had removed her petticoats! But even as she could more easily move her legs, the water's cold seemed to suck the very life from her. Lord Plymouth, having surfaced several feet away from her, swam in her direction and captured one of her hands.

"Hang on!" he managed to get out. In the darkness, his face was barely visible until lightning once again split the dark. For a moment, she was sure his lips were blue and wondered about her own.

"To what?" she managed to croak, almost wishing he had removed her gown when he had been seeing to her petticoats.

"Me!" he shouted as he held her hand out of the water and moved it to his neck.

Samantha nodded as best she could and grasped the back of his waistcoat, her gloved fingers warm enough to take hold. *Had the man shed his topcoat whilst he was underwater?* she wondered.

When he moved to swim, she did so as well with her free arm and kicked as hard as she could, hoping her feeble attempts were helping more than hindering him. When they seemed to swim into a solid mass, Lord Plymouth let out a shout and everything went black.

ABOUT THE AUTHOR

A self-described nerd and lover of science, Linda Rae spent many years as a published technical writer specializing in 3D graphics workstations, software and 3D animation (her movie credits include SHREK and SHREK 2). Mythology, immortality, and ancient Greece have been lifelong interests.

A fan of action-adventure movies, she can frequently be found at the local cinema. Although she no longer has any tropical fish, she does follow the San Jose Sharks. She makes her home in Cody, Wyoming. o

For more information:
www.lindaraesande.com
Sign up for Linda Rae's newsletter:
Regency Romance with a Twist

www.ingramcontent.com/pod-product-compliance
Lightning Source LLC
Chambersburg PA
CBHW031212120726
47905CB00002B/302

9 780099 150751 1